Marius' Mules XV

The Ides of March

by S. J. A. Turney

1st Edition

"Marius' Mules: nickname acquired by the legions after the general Marius made it standard practice for the soldier to carry all of his kit about his person."

For Sarah, a light in the darkness, a friend beyond compare, a soul sorely missed.

ALSO BY S. J. A. TURNEY:

Completing the Marius' Mules Series

Marius' Mules I: The Invasion of Gaul (2009)
Marius' Mules II: The Belgae (2010)
Marius' Mules III: Gallia Invicta (2011)
Marius' Mules IV: Conspiracy of Eagles (2012)
Marius' Mules V: Hades' Gate (2013)
Marius' Mules VI: Caesar's Vow (2014)
Marius' Mules: Prelude to War (2014)
Marius' Mules VII: The Great Revolt (2014)
Marius' Mules VIII: Sons of Taranis (2015)
Marius' Mules IX: Pax Gallica (2016)
Marius' Mules X: Fields of Mars (2017)
Marius' Mules XI: Tides of War (2018)
Marius' Mules XII: Sands of Egypt (2019)
Marius' Mules XIII: Civil War (2020)
Marius' Mules XIV: The Last Battle (2021)

The Praetorian Series

The Great Game (2015)
The Price of Treason (2015)
Eagles of Dacia (2017)
Lions of Rome (2019)
The Cleansing Fire (2020)
Blades of Antioch (2021)

The Damned Emperors Series

Caligula (2018)
Commodus (2019)
Domitian (2022)

The Legion XXII Series

Capsarius (2022)
Bellatrix (2023)

The Rise of Emperors Series (with Gordon Doherty)

Sons of Rome (2020)
Masters of Rome (2021)
Gods of Rome (2021)

The Ottoman Cycle

The Thief's Tale (2013)
The Priest's Tale (2013)
The Assassin's Tale (2014)
The Pasha's Tale (2015)

The Knights Templar Series

Daughter of War (2018)
The Last Emir (2018)
City of God (2019)
The Winter Knight (2019)
The Crescent and the Cross (2020)
The Last Crusade (2021)

Wolves of Odin

Blood Feud (2021)
Bear of Byzantium (2021)
Iron and Gold (2022)

Tales of the Empire

Interregnum (2009)
Ironroot (2010)
Dark Empress (2011)
Insurgency (2016)

Invasion (2017)
Jade Empire (2017)

Standalone Novels

Para Bellum (2023)

Roman Adventures (with Dave Slaney)

Crocodile Legion (2016)
Pirate Legion (Summer 2017)

Short story compilations & contributions:

A Year of Ravens – Various (2015)
A Song of War – Various (2016)
Rubicon – Various (2020)
Hauntings (2021)

For more information visit www.simonturney.com or
www.facebook.com/SJATurney or follow Simon on Twitter
@SJATurney

ROME
44 BC

PINCIAN

QUIRINAL

VIMINAL

CAMPUS
MARTIUS

SUBURA

ESQUILINE

CAPITOL

TRANS
TIBERIM

FORUM
BOARIUM

FORUM

VELIA

PALATINE

CAELIAN

AVENTINE

1 House of Calvinus
2 House of Cassius
3 House of Hypsaeus
4 House of Vatia
5 House of Fronto
6 House of Cicero
7 House of Caesar
8 House of Antonius
9 Caesarian Collegium
10 Pompeian Collegium
11 Burial Pits Warehouse
12 Temple of Venus Genetrix
13 Basilica Aemilia
14 Rostra
15 Tabularium
16 Bath House
17 Circus Maximus
18 Lupercal
19 Temple of Mars
20 Theare and Curia of Pompey
21 Navalia

DECEMBER

"Caesar, having ended the civil wars, hastened to Rome, honoured and feared as no one had ever been before. All kinds of honours were devised for his gratification without restraint, even such as were divine."

– Appian: Civil Wars II. 106

CHAPTER ONE

'Try to control your temper this time.'

Marcus Antonius, alighting from his litter with a sour expression, fixed his wife Fulvia with a glare. 'That depends entirely on how reasonable he is, as always.'

'Even when he is hard on you, Marcus, it is always in your best interest, or at least he believes it is. You are too quick to anger, and that does little to mend any fences.' She apparently saw something pass across his eyes, for her own gaze hardened. 'And do not think of turning your anger on me.'

Antonius took a deep breath. She was right, of course, about both him and Caesar. But more than that, as the sole heiress of two of Rome's most prominent houses, despite her sex she was more powerful than most senators. Pissing her off could very well make him a lot poorer. He contented himself with giving her a nod. She returned it, satisfied, and sat back in the litter, pulling closed the curtains so that the passing life of the city could not ogle her, while their guards and slaves huddled around, keeping all and sundry at a safe distance. The small entourage turned with the litter and began to move away, for Fulvia had her own business to attend to, and Antonius would return on foot with his own people.

It was said that a few short generations ago the city had been safe to walk alone, barring potential encounters with the petty criminals prevalent in all cities. Even Antonius found that hard to believe really, even though his mother had claimed to remember such days, before the civil wars of Sulla and Marius. These days, even the hardiest of noblemen would not dare brave the streets without a stream of lictors or a private bodyguard. Petty criminals were the least concern in a city where everyone with status had an agenda and everyone who did not have money brandished a knife on behalf of those who did. 'See Rome and die,' was a saying in the provinces, but it had never been meant as literally as it appeared to these days.

Antonius took another breath as a slave adjusted and rearranged his toga, making him as noble-looking as possible. Suitably arrayed, he nodded to the chief of his guards, who stepped forward and approached the gate. As the man hammered the decorative bronze knocker on the timber, Antonius looked around himself.

Caesar did himself no favours with his detractors, really. His family had originally had modest estates and town houses, actually not as grand as those of Antonius' forebears, but at some point during his fourteen years of campaigning all over the republic and beyond, one of Caesar's factors had used some of the enormous sums of money he'd acquired in purchasing land and building a grand villa here. There were plenty in Rome who maintained the notion that Caesar had his eyes set on nothing less than monarchy, and this palatial home could only fuel that fire.

A high wall with no windows and just this one gate enclosed a set of grand sculpted gardens that spread up the slope above the Tiber, opposite the city. Such was the gradient that even over the walls, Antonius could see the avenues of cypress trees, the jetting fountains, the beautiful statues and there, above it all, the towering villa of Rome's dictator.

He felt a familiar twitch reach his face and tug at the corner of his lip as the guard knocked again and finally the gate opened. The sight of what emerged set that twitch off all the more, and he thrust out his hand. A faceless lackey placed a cup of wine in it, and Antonius slugged down the rich, unwatered liquid with a sense of relief, for even in an instant, he felt its familiar warmth take the edge off his nerves. The slave retrieved the empty cup and Antonius took a step forward while his guard announced him to Caesar's soldiers... for that was what they were. There was little really to distinguish the guards on Caesar's estate from the legionaries that had traipsed across the world with him, and with good reason. Most of them were drawn from those very legions, veteran killers who owed the general everything – men loyal beyond all doubt. Their arms and uniform were very familiar. Of course, they openly brandished weapons of war for here they were

4

outside the pomerium, and the laws of Rome did not apply, leaving them free to move about fully armed.

As the almost-legionaries opened the gates fully and stepped back to allow them entrance, Antonius, feeling a familiar prickling sensation of warning, turned. The street was wide and spacious, this side of the river not packed tight like the bulk of the city, and there were considerably fewer people about, but those who were generally looked his way. A toga-clad man with a large entourage at the gate of the city's most eminent citizen would draw attention naturally. Nothing really seemed out of place, and yet something out there had set off a warning with Antonius. He noted it, and tried to commit that ordinary scene to memory before turning once more and walking through the archway into the grand gardens.

Antonius' lip twitch began again. A set of steps led up directly through the gardens between lawns, flower beds, fountains, pools and avenues, straight from the gate to the villa itself, and Antonius knew why. Anyone approaching Caesar would be exhausted and trembling from the climb by the time they arrived, putting the general immediately at an advantage. The old bastard knew every trick there was. For those in the know, and favoured by the general, of course, there was an alternative. A litter had been brought round and lowered to the ground for him. The eight men bearing it were Hispanics, Antonius thought, from the look of them. Big men, but then they had to be, really. Stepping inside, Antonius settled himself as the vehicle was lifted up onto shoulders and began to move. His entourage followed, bracing themselves for the climb. They need not use those awful steps, though. A second approach wound like a snake up the hill at the side of the estate, the journey twice as long, but half as steep. Antonius looked out of the window as he climbed, noting how expertly the men changed their stance and grip to keep the litter horizontal despite the slope.

He couldn't decide whether what he was seeing on the journey was meant as honest tribute or as some sort of joke. At every second turn of the winding path, they passed a small shrine with tumbling waters, each dominated by a statue. From the very start they drew the eye, for that first one was truly familiar. Antonius had commanded cavalry at Alesia almost a decade ago, and he knew Vercingetorix as few would. He could see how well the sculptor had rendered the image of the Gallic chief. From there, the statues were no less familiar as they climbed. Pompey. Scipio. Ptolemy. Pharnaces the Second. More. All men vanquished by Caesar. It was a rather tasteless display, really. As they reached the top of the hill, Antonius was interested to note only one face conspicuously missing from the list of foes.

Caesar would never again look upon the face of Titus Labienus, the man who had been his closest ally and betrayed him to become his greatest foe.

Approaching the villa, the litter slowed, and finally touched to the ground. Antonius alighted and once again his slave, puffing with the effort of the hill, hurried forward to adjust his toga. As his weary men gathered, Antonius approached the door of the house, where Caesar's slaves were waiting, heads bowed in respect. Without a glance at any of them, he walked in through the door. Numerous voices were audible across the house, from far ahead and from various rooms nearby and, as he strode past the altar to the household gods and the brightly painted scenes of Venus's exploits on the vestibule walls, he could also hear voices from the staircase that led to the second floor.

'…in preparation for any event. I must look as though…' the start and end of the sentence, delivered haughtily to a slave, were lost as the speaker moved close to the stairs and then away again. Even dulled slightly with wine, though, Antonius' senses identified the voice's owner in an instant. That sibilant drawl with the heady accent that spoke of Aegyptus. That honeyed voice that could persuade a man to anything. Cleopatra, Queen of Aegyptus and… *what* of Caesar? Not wife, certainly, for Antonius could also hear from ahead the aristocratic tones of Calpurnia, the dictator's spouse. Antonius winced. He was no celibate himself, and he knew Fulvia was well aware of his periodic dalliances with rich ladies around Rome, but that was all they ever were: a bit of fun. Fulvia knew that, and knew that at the end of the day he was hers and hers alone. How Caesar had the gall to have that woman here as a consort, living under his roof with their child, sharing a house with his own wife, Antonius could not imagine. It felt uncomfortable even to him, and he didn't have to *live* here. The great man's decision-making needed to be questioned from time to time.

Passing the stairs and the fading Aegyptian drawl, he passed through the atrium, again loaded with images of Venus, the founder of Caesar's line, back in the mists of time. He could hear Calpurnia better now, and she sounded angry. Her voice was lowered, so he could just hear her tone, though not the words, and, as he passed through the next corridor and out into the huge peristyle garden, he was just in time to see her disappear into another room at speed, slaves falling over one another in her wake to get to the mistress and help.

Gaius Julius Caesar, consul and Dictator of Rome, pontifex maximus, master of the senate, conqueror of Gaul, stood on the far side of the garden, eyes narrowed as his gaze remained on the doorway into which his wife had vanished. He was almost vibrating. Antonius girded himself. He was not feeling particularly at ease, and Caesar looked angry. Such was often not a good combination between them, but he could not really put this off again. He'd done so often enough.

The memory flashed up once more, into the back of his mind: Trebonius in that office in Narbo, speaking words of murder and treachery.

'I am not alone, Antonius. There are others.'

Antonius had told him flatly to put aside any such idea, and had even threatened him, but had said that he would forget he'd ever heard such words. Over the three months since then, though, the scene had replayed time and again, and Trebonius' last words had nagged at him as he settled into Rome once more and summer slid through autumn into winter.

'There are others.'

He'd told no one, just as he said he would, but every passing day made him feel more and more uncomfortable with that decision. In truth, he would probably have told Caesar about the possible plot months ago, had things been easier between the two of them. But Caesar had changed; was changing still. He was not the poor, hungry, ambitious son of Rome that Antonius had known in the old days. He had become something altogether different, and every passing day made those rumours of his intended kingship seem more and more realistic.

He'd not told Fulvia, even, about the plot. He *had* told her that he had very important information for Caesar, and she had urged him over the months to mend whatever had broken between them and to reveal whatever it was that had increased his drinking and kept him awake at nights. He'd made two visits to Caesar over the autumn, outside official business, thinking to finally tell the general of the potential plot that lurked among men he had once trusted. Trebonius was back in Rome now, and spending time with other senators, after all. But both times Antonius had visited, Caesar had either done or said something that pissed him off and pushed the words back down into his throat. Perhaps this was the time. Perhaps, he noted, looking at the angry dictator across the garden, not.

'Marcus Antonius,' Caesar said, his voice not over-friendly, without even looking his way, eyes still on the doorway to Calpurnia's rooms.

'Caesar.'

'You have come to speak of position and war again?'

Antonius felt his jaw tighten, that twitch increase again. The old bastard. Why bring that up straight away? As if that matter had not already brought them into direct argument even in official meetings among senators. For a moment, he felt a different irritation arise, one that was nothing to do with plots or with Caesar's increasing autocracy in the city. Perhaps it was better to speak of something else first and work up to the matter of the plot, for that would likely cause a whole new argument. Caesar would want to know when and how he found out, and would inevitably be angered that Antonius had known for three months and yet said nothing. The longer that went on, the harder it would be to tell him. Yes. A different argument, to put him in the right frame of mind to stand up to Caesar's ire.

'I hadn't, but what better time.'

8

'I have made up my mind, Antonius. I have made the assignments.'

'I am a warhorse, Gaius, and you know that. Don't put me in a fucking stable again to moulder over the summer while you charge around the provinces making war. My place is with your cavalry, or even more, commanding whole armies on the battlefield.'

'Look at you, Marcus. You're drunk already. It's not even noon.'

'Sober, I'd never have come,' he snapped in reply.

'I have the men already assigned to legion commands, I have all the legates and prefects I could need. And though I have yet to secure his aid, I have my overall strategist in mind. You are not it. You are none of them. But that does not mean I do not value you, Antonius. In my absence, Rome will need a firm hand on the reins.'

'I am not a baby-sitter for your pet *kingdom*, Gaius.'

Caesar's eyes became flinty. 'Be careful what you say Marcus. We have known each other all our lives, but I will accept certain accusations from no man.'

Antonius felt that twitch threatening to pull his face off now. 'Don't try and threaten me, Gaius. I've known you too long. You conquered Gaul. Well done. All Rome bows to you for that. You settled Aegyptus, but that little coup has somewhat soured, since you brought the queen back here as your whore.' He saw Caesar's eye flicker then. That had hit the man where it hurt, but he didn't let up. He knew he was making dangerous points and straying ever further from the reason he was actually here, but he just couldn't stop himself. He had set the boulder of his anger rolling, and the slope was long. 'Rome faltered with you when you went to war against our own, and yet I supported you. I went with you, fought Romans for you. You seem to have come through that largely unscathed.' *So far. Barring possible plots...* 'And now, at last, you turn your sights once more to enemies of Rome. Something no one will argue with. Parthia has been the thorn in Rome's side for as long as we have known them. There will never be peace between they and us, and their conquest will truly consolidate the republic and will be your greatest triumph of all. But we all know it will also be your last. You're not a young man, Gaius, but neither am I.

9

This will be *my* last chance at a great conquest too, and instead you want to leave me here, arguing senators back into their seats, negotiating with moneyers so that they can put on coins images of victories I cannot be part of.'

'You should bear in mind,' Caesar answered in a slight hiss, his face stony, 'that you cannot be trusted.'

Antonius felt the fury rise in him then, ready to launch into a tirade, but Caesar did not give him space to interrupt. 'All that business with Dolabella,' the dictator went on, 'and almost war in the forum? Even in asking you to maintain peace in Rome, I am putting in you a trust that many say you do not deserve. What's more, you know that Parthia will last more than one season of campaigning, perhaps even as long as Gaul. Maybe if this time you prove you can be trusted to do the job in Rome, I might look at a position for you out east. Although that might be a sizeable "if".'

'You arrogant shit,' Antonius snapped. 'You might think you rule Rome like a king, and we are all your minions to assign as you see fit, but some of us have blood as old as yours. I have commanded armies for Rome, led sessions in the senate, overseen festivals, given games. I am not your lackey, Caesar.'

'No. *Lackeys* know their place,' Caesar countered, eyes flashing.

'Fuck you,' Antonius spat. 'I should have known better than to come here and try to speak to you like a friend. Like an equal. Because in your eyes you *have* no equal these days, and precious few friends, I'd wager, too. Those you *do* have are deserting you daily. Watch your back, Caesar. That's all I'm saying. Just watch your back.'

He turned, ignoring the dictator's blustering fury as Caesar launched arrows of words at his back, and stormed away across the garden. By the time he entered the atrium once more and was lost to Caesar's sight, he was shaking. By the time he was at the front door, he was scolding himself for having once again allowed himself to get side-tracked from his main purpose. Again, he had come to tell Caesar about Trebonius and a potential plot. Again, he had ended up arguing with the man for not allowing him a role that he deserved, and had gone away without revealing the plot. And now it would be a month before he could even hope to find

10

sufficient inner strength to try again, by which time telling him would be all the harder, for more time would have elapsed.

The eight Spaniards opened the litter door for him. He ignored them, instead bounding down that enormous staircase towards the gate at the bottom. His entourage, surprised, leapt to follow, scampering in his wake.

It was somewhere about halfway down the gardens that his blood began to cool, but where usually he would now feel regret worming its way into his soul, this time things were different. The anger had cooled, but it had not gone. Instead, it had formed into a diamond and frozen there. He had failed to tell Caesar about the plot. Of course, Trebonius had probably forgotten all about it anyway. There probably *was* no plot. And in a way Antonius *had* warned him, had he not?

Watch your back, Caesar.

He felt the anger, nestling there, cankering. Maybe it was all in the lap of the gods now. What was meant to be would be. He would not try again. Let Caesar live with his own decisions.

Indeed, by the time he had reached the bottom of the stairs, he had found that his fiery anger at Caesar *had* faded, but only because it had become something new. A cold ire that glittered in his heart. One thing he would do, though, was to prove the old bastard wrong. If Caesar would not take him to Parthia with the army, Antonius could not force his way into a position. No one with the authority to assign him was going to do so against Caesar's wishes. Such was the man's power and authority these days that even Antonius, scion of one of the republic's most noble and ancient houses, married to an heiress of unimaginable wealth, could not hope to deny him. Angry though he might be, he was going to be left to run Rome, and if that was inevitable, he would prove that no one could run Rome better. He would be consul this year, that was part of the deal, alongside Caesar. But from March, Caesar would be off fighting in the east, and so in his absence, Antonius would have almost unlimited power in the city. He would prove himself. He had to admit that the Dolabella episode had rather battered his reputation, and he knew he'd cocked that up properly. But this year he would redeem himself in that regard, and prove himself.

Fuck Caesar.

Moments later, he was back out of the estate and on the street of Transtiberim. His people were still with him, but he was striding ahead now. Anger was still driving him, but it had now been joined by purpose, and the twin powers were pushing him on. He stormed along the road towards the Aemilian Bridge. Some of his guards had managed, tired though they were, to forge on ahead and manage to get in front as a vanguard. Others were keeping pace to the sides, while more followed on behind, along with the slaves. Twelve guards and five slaves. About the minimum he ever travelled the city with these days, and only so few because half had gone with Fulvia about her business.

He was so angry he never felt it this time. Never felt the eyes on him, that should have raised the hairs on his neck. The wine, the anger, both had dulled that reflex that had kept him alive on so many battlefields in his life. The prickling sensation went unnoticed. And so focused on his internal troubles was he that his people's attention was likewise on him, much more than on their surroundings.

They failed to see the figures near the river, in the archways of buildings and alleyways, watching as he emerged from Caesar's gate. They failed to see those same figures flitting from block to block, keeping pace with them. They even failed to see them emerge ahead of Antonius onto the bridge that crossed back into the city proper. And that was why what happened next came as a shock.

Antonius, still wrapped up in his irritations, stormed across the bridge at pace, passing the warehouse by the river that stored all that was needed for the cattle markets in the forum boarium. He passed the temple of Portunus and the hall of the flower market, marching around the edge of that wide open space and into the narrower streets that lead into the Velabrum and would carry him to the forum and beyond.

It was only as the turned into the Vicus Canarius that he finally realised something was wrong, for it was then that their shadowing observers struck. The two guards who had led the van, out of breath from the hillside and their hurrying to keep up with their angry master, fell first. Half a dozen thugs stepped out of a side alley with surprising speed and struck their blows before Antonius' guards were even aware of the danger. They were armed with stout clubs, much like the guards, for only the truly brave broke Rome's ancient law against carrying a weapon of war within the pomerium. That, of course, was why they had not struck on the far side of the river, where Caesar's guards were close, brandishing steel blades, safely outside the sacred boundary. Here, they could fight on their terms.

Antonius blinked, shock pulling him out of his internal monologue as the leader of his guards died in an instant, half his head mashed in with a massive swing of heavy oak that smashed the man's cranium, eye socket, cheek and jaw. The guard collapsed to the ground, shaking uncontrollably as the body tried to react to the damage without the control of the brain. The other man perhaps had it worse, for a well-aimed blow with a length of ash took him in the throat, flattening his windpipe and crushing his throat-apple. The man dropped the weapon he had only just begun to draw as he fell to his knees, clutching at a neck that no longer allowed the passage of air, gagging and hissing in pain and panic.

Antonius stared at the two dying guards, and the four others that leapt forward to help, their own clubs coming out. The tactician in him took over in an instant. He spun, checking his surroundings. The pair who'd attacked from the front were not alone. Even as his own guards leapt in to take them on, their own mates were pouring from the alley to swamp Antonius' party. To the right of him, the street held the large, forbidding gates of guarded warehouses, and there was no sign of respite there. There would be no retreat, either. Behind him, more men were looming at the end of the street, converging from the open space of the cattle markets. Some of those men brandished not only clubs, but had acquired sharp animal goads in passing, which they now waved eagerly. The way back was sealed off. Fear rising, he glanced left. Several shops lined the street, and he wondered as his eyes played across them whether any of them would have a rear exit that they could use to flee through, escaping this street. There was no way he intended to stay and fight, whoever the assailants were. He had only ten guards

13

with him, and the slaves would be of no use whatsoever, while the enemy were far more numerous, like a criminal gang.

His eyes fell on a sign – an old sign with peeling paint beside an open dark door. A sign that showed a bunch of grapes. The name of the caupona had long since worn away, though it was clearly a low-class establishment, from the condition of the building, the lack of proper signage and the proximity to the extremely pungent cattle market. It crossed his mind for a moment that only the lowest of Rome's society would eat or drink in such a place, and so there was every chance of finding even more hostile foes inside, yet it looked very much as though he'd been left with no choice. Superior numbers of the enemy both ahead and behind, the impassable facades of sealed warehouses to one side, and shops that would have no rear exit because they backed onto housing everywhere else. Only the caupona gave even the slightest hope of escape.

Many cauponae would be much the same as the shops to either side, simple single-room establishments rented from the owner of the building whose frontage they occupied, their back wall the outer one of that house.

This one, he reasoned, had to be different, and for just one reason. Wine could be transported in amphorae and jars of all sorts of sizes and so could easily be brought in to most establishments. But in the past decade, since Caesar's campaigns in Gaul and, most particularly, since the more noble among the Gauls had been admitted to the senate, the city had gained a peculiar and unexpected interest in beer. Gone were the days when beer was a barbarian abhorrence. Now it was a fascinating foreign beverage. Not for the patrician elite, of course, but then the patrician elite wouldn't be caught dead in a caupona like this one. This served the poor and the hard-working, and it was almost certain it served them beer. Beer came in barrels. And while all manner of wine jars might fit through the narrow doorway of this unnamed drinking pit, there was no way a barrel was getting through. That meant a rear access, and a rear access meant potential escape.

Antonius returned his attention to the fight. They were in trouble. Five of his twelve men were already down, and there were now more enemies visible on the street than there had been when he'd first seen them. Even as he cleared his throat, the sixth of his guard was felled by blows from three sides, one of the unarmed slaves running forward to try and pull him away, only to join him in the world of the mortally wounded.

'Back,' Antonius bellowed, waving to his men. 'Back to the caupona.'

'There?' cried out one of the guards who'd just freed himself from a struggle and managed to step back into the open. 'In *there*?'

'Or stay here and get beaten to death,' Antonius snapped back at him as he turned and began to run for the doorway. On the way, he passed another fight, ducked, swept up a fallen club, and swung it at the nearest of the attackers. The shock of the weapon's contact sent a numbness up his arm, for he was out of practice, and it had been a number of years since he'd had to swing a weapon. But it had the desired effect. The street ruffian's head snapped around sharply as blood and teeth flew through the air, and he fell into the next man, fortuitously freeing the nearby guard from his own fight. That man gave his falling opponent a last thump for good measure and ran after his master.

'Please, Fortuna,' Antonius hissed under his breath as he made for the dingy entrance, 'let this shithole have a back door.'

CHAPTER TWO

'Can you go ask for more wine?' Fronto said, gesturing to Aurelius.

'Of course, *Domine*,' the former legionary grinned, rising.

'Domine?'

Aurelius pointed to Fronto's garment, still grinning, then turned and gestured to the proprietor. Fronto looked down. His tunic was white, or at least had been when he'd put it on, though now it had a large splash of grease from the suspicious meat-on-a-stick they had all eaten for lunch and two stained trickles of red wine that were slowly becoming a permanent feature. It was neither the white tunic nor its new stains that Aurelius was indicating, though. That was the two wide dark red stripes running down it on either side of the neck, indicating the rank of a senator.

He felt his lip curling in distaste.

He had fought political advancement for so long he'd assumed himself free of it, but it seemed that politics was an expert hunter and had caught him in the end, in his old age. He was damned if he was going to accept it gracefully, though.

'What wine, your senatorship?' Aurelius called across the room. Fronto glared at him until he collapsed in a fit of laughter and then ordered a new jar. Clearly this joke was the gift that was going to keep on giving for his friends.

He sighed. He'd done so well. His family were, of course, of extremely noble lineage, an offshoot of the Valerii, and expected to sit in the senate. His mother had been so proud when at twenty-two he had taken his first step on the cursus honorum, accepting a military tribuneship in Hispania, where he served with Caesar, the great man himself assigned there as quaestor. He'd excelled in the post, showing a natural talent for war. Unfortunately, for his

16

ambitious mother at least, he'd returned three years later a grizzled soldier with a mistrust of politicians. She'd urged him to take a position as quaestor, and in the end he'd accepted, largely to shut her up. He'd managed, more through luck than judgement, to secure the quaestorship in charge of military pay, something he understood without too much difficulty and which kept him close to the army and as far from the politics of Rome as the position would allow.

In theory, he would have needed to serve as an aedile or a praetor next, though in those days, in the aftermath of the civil war of Sulla and Marius, things were a little flexible, and many of the age and career requirements for postings were easily ignored with the odd promise and a passing of coins. Thus had Fronto managed to skip the next postings and secure his command of the Tenth at the tender age of thirty two. Then had come Gaul, and everything had marched on from there, all focused on the military with no further thought of a military career.

He'd married, had his boys, and fought his way across the republic and back under Caesar's banner. Last summer, in Hispania, the wars had finally ended, the first time in well over a decade when there was nowhere waiting to be fought in next. He'd returned to Rome a happy, forty-seven year old man, knowing he had a wonderful wife, two eight year old boys, plenty of cash and estates protected by Rome's most powerful men, as well as a burgeoning wine business. He'd had visions of a happy retirement, spending time sitting in an arbour in the villa near Tarraco perhaps, drinking wine and watching the sea, or here in the city, spending the days in the baths and at the games.

He'd reckoned without Lucilia.

He had been home three days when her plans were laid out in stark detail. He had avoided climbing the Cursus Honorum through military service throughout Caesar's wars, but now he was home and there was no excuse.

He'd argued. He had already had a career and was ready for retirement. He'd acceded to her wishes and ended his military career. No more legions. No more war. Home and peace. She had asked him how he was going to keep busy? He was not a man given to quietude and introspection. He had made the horrible mistake of bringing up baths, games, races and wine, and had winced as her eyes hardened. She had no intention of retrieving her husband from years of war only to lose him to a daily round of bars and games.

'And if you care little for your own advancement, and as little for me, then at least think of your sons,' she had said in a tone of voice that labelled him an arsehole of the first order. He'd winced again, and she had gone on to point out that if his sons wanted the chance to reach high position in the republic they would need whatever leg-up Fronto could provide. A father who had served in the senate, held important positions, and had built up a clientele of Rome's more useful men would give the boys a head start in life. If Fronto really pushed, given his connections, he might even secure the consulship in time, and that would set the boys up for good.

He'd felt so battered after that conversation he'd found himself promising that he would ask Caesar to use his power and influence to secure Fronto some higher position. That was when the other boot hit the floor. Lucilia had told him there was no need. She had already been in conversation with Caesar's wife Calpurnia while the men were still on their way back from Hispania. The woman had promised to persuade Caesar. Within a day of their return to Rome, Caesar had relented to his wife and made a place available in the senate. Lucilia had spoken to one of the city's best artisans and ordered suitable garments.

And so within a month of his return, Fronto had found himself in the position he'd managed to avoid for the past thirty years or so. He was a senator. It was little comfort that Galronus still sat too, for his friend seemed to have acquired a talent for politics and persuasion and was already far better a senator than Fronto would ever be. And somehow *he* managed to keep his broad-striped tunic clean, even though he was eating and drinking the same stuff as Fronto.

And the less said about having to wear a toga, the better. Why their forebears had decided to create and to pin their social status on a garment that seemed designed to unravel as you walked was beyond him, but he always seemed to arrive at social occasions with an armful of folds that had slid to the ground on the way.

Aurelius returned with a slave at his shoulder carrying a tray of wine jar and cups. 'There we go.'

'Thank you...' Fronto said, pausing for a moment while trying to think of a cutting, scathing nickname to use.

'Lucius Aurelius, son of Marcus Aurelius Cotta,' helpfully supplied a voice behind him.

Fronto turned and shot an angry glance at the man. That was another problem. Apparently sitting in the senate and having to wear important clothing was not enough. As a senator, Lucilia was determined he would hold his own, and so he had a proper senatorial entourage. Despite Fronto's tradition of keeping only freed servants in his house, a habit inherited from his father's fear of slave uprisings, Lucilia had been insistent, and now five slaves stood idly by a wall, waiting to hurry over at his gesture, all a little confused that their master seemed determined to do things himself or let his important friends do them. Then there was his personal attendant, who had quickly learned not to surreptitiously comb Fronto's hair when he sat down, and still sported a black eye from when he'd tried to apply perfume.

But the worst of all the slaves was Abronius, the nomenclator. Every senator had one, a clever and well-trained slave who attended them in public and whose entire job was to remember the name of everyone of even remote importance, and to supply their name, the names of their family, their history, and anything pertinent about them at the drop of a hat. Abronius was good at his job. Fronto had yet to find someone of any remote rank the man did not know all about, despite repeated attempts to trip him up. But Abronius was also far too over eager, and spent much of his time barraging Fronto with names and information, whether he wanted them or not.

He'd also acquired a new guard unit, mercenaries drawn from the retirees of Caesar's legions, requested by Lucilia and selected by Masgava and Aurelius. There were forty of them, and half that number went everywhere with Fronto, making it very hard to be incognito, one of Fronto's favourite conditions. The twenty men were currently out back in the cold air, out of sight, where Fronto preferred them. They weren't happy about it, but stuff 'em. He was safe here with his friends, Galronus, Aurelius, Masgava and Arcadios.

'When are we going home?' Galronus asked quietly.

Fronto winced again. He was trying not to think about home. He'd been trying to stay out of the way all day. He'd claimed a meeting of the senate, which he'd attended just long enough to be noted as present, and then slipped out. Not expected home, he'd then been to watch the early afternoon races, which had become an extremely troublesome pastime when one was accompanied by an entourage. Then they'd eaten, Fronto dropping food down his tunic. At least it wasn't his toga, which he'd taken off as soon as possible and was now being carried by one of the slaves. Since then they had been in the bar, hiding. Hiding anywhere was preferable to going home.

Lucilia was in organisation mode. She was throwing a small soiree this evening for some of Rome's more important senators and their wives. Fronto had quickly learned that the more important a senator was, the higher the chance he was an unbearable arse. So he was not looking forward to tonight. And even before the party, the house would be chaos and whatever he did would be wrong and in the wrong place. Thus they hid here, and remained hiding, somewhere Lucilia would not look.

'As late as we can reasonably get away with,' he answered. 'If we could go home once the party's over, that would be a win for me.'

'Is Caesar coming?' Arcadios put in.

'I don't think so. He was invited, of course, but he's got rather a lot to do at the moment.'

Aurelius gave him a lascivious grin. 'I'll bet he does with two women in his house.'

Another wince. If Fronto kept this up he was going to have a face like a prune, or at least that was what Lucilia kept telling him. 'At least it means he doesn't need to decide whether to bring Calpurnia or Cleopatra with him.'

That comment caused an outbreak of laughter among the others. Once it settled, it was Galronus who spoke quietly. 'He'll have to send her back to Aegyptus, won't he? I mean, he already has a wife. And he's not allowing the boy to inherit.'

20

They all nodded at this. Caesar's will had been witnessed by Fronto among others, so he knew clearly what was in it. The lion's share of all he had would go to Octavian, with a reasonable sum to his other nephews, Pedius and Pinarius. Caesarion was not even named in the will. Oh, they all knew the boy would be looked after, but Caesar had to be careful. Rome grudgingly accepted the presence of the Aegyptian queen, so long as she held no actual power, but to legitimise Caesarion would turn many a senator against him.

'Personally,' Masgava put in, 'if I were Caesar I would send her back to Alexandria as a client queen of Rome with the boy set to inherit. He would be pharaoh of Aegyptus in good time, and with close ties to Rome. He would owe Rome and he'd know it. The place would be a staunch ally. It's the only feasible way.'

They all acknowledged the sense in this with nods as Aurelius poured wine into the cheap, cracked krater and added the water for a sensible mix, dipping the cups in and passing them round. In the moment's silence, Fronto looked around, suddenly acutely aware they were discussing a rather sensitive topic in a very public place. He relaxed a little. There were only half a dozen other occupants, and they were over at the far side, trying to stay out of the way of the senator in their midst. This was not the sort of place a senator stooped to visit, which was precisely why it attracted Fronto, with the added bonus that Lucilia would never think to look for him here.

It was as he was considering the poor quality of his surroundings that the world exploded into action.

A man barrelled in through the doorway at speed and skidded to a halt in the middle of the room, looking around and blinking, adjusting to the dim interior. He was a swarthy fellow in a well-cut but very miscellaneous tunic, solid boots, and wielding a nightstick of solid ash that was already stained with blood and seemed to have hair stuck to it. Fronto was just staring in surprise at the man when a more familiar figure charged in after him and staggered to a halt beside the club man.

Marcus Antonius spun, focusing on the caupona's owner.

'You have a back door?'

21

The barman stared at him in shock. He was probably still reeling from a senator coming in with his retinue, which had driven out half his regulars in a heartbeat, and most certainly would not be prepared for one of Rome's most important persons darkening his door. Antonius snapped the fingers of the hand not holding a club, with some urgency. 'Come on, man. A back door.' He turned to his guard. 'Pay the man.'

Fronto found his voice from somewhere.

'Antonius?'

The luminary in the centre of the room turned slowly, brow furrowing. 'Fronto?'

'What in the name of Venus's left tit are *you* doing here?'

'Bit of a problem outside,' Antonius replied. 'Is there a back door?'

'There is,' Fronto replied with a grin, then raised his voice and cupped his hands to his mouth as two more of Antonius' men staggered in, one of them bleeding from the head. 'Sinna?'

As a door opened near the bar, Antonius turned in fresh surprise. Fronto's guards burst in, alarmed at being summoned, their leader looking this way and that for potential danger, his gaze falling on Antonius and the three of his men. The last of Antonius' guard from outside arrived, backing through the door, struggling, fighting someone off.

'How many men have you got?' Antonius hissed.

'Twenty, plus us.' He looked at the man fighting a valiant defence at the door. The state of Antonius and his people suggested that they were up against serious odds. Fronto rose and waved at the half dozen deadbeats at the far side of the caupona. 'A free day's drinking for anyone who helps protect my friend here.'

As the six men rose greedily and picked up jugs, chairs and sticks, Fronto grinned. 'That makes near forty of us altogether.'

Now, Antonius grinned. 'That sounds more like it.'

He hefted his club as the man in the doorway took a blow to the chest and fell back, coughing, into the room. Fronto reached out behind him with an empty palm. 'Stick.'

He was grateful that his people were already coming to know him and his ways, for one of the slaves somehow immediately managed to lay his hand on a length of vine wood not unlike a centurion's rod, and slapped it into his palm. He wrapped his fingers around it as he rose, then swore for a moment as his knee gave a little wobble, having been sat so long, before he straightened it.

The enemy poured into the caupona now, the doorway unobstructed. They looked this way and that, and an aura of doubt began to manifest as they realised Antonius seemed to have found friends. Still, this did not deter them for long, and moments later they were running at the men in the bar. Fronto's guards were still entering, pouring in through the back door, and all present were piling in, engaging with the mob.

Fronto swished his vine stick for a moment, a grin settling onto his face. Screw the senate. *This* was *his* kind of Roman politics. He looked at the men advancing slowly and carefully on them in the rather restrictive confines of the caupona. They were all dressed differently, all in relatively poor gear. They all looked Roman enough, and among them he could see a smattering of old legionary tunics and military boots, though only here and there. They appeared to be a mob of the ordinary people of Rome, with no other identifying mark than that some of them were ex-soldiers.

One thing that defined them, though, was that they were armed, and they were enemies, and sometimes that was all that was needed.

Fronto selected a man with dark, slightly oiled hair and a beige tunic fastened with a plain leather belt. The man had a stout length of wood in one hand, but was gripping and ungripping the other as though in pain, presumably having suffered some injury outside. As the man came for him, Fronto grinned nastily and hefted his vine stick ready. He was just identifying weaknesses and deciding where to hit the man when two of his own guard pushed in front of him and created a defensive wall between him and the man.

Fronto growled angrily, but his guards ignored him as they laid into the man he'd targeted, pulverising him repeatedly until he fell, whereupon one of them kept beating him to be sure, while the other moved on to find another opponent. Angrily, Fronto pushed around them and set his sights on another opponent. A pale man with spiky blond hair spotted him and ran, stick held above his head. Fronto grinned and pulled his own stick back at waist height.

As the man approached, Fronto began to duck in order to avoid the coming downward blow while jabbing out at the man's gut.

His shock as he found himself pulled backwards was only overcome by his anger as Masgava stepped into the gap between him and the man and slammed his fist into the attacker's gut, forcing the enemy to double over with a squawk. Fronto looked around to find Arcadios gripping him, having pulled him from danger. He glared at his friend.

'You'd better have a bloody good reason for that.'

The look Arcadios gave him as he moved on to another target made it clear that he had, and Fronto, even in the midst of a fight, pieced it together in a moment. This was Lucilia's doing. They had all been told to under no circumstances let Fronto get into trouble. And every man here, even Galronus, was absolutely loyal to Fronto and would never ignore his orders for anything… except a command from Lucilia, a woman they considered Fronto's commanding officer.

He roared, partly in anger, partly frustration, as he found himself at the back of the fight, thoroughly protected by friends and strangers alike. Off to his left, Marcus Antonius was in a similar position, safe behind everyone. He looked as frustrated as Fronto. The man was every bit as much the soldier as him, after all.

Fronto chewed his lip for a moment, looking this way and that, then his eyes fell on one of his new guards who had just taken a glancing blow to the head and was reeling, holding up his own club in an attempt to ward off further attacks while his head spun. He was going to be hit again, obviously, and the next blow might be either fatal or debilitating. In a heartbeat, Fronto was there. His vine stick lanced out, caught a blow that would have struck the beleaguered guard on the head, and, grabbing the man's tunic by the neck at the back, hauled as hard as he could. The man lurched backwards with a gasping cry, half-strangled by his tunic neck as Fronto pulled him from danger. The man was still dazed and unbalanced and as he fell back he dropped to the floor, swooning. Fronto was in his place in a heartbeat, and that old familiar battle buzz was back.

He hadn't realised quite how much he'd missed it, though it had only been a matter of months since he'd been at Munda facing off against the enemies of the republic. A paean to Mars played in his heart as he leapt forward, sprightly for his age, his vine stick tapping his opponent's club out of the way and then smacking the man rather hard between the eyes. The man lurched, his own club lowering.

'Get back, sir,' called the man to his left, his tone urgent as he fought hard with the man before him.

'You look to your own trouble,' Fronto snorted as he smacked the man in front again in exactly the same place, between the eyes. This time there was an audible crack and the man staggered and then collapsed to his knees, the club falling from his fingers to bounce across the floor. Fronto was no novice to combat of any sort, and knew damn well the dangers of assuming a man to be down only to find him coming back at your unexpectedly. Consequently, even as he selected another target, he slammed his hard leather boot into the man's head, snapping it back and quite possibly snapping the neck in the process. The man dropped backwards to the filthy floor, shaking into unconsciousness or death.

He could hear warnings being bellowed now, and was vaguely aware of a thinning in the ranks of their opposition. Indeed, as he moved towards the next man, that assailant was already looking over his shoulder, faltering, ready to run. Fronto, his battle face well and truly on now, found himself reluctant to let the man go, and took a quick step forward, then another, and then slammed his foot down hard. As the man was turning, preparing to flee, suddenly the bones of his left foot were being turned to shards and splinters under Fronto's merciless stamp. The man screamed, turning wide eyes on Fronto, who replied with his vicious smile as he completed his double attack. His forehead met that of his opponent, connecting with the lower edge at the top of his eyes. He both felt and heard bones breaking, and knew them not to be his. The man's screaming stepped up a notch as Fronto took a step back. His own head was a little swimmy from the blow, though he knew in his case it would pass in moments. The man he'd struck might live, might not, but if he did, he'd have cause to remember that blow for the rest of his miserable life through broken eye sockets.

25

As Fronto stood, shaking his head in an attempt to clear it, he was vaguely aware the enemy were pulling back from the caupona into the street, fleeing. Hands were on him then, helping him, guiding him towards a chair. With angry grumbles he waved them away. As he blinked, recovering quickly, he became aware of a warm trickle just as blood ran into the corner of his eye. He blinked again and when he'd cleared it, Masgava was standing in front of him.

'That had better not be *your* blood,' the Numidian said flatly. 'If it is, your wife will crucify us.'

Fronto reached up and probed across his head. Bits of it felt slightly sore, but he could find no actual wounds. He shook it, and wiped the blood from his forehead with the sleeve of his tunic, then looked at it with a sinking feeling. It was going to be really hard to explain away that particular stain when he got back.

'Listen, when we get home, I have a job for you and Aurelius. Keep Lucilia busy while I run and find my spare tunic.'

Masgava gave him a scathing look. 'You're not going to hide this one. Not without an hour in the baths, new tunic and boots and, if that head butt was as hard as it looked, you're not going to be able to hide the bruises in a day or two.'

Fronto sighed and turned to see Marcus Antonius striding towards him with a smile. 'Your presence here is most welcome, Fronto,' the man laughed. 'Thank you for your timely assistance.'

'If you want to thank me, explain it to my wife, who's going to do me far more damage than they ever could.'

Antonius laughed. 'As it happens, I am at your soiree this evening. I shall make sure to tell Lucilia of your valiant part in saving me from ruffians.'

'If you really want to help, downplay my part in it as much as you can.'

The man laughed again. 'I actually feared for my life out there for the first time in a while.'

'Who are they?'

Antonius shrugged. 'No idea. I had been at Caesar's villa, and crossed back over from Transtiberim. They jumped us just out there, past the forum boarium, though looking back on it, I think I was vaguely aware of them even at Caesar's before I went in.'

'So they followed you from Caesar's. I wonder why. They look like a street gang, but some of them are ex-soldiers.' Fronto turned to his friends. 'Any ideas who they are?'

The others began to move around, crouching, examining the bodies. It seemed that the defenders had proved excellent soldiers and the attackers had been shrewd and careful, for only the dead remained. Anyone with a chance of living had been helped up and fled with the rest. As Fronto finished cleaning himself up at the expense of his tunic, finally Aurelius called 'aha!'

'What is it?'

The former legionary moved to another body and lifted his sleeve, looking at his bicep just below the shoulder. A third and fourth seemed to confirm his diagnosis.

'What?' Fronto urged.

'They all have the same tattoo. These are all members of one of the collegia.'

Fronto nodded slowly. The collegia were organised guilds in Rome. Some were professional, such as the college of fetial priests, the college of fishmongers of the Aventine, the college of Oppian scribes and so on. Others were regional, based on location more than on profession, such as the college of the northern Esquiline or the college of the left-side Velabrum. Then there were others, and plenty of them. In fact, Rome was almost as full of collegia as it was of criminals or senators, two labels Fronto had decided were often interchangeable.

'Any idea which college?'

'Given the wreath and the eagle on them all, they have to be a college of ex legionaries, and the 'I'? Well Caesar's First are still relatively new and mustered in Dalmatia ready for the Parthian campaign. Logic says they're the First Legion that Pompey commanded at Pharsalus.'

Fronto took a deep breath. 'That might go a way to explaining it. Former Pompeians. They could have been watching Caesar's villa waiting for opportunities for revenge. And seeing you would be perfect. They would love you or me little more than they would Caesar. I tell you, Antonius, the streets are becoming downright dangerous. I would be much happier moving back to Tarraco, if Lucilia would let me off this cursed cursus.'

27

Antonius laughed. 'I watched you in the middle of all that. You were in your element. I can't picture you rocking back on your chair at that lovely villa in Hispania and discussing the harvest. Have you sold that wine business, by the way?'

Fronto's lip curled. 'Not yet. It's not mine, now, though.'

That had been another sore point. He was fond of his wine business. It was one thing he'd done himself, albeit with the help of knowledgeable associates. It was now a growing concern and one of the more important wine import businesses of the city. But senators were forbidden from indulging in business. All his income was to come from rents. He was going to have to sell the business and buy up some land. In the meantime, he had transferred the company deeds to Catháin, while taking a healthy share of the profits.

'It might not be as simple as Pompeians taking pot shots at Caesarian officers,' Arcadios put in, looking down at the bodies.

'Oh?'

'From what I hear it's increasingly common for the collegia to be working for someone with money, more or less a private army made up of ordinary people in the street.'

Masgava nodded. 'It's true. You remember Clodius and Milo? Their gangs?'

Fronto nodded. He remembered them all too well.

'Clodius and Milo used the collegia in their gang wars. It might be that someone is targeting Caesar, or Marcus Antonius, or both. And if they are, then you might well appear on their list, too.'

Fronto shook his head. 'Who would care about me?'

Antonius answered that. 'Anyone who lives and has a grudge against Caesar. Cicero? Minucius Basilus, Antistius Labeo? Petronius? The Caecilii? It's a pretty long list, Fronto. I wonder whether it's worth investigating.'

'Maybe,' conceded Fronto doubtfully. 'Personally, I'll mark it up to opportunity and bad luck unless it happens again. Anyway, I'd best head off. I need to get myself cleaned up and changed before Lucilia sees me.'

Antonius laughed. 'Good. I'll see you at your place tonight, then.'

Fronto gave him a scathing look. 'And I'll go and lock the wine cellar ready.'

CHAPTER THREE

'Should you be getting involved?'

Fronto sighed as he belted his tunic, Lucilia's concerned tone hanging in the still winter air. 'I am involved, whether I like it or not.'

'But there are *levels* of involvement. Try to stay on the edge, Marcus.'

'It's probably an isolated incident. Caesar isn't short of enemies, even with the wars over. They're just a different sort of enemy now, in the city, pretending to be peaceful citizens. These men were veterans of Pompey's legions. The wars are over and most of the legions disbanded, but those who served Pompey have found themselves without the benefits of Caesar's veterans. There's always going to be bad feeling. I think this was just disenfranchised ex-soldiers trying to take out their anger on Caesar and finding the next best thing in Marcus Antonius.'

'But *you're* the next best thing to *him*. If armed ruffians feel content to go attacking Caesar's former officers in the street, none of you are safe. You, Antonius, Galronus, Brutus. Steer clear of any involvement with Antonius, dear, in case they come back for more. You'll find yourself dragged into trouble.'

'Trouble finds me,' Fronto grunted. 'You know that.'

'So take a stand, Marcus. Maybe you can be the one to bring these people back into line, make them law-abiding citizens.'

'How?'

'You're a senator now, and I'm sure Caesar will be able to find a praetorship for you. You finally have influence in the upper circles of Rome, and with men like Galronus sitting in the senate, too, you'll have support. Try to help these people. Show them Caesar's vaunted clemency. Persuade the senate to grant extra pension bonuses to the veterans of the losing side in the war, as well as the winners.'

Fronto frowned. He'd actually been intending to do as little as possible in the senate, to sit in the back row and snooze if possible, and do nothing of any import. But now that Lucilia said it, that was actually a damn good idea. He found that a small smile had crept onto his face. He didn't want to be a law-maker, but if Rome was going to remember him for anything political, why not re-enfranchising the army?'

'I'll have a think on it, dear.'

'A senator has a duty to make the world a better place, Marcus.'

'Yes, dear.'

She gave him a look that he knew well. She was aware that when he said 'yes dear,' he was effectively trying to end a conversation he wasn't enjoying. She straightened, but at that moment one of the household slaves appeared in the doorway, clearing his throat.

Fronto looked across at the man, as did Lucilia.

'The doorman reports visitors approaching, Domine,' the man said, addressing Fronto, eyes lowered in respect.

'Who?'

'It would appear to be the dictator, Domine, Gaius Julius Caesar.'

Fronto's brows arched as he looked across at his wife. 'An unexpected visit, especially so early in the morning. Caesar's usually having his salutatio at this time, and he's then wrapped up in admin for hours.'

Lucilia gave him a smile. 'How fortunate we are that the house is in good order.'

And it was. The house was often a little untidy, partly through the activity of the two boys, partly because Fronto was used to simply leaving things around in his campaign tent with no one to complain, a habit he was finding hard to break back in the city. But the grand party the other night had required a large clear up, and the house was still in good condition from that.

'It's too late for him to want breakfast,' Fronto mused, then gestured to the slave. 'But have wine and water brought to the winter triclinium, and arrange some trays of pastries and the like, just in case.'

31

Lucilia nodded. 'Bring out the *best* pastries, the ones from Eurysaces' place. And the very best tableware. And the vintage Falernian.'

'I have plenty of good wines I've imported myself,' Fronto grumbled. 'The stuff in my private supply costs a fortune.'

'This is Rome, Marcus, and these men are Rome's masters. You really have to learn to play the game.'

Fronto gave her a noncommittal grunt, then shuffled out of the room, adjusting his attire and swatting away the hands of the slave who hurried over to help. Servants had a bit more pride, in his experience. Slaves were always too desperate and eager to help, but some things he didn't *want* help with. That message was slowly sinking in across the household, though. The turning point had probably been when he'd been in the latrine and couldn't find the shit sponge. He'd begun to get a little worried about what he was going to do when the slave had turned up with the sponge, ready to wipe him. That particular slave had left the latrines pale and shaking under Fronto's threat of what he would do it that slave came within three feet of his backside.

He was about to take a seat in the triclinium when Lucilia appeared in the doorway, attended by three slaves, one with an armful of white material. She snapped her fingers and pointed at Fronto, and the slave hurried across, looking hopelessly apologetic. Fronto paused, considering arguing, but knew he would lose, and gave up with a sigh. He stood with his arms out as two of the slaves hurriedly wound and draped the toga around him in the traditional manner. As they finished adjusting and stepped back, Fronto felt the massive weight of wool and wondered briefly if this was how the Aegyptian kings had felt, wrapped in their tomb bindings.

He remained standing. Sitting and rising too often was hard in all this, and often resulted in a certain amount of unravelling. Mere moments later he could hear a familiar commanding voice out across the atrium, and the murmuring of both guests and household staff. Two slaves appeared with wine and krater and fine glasses, ten in number, just in case, while three more brought platters of sweet-smelling pastries that were placed artistically on the tables.

32

The slaves just managed to reach the edge of the room and stand attentively, eyes downcast, as the visitors were led into the room.

It occurred to Fronto that 'Politician Caesar' was different to 'General Caesar'. There was still something commanding and authoritative about the man, but somehow over the years of war, he had seemed naturally martial, as though Mars' blood flowed through him rather than that of Venus. But now, back in Rome, he was different. He seemed to fit the toga as though the garment had been designed solely for him. Moreover, he could somehow walk in it without it sliding down his arm and unravelling. He carried the authority of generations of Roman aristocrats just in his bearing. No wonder the senate kept falling over itself to heap new honours upon him.

Caesar gave the warmest of smiles, first to Lucilia, then to Fronto. Behind him came an entourage, but only a small and intimate one. Undoubtedly his lictors and a small army of slaves waited out in the street or in one of the waiting rooms off the atrium. The men with Caesar, though, were eminent in themselves.

Aulus Hirtius was as familiar a figure as could be, a man who had been Caesar's secretary throughout most of his wars, a confidante, a military commander in his own right, and a man even Fronto considered trustworthy and above reproach. Cornelius Balbus was a recent addition to the retinue, Caesar's current secretary, but was already proving to be a good man, and one Fronto quite liked. Gaius Oppius he was less sure of. The man had inveigled his way into Caesar's close amici a few times over the years, whenever he was in Rome, and it had taken only days on the return this time for the man to secure himself a place as one of Caesar's closest confidantes. There was nothing actually *wrong* with him, and he seemed to be perfectly reasonable and sensible. There was no reason really for Fronto to mistrust him, yet for some reason he did. The other two were more familiar and more welcome: Decimus Junius Brutus Albinus, an old friend of Fronto's going right back to the campaign against the Venetii a dozen years ago, and his cousin Marcus Junius Brutus, longstanding friend of Caesar's and, if carefully-spoken, scandalous rumour were true, his son by Servilia. Five luminaries of high rank themselves, all attendant upon the man who had been made Dictator of Rome for an unprecedented period of ten years.

'My dearest lady,' Caesar said, flashing his most engaging smile at Lucilia, 'it is a joy to see you once more, and looking so glorious. I must apologise for invading your wonderful home with a cohort of politicians.'

Lucilia gave a light laugh, murmuring her thanks and downplaying any trouble this might be. Fronto waited for the niceties to be out of the way. Caesar always had much to do, and since his return to Rome his free time had disappeared entirely, to the extent that he continued to enact laws even while attending the circus, his secretary taking dictated notes even as chariots piled up and riders died. He certainly had not had time for social visits. This, then, was clearly no such thing.

'Fronto, how has civilian life been treating you? I have spotted you in senate meetings, skulking at the back like a mischievous schoolboy, but you have yet to really make your mark. You are missing the battlefield too much perhaps?' He flashed a look to Lucilia, knowing damn well what she would think of that. Fronto twitched. Why was the bastard poking that little sore point?

'I was, in fact, looking forward to a comfortable retirement,' he replied. 'Just me and Lucilia, and the boys. I've no wish to play politician, but really, I've no wish to stand on a battlefield any more, either. I'm getting too old for that.'

He saw Lucilia's expression ease and congratulated himself on playing that particularly well. Caesar, however, greeted the comment with a smirk of disbelief. 'Come now, Marcus, I know you of old. You have walked away from war more than once, but you always found your way back. And age is no great leveller. Look at me, for I am some years your senior, yet come the Spring I will take to my horse and my cuirass, and let Parthia tremble at my coming.'

'Each to his own,' Fronto said quietly.

'And that is what I wish to see you about.'

Fronto saw Lucilia's expression harden again, and stepped in before anything else prompted an outburst. 'Caesar, if you are about to offer me a place on the field in Parthia, please do save your breath. I am adamant. I will not be returning to active service.'

Caesar laughed. 'A wager, then. I have a small, delightful estate on Capreae with its own cove of the most glorious blue water. I will *give* it to you if you make it to the next winter without relenting and seeking a position in the legions. I *know* you, Fronto.' He turned to Lucilia. 'But I also know that your lovely wife would rather you remain at her side and not in the sands of Parthia, so fear not, I am not here to offer you a role in my army.'

Again, Lucilia recovered her smile, though Fronto's eyes narrowed. What did the old goat want then? Fronto wasn't going east, he was adamant. Let Caesar wager his property, and Fronto would walk away with a new summer home. But if Caesar didn't want Fronto as an officer...'

'I have four months before I intend to depart,' the dictator said. 'I shall leave Rome three days after the Ides of March with my staff, which should give me just the right time to join the army on the other side of the Adriaticum before the campaigning season starts five days later. Oppius and Cornelius here will serve as proxies in Rome during the campaign, with Marcus Antonius standing as my fellow consul.'

His eyes darkened a little, then, and Fronto wondered if the man was having second thoughts about that. Certainly he and Antonius had not been seeing particularly eye to eye recently.

'It is the planning that I am finding difficult, Fronto. I prefer, as you know, to create the strategy of my own campaigns. I have done so as often as possible. But I find that with only a few months available to me in Rome before I depart, I am pulled in every direction every hour of the day by jobs that need doing. I simply do not have the time to fully prepare this campaign. I have achieved a certain level of planning. Many units have already been recalled and sent to Illyricum ready for the campaign, and I have put the main fleet on alert, but I have had little time to assign the staff, to plan the transport of the army, organise a sufficient supply system, assign depots, or to even look at the maps of Parthia and the East. And that is where you come in.'

Fronto glanced across at Lucilia. He half expected to see her glaring at either Caesar or himself, but was surprised to find her nodding along thoughtfully. He coughed. 'You need my help?'

Caesar nodded. 'I find that many of my best strategists are no longer able to help me. Your greatly-missed father-in-law was a man upon whose talents I used to rely, as also Paetus and others long-gone, not to mention a certain lieutenant of mine, damn his memory.'

An image of Titus Labienus flashed into Fronto mind, and he swiftly pushed it away again. The man had been a strategist and general to rival Caesar and, in the end, that was precisely what he'd done. To Fronto's knowledge, since the man's demise at Munda in the summer, Caesar had yet to speak his name.

'Suffice it to say,' Caesar added, taking a deep breath and straightening, 'all the men in whom I might place my trust with the planning of a grand campaign are gone. All bar one.'

'Two,' corrected Fronto, gesturing to the Junii cousins.

Decimus Brutus shook his head. 'I might have been able to help with the fleet, but I'm too busy anyway, Fronto. In the new year I'll be Praetor Peregrinus, and my duties will fully occupy my time. And Marcus here,' he nodded to the other Brutus, 'will be urban praetor.'

'Please, sit,' Lucilia said, 'and have wine and pastries.'

With grateful smiles, the visitors moved around the room and sank to couches. Fronto did the same, hurriedly grabbing the fold of his toga that began to slide free and throwing a glare at the slave who had stepped towards him to help and then stumbled to a halt.

As wine was poured and handed out and Cornelius Balbus took the first bite of one of the sweet treats, nodding appreciatively, Caesar leaned back a little, took a sip and then fixed Fronto with a level look.

'The thing is, Fronto, that you are hardly busy. As I said before, I've been watching you in the senate, and all you do is sit at the back, waiting for it to finish, occasionally standing and agreeing with people if you can't avoid it. I'm sure I've even seen you asleep a few times. You have the combined benefits of being one of my most experienced strategists with decades of service in the field across most of the republic, of being above reproach and utterly trustworthy, and of being, despite your position, mostly bored and free.'

Fronto sagged a little. That last was hard to argue. He'd assiduously avoided anything that smacked of actual work since his first senate session. He'd even toyed with hiring a lookalike to dress in a toga and sit there for him while he spent the time in the bars of the city. But he'd meant what he said. He was retired. He had absolutely no intention of going off to war again, and was adamant that he would be around for the rest of his boys' childhood. He would not leave them fatherless as his own sire had done. And, yes, Caesar had assured Fronto and Lucilia that he didn't want him out in Parthia. He just wanted someone to plan the campaign. But Fronto also knew both Caesar and himself. It would change. Without any intention, by the time Spring came around, Fronto would somehow be further involved. By summer he would be commanding a legion and stomping around some godsforsaken sandy shithole in the east, without even being able to remember how it was that he came to be there. It was a simple matter of Caesar being wily and persuasive beyond the level of common mortals and Fronto having one of the weakest wills ever encountered. It was inevitable. If he dipped his toe in this particular pond, he'd be doing backstroke by summer.

'No,' he said.

'Marcus, I need your help. I simply do not have the time to deal with so many minutiae, and you do. I will owe you. I will reward you. What is it that you seek? A praetorship? Governorship of a good province? Sicilia perhaps? What is it that you want? Plan Parthia for me and it is yours.'

Fronto blinked. That easy? And what did it say about the ridiculous level of power Caesar now wielded that he could make such an offer, when really it should be the senate appointing such positions. He found himself drifting, wondering, picturing life as the governor of Sicilia, or Sardinia. Perhaps even Hispania Citerior. He could govern from Tarraco, which meant he could live in the villa. They could move back to Hispania and enjoy the good life, and he could make a lot of money there. It was almost a second home to him, anyway. And...'

He shook his head. Bloody hell, but the man had almost had him, with just a governorship dangled before his eyes. But that dream evaporated when he realised what would actually happen. He would be appointed governor, but somehow he would still end up on a horse in the sands of the east bellowing for centurions to check ridges for Parthian cavalry, while his governorship went into abeyance for a future time, someone else occupying the seat in the meantime.

'No. This is not the job for me, Caesar.'

'You refuse me, Marcus? When I offer you greatness in return?' A suspicious look fell across the older man's features. 'Is this about the events the other day? Antonius attacked in the street, for merely being one of my amici? Do you fear being my amicus and drawing the anger of a rabble of ex-soldiers?'

Fronto snorted. 'Hardly. And anyway, I intend to do something about that. I'm going to raise it in the senate. A grand amnesty for all the survivors of the war who fought for Pompey and his people. Restitution. Payments of bonuses and grants to allow those enemy veterans to re-enter our society with no shame and no difficulty.' He grinned. 'And that will occupy far too much of my time to allow me the freedom to plan campaigns, I'm afraid. You see I finally have a purpose in the senate.'

He sat back and pulled up a fallen fold of toga, feeling smug. The dictator had thought the game won before it began, but Fronto had pulled a surprise move and put a playing piece right in Caesar's way, blocking him. Game over.

Caesar gave him an infuriating smile and Fronto's confidence slipped. Caesar had spotted a way round that blocking piece.

'Oh if that's the trouble, Fronto, let me help.'

'What?'

'Your proposal. It is an excellent idea. In fact, it should have been done already, and I cannot think of a senator who would vote against it. Spend a day or two scribbling down the details and have it sent to me. I will rush it through at the next meeting of the senate. We'll have it enacted before the consuls are chosen in the new year.'

Fronto sagged again, like an inflated pig bladder with a leak.

'Still, no.'

'Come, now, Marcus, I need only three or four months of your time. You can do this all from Rome, with perhaps a trip or two to Ostia. You will be home with your family every night, and I will offer your whatever you desire in return.'

'What I desire is not to plan a campaign. Can you offer me that?'

'What about the consulship.'

The room fell suddenly silent. Fronto's face passed through a dozen expressions in a matter of heartbeats, settling on bafflement. 'I cannot be consul. I've not held enough public posts.'

'You would be amazed at how many corners can easily be cut. And your reputation being one of scrupulous honesty and nobility, I doubt a single voice would be raised against your appointment.'

It was Marcus Brutus who spoke then. 'But the consuls for the year have already been decided, Caesar.'

Oppius nodded. 'Your noble self, and that cannot be changed. You need the consulship for the campaign. And Marcus Antonius. And he will need the position to deal with Rome in your absence.'

Caesar gave a humourless chuckle. 'Antonius' position as of my departure in March is still uncertain. I had him in mind as my Master of the Horse, controlling the equestrian order and dealing with Rome in my absence, but he continues to argue and raise difficulties. If he goes on the way he is, demanding a place in my army, I may have to reduce his authority and pass that on to Lepidus. And you gentlemen here will be heavily involved too, of course. Antonius can have the ordinary consulship in the new year, and lay it down in March. Then I will grant the suffect consulship to you, Fronto. Consul of Rome for nine months? How does that sound?'

Fronto was staring at him. Behind Caesar there was no higher position to be had in Rome, and no honour higher than could be bestowed upon a family. He found he was holding his breath and forced himself to breathe slowly.

'Unless I am much mistaken,' Caesar said with that infuriating smile back in place, 'no member of the Falerii have ever held the consulship? The *Valerii*, yes. They have held the esteemed place of consul repeatedly from the expulsion of the kings right down to the year we dealt with the revolt of Ambiorix. The Valerii are an honoured and respected gens of Rome. Sadly, your own offshoot of that great tree has yet to sprout such golden buds. I do remember hearing that your father was in line for the consulship but did something unfortunate and was removed from the running. The consulship for the Falerii, Marcus... their name forever in the annals of Rome.'

Fronto was still silent, actually lost for words.

'Marcus?' Caesar's tone was honeyed, enticing. Damn the man, but it was tempting. And it was only four months, all in Rome. That was the promise. It was the most incredible offer, and with no downside. Too good to be true.

And that was because it wasn't. That was the offer now, but like a good market trader with poor meat, the offer would change during the negotiation, and by the time Fronto walked away he'd have no money and only rotten meat. The consulship and working from Rome was the offer now, but by March, that would depend on Fronto being involved in Parthia. Caesar couldn't realistically take the consulship off Antonius this year, no matter what he said, not without turning the man against him. And he couldn't let it go himself, for he needed the authority to make war. This next year would have to still be Caesar in Parthia and Antonius in Rome, the two consuls. So, Fronto's offered consulship would slip to the next year instead, and it would transpire that this would give him a season to devote to Parthia. He would be consul designate, but he could guarantee he'd be leading a legion beforehand. That was how Caesar worked.

'No.'

He would not go to war again.

'Fronto? Really?' Caesar almost looked defeated, though he was rallying already.

Fronto knew the man, knew that if Caesar kept badgering and no one came to his aid, he would inevitably collapse under the weight of the pressure. He looked at the other gathered luminaries as Caesar continued to make promises and offers, but none of them looked like leaping in to interrupt. They were all hanging on Caesar's every word, in fact, nodding. In desperation, he glanced across at Lucilia. Of all people, she would be the one to stand and deny Caesar. She would not want Fronto going east, and she must know the man well enough now to know that was what would happen in the end. To his frustration, she also was nodding along to Caesar's words, hanging on them just like the rest.

He had to resist all temptation. He conjured up images in his mind that would help defend him against Caesar's words. Memories of Labienus standing in a field of dead Belgae, lamenting a war he deemed unnecessary. Pompey's head, removed in the most horrifying way just to appease Caesar. Gnaeus Verginius, Fronto's oldest friend, lying broken and dying in a quarry in Hispania, cursing Caesar with his last breath, and forcing a promise from Fronto that he really couldn't dare to think about. It was all so dark, so unpleasant that it kept a smile from his face throughout the next half hour.

Caesar's amici drank their wine, ate their pastries, commented occasionally and intelligently. Caesar hardly touched anything. His offers never changed in essence, for they could not. He had offered the greatest things he could, and yet Fronto had turned them down. He tried many approaches over that time, and only Fronto focusing on internal images that turned Caesar into a monster stopped him folding under the pressure and accepting.

Finally, eventually, Caesar stood and stretched with a sigh. 'I am surprised, Fronto. Surprised and not a little disappointed. But I know you, and I know how hard it is for you to deny this. The offer shall remain open. You have but to accept.'

He turned to Lucilia, complimenting her with the warmest of smiles, and, with a gesture to the others, he turned and strode from the room, gathering his people at the atrium and leaving the house. Fronto hardly dared breathe until he heard the doorman seeing them out and the door clicking shut. When he finally felt safe once more, master of his own destiny, he sagged.

'Phew.'

'You should accept, Marcus.'

Fronto blinked and turned to Lucilia, who had fixed him with an earnest look. 'What?'

'Caesar's offer. You should accept.'

Fronto frowned. This, he had not expected. He shook his head. 'I thought you knew Caesar better than that. It's all words, no substance. He promises me big things that he will hang in front of me like a carrot on a stick, and it starts now with planning a campaign for him, but by Spring, he will have me in a cuirass and on a horse in desert sands. That is how he works.'

'No. You have more strength of will now than you had back in the days you couldn't help running to his side. Having a family has changed you, Marcus. I've seen it. Galronus tells me how many times since Pharsalus you have promised Caesar just one more season until the war ends. And now it has. There are no more seasons, and you have broken free. I know you can refuse him, because I saw you do just that this past hour. I was so proud of you. And if you can do it now, you can do it again, and refuse to go east. But if Caesar offers you the consulship, he *will* grant it. If he vacillates, I will make it very difficult for him.'

Fronto blinked. 'You? How?'

'You do not think I have been throwing all these soirees for fun? Men are not the only ones who create networks, Marcus. I have the ear of many of Rome's most important women, the wives of its most important men, including Calpurnia, who is a darling. All you have to do is accept Caesar's offer and stand firm when the time comes. I will make sure that anything he offers you actually comes to pass.'

Fronto laughed. 'Gods, but Rome harbours Amazons without knowing it.'

Lucilia shook her head. 'Rome knows it. They came from Troy with Aeneas, you know? But I will have you accept that offer whether you like it or not, because our boys are a tender eight years old, but in only a decade they will be military tribunes and start climbing the Cursus Honorum. I do not want them to become bone-hard soldiers, Marcus. I want them to make their mark on Rome and to achieve greatness. And anything we can do to give them a leg-up on the ladder, we need to do. Having a father who has been consul will open doors that nothing else can. You know that.'

Fronto tapped his lip. She was nearly as convincing as Caesar, damn the woman. He didn't know why he was waiting. If Lucilia wanted it, he was never going to refuse. He cleared his throat and pointed to a slave. 'Find Catháin, Aurelius and Arcadios. I have a message for Caesar.' He turned to Lucilia. 'Catháin is an expert negotiator. He can carry my acceptance and guarantee not to accidentally agree to anything else.'

'Good,' Lucilia smiled. 'Then it is done.'

CHAPTER FOUR

For an hour following the departure of Caesar and then of his messengers, Fronto had sat in the triclinium with Lucilia, talking about the future and what these changes might mean. He was still unsure and more than a little conflicted in what he'd agreed to, yet when Lucilia spoke about it, as always, it all sounded too simple and sensible. It was only in the silences in between that he began to ponder once more on the probability that the only thing that would come of all this was Caesar arguing him back into active service by the summer. By the time an hour had passed, though, she had more or less convinced him that it was the right decision.

Then the boys had come in, having finished their morning chores and waiting for Gerontius, their tutor, to arrive for lessons. As was becoming more frequent by the day, trapped in the house by both winter weather and duty, Marcus and Lucius had spent that brief free time playing and causing trouble together. Predictably, that had quickly descended into play fighting, followed by a minor injury that had them shouting at one another until Lucilia intervened.

'He hit me.'

'Did not. The *wall* hit you. I just pushed.'

Fronto nodded earnestly at what seemed an important distinction there.

'Go to your rooms, separate, until Gerontius gets here,' Lucilia said, her tone brooking no argument. Such was her authority in the house that Fronto was halfway through rising to obey the command before he acknowledged that it had been meant for the kids.

Marcus and Lucius stomped out of the room glaring at one another. As soon as they were out of sight, Lucilia chuckled. 'One sestertius gets you ten that they're friends and causing trouble again before they even reach their rooms.'

'Domine?' came a call, echoing through the atrium.

Fronto turned a frown on Lucilia. It was not common practice for the doorman, whose voice it was, to call for them, rather than hurrying to find them and report. Rising, suddenly tense, Fronto padded from the room, Lucilia at his heel. More visitors? Trouble?

He passed through the atrium and turned into the vestibule, its little shrine to the household gods dominating the room with its statues, including Fronto's figurines of Fortuna and Nemesis that had travelled across the republic with him from war to war. The sight that greeted him in the doorway put him fully on the alert and without even looking, he waved a hand to attract the attention of whatever slaves or servants were in attendance.

'Go bring my guards. All of them.'

The doorman was crouched on the mosaic of Vesta with lamp and patera, over a heap that looked a lot like Aurelius, while Arcadios leaned against the wall nearby, his scarf tied around his thigh to staunch the blood that had poured from a deep wound in his calf. Blood was smeared all across the mosaic and the marble tiles. Two only had returned intact. Possible even one.

He hurried over, issuing further orders. 'Find the physician. He'll be in Salvius' room. Bring him here. Now.'

The medicus, one of Rome's best, for whom Fronto was paying a horribly high retainer, had been with them since their return, looking after Salvius Cursor, who was alive and breathing, yet still to wake from his comatose state after an attempted poisoning in the Spring. The physician had identified signs that the invalid was close to a return and had almost thought him waking a couple of times. Fronto harboured the private suspicion that Salvius was actually done for and that the physician was just giving them hope in order to continue his rather cushy position, well-paid and with room and board for the simple task of looking in on Salvius a few times a day. Well now there were actual wounds, the man could earn his keep.

Fronto hurried over. Arcadios was alright. The wound was deep, but the bone remained intact and the blood flow was curtailed for now. Fronto had seen enough battle wounds over the years, including a number of his own, to recognise injuries for what they were, and even to attempt an amateur triage.

'You ok?' he called to the Greek archer, throwing him a glance as he approached the heap on the floor.'

'I'll live,' grunted Arcadios.

But would Aurelius? His head was covered in blood and he was unmoving. Fronto checked his pulse and his breathing. He was still alive and steady. Perhaps he wasn't as bad as he looked. As the doorman held the former legionary up, Fronto probed his head for damage. He found a matted patch of hair where the skin was broken, and recognised the signs of a good thump from something hard. He chewed his lip. 'I think he'll be alright, too. Think he got his wits knocked from him.'

Arcadios nodded. 'I thought so too. With this leg, I could only bring one back, and Aurelius might live. Catháin...' he began, tailing off.

'Tell me.'

As the medicus arrived, several slaves with him carrying a bowl of warm water, fresh linen and his medical kit, and the guards of the household began to gather, moving out through the door to check the street nearby, Fronto wandered across to Arcadios by the wall.

'We got most of the way from here to Caesar's house. Just crossing the Aemilian Bridge we were attacked. They came from the far side, but it seems they had a few men following us too. When we saw them cutting us off, we turned to run, but found the way back blocked. No one around seemed inclined to interfere. We tried to retreat anyway.'

Fronto nodded, gesturing to Arcadios' wound. 'They let you get outside the pomerium, where some of them were armed for war. Wily bastards.'

'We gave better than we got. I reckon we downed at least six. Unfortunately, by the time we got back to the near bank, Catháin was done for. He'd taken a wound in the back, and I could see it killing him even as we ran.'

'How did you escape?'

'Catháin, clever sod even mortally wounded. He threw his purse of coins in the air, and all the locals flooded the area, chasing money. We managed to slip free, but a thrown rock caught Aurelius even as we got away. Catháin fell halfway across the cattle markets, and I checked, but he was gone before he hit the ground. I grabbed Aurelius as he passed out and dragged him until I found a baker's handcart, which I stole to bring him back.'

'Were they the same people who attacked Marcus Antonius?'

'I don't know. We didn't stick around to ask.'

Fronto chewed on his lip. It seemed likely. If they had been watching Caesar and had attacked Marcus Antonius just as a target of opportunity, there was every chance they watched Caesar come to Fronto's and had a go at the first group of men they could. If so, it represented another step towards open confrontation. 'I presume they'll have taken their dead or wounded.'

'Maybe,' Arcadios replied, 'but at least two of them went over the bridge parapet.'

Fronto nodded to himself and then turned to the others. 'Take care of Arcadios and Aurelius,' he said to the physician, then to the leader of his guards: 'Detail six men to stay here and watch. Don't open the door for anyone but me, understand?' They all nodded. 'The rest of you come with me. It's not far to the bridge.'

With that, he threw an apologetic look at Lucilia, who was ordering around the slaves, and dipped out of the door into the cold December air. It was not quite cold enough yet for snow or ice, but there remained the promise of such weather in the crisp morning. His men had already spread out into the street around the house, securing it and making sure no gang members were lurking in doorways. Once he was out with the others, they all gathered around and moved off down the slope of the Aventine towards the river, the house door closing resolutely behind them.

They descended to the wide street running along the side of the Circus Maximus, the upgraded seating stands donated by Caesar only recently completed and dedicated. Within a few short moments they were hurrying across the open square of the forum boarium with its merchants already doing business for the day. As they moved at a jog, Fronto kept his attention on the ground. There was no sign of Catháin, and given the amount of detritus on the ground of the cattle markets, there was no real way of telling where he'd been. No point in asking, either. The ordinary people of

Rome were infamously reticent when it came to remembering trouble when questioned.

Reaching the river, they hurried along the bank towards the bridge, but Fronto was looking down the slope and steps to the waterside rather than up at the parapet. There would be no bodies left on the bridge, but…

He spotted three shapes quickly, though they all needed more than a single look. Bodies in the Tiber were hardly an unexpected thing. Rarely did a day go past without some unfortunate washing up on the bank. Indeed, as they skittered down the slope towards the first shape, Fronto could see that it was a young woman with the remnants of a gown that left little to the imagination. Despite the lack of connection to his own problem, out of sheer interest, he turned her over. Through the grime and the discolouration of a day or two in the water, he could see the marks of strangulation around her throat. Hardening his heart against the poor girl's fate, he turned his attention to the next body.

A little further along, he found the remains of Catháin, thrown down the slope, out of the way of city life. Fronto felt the anger boiling up afresh. Until now, the trouble they'd had had been simple politics, and something he could at least try to look at objectively. Now, it was personal. Catháin had been his right hand man in business, had become a friend, and even a close one, a member of his familia. And the bastards had stabbed him in the back as he ran. And for what? Because he worked for a man who had a connection with Caesar?

He could feel his lip curling. He was becoming properly angry now. He gestured to two of his men. 'Pick him up. We take him with us.'

They did so, carefully, as Fronto moved on to the next huddled shape. The man initially appeared uninjured, but as Fronto turned the body, the head lolled at unnatural angles, confirming that the neck had been expertly broken, a move Fronto knew to be a favourite of Aurelius', when he was unarmed. He looked carefully at the man. He was scarred and weather-beaten, a general look that was highly suggestive of a former soldier. Remembering what Aurelius had found after the first attack, he pushed up the man's tunic sleeve. Sure enough there was a tattoo there. A wreath and a

V. Unlikely to be the Fifth Legion alongside whom Fronto had fought more than once in Caesar's wars. More likely a different Fifth, raised by Pompey. It more or less confirmed what he'd suspected. He realised he was gritting his teeth now, angry that this urban war of revenge had spilled over into Fronto's household. He looked around at the faces of his men. They looked little happier than he.

'Who knows anything about ex-legionary collegia?'

There was a ripple of head shakes, though two men stepped forward at one end. 'I know where there's a collegium of Caesar's veterans,' one supplied, while the other frowned. 'My da belonged to Marius' veterans on the Oppian, sir.'

'How do I find out where this lot meet?'

There was an extended pause, until a man cleared his throat. 'Surely it'll have to be logged in the tabularium, sir?'

Fronto blinked. Of course it would. Collegia were official guilds. They would have to be registered with the city's government. He nodded to himself, then gestured to them. Four of you take Catháin home and tell my wife that I'll be back by noon. The rest of you, pick up that piece of shit and come with me.'

As two of his guards heaved the body of the attacker up, Fronto marched off with purpose. With his men in tow, he strode through the flower market, considerably better smelling than the cattle market, gathering interested looks as he went, what with his private army and a body borne aloft. Beneath the infamous Tarpeian Rock they marched, then up to the Capitol. The tabularium, Rome's central records office, occupied the slope overlooking the forum, rising on massive substructures, a two-tier arcade running along the hillside fronting a building that housed dozens and dozens of offices. It took only a few enquiries to locate the office that held records of all the city's collegia. Fronto's men gathered around in the wide corridor, still carrying the corpse, while he stepped inside.

'I need to know the location of any collegia in the city formed of veterans of Pompey's legions,' he told the worried looking clerk. The man shot his nervous glance out through the door, where a body was bobbing around among a large group of hard-looking men. Quickly, he turned to his records, crossing to a large rack on the wall, filled with small wooden tablets. Moments later, he returned to the desk with two of them.

'Here we are, sir. Two such colleges, though only one is active. This one draws its members from the Esquiline, the Quirinal and the Viminal. It's a sizeable college with a recorded two hundred and eleven members.'

'A few less now, I suspect,' Fronto said darkly. 'The other?'

'The other was smaller and based on the Caelian. But it was disbanded two months ago after a number of local thefts were linked to the house. They had their charter removed, their meeting house was impounded, and the leaders were sentenced to exile.'

'Seems likely I'm after the other one, then. Where's their meeting house?'

'Err, on the corner where Lampmakers meets Tibur Street, just north of the Clivus Suburanus.'

Fronto smiled a hard smile at the man. 'Thank you.' And with that, he turned and exited once more. 'Come with me,' he said to his men.'

In moments they had exited the great office complex and were marching across the city, passing the grand forum that had recently been completed in Caesar's name, housing at its heart the temple of Venus Genetrix, honouring the great man's divine ancestor.

Given a long walk across half the city, it should be possible for a man to cool down a little, to gain perspective and calm his anger. Fronto was not such a man today. Every footstep made him a little bit more angry, and by the time they turned into the Lampmakers Street and marched up towards the crossroads they sought, he was aware that he was probably more angry than was really good for him. He was about ready to start breaking heads, and had to force himself to gain a little more control, given that there might well be the better part of two hundred of them in there, while he had just a small guard with him.

It was not hard to identify the meeting house of the collegium. Where the road met Tibur Street, one corner building was clearly neither residential nor commercial, lacking the standard store fronts, instead with a single unmarked door and a row of large windows well above head height. Fronto looked at the door for a moment, and identified a wreath motif expertly carved into the timber panels. This was definitely the place. Reaching up, he hammered on the wood.

No answer. He waited for a short while, and then repeated his heavy knock. Still nothing. Listening carefully, he could hear the distant sounds of movement and conversation within through those high, open windows. They had to know he was knocking, which meant the lack of an answer was deliberate. Just to be sure, he hammered a third time, even harder, and immediately put his ear to the door. They knew.

When there was still no answer, he looked this way and that, and then up. The windows were not shuttered, allowing daylight into the building. What he would give for a cart, but vehicles were forbidden in the city streets in the hours of daylight, without special permission being sought. His eyes fell upon a man further down the street, busily painting the outside of a shop, standing near the top rung of a ladder, paint tub balanced precariously as he worked.

In a matter of moments, and with the exchange of a few coins, Fronto and his men were carrying the ladder back. While Fronto stood at the door once more with most of his men, three of them climbed the ladder towards the open window, and manhandling the body of the attacker with the broken neck up between them. They reached the top and, at a nod from Fronto, threw the body in through the window, quickly sliding back down the ladder and hurrying over to join him, while the painter retrieved his property.

Fronto listened for a moment and as soon as he heard the shouting begin inside, he hammered on the door once more. This time, as he stepped back, he heard approaching footsteps. Preparing, he folded his arms. His men needed no cue to gather around him and look menacing.

The door opened. A single man, maybe in his early fifties, stood in the hallway. He leaned on a stick, though Fronto noted the stout shape of the cane and surmised it was used for combat at least as much as support. The man's expression was distinctly unfriendly.

'Take me to your leaders,' Fronto said, expression flat.

The man's eyes narrowed for a moment, then he went for the door, as if to close it again. Fronto reached out and slapped his palm against the timbers, pushing it wider.

'You've no right,' began the man.

'Now,' snapped Fronto, glaring at him.

Behind, some way along the corridor, two more figures emerged from a door. 'It's alright, Tellus,' one of them said, 'let him in.'

The man stepped to one side, and Fronto walked in, his men following him two-abreast. Ahead, those two men disappeared back into that doorway, from which pale light leaked. Fronto marched to the door and turned. Beyond it was a large hall, those high windows bathing it in cold morning light. Perhaps two score men were gathered on three tiers of stepped seating around the edge. Four men stood at the far end, and Fronto assumed the pair who'd granted him entrance to be two of them.

'Greetings, Marcus Falerius Fronto,' one of them said in a cold, carefully neutral tone. 'You have our thanks for returning to us the body of a fallen brother. I trust he has presented no difficulty.'

Fronto marched on. His men had stopped in the centre, but Fronto strode straight forward until he came face to face with the man who'd just spoken, and only stopped an arm length away. He lifted his hand and pointed his finger at the man's nose.

'I don't know whether you lot are working for some shit-brick who has a problem with Caesar, or whether you're just disgruntled and feeling hard done by, and taking it out on the man who beat you at Pharsalus and in Africa, and frankly, I don't care.'

His words echoed, bouncing around the high, bare walls of the large hall. The man before him made no reply, nor did his friends. He simply stood, stony faced, watching, waiting.

'I was prepared to take your case to the senate, to ask for bonus payments to all veterans of the wars, regardless of who they fought for. Because the wars are theoretically over, and Rome is supposed to be at peace. But you lot cannot let the war end, can you?'

'You do not know of what you speak, senator,' the man said, still stony faced.

'Yes I fucking do. You can take your grievances to Caesar and do what you like, even when it moves on to his friends, men like Marcus Antonius. They're big boys. They can handle a little opposition. And I might even have been able to allow you to set yourselves against me. I know I probably led men against you

52

more than once, and my lads are growing fat and happy on war profits while you lot have at the best a small pension.' He paused. 'But when you start attacking my people, that makes it personal. The man you killed on the bridge today was no soldier. He never fought against you, or against anyone. He was a wine merchant, for gods' sake.'

'Unfortunate,' said stony-face. 'Perhaps one day you will find the culprits. But you will not find them here.'

'Don't bullshit me. I've met much better liars than you. The senate meets again once more before the new year. If there are no repeats of this unacceptable violence in the city and my people feel safe to walk the streets once more, I will carry through my promise and see your veterans settled comfortably with the conviction of the senate. If, however, there is any further incident I can link to you, or a single one of my people meets with an unfortunate accident, not only will I do no such thing, but I will make it my life's work to be a personal plague to your collegium, burning through your people until you can't supply enough members to play a board game. I will end you all. That is a promise. Now take my words to heart and I will leave in peace. Your move. Be very careful what you do.'

With that, he turned and strolled back across the room. Reaching his men, they gathered around him, and strode with him back to the outer door, which had been opened ready. Silence reigned in the room as he left, and it was only once they were a little way down the street that Fronto took a deep breath and spoke again.

'What did you think?' he asked the guards about him.

'Beggin' your pardon, sir, but I wouldn't trust any one of them as far as I could shit him down a pipe.'

'Quite. I formed the distinct impression that my threat fell on deaf ears. There were a lot of them, and if the numbers on record are anything like correct, that was less than a quarter of them. They're almost an army. If they're going to be roaming the street, taking it out on Caesarians, it's time those of us who stand to be targets organised more of a defence. You lads are good, for Masgava would choose no fool, but against two hundred veterans even you lot will get battered. I need to warn Caesar, Antonius,

Brutus and the others that they need to increase their own security. As for me, I have my own idea. This lot are an army of veterans, then so we shall get our own.' He looked back across the heads of his guards and identified the man who'd spoken earlier. 'You said you knew of a collegium of Caesar's veterans?'

The man nodded. 'Yessir. They meet in a house not far from the Navalia.'

'Show me.'

With that guard now leading, they descended the Esquiline and headed across town for the Tiber once more. Even from some distance away it was always easy to spot the Navalia, Rome's riverside military harbour. It was a rare day when there were not at least three triremes docked there, large masts and sails rising above the level of the open spaces around, showing at the end of streets. For a while they seemed to be making directly for the port, but just before they emerged out into the main street opposite, they turned and moved down the Vicus Stabularius. They came to a halt opposite the Baths of Fortunatus, and the guard indicated a door in a largely featureless wall. Much like the last collegium, identifiable only from the wreath carvings on the door, this house was unnamed, barring a single carving of a bull above the door, the symbol of Caesar's legions, sported on their shields across the whole world for a decade and a half now.

Stepping across to the door, Fronto reached up and rapped upon it. There was a prolonged silence, and finally the approach of solitary footsteps. The door edged open halfway and an old grey-hair appeared in the gap. Fronto adjusted his thinking in that moment. The man was probably only a few short years older than him. Mentally Fronto might still feel thirty, but the body containing him had aged considerably.

'Could...' he began, quietly, but the veteran's eyes widened in surprise, and he bowed his head respectfully.

'Senator,' he said, his voice reedy but proud. 'It is an honour.'

As Fronto frowned, unused to such treatment, the man reached across and pulled up his sleeve to display a tattoo of rearing horse and bull, either side of an X.

'Tenth legion,' Fronto said with a smile.

'Glorious Tenth, sir,' the man grinned. 'Good to see the commander looking so well.'

Fronto laughed. 'And so old,' he added. He frowned, estimating the man's age again. 'You would have been at the Sabis. Maybe at Vesontio and even Geneva?'

The man's grin widened. 'I marched out of Cremona with you, sir, against the Helvetii. And I rode with the Tenth against Ariovistus.'

'I need to speak to your collegium,' Fronto said quietly. 'When do they gather?'

'We've maybe half a dozen of the seniors here today, sir, including a representative. Whatever you need to say, you can say to them.'

Fronto nodded. 'Please lead on.'

With his men at his heel he entered the building. The old veteran waited for them all to pass the threshold and then closed the door behind them and locked it, before hurrying to the front again, head bowed as he led them on into the building. Where he brought Fronto was no great hall, though, like the other meeting house. He was led instead into an office large enough only for a few people. Three men were seated around a table, all in good quality tunics that bore a marked resemblance to a military cut. On the wall behind them was a replica of a legionary standard with a bull emblazoned upon it.

As they entered, the three men stopped talking, a set of lists lying on the table between them, and all three faces turned to Fronto. In the blink of an eye, the man directly opposite seemed to recognise the visitor and rose to his feet.

'Good morning,' Fronto said, smiling. His guards he'd now left out in the corridor, for surely there was no danger here.

'Legate Fronto,' the man said, head bowed. '*Senator*, Fronto, I'm sorry.'

'I come seeking help. Or perhaps it might be said with a proposition.'

'Sir?'

'It would appear that a nefarious bunch of ex Pompeian veterans are targeting Caesar and his allies. With the streets becoming increasingly dangerous, I wondered whether it may be that your collegium is looking to pick up a little extra work, for appropriate payment, of course.'

There was a strange silence for a moment, then one of the other men at the table clicked his tongue, and rubbed his chin. 'Protection duties, you mean, sir?'

'More or less. Just to be on hand and do what needs to be done to protect Caesarian interests in the city.'

'It would have to be strictly protection, sir,' the first speaker said.

'Oh?'

'One of the conditions of the charter for our collegium, indeed for every ex-military collegium, is an agreement not to become involved in any breach of the city's peace. We are permitted to protect ourselves and our members, and to deal with criminals appropriately, but if we are found to be connected to any reported menacing behaviour we could have our charter revoked, and lose all our benefits.'

Fronto nodded. 'That sounds fair. And protection was largely the point. I would be happy to offer your members a stipend to match what I pay my own bodyguards, monthly and on an ad hoc basis.'

The man chewed his lip. 'I will have to put it to a full vote of the members, sir.'

'You're an expert on legal nuances now, are you Fontalis?' called a new voice as a figure stepped into the room. The man who'd been addressing Fronto took a step back, lowering his eyes.

Fronto turned to the newcomer and blinked in surprise. Carbo looked much the same. A little older, a little smaller, but still stocky and with that pink, shiny pate he remembered so well. He'd not seen the former primus pilus of the Tenth for half a decade, the man last heard of in the role of camp prefect of the Thirteenth.

'Carbo?'

'Legate. Don't worry about us. We're with you. And if the worst comes to the worst, I know men who can argue our case in the courts. Can't have the general's men being targeted can we?'

Fronto grinned. 'Good. I'll return tomorrow, if that's alright, once you've had a chance to call your meeting? How many members do you have?'

'One hundred and nine, sir,' Carbo replied.

Fronto smiled at the thought that, including his guards and friends, he now had the better part of two centuries of ex-soldiers working for him, including a man he trusted implicitly. That smiled lasted all the way out into the street, when his calculations had been mentally completed and he'd worked out how much money one hundred and nine new men were going to cost on a monthly basis. In a good Roman household, it was always the wife who controlled the purse. He was going to have to be very nice to Lucilia this afternoon.

CHAPTER FIVE

Fronto, standing in the archway, accepted a pastry-wrapped wad of greasy meat from Galronus. He eyed the contents suspiciously as drips fell from the bottom, slapping onto the cobbles as something brown and unidentifiable steamed up at him. He glanced across at his friend, who was busy tucking into another wrapper with gusto, shrugged, and took a bite, looking over his shoulder now. Away down the street he could see the gathering of Caesarean veterans with Aurelius at the fore, sporting crisp white bandages around his head. They lurked in arcades and doorways in small gatherings and pairs, and unless you knew they were all one group it would be easy to mistake them for just another part of the ordinary life in the street.

'How many do you suppose there are?' he asked, taking another mouthful of the suspicious snack.

Galronus looked out of their shadowy hiding place, glancing back down the street. 'All of them,' he frowned.

'Not them,' Fronto sighed. *'Them,'* he added, pointing out through the archway.

Across the street, a gathering of tunic'd men armed with stout cudgels were gathered around the doorway of a grand house, the shops built into its outer walls occupied by nervous looking proprietors keeping out of the way of the armed gang.

'Forty or so. Maybe fifty.'

Fronto nodded. That confirmed his own estimate. It also meant that they outnumbered Fronto's gang by three men to two, or thereabouts.

'What are they up to?'

Galronus remained silent, the question rhetorical. Fronto was in half a mind as to whether this whole thing had been a good idea or not. It had seemed so initially.

58

The man he'd set watching the meeting house of Pompey's veterans had sent a message via a street urchin that had interrupted Fronto's salutatio. That alone had been worth it, really. Now that he was a senator, and a serving one in the city, Fronto had rapidly acquired a cadre of clients, helped along by Lucilia's social networking, and now it seemed his mornings were to be taken up in granting an endless stream of favours to oily would-be politicians and desperate shopkeepers. Lucilia had assured him they would be of value in due course, but for now they were little more than an irritation. Still, when the messenger had arrived, he'd found the perfect excuse to draw the session to an early close and send disappointed clients away. Standing here in a clandestine manner and in potential danger was a great deal more satisfying than sitting in a big room and listening to people complain and beg, after all.

The Pompeians had gathered in numbers in the street outside the meeting house, according to the message, and that had piqued his interest. Over the days since his visit, he'd made sure to keep the place under surveillance, and the collegium had met at least every other day, though rarely with more than a dozen members. From what he understood, full meetings were called once a month at most. But they always gathered inside their house, for their private meetings. Not in the street. This was different enough to draw attention.

Gathering his things, shunning the toga and throwing on his military cloak, Fronto had grabbed Galronus and sent Aurelius to seek the aid of his own pet collegium, telling them to gather two streets across from the Pompeian meeting house. He and the Remi noble had then left the house with a small entourage of guards, waving away slaves, servants, litters and all the trappings of nobility. He had to move fast and draw little attention. He wanted to know what would cause a gathering of Pompeian veterans in the street, and that meant subtlety, not entourage.

He and Galronus had reached the house in time to see a sizeable gathering having formed, three of them handing out clubs to each member present. Their being armed set off a number of extra alarms with Fronto and he was immediately grateful that he'd sent for help.

Watching them from the shadows of a side street, he kept one guard with him and sent Galronus off to meet the Caesarian collegium and keep them close, but out of sight. He'd tried to count the enemy heads several times, but as they moved about he repeatedly lost count. Finally, some consensus was reached and an order given, and they began to move, flowing away up the street, military boots clacking on the dirty stones, and Fronto waited until they were all on the move, the last man glancing over his shoulder briefly before following on. Then he emerged from his side alley some distance behind them, and moved along the street wrapped in his cloak, his guard close by, just two figures swathed against the cold in a street of similar people. He made sure occasionally to move from one side of the street to the other, or to pause at stalls or shop fronts, to minimise the impression that he was actively following them.

Two blocks up the street, he glanced left and right and spotted Galronus and Aurelius standing in conversation, blending in with the general street life. He couldn't see a gathering of his own veterans, but then that had to be a good thing, since they were supposed to be hidden. As he moved on, Galronus caught up and walked alongside him nonchalantly.

'Aurelius has about twenty men, one block across. They'll move parallel with us, close enough to help if need be but out of sight.'

Fronto nodded. 'What are this lot up to? They're armed for trouble.'

Galronus had simply shrugged, and, with the guard close behind, they followed on, chatting calmly like any pair of citizens in the street. The Pompeian collegium moved with purpose, heading across the saddle of the Esquiline and Viminal hills, moving into a more salubrious area, spotted with the houses of the wealthy, the streets wider and cleaner than those down towards the heart of the city.

That was where the Pompeians halted.

Fronto and Galronus had continued to walk a little, making sure not to draw their attention, and had then turned into the archway of a passage leading under a brick building, where they slipped into the shadows and watched. His guard, sent away before they had stopped, had gone to liaise with Aurelius, and as the two watchers had settled into position under the arch, and the crowd of Pompeians had massed outside the building opposite, Fronto's own collegium had emerged from the side street in small groups and gathered a little down the street. They weren't as subtle as they probably thought they were, but the Pompeians had all their attention locked on their destination and failed to notice the gathering behind them.

One of the men emerged from the enemy crowd and approached the door. As he moved, he handed his club to one of his compatriots, then rapped on the timber. The door opened a little and Fronto could just see across the street, past the visitor, the shape of a bulky doorman within, gripping his own cudgel. There was a brief verbal exchange, and the man was admitted, disappearing into the gloom, the door shut behind him.

Outside, there was a sense of anticipation among the gathered Pompeians.

'Whose house is that?' Galronus murmured.

'No idea,' Fronto answered. 'Someone wealthy, though. A senator I imagine.'

They continued to wait, though they moved a little further back into the shadows, since now the gathered Pompeians were at a loss for something to occupy them and turned this way and that, taking in their surroundings. Fronto prayed that Aurelius was alert enough to keep the others looking like ordinary street life, and since there was no sign of sudden alertness among the Pompeians, it seemed he had succeeded.

The following quarter of an hour was strange and tense, and Fronto was rather grateful when finally the door of the house opened once more and the leader of the collegium emerged and re-joined his people. Half a dozen of them crowded close and there was a brief discussion, which ended with the man nodding in confirmation of something, and a sense of increased anticipation in the street.

As the crowd moved off once more, Fronto looked all about, noting everything he could about their location. He would want to identify the house's owner later, and would need to know exactly where he was. Observations complete, he and Galronus moved up to the archway once more and looked along the street. The Pompeians had moved on, but were clearly not returning to their meeting house, for they turned into another side road, heading in the direction of the Quirinal hill.

'I wish I had even a clue what they were up to,' Fronto grumbled as he and Galronus followed on, once more trying to blend in with the ordinary street life. Glancing over his shoulder, he could see the general shift in the street as the Caesarians followed on in small groups, trying not to draw attention.

'Maybe they've just received instructions?' The Remi mused.

Fronto chewed his lip, nodding. Certainly that house was the house of a rich and powerful man, and only one man had gone in, unarmed. It was more than possible that all the collegium's activity was directed by a powerful master with a deep purse, rather than by their collective anger and sense of inequality. Was this their master's house? Had he given them fresh instructions? A new target to hunt?

'Where are we now?' Galronus asked as they turned another corner and moved into narrower, less wealthy streets. The Remi had spent much time in the city's centre and on the Aventine and Caelian hills, but a lot less on the heights of Rome's hills to the north of the forum. There was little in the way of entertainment venues and taverns up here, so nothing to attract Galronus. Or Fronto, for that matter.

'That big temple,' Fronto said, pointing to the back of a huge building just visible off to their left along a side street, 'is the temple of Quirinus. We're just coming down from the Quirinal. No more houses of the rich this way. Just insulae, shops and shitty streets.'

The Remi nodded to himself as they moved to lower ground, back into the built-up body of the city. The pair of them almost walked into trouble as the crowd of Pompeians stopped at another building, and Fronto and Galronus backed off hurriedly into another shadowy doorway. Fortunately they didn't seem to have been spotted, and the two men watched, a sense of foreboding building.

The structure opposite was a simple insula of brick, not unlike many in the region, better quality than the more common wooden blocks, and with far less chance of burning down, but still generally the home to less wealthy citizens, shops built into the ground floor, stairways leading up between them into the landings from which apartments led off. The Pompeians largely remained gathered in the street, though this time they were not so much waiting, as guarding. While eight of their number disappeared into a stairwell, the rest turned their attention to their surroundings, guarding the doorway, watching the street crowd.

Careful, Fronto and Galronus made sure to keep to the shadowy interior of the doorway, watching.

There was a prolonged silence, other than the standard background noise of the street, and every moment they waited, Fronto felt a greater and greater sense of building trouble. His ear twitched at a sound. Somewhere beneath the blanket of city noise, he could just hear trouble. Closing his eyes, he focused. Definitely trouble. Muffled, indoors, somewhere in that tenement building, high up, several storeys above street level. Just about where those eight men would have got to by now.

He opened his eyes and looked up, gaze tracking the sound from one open window to the next as it climbed the side of the insula. As his eyes locked onto the aperture that was the source of the fracas, he blinked in shock to see a figure emerge.

The man gave a howl of terror as he hurtled from the window out into the open air some forty feet above the street. The gathered Pompeians in that direction scattered, many of them having been looking up in anticipation. The waiting collegium surged out of the way as a plain tunic'd figure plummeted through the air and hit the stone flags and gathered ordure of the street with a wet crunch.

Fronto stared in shock, the killing replaying in his mind as his gaze rose from the body to the window and back several times. Figures appeared in that window, looking down at their victim, and then retreated into the shadowy interior once more. The body in the street lay still, a dark lake forming around it, liquid cascading down the gentle slope between the cobbles.

Fronto fought the urge to shout. For just a moment, he'd felt the distinct desire to call together his own men and lay into this bunch of murdering bastards, but he bit down on the command. Starting a small war in the street right now was not an appropriate response.

Not yet, at least. Not without knowing more about what was going on.

He watched, lip twitching, as members of the Pompeian collegium came close, examining the fallen man, careful not to step in the blood. Two of them gave the broken corpse an extra kick for good measure, and a number of them spat on him. Finally, the killers emerged from the doorway and re-joined the crowd, which gave a victorious rumble of satisfaction, and then turned and surged off up the street the way they'd come.

Fronto waited, trembling with anger, as they moved, and then, as they became suitably distant, emerged from the shadows and beckoned down the street. Aurelius and the Caesarians began to move up to join him.

'Aurelius, take half the men and follow them. Keep yourselves hidden. I suspect they're heading home, given their direction, but if they get up to anything else, send a runner back here and home.'

The bandaged veteran nodded and gestured for a number of the collegium to join him, then moved off up the street in pursuit of the Pompeians. Once they were alone, Fronto looked at the gathered faces of his men. Carbo had not been one of veterans in attendance that morning, and he found that he was disappointed in that. He'd have felt better with the sturdy former centurion by his side.

The ordinary citizens of Rome had now emerged from their shops and houses, gingerly approaching the body, looking up at the window, pointing and murmuring to one another. Fronto huffed, wondering what to do. Policing the streets wasn't the job of a senator, but then it wasn't really *anyone's* job. In the legions, crime was handled by men assigned to keep order, directed by centurions. The city had no such measures. Perhaps it was time Rome had a peace keeping force of its own.

'Everyone back,' he shouted, stepping across the street towards the body. He had no badge of office, lacking even his toga, but his commanding tone and his accompanying veterans were enough authority to send the civilians scattering back to their doors, away from the corpse.

With the others at his shoulders, Fronto approached the dead man. He was dressed in a tunic and boots of average quality, unadorned by anything but a single ring on his finger. He looked at the body. He could just see the edge of a legion tattoo peeking out from beneath the tunic sleeve, and though he couldn't see enough for detail, he already felt sure it had to be one of Caesar's legions. As he crouched, a voice behind him gasped in surprise.

'I *know* him.'

Fronto paused, straightening again and turning. One of the veterans of his collegium had stepped out front and was pointing down at the body. The corpse's face was bloody but intact, for it had been the back of the man's skull that had exploded on impact.

'Who is it?'

'His name's Sallentius, sir. I served with him in the Thirteenth. We were with you at the Rubicon, sir, when we marched on Rome. He was a centurion's clerk, sir.'

'A clerk?' Fronto frowned. Targeting Caesar, Antonius and Fronto made sense in some way, for they were the men who had commanded, who had led legions against the Pompeians. A clerk, though? An ordinary soldier? What could be important enough to drive them to find his home and murder him in public?

'Third Century, First Cohort, sir. His centurion was in charge of transfers, recruitment and personnel records for the Thirteenth.'

Fronto sucked on his teeth. That made him a little more important than most military clerks, but still this seemed odd. 'Take a note of the window he fell from and follow me, eight of you. Including you,' he added, pointing at the man from the Thirteenth.

With them in tow and the others gathering near the body to keep people away, Fronto made his way across to the open doorway at the bottom of the insula. It only occurred to him as he turned the dark corner of the stairwell onto the first landing that he'd not counted the killers as they re-emerged, and it was faintly possible that they had left one or more of their number in the building. Gripping his hands into fists and wishing for a sword, he turned the next few corners very quietly and carefully. His lungs beginning to feel the effort of the climb, he reached the top of the flight that led to the floor he estimated to be that of the clerk's home. As his men joined him, Fronto crossed to a window and looked down. A dim side alley was all he could see. He moved around to another window and when he looked down from it, he could see the body and his men below. Orientation confirmed, he worked out where the fatal window would be, and approached a closed door in that direction. He felt the anticipation build once more, and motioned for the others to be ready. If the door was properly sealed, that meant there was still someone inside.

He reached out, slowly, carefully, and gave the door a push. It swung inwards by a foot, then scraped on the floor. A little extra push and it opened fully to reveal a well-kept, if not particularly high class apartment. Two rooms, every space visible pretty much from the door, unless someone was hiding in a corner. Fronto peered left and right, making sure no one was lurking behind the door, then stepped inside and beckoned to the others. Using hand signals he ordered men to search the place, while he crossed to the window and looked down. It made him shiver, and he stepped back swiftly, having confirmed this was most definitely the place. It was hard looking out from there and not imagining being tipped through it.

'Clear,' called two voices from the little kitchen-dining room that led off this bedroom.

Fronto let his tension ebb. The enemy had all gone, and the home had had but one occupant. Something caught his eye, then, and he crossed to a small desk with a single rickety chair. A pen and well of ink sat there, the nib still wet from writing. There was no parchment or vellum, though. Whatever he'd been writing had been taken. Damn it.

Scouring the table, he found a stack of clean, unused parchment in a box, and three wooden cases for wax tablets. On the off-chance, he opened each of them. Two had a good wax layer within, one clean and freshly scraped, one containing what could only be a shopping list. The third was empty of wax and discoloured with smoky black, awaiting the pouring of fresh wax to revitalise it.

A suspicion upon him, Fronto looked about and then moved into the kitchen. It didn't take too long to find what he was looking for. A simple pottery bowl sat on a kitchen worktop with an extinguished candle nearby, and in the bowl was a small, hard puddle of dried plain wax.

'Bollocks.'

Galronus crossed to him. 'What is it?'

'Whatever he was writing has been taken, and whatever was on this tablet, he destroyed. Look, he melted the wax over a candle and let the message run into the bowl. Must have been important. He couldn't risk scraping the wax and leaving any sign of the message.'

'I think, sir,' the man from the Thirteenth said, appearing at his shoulder, 'that there wasn't enough wax to scrape easily. There's hardly any wax in the bowl. There can only have been a thin layer in the tablet. It was well used.'

Fronto sighed. 'Same problem, though. The message is gone.'

'Maybe not, sir.'

He turned a frown on the man. 'Oh?'

'I served as a clerk for a year or two as well, sir. You learn a few tricks.'

As he reached out to take the tablet case, Fronto relinquished it readily. The man found a piece of cloth from one of the surfaces and looked at the soot-discoloured wood. Placing it on the worktop, he put the cloth into the case and rubbed the surface hard. After a little work, he lifted away the cloth and leaned back.

Fronto blinked. The soot had been pushed into indentations in the wood, leaving faint traces of words. 'Impressive.'

'When there's not much wax, if the writer presses hard, it leaves a trace of the message on the wood below,' the man said.

Fronto took the case back and peered at it. 'I can only make out parts. I can see the word 'singulares.' And 'recruit.' And 'contubernium' And something at the bottom. Looks like a name. The sender, I guess.'

'What does it mean?' Galronus mused.

'He was a trained clerk with a history of dealing with transfers and recruitment. If you wanted to recruit a singulares – a bodyguard – of, say, a contubernium of eight men, who would you approach to help?'

Galronus frowned. 'Him.'

'Quite. Someone had him building a bodyguard. And I would hazard that the list he was writing was potential recruits, all of whose names are now in the hands of those Pompeians. That smacks of an impending eight-man bloodbath to me.'

'I think this name is Cornelius, sir,' the veteran said, pointing to the tablet case. 'And the next word starts with a B, I reckon.'

Fronto peered at it. 'I think you're right. And that second name is Balbus. Cornelius Balbus.'

'Who's that?' Galronus asked.

'Caesar's secretary. Caesar's putting himself together a small extra bodyguard in addition to his lictors. Or maybe someone is doing it for him. Though I don't think they'll make it through the night.'

Galronus drummed his fingers on his folded arms. 'Can we stop them?'

'We can't anticipate it, because we don't have the list, so we can't warn anyone. All we could do is follow them and attack them when they find the first man. That way a small street war looks likely.' He thought about the body in the street. 'Tempting, though. The enemy outnumber our lads quite heavily, but if we could get enough men, we might be able to do something about it.' He looked at the veteran from the Thirteenth. 'Take the others. Head back to the Pompeian collegium house. If they go home, just have them watched. If they go after anyone else, I want you lot to use your brains. If you can stop them without a disaster, do it, but if you're outnumbered enough that you're unlikely to win, just keep watch and report back.'

The man saluted and he and the others moved off.

'And what are *we* going to do?' Galronus asked.

'We're going to find out who's behind all this.'

With the Remi at his heel, Fronto descended the stairs once more. There, he posted one of the men to wait for any news from the others, with orders to pass it on to Fronto's house on the Aventine. Four men had stayed in the street, waiting for him, and with the other three in tow, he turned and headed south, making for the heart of the city once more. Back at the centre, he passed the new forum of Caesar's and the great new temple of Venus Genetrix and climbed the slope of the Capitol. The city records office was as busy as always, but a simple enquiry was enough to guide him to the appropriate office. Finding the signed door, he made his way in. Three clerks were busy filing, and one, noticing

68

the new arrivals, put down his pile of records and approached them.

'Can I help, sir?'

'I'm seeking the owner of a specific property.'

'Naturally, sir, otherwise you wouldn't be here.'

Fronto frowned. Sarcasm. Great. 'It's on the Viminal.'

'Perhaps we could narrow it down a little more, sir?'

He glared at the clerk. 'Large estate on the Vicus Porta Collina, not far from the gate end of the street. Just down the slope a little from the reservoir of the Aqua Marcia, on the opposite side of the street.'

The clerk nodded. 'That should be enough, sir. Bear with me.' And with that, he scurried off to the racks of documents, located the one he was looking for, and withdrew it, crossing to a table near Fronto. There, he removed the lid from the scroll case and pulled free the contents, laying it on the table and flattening it out, one hand at the top, one at the bottom as he examined the listings.

'From that end, we have the office of a scribe, the house of a tutor in eastern languages, and a rug shop. The first proper residential property sits behind them, and I believe this is the one you're looking for. The estate is just short of two hundred and fifty iugeri in area, including gardens and bath house, with the main entrance facing onto the Vicus Porta Collina. Last valued several decades ago, but was worth five hundred and sixty thousand sesterces at the time.'

Fronto nodded, lip twitching. That sounded about right. Enough value to qualify for the senate at least. 'Who?'

The man ran his finger down the listings. 'One Publius Plautius Hypsaeus, sir.'

Fronto straightened, folding his arms. 'Hypsaeus. Interesting.'

The man remained ready with the scroll until Fronto waved it away with one hand. Beside him, Galronus coughed. 'Who is that?'

'Do you remember Clodius? And Milo?'

The Remi nodded. Who could forget the gangsters who had supported Caesar and Pompey, who had led small wars in the streets of Rome, burning down buildings and running crime in whole regions. Both men were long dead now, and their absence had only improved life for most of the city.

'Well Hypsaeus was another of their kind. A man with enough influence and money to have done great things, but who was more interested in amassing personal power and control. In a way, he was brighter than both Milo and Clodius, if less ambitious. He was clever enough not to get involved in the Caesar-Pompey conflict that caused the death of the others. But he was also shrewd enough to disappear from the limelight when Caesar gained full control of the city. I wouldn't have said he was ever an enemy of Caesar directly, but he was certainly never his ally. He ran gangs years ago, and if there was a man around now with the knowledge, experience and finance to hire a strong collegium, he certainly fits the bill.'

'So now we have a potential name.'

Fronto nodded. 'We'd best get home. If our Collegium has found out anything, they'll have sent messages there.'

Leaving the tabularium and thanking, rather tersely, the officious clerk, they descended the hill and left the centre of the city, passing around the edge of the Palatine, the end of the Circus Maximus, and climbing the slope back up the Aventine. They had been walking for perhaps a quarter of an hour when the door opened and the doorman admitted them.

'Domine.'

'Any messages left for me?'

'No, sir.'

Fronto nodded. 'Perhaps the Pompeians are going home first to plan. Good. That buys us some time.'

'Ah, Domine,' called one of the slaves, turning and making his way over, head bowed in respect.

'Yes?'

'The medicus asked me to let him know when you were home, sir.'

'Oh?'

'Your guest is awake, Domine.'

It took Fronto a moment of frowning to work out what that meant, but then he turned to Galronus, blinking in surprise.

Salvius Cursor was back.

CHAPTER SIX

Fronto watched the last of his clients leave after the morning salutatio, this particular fellow rankling slightly, given that he was a successful wine merchant, while Fronto was still trying to offload his own wine business that, by law, he should no longer really own while sitting in the senate. *Everything* was pissing him off a little this morning. Everything seemed to be hovering on the edge of something but not quite there, and not just the wine business.

It had started last night, with Salvius Cursor. Fronto had hurried to the medicus he'd hired at excessive cost, hungry for news of the injured officer. Would Salvius remember anything from his attempted poisoning? Would he have information on Octavian, the man behind the lethal mushrooms? Would he even really be the same Salvius Cursor? Although on that last, Fronto would privately admit that a little change here and there might not be a bad thing. Unfortunately, when he found the medicus, the report was less informative and useful than he'd hoped. Sometime during Fronto's absence yesterday, the man had suddenly lurched upright with a blood-curdling howl that had brought slaves, servants and medical personnel running. He had then babbled incoherently at everyone who flooded into the room, and promptly passed out again. Still, that one waking moment was more than the medicus had realistically hoped for, and he regarded it as a solid sign. Indeed, apparently Salvius had woken again during the hours of darkness, grabbed a slave by the scruff of the neck when he hurried over to the bed, demanded to know where he was, and, when informed, gave a relieved huff and passed out once more. So far, Fronto had missed both waking moments and the medicus was insistent that he not disturb the patient and let him recover naturally at his own pace.

So that was another frustration on top of the tedium of salutatio and wine merchants. Then there was the Pompeian veterans. Fronto had anticipated two possible outcomes of the death of the clerk and the stolen list. Firstly that the collegium would immediately chase down every name on the list and butcher them, which would at least allow Fronto and his men the faint chance of following them and saving some of the targets. Or secondly, perhaps they would return to their meeting house and plan the downfall of each of the names first.

What Fronto now assumed was happening was a third, unanticipated option. His watchers had reported in over the afternoon and evening that the enemy collegium had returned to their meeting house and spent much of the day there before going their own ways, returning to their homes. Unable to do anything of great use, the Caesarian veterans had similarly returned to their dwellings, while Fronto's watchers had continued to keep the house under observation in shifts.

Then, this morning had brought unpleasant news. Three decorated veterans of Caesar's campaigns had met their end during the night, presumably the first three of the eight on the list. The first had been a former cavalryman who had served at both Alesia and Pharsalus, a member of the collegium Fronto now controlled, who had been jumped in an alleyway on the way home after the day's events. His arm purse and all valuables were taken, and by anyone else it would be assumed to be a random robbery in the dangerous streets. Given the man's history, Fronto assumed otherwise as the report was delivered early morning, especially given the other two reports that came in quick succession. A second member of the collegium had met his end in a private bathhouse in his neighbourhood. The former centurion was found floating face down in the warm bath by one of the other exclusive members. All visitors had been checked out, and none seemed to be guilty, each with a solid alibi. Again, it had all the hallmarks of an accident, but for the fact that it clearly wasn't. The third death was the most public, but the least expected. A soldier that had been in Fronto's own party during that attack against the Veneti over a decade ago and who had later served as one of Caesar's singulares, but who had not been a member of the veteran collegium. He had been quietly walking down a street in the heart of Rome when a heavy roof tile had fallen from high up and struck him on the top of the head, smashing his skull and pulping his brain. So clearly an unhappy accident. And yet so clearly not, to Fronto. And while the first two had suggested that the eight names were all men to be drawn from the ranks of the collegium of veterans, this one changed that. There would be no predicting the targets, other than that there was a good chance they were part of the collegium. Its members were now on the alert, going about their business in pairs or groups.

Would they stand even a small chance of saving the other five? Fronto doubted it. The three attacks had clearly been carried out by individuals or small groups, and so watching the collegium meeting house would be of no value without watching each member at all times.

It was all so frustrating. Wine, clients, Salvius and the killings. And all Fronto could do was go about his daily tedium as the reports rolled in. As the wine merchant left the room, Fronto mulling over his myriad irritations, he rose from his seat, cast away the toga he'd been wearing for the look of things and traipsed through the house in his tunic, drawn by the sound of voices from the peristyle.

He had his first smile of the morning as he rounded the corner. The boys were in the garden, ignoring the insistent chill of the air as they leapt about over low hedges and around statues and planters, wielding wooden swords and yelling curses and imprecations at one another. He wandered across to where Galronus stood beside a column watching, and leaned next to him.

'Curse you, dog of Ilium,' bellowed Lucius, already bulky and muscled for an eight year old.

'Up yours, Achaean,' grinned Marcus as he flung a clod of earth from a planter, hitting his brother full in the face.

'Ilium? Achaea?' Fronto murmured.

'This is apparently a duel between someone called Achilles and someone called Hector. I am not aware of these Roman heroes,' the Remi admitted.

'That's because they're not Roman. This is about the war between the Greeks and the Trojans.' It made him smile to see. Since spending more time back in Rome and reacquainting himself with the twins, he had come to know them a great deal more. It was no surprise the roles they had chosen to play for the game, heavy, strong Lucius taking the role of the Greek demigod, with thoughtful, wily Marcus playing the part of the tragic Trojan prince.

'Who wins?' Galronus asked.

'In the tales, Achilles. He is the greatest warrior in the world, invincible, apart from one weak ankle.'

'Hector should stamp on his foot, then.'

'I wouldn't put it past him in this interpretation,' grinned Fronto.

Unfortunately, it seemed the duel was destined to remain unfinished, for at that moment Lucilia appeared in a doorway opposite, barking the boys' names.

'There you are. Your tutor sits in the tablinum waiting for you and here you are covered in mud. Go clean yourselves up and get in there swiftly. Catullus awaits.'

The boys continued their play fight as long as they thought they could get away with it, until Lucilia began to tap her foot, arms folded, eyebrow arched, and, recognising the danger signs, they brushed themselves down, put aside their swords and hurried inside past her. Fronto and Galronus both chuckled, leading Lucilia to look across the garden at the pair of them, a silent admonishment in her eyes.

'Have there been any more messages?' Fronto asked as Lucilia disappeared inside.

Galronus shook his head. 'Nothing in the last hour. Your meetings have finished?'

'Thank the gods. Now, time for a quick trip to the baths, and then I've put aside much of this afternoon to go through troop muster reports. I think it's time I got into a little more detail of this whole Parthia plan. We've only got three months really to pull it all together.'

Galronus nodded. 'I'll come with you and lend a hand.'

'Thanks. Think I'll just make a side visit on the way. You never know. Maybe Salvius will be awake again.'

'See you in the atrium on the hour, then.' Galronus slapped him on the shoulder and then went his own way. Fronto took a deep breath of the cold morning air and then turned and made his way back through the sprawling house. His injured house guest had occupied a room in a largely empty wing since their return, and Lucilia had devoted a small staff of slaves to look after him, to change his sheets and to bathe the comatose man and make sure some nourishment passed his lips. Fronto had been impressed with that. They fed him water and soup three times a day, prising open his mouth and pouring the foods in, for it seemed that even in his absent state, Salvius still automatically swallowed.

Fronto passed a pair of slaves in the corridor, the two young lads dipping respectfully out of his way, and waiting for him to pass them. Then, turning a corner, Fronto, much to his surprise, found strangers in his house.

'What's going on?' he demanded of the three large, well-muscled brutes blocking the passage. Two with local colouring and a third dark skinned giant from the southern lands, all three were wearing bland tunics but with military belts and boots, and knives at their sides that could be argued as work knives rather than weapons of war, but edged towards the latter.

'Who are you?' one of them asked, insolent.

Fronto felt his lip twitch and pulled himself up to his full height, which was a head shorter than even the shortest of these men. For the first time in a while, he wished he'd not discarded the toga, for in just a tunic, he could really be anyone.

'I am Marcus Falerius Fronto, the owner of this house.'

If he'd expected apology and contrition, he was disappointed. The three men looked him up and down as if trying to decide whether he was lying. Just as he was about to issue a growled threat, the man spoke again.

'The master is not to be disturbed, Senator.'

Fronto blinked. The master? Who was that? Salvius Cursor? Who *were* these people?

He was about to open up into a whirlwind of verbal abuse when the door behind them, along the corridor, opened, and several more

75

figures emerged into view. Fronto's questions were answered as two slaves stepped aside to allow Octavian to take the lead.

Caesar's great nephew was no longer a boy, and Fronto recalled now the rangy eighteen year old he had encountered in Hispania earlier in the year. Octavian's gaze fell on him, and the young man gave him a smile that was calculated to appear warm and friendly, betrayed only by that half heartbeat when the smile had been assembled.

'I am not accustomed to my home being invaded without my knowledge,' Fronto said, drily.

Octavian laughed. No humour. Another construct. 'Your doorman checked with your good lady wife. She did not wish to disturb you during an important salutatio, especially since I was not here to see you, but to visit your guest. I must apologise for my guards. My uncle insists that I am protected at all times.'

'A wise precaution, though not one people usually need to take in my house. *Usually*. You've been to see your victim, then?'

He noted a tiny twitch in Octavian's eye at that, a tacit reminder that Fronto knew all about what he'd been up to the previous year.

'The noble Salvius Cursor is fully awake,' the young man said, with no acknowledgement of Fronto's subtle reminder.

'I've not had a chance to speak to him yet,' Fronto snapped. 'Funny how he's only recovered over the last half day, and somehow you contrive to be here to visit before even I have seen him. Just how many spies do you have in my house, Octavian?'

'Please,' the young man smiled. 'I have no need of spies. It was lucky timing, that is all.'

'So no more than three, yes?'

Octavian's answering smile was infuriating. 'He is far from full recovery, I fear.'

'Maybe you'd like to find some mushrooms, help him along?'

Again, that tic hit Octavian's eye, but that was the only sign as the young man smiled broadly. 'Physically, he is weak, I think, after so long unconscious. But his muscles will return. It is his mind, sadly. Not his reasoning, for he seems to have wit aplenty, but he lacks large parts of his memory. Perhaps that too will return with time. I trust you will help him recover his memories… *carefully*.'

76

The stress on that last word was rather hard to miss, and rarely had Fronto felt a greater urge to punch the young man. He was far too clever for his own good, and ambitious and ruthless, too. A man in Caesar's mould, clearly.

'I'm going to have every slave and servant in this house thoroughly interrogated and investigated until I find your spies. Then I'm going to have them delivered to your front door in packages no larger than a foot long.'

Octavian snorted. 'Oh, Marcus, do stop. We are all on the same side, you know? The dissenters are all gone now, the last of their power broken on the field of Munda. When will you learn to trust me.'

'When you prove yourself trustworthy.'

Again, Octavian chuckled. 'Very well. I will take my leave. I must visit my uncle. I will pass on your regards. He is looking forward to an update on your preparations for Parthia.'

As the young man swept past him, making for the atrium, Fronto held his angry retorts back. He really did have to spend more time on those preparations. He'd done a few hours' work here and there, but this business with the collegia had rather occupied a lot of his time recently. He waited until Octavian and his entourage had left, and then strode across to the door and poked his head through. Salvius Cursor was half upright in bed, propped up against large pillows. He looked pale and thin, but his eyes were clear and his expression thoughtful.

'How are you feeling?'

Cursor turned to the door and an odd smile crossed his face.

'A little weak. A little wobbly. Otherwise not bad. Very hungry. I could eat a whole cow. Raw.'

Fronto laughed. 'I'll bet. Months of nothing but soup will do that to a man. You're like a skeleton. A shadow of yourself. I swear if I didn't know it was you, I'd not have recognised you. I'm surprised Octavian didn't kill off your appetite, though.'

'He is nervous. Hides it well.'

'He's nervous of you. I think he's more than a little relieved that your memory is patchy.'

'There's nothing wrong with my memory, Fronto.'

'Ha. So you do remember.'

'Not the sort of thing you forget in a hurry. But I also know that Octavian is currently the most powerful man in Rome after his great uncle, and I think my life expectancy will improve endlessly if Octavian thinks I have nothing on him. Given that he still walks and breathes, I presume you've confronted him since my near demise?'

Fronto nodded. 'You were not one of the potential impediments to his inheritance, but your investigation threatened him. I warned him to pull in his horns. Despite his little run of incidents, he's still his uncle's favourite, and there will soon be a new will to reflect that. I think Rome would rather see Octavian inherit Caesar's estate than his son with Cleopatra. You won't seek revenge?'

It was a good question. Fronto himself had thought long and hard about whether Octavian deserved any kind of punishment for what he'd done, but in the end he'd decided to leave things as they were and trust to luck and the gods. Salvius Cursor was a much less forgiving man, though, and one given to violence as a solution to most problems.

'I have yet to decide. Right now, I feel I need to catch up on events. I've been rather out of things.'

Fronto nodded. 'A brief rundown of everything that's happened?'

'If you feel up to it. I suspect that if I'm to catch up, you might be able to do it without expanding too much on trivialities.'

Fronto nodded. 'Let me begin with Hispania.'

He spent the next hour in that room, trying to give an abbreviated history of the campaign against Labienus and the younger Pompey, while not wanting to miss any pertinent detail. Ending his account of the campaign, he moved on to the return to Rome, and then to Caesar's living arrangements with the Aegyptian queen and her young son under the same roof as Caesar's wife.

'Is that not awkward?'

'I would have thought so. Had it been me, Lucilia would have scratched out her eyes, buried the boy in the garden and had me crucified all within the hour. Calpurnia seems to be content to accept her lot. I suppose with Caesar's history of women and affairs, she's had plenty of practice at putting up with such things.'

'So what is Caesar doing with his unprecedented long-term dictatorship?'

Fronto shrugged. Right now he's making laws on a daily basis, trying to drag Rome out of the cycle of corruption it's endured for years. And he's finishing all his building projects. He's started a new curia for the senate to meet in and demolished the old one. This one will be larger, to accommodate an expanded senate.'

'So where do they meet now, if one's destroyed and the replacement not finished?'

'In a great room in Pompey's theatre complex. I think it appeals to Caesar's sense of irony to hold the senate meetings there. Oh, and he's extended the seating in the circus. He was already working on his new forum when you fell ill, yes?'

'Yes.'

'Well that's done, and mostly dedicated and open. So yes, he's on with legal and construction projects. Come late Martius, and the start of the campaigning season, he's to war again. It seems he never tires of the battlefield.'

'Or more likely the glory and loot he reaps from it. Where this time? Britannia?'

'Parthia.'

Salvius whistled through his teeth. '*Big* fish this time, then.'

'Yes, and somehow he's managed to persuade me to plan it for him, though he's inclined to base himself in Aegyptus, while Antioch would be the clear choice.'

'I wonder why,' Salvius replied drily.

'Quite. There are fears among certain sectors that Caesar actually intends to move the whole of government to Alexandria.'

Salvius shook his head. 'He'd never do that.'

'Probably not, but people are usually ready to believe the worst of people, after all. In the meantime, we have our own little problems.'

'Oh?'

'There's a collegium of former Pompeian veterans who are picking off Caesar's allies and supporters. Whether they're acting on their own or being directed by some villain we can't be sure, but they've already attacked Marcus Antonius in the street, killed Catháin and started working through Caesar's veterans. We followed them back to a house owned by Publius Plautius Hypsaeus, and it's our current working theory that he's behind it all. I need to spend some time investigating him, since he's been something of a recluse these past few years, but Caesar is beginning to nudge me about Parthia, so I'm getting short on time to spend on such things.'

Salvius gave him a smile. 'What you need is an inside man.'

Fronto snorted. 'They're a fraternity. I'm more likely to find an uncorrupt priest in Rome than an ally among their number.'

'You seem to be forgetting something,' Salvius said with an odd smile, pulling up his tunic sleeve a little. Fronto's gaze fell upon the tattoo on the man's bicep. He'd seen it plenty of times over the years, often enough that the fact that it was actually the tattoo of a Pompeian legion usually completely bypassed him. He stared at it. Salvius Cursor, of course, had been an officer in Pompey's legions before his defection to the Caesarian forces. Indeed, his history had been part of the reason it had taken years for Fronto to find any trust in the man. That, and Salvius' blind need to drench himself in blood at any given moment.

'You're bedridden, Salvius. You've been comatose for months. You've only been awake three times since last Spring.'

'I'm weak, and I'm hungry, Fronto, but my mind is working just fine, and it's that you need.'

'If you walk into a Pompeian collegium, you'll be dead in hours. You're quite well known, Salvius. You're one of the officers from plenty of famous battles, and the recent commander of Caesar's bodyguard.'

'And yet you said it yourself: I'm so skeletal right now that I look nothing like myself. All I need to be able to do is walk and think fast. For Jove's sake, Fronto, I've been in bed for the better part of a year. I need to be up and about and doing something.'

Fronto frowned. 'I can't say it wouldn't be useful. And I have to devote the next few days to troop movements if I'm to coordinate the mustering of the army across the water. Let me tell you everything I know. The better informed you are, the better your chances.'

Salvius nodded and propped himself up a little straighter.

* * *

One thing, Salvius Cursor would only admit in the silent corners of his own mind, which had held him back more than once in his life was his impulsive urge to throw himself into danger without thinking things through adequately first. His current situation was most definitely an example of this troublesome character flaw.

For a start, he was a lot less well than he'd let on. Fronto had been insistent that he not do anything until he proved he was strong enough. He'd agreed to walk from his bed the entire length of Fronto's house to prove his fitness. He'd not realised how large Fronto's house was when he'd come up with that brilliant idea. He'd clenched his teeth and risen from bed for the first time in many months, and almost collapsed like a jelly straight away, only monumental efforts of will and a healthy ladleful of luck keeping him upright. He'd taken some time to gain the strength and balance to put one foot in front of the other, and had finally managed to totter to the door before having to grab the wall to hold himself up.

Fronto had made negative noises, declaring him stupid to even be out of bed. There had followed half an hour of sporadic lurching and shambling through rooms, along corridors and across gardens, culminating in having reached the very far end of the house. He'd given Fronto a defiant smile, while inside everything had gone all wobbly and the only thing that stopped him shitting or throwing up was that he couldn't decide which orifice was more urgent.

Fronto had snorted. 'And what are you going to do now?'

That statement, that challenge, had been just what Salvius had needed to push him, and with a grunt he had turned and done the walk back, slightly faster than before, though largely because half the time he was more falling forward than walking.

When he had announced that he would heal and eat for one more day and then go and find his fellow Pompeian veterans, Fronto had still declared him unfit. Salvius had enlisted the aid of the medicus and, with carefully worded questions, had managed to elicit a medical opinion that the more he walked and exercised, with appropriate caution, the stronger he would get, and that nothing should be out of his capabilities, as long as he took things easy. Perhaps using a walking stick.

Fronto had still argued and had told him he would need to recuperate for many days yet before they would let him do anything as foolish as attempt to walk the streets alone, let alone attempt to infiltrate an enemy fortress. That was why he'd waited until Fronto was out the next afternoon, chasing up troop reports at the Navalia, before leaving the house alone and without asking. He'd stolen a small purse of money from Fronto's office on the way, and swatted away slaves who came to interfere.

He'd tottered out into the cold sunlight and made it almost halfway down the Aventine's slope before he collapsed and had to have a rest. He'd almost brought up the three solid meals he'd been fed since waking, but had managed to keep them down by some miraculous feat of will.

Near the Circus, he'd found an apothecary and had managed to purchase both henbane in a liquid tincture and a walking stick. With the support of the latter and the numbing, soothing pain relief of the former, he'd pressed on with fresh energy. Still, it had taken him much of the afternoon to reach the location of the meeting house Fronto had described.

Since then, it had been a whirlwind of activity.

The man who'd answered the door of the meeting house had admitted him with a little suspicion, though much of that had been allayed by the tattoo that clearly placed Salvius with Pompey's legions back in the day. He had been led to another man, who had taken his details. He'd thought on his feet, using names and locations and histories that stood out, which he would remember. Marcus Saturninus was his assumed name, a name lodged firmly in his memory as the first man he had ever killed. His address he gave as a house on the lower slope of the Caelian, the house of a childhood friend of his, and he placed himself militarily most recently at Thapsus. He didn't want to risk involvement in the Hispanic campaign, for it would be too easy to trip him up. He remembered Thapsus, though. He claimed to have settled in Africa after the battle, and to have returned to Rome only this last summer. His weakness he put down to a winter illness from which he was now recovering. It was all apparently satisfactory. Then he'd been taken to someone even more important.

That man, leaning back at the table across from him, clearly had trust issues. He'd not let anything slip in quarter of an hour of questions.

'Tell me again why you seek our brotherhood?'

That was the prime one, of course, and he kept coming back to it, apparently unconvinced.

'Protection,' he answered again. 'Stability.'

'Explain.'

He nodded. He needed to lay it on thicker, this time.

'I lost everything in Africa. I was wounded at Thapsus, left for dead. I had no pension, nothing. What I had was what I stole in the aftermath of the battle. I signed on as a mercenary guarding caravans, but the desert is no place for a sane man, so I stopped that after one season. I used what I had to set up as a smith near Uthina, but last winter the rains and storms flooded us, ruined my house, and the village moved away. I sold what I had left and decided to come to Rome. After all, the streets are paved with gold, or so everyone says. It cost nearly everything I had left. I now have a small apartment and a small purse of coins. I've been spending my time teaching people self-defence, but with this illness laying me low over winter, I had to stop that. Now I've very little, and I've been learning how dangerous this city is, especially for men like us, with Caesar on the *throne* of Rome. I need likeminded people, and somewhere to turn.'

The man nodded slowly. 'We don't pay our members, of course. We can help in many ways, but we are not a substitute for an employer.'

Salvius shifted in his seat and dropped his elbows to the table, steepling his fingers. 'Word has it that if you need money, and you're not too fussy about how you get it, the collegia can help.'

The man's expression became bland, unreadable. 'If that's your goal, you need criminals, not veterans.'

'You know what I mean,' Salvius hissed. 'Some jobs only go to the boys, yes?'

'If you mean to impugn the reputation of this fraternity…'

'I don't. I just need money, and from a source I trust. There are plenty of powerful men hiring these days, but they all seem to be *Caesar's* men. One look at my arm and I'm not good enough.'

Finally, this seemed to elicit a little sympathy. 'Our collegium does, from time to time, find patrons of its own. We had one such until relatively recently, though we have since endured a time of freedom. We may now have a new patron, but any work for him will not be handed out blind to newcomers. You will need to prove your worth and loyalty first.'

'Naturally. I will do what I can, and as I shake off the last of this illness, I should become a lot more useful.'

The man seemed to consider this for some time, chewing the inside of this cheek, and finally nodded curtly. 'Very well. I will have your membership logged with the authorities. For now, I expect you to attend here every day and do whatever is required of you. In time, as you prove yourself, those duties may become more important and more... lucrative.'

Salvius Cursor bowed his head. 'Thank you. You have no idea what this means.'

'You may live to regret it, Marcus Saturninus. For now, welcome to the Pompeian Collegium of Upper Rome.'

CHAPTER SEVEN

'I can spare only a moment, Marcus.'

Fronto clenched his teeth against the irritation. After all, it was *him* doing *Caesar* a favour, not the other way around. 'This is important.'

'We have business in the forum, Marcus, as you know. I am expected in less than half an hour.'

The dictator lifted his arm as his dress slave wound the toga carefully, settling every crease and fold in the perfect position. Fronto was acutely aware that his own toga was crumpled and skewwhiff, and kept slipping down his arm, causing him to retrieve it and pull it up every ten or fifteen heartbeats.

'Very quickly, then, are you really honestly intending on defeating the Getae on the way?'

'Fronto, the region has been unstable for five years since the coalition defeated Hybrida. I cannot undertake any campaign against Parthia while the land to the north is in danger. What happens if I take the entire army across to Parthia and the Getae and their allies pour south into our lands behind me? No, the Getae have to be put in their place before the Parthians. But I do not anticipate this action taking more than a month, and should be possible with only a small force, allowing much of the army to continue on to the east and begin preparations for my arrival there. I presume you can adjust your plans appropriately?'

Fronto took a deep breath and tried to stop grinding his teeth. For the past few days, every time he had brought to the dictator's attention even the most minor aspect of the campaign, Caesar would claim that he was too busy to talk, and throw chaos Fronto's way by changing the goals before walking away and leaving him to it. The army was already assembling, with the dictator scheduled to leave just after the Ides of March to bring vengeance to Parthia for their humiliation of Crassus and his army, and now, with less than three months to go, the general had added a whole new branch to the campaign, which would completely change all Fronto's current plans for the transport of the army east. He closed his eyes, forced him not to tell Caesar into which dark orifice he could shove his campaign plans, and counted silently to ten. Lucilia would be extremely irked if he walked away from this, as she had made plain the last three times he'd threatened to do so.

'I currently have sixteen legions either already gathered across the Mare Adriaticum or on their way there from previous locations. Sixteen! From all over the republic. I have the better part of ten thousand auxiliary cavalry making their way there, too. By the Ides of Februarius, they will all be assembled. Every officer in every unit involved has been sent full details of their plans, including any sea transport, departure points and dates. Every ship we have managed to drag together has the orders for where to meet, embark and disembark their loads. This miracle I have pulled together in less than half a month. And now you ask me to change half those orders before they have even reached the men for whom they're intended?'

'It's a simple thing,' Caesar said, with infuriating ease. 'Five legions should be sufficient to put the Getae in their place and secure the north. Have five of the legions that are already in position form a separate force. I will collect them when I leave Rome, and we shall march east across Thrace and put the Getae down, then turn south and meet with the rest of the army, using your many ships, close to Parthian lands.'

'You make it sound so easy,' Fronto grumbled, 'but you have absolutely no idea how much work that creates.'

'Do I not? Have I not planned campaigns every year for over a decade now? Come, Marcus, I know you can do this. You have my utmost trust and support.'

Fronto clenched his teeth again. Now was perhaps the perfect time to raise that other matter once more.

'If that is the case, Caesar, I will once again ask you to put aside this foolish notion of basing the campaign in Alexandria, and instead settle on Antioch. Gods, but from Getae lands you'd have to go *past* Antioch to get to Alexandria.'

Caesar turned then, and there was an odd look in his eye. 'No. It must be Alexandria.'

Fronto sagged, rolling his eyes. Every time, a flat refusal. 'Why? You've cited so many reasons of logistics and politics, but you know I can see through that. They're all valid points, but none of them, even all together, are sufficient to shift a campaign base from somewhere practical to somewhere distant. If this is just about your pet queen...'

Caesar's eyes flashed angrily for just a moment before he recovered his composure. He looked deep into Fronto's own eyes and seemed to come to some decision. The dictator turned to the various slaves and clerks in the room. 'Go. Have the retinue prepare. We leave for the forum presently.'

He waited until the slaves and servants had all departed, the last closing the door behind him, and then paused a little longer, listening to the footsteps outside recede, making sure they were alone.

'Very well. You are closely involved in this. Perhaps it is best you know everything, though this I cannot have revealed publicly yet, for it could do irreparable harm if this information is disseminated without the appropriate contexts. You are aware of the rumours about the Sibylline books?'

Fronto nodded. 'Yes. And I can't say it doesn't concern me, but we all know that the oracles are all about interpretation, and there are nuances that could entirely change the current perception.'

Yet despite that, he felt, deep down, rather uncomfortable with the coming campaign in light of the prophecies. The quindecemviri had been asked to consult the great books of oracular prophecy as was the norm before any new campaign, and their findings had been rather more direct and clear than usual. The Parthians, they had said, were ruled by a king of kings, and they could not be subdued by anyone less than a king. This had led to a flood of suggestions among the people of Rome, from crowning Caesar to calling off the campaign entirely, and everything in between.

'You and I know that the prophecy was clear, and whether or not we believe it, Rome does. And the republic's history of sending powerful armies to Parthia, only to watch them destroyed, lends some weight to the prophecy. I do, I think, have a solution.'

'You will not let them crown you,' Fronto said flatly. He wasn't sure whether it was a plea or a demand. Possibly both.

'Of course not. Rome flourished because it ejected its kings and became a republic. And no matter what any man says about me, I have never intended sole rule of the republic. My goal was to pull her together after decades of corruption and war, to make her strong once more, and to leave behind me a republic unassailable, and a legacy of greatness for my descendants, just like those of Brutus, who had ejected the last king.'

'So you will be no king. I don't follow.'

Caesar smiled. 'Don't you? I'd always thought you brighter than that.'

Fronto tried not to bridle at the jab. 'Explain.'

'Why do you think I keep Cleopatra at my side?'

Fronto frowned. 'She's your concubine. The mother of your son.'

'She is also…'

'The queen of Aegyptus.' Fronto blinked. Gods, really? That was his plan?

'I see you have connected those dots. Yes, Fronto, I shall divorce Calpurnia before I depart, and once the Getae are defeated, and I reach Alexandria, I shall marry Cleopatra. I will be a king, after all. Yet to Rome I shall continue to be but a senator and a son of the republic.'

'Do you really think the people are going to support you as pharaoh of Aegyptus?'

'I will be king there only for the duration of the campaign, Fronto. I will be king to defeat the Parthians, for it must be so. Then, when Ctesiphon lies in smouldering ruins and the Parthian Shahanshar grovels at my feet, I can step aside once more. Then young Ptolemy, Caesarion as he is known, can take my place as is his birth right.'

Fronto shook his head, not to deny this, but in wonder. It was such a neat and elegant solution. He would fulfil the prophecy of the Sibyl, and would thus be able to conquer Parthia where no other Roman could ever hope to. And if he could do so with sufficient speed and efficiency, he would be able to lay down that crown and return to Rome an ordinary citizen before dissent could really spread. And into the bargain he would settle Caesarion as a client king of Rome, securing his son's inheritance along with the loyalty of Aegyptus. It was masterful, as long as it all worked out as planned.

'There will be those who will argue against such a move.'

Caesar nodded. 'And that is why I have been very careful with who I have assigned to the army we take east. That is why you are so heavily involved, Marcus, because you have been at my side all these years, and you know me for a man of my word. That is why men such as Cassius and Trebonius must remain in Rome, and that is why I will set Antonius here as my co-consul, and Lepidus as my magister equitum. Between the pair they can keep control of any who might defy me while I do what must be done. That, Fronto, is the point of the dictatorship. That is why it exists, and why I hold the office. To do what must be done for the safety and future of Rome. I will have Rome controlled with an iron grip while I wear a gilded crown in the east long enough to put Parthia on its knees and remove the threat from the east forever. Then I can put aside such trappings, return to Rome, loosen my grip, and all will be well.'

Fronto found himself staring, eyes defocused, at Caesar, and pulled himself together. That was the problem with Caesar. Sometimes his logic and his planning was so clever and mercurial that you found yourself almost hypnotised by it. Yet even thinking with the cold mind of a republican senator, Fronto had to admit that it was all very neat, and the way Caesar described it, it was more or less the perfect plan.

'If this goes wrong, it could be a disaster.'

Caesar smiled. 'The same can be said of most plans that are worthwhile, Marcus. For now, I must attend the forum as planned, and you must alter your plans so that I can take a force against the Getae. You know now why I must launch the campaign from Alexandria, and I must ask you not to pass on this information. I will have everything in place to contain trouble, but we are not quite there yet.'

Fronto nodded and, satisfied, Caesar gripped the folds of his toga and made for the door. Fronto followed on, the comedy figure constantly hitching up his own garments in the wake of the great man. Pulling open the door, Caesar was immediately flooded by an entourage of slaves, servants, guards and other hangers-on. Several leading senators, including Cornelius Balbus and Gaius Oppius, fell in behind, and Fronto shuffled over to join them.

'You'd think he was dedicating the temple, given all this pomp,' one of them said, not disparagingly, but resignedly.

Fronto could only nod. Caesar's forum had been being constructed for years, and the temple itself had been started just after Pharsalus. It had been dedicated the previous year, while Caesar was passing through Rome, between Africa and Hispania, though in truth it had only been half-built at the time. Now, it was finished, along with the rest of the new forum, though not the new senate house yet. It was a statement, what Caesar had planned this morning, but then everything Caesar *ever did* was a statement.

Like every Roman nobleman, Caesar held his morning salutatio, in which he met his clients and granted boons and requests, heard pleas and so on. But this morning, he would do so in a new and grand manner. With the final completion of his great project, he would do so atop the steps of the great new temple of Venus Genetrix, allowing all those who came to him to appreciate the majesty of his creation. Sly bastard.

And given the importance of the day, the dictator had politely requested the attendance of many of those senators who had constantly shown him their support. Fronto had to hand it to the man, Caesar knew how to play to a crowd. As the entourage filed through the atrium and vestibule, out into the grounds of the grand villa beyond the Tiber, Fronto looked down the slope and could see how the streets were already lined with citizens waiting to see the great man pass.

They set off down the steps towards the lower ground close to the river, and beside Fronto, Oppius sighed. 'I'm sure we could all be just as impressive either on a horse or in a litter.'

Fronto declined to comment, though he knew that by the time he reached the bottom of the steps and his knee was screaming at him, he would similarly be regretting the lack of transport. But Caesar knew the value of appearance. There were minor, but persistent, rumours in the city of his desire for a throne, and his traversing the city on foot, preceded by a dozen lictors, wrapped in tradition in the form of the toga, would go a long way to restoring his humility in the eyes of the people.

The long train of white-clad humanity descended the steps with only a little subdued swearing, and reached the gates of the estate, where they gathered once more, forming into an appropriate procession. As the gates swung open and the people of Rome cheered for the man who had brought stability back to Rome, the lictors emerged, splitting into two lines of six, where they moved to the edges, a line of rod-wielding men keeping the crowd from getting too close to Caesar. From there they moved at a steady pace along the river to the Cestian bridge, crossing the flow via Tiber Island and the Fabrician bridge. On the far bank, just a quarter of an hour's walk brought them around the lower slope of the Capitol and to the new forum of Caesar.

This morning's salutatio was not to be the private audience that such events traditionally were, held within the patron's office, with a steady flow of applicant clients. Today's was more spectacle than anything, as was clear to Fronto as they approached the great, glorious, finally-completed temple. The great bronze temple doors stood wide open and a warm golden glow emerged from within, where lamps and braziers burned in large numbers, illuminating the interior and warding off the cold of a midwinter morning. Drapes of crimson hung from the walls of the temple, their blood-red making the white columns in front stand out in brilliant glory. A single chair stood on the podium of the temple before the doors, atop the steps, a curule chair, simple in design, yet auspicious and powerful in meaning, that sat awaiting the dictator. No other chairs were in evidence. The patron would be expected to sit, with his clients standing.

As they reached the temple and climbed the steps, the lictors took their positions around the podium, ready to protect their master, Caesar sank into the seat and arranged his toga appropriately, his personal slaves and attendants close by, while his allied senators gathered in a small crowd behind him, beneath the colonnade of the temple.

Fronto stood there for a while, his knee throbbing with all the exercise of a hill descent and then a hike across the city, while Caesar cleared his throat and began to address the crowd. Before beginning his salutatio, he announced the completion of the forum at last, and dedicated the whole complex to the people of Rome, for their convenience and enjoyment. There was a huge roar of approval as he finished, and then the tedium of the actual event began. Those equestrians, plebeians, and the less important patricians, began to approach the temple, one by one, climbing the steps to stand a head below Caesar, even though he remained seated, asking for boons and favours. Fronto half listened to the first few, but became excruciatingly bored very quickly.

He looked around and smiled to himself. He was near the back of the gaggle of senators, not feeling the greatest need to be seen in the dictator's company, and really, he might as well not be there, for all his visibility. He was just another togate figure among the crowd. He had to strain and crane to see what was going on, and if that was the case, then hardly anyone would be able to see him. He could hardly head down the steps and leave, but he was sick of standing, with his sore knee, and it was cold here doing nothing. Consequently, moments later, he was stepping quietly backwards in through the temple doors.

The moment he was inside and out of the view of the general public, he turned and walked to the centre of the chamber, letting his eyes adjust to the relative gloom as the blessed heat of the place flowed over him. He could really do with somewhere to sit down. His eyes fell first on the great statue of Venus commissioned from the talented sculptor Arcesilas, and he considered whether it would be sacrilegious to sit on the base of the goddess' likeness. He would do so if there was nowhere better, he decided, and looked around, taking in the various displays of riches and piety that Caesar had donated to his new temple.

That was when his gaze fell upon the latest addition.

He winced.

'Really?' he murmured aloud, but to himself, as he took in the immeasurable riches shown in the gleaming statues. They were both solid gold. One was clearly meant to be Venus, while the other could only be Eros, yet only a fool would miss the clear resemblance to Cleopatra and Caesarion. What was he thinking?

'Tasteless, isn't it?' mused a familiar voice just behind him. He turned to see Decimus Brutus, arms folded, shaking his head sadly.

'Just a little.'

'He spends so much time making pains to be seen as a republican senator and a man of the people, and in between he displays excesses like this. It's no wonder there are so many rumours and half the senate think he's a king in his own head already.'

Fronto just nodded. He knew the truth, had heard it from Caesar's own lips and knew it to *be* the truth. But he was in the minority, and no matter how many times Caesar walked across the city like a normal citizen, commissioning gold statues of his mistress to display in temples could only diminish public opinion of him, among the senate, at least.

'He's going too far, Fronto. Too far and too fast. He'll make more and more enemies unless he reins back in a little.'

'He'll be alright, Brutus. He just needs to get through to the campaigning season without pissing off anyone else, and then he can go fight the Parthians, win us Alexander the Great's empire and come back to lay down his powers.'

'And you think he will?'

'I really do.'

'I hope you're right,' Brutus sighed. 'I see the way some of our peers look at him, with eyes of daggers. He's got to start building bridges and stop burning them.'

Fronto sighed and crossed to the cult statue, sinking to the base and rubbing his knee with relief. Brutus leaned close by, and the two of them began to discuss the coming campaign. Fronto dropped in the news that the Getae now featured in the plan, though he carefully avoided mentioning Alexandria or the Sibylline prophecy. For perhaps half an hour the two men talked earnestly, Brutus lending his not inconsiderable knowledge of naval operations to the plan. By the time they heard the end of the salutatio being announced outside, the young nobleman had solved a number of Fronto's logistical problems for him.

Acknowledging the need to return to the public eye, Brutus helped Fronto up, and the two of them strolled out of the temple, with a last look of disapproval at the golden Cleopatra in the corner. Something was happening, though, as they emerged. The line of applicants may have finished, but Caesar remained seated, and there was an almost reverent hush, broken by the sounds of several dozen soft-booted feet approaching.

Brutus held sufficient rank among the gathered senators that as he moved forward, most of them stepped aside for him, and Fronto followed in his wake, moving to the front of the crowd, close to Caesar in his seat. He looked down the steps and his brow rose in surprise. The approaching gathering were similarly toga-clad, senators all, led by the two consuls, mere days away from ending their term: Fabius Maximus and Gaius Trebonius. The party reached the steps and climbed without delay. There was an odd and awkward moment when the lictors accompanying the consuls, each of whom had the same number as Caesar, came into conflict, confused as to where they should stand with regard to each other and to Caesar's own lictors. Fabius and Trebonius and the senators at their heels ignored the confusion as they neared Caesar. They stopped an appropriate distance from the dictator and looked at one another, both aware that they were looking up at a seated man. Fronto winced. Dictator or not, this was not the way to treat a consul of Rome.

The two men took another two steps up, so that at least their heads were above Caesar's, though this brought them uncomfortably close to him. It was all so stilted and awkward that Fronto silently berated them, urging them to hurry about their business and leave.

Behind the two consuls, one of the senators climbed two more steps closer and unfurled a scroll he held.

'Gaius Julius Caesar, by the will of the senate and the people of Rome, you are hereby granted the consulship, beginning in the new year, for a period of ten years without break, your co-consul to be allotted annually as tradition demands. Furthermore, you are granted...'

'No.'

The man stopped, frowning. He looked up at Caesar, whose voice it was that had interrupted.

'Caesar?'

'No. No ten year consulship. It is not legal. I...' he paused, and Fronto began to suspect something. 'I accepted the dictatorship to save Rome, not for glory. The consulship can be mine for only a year. I will hear nothing else.'

Before the senator could respond, though, it was the consul Trebonius whose voice cut through the cold morning air. 'Will you not rise, Caesar?'

The dictator was silent, and Fronto could see the anger rising in Trebonius' face. 'Dictator or not, it is customary to rise when addressed by the senate, let alone by a consul of Rome.'

'I am done here,' Caesar said, and Fronto winced again at the surge of anger in the faces of both consuls, as well as a number of the senators behind him. But Fronto had been listening to Caesar's voice, and the strain in the tone, and now the dictator's fingers were gripping the sides of his chair so tight they had gone white. He *was*. He *was* done here. And it was not through choice. Oppius was suddenly stepping between Caesar and the consuls, suggesting flatly that it was time they withdrew, while Cornelius Balbus crouched at Caesar's side, as though discussing something private with him. In heartbeats, the consuls and the senators were retreating down the steps, and many of the gathering with Caesar were stepping out, crowding around the dictator. It came as no surprise to Fronto when, as Caesar rose and turned, his eyes were twitching and there was foamy drool at the corner of his mouth. He had come surprisingly close to enduring one of his fits in public view. Only the quick thinking of Oppius and Cornelius had covered him and removed him from view just in time.

As Caesar began to choke and convulse, his closest friends and allies helped him back and into the warm interior of the temple. Fronto waited. He would follow on in a moment. He knew these fits, and he knew that Caesar would be fine in an hour, as long as they stopped him biting through his own tongue. Instead, Fronto looked down the steps with a sinking feeling.

That had been terrible timing. Caesar had not risen to address the consuls, had refused their honours, had dismissed the senate and turned his back on them, and all in a matter of moments. And it had been his desperate need to get away, into somewhere private, that had led to such precipitous actions. But Fronto could hear the angry rumble of the senators as they departed, and even the faces of the ordinary citizens gathered around displayed plenty of disapproval.

This one was going to hurt his reputation properly.

ROME. THE DAY BEFORE THE KALENDS OF FEBRUARIUS.

Gaius Cassius Longinus looked about the room at the others. Trebonius was carefully expressionless, though his lip danced a merry twitch that said it all. Rubrius Ruga wore a sour look as though he'd been sucking bitter vetch, the result of that display at the temple which had caused this impromptu meeting. Calavius Sabinus looked nervous, and well he might, being one of the newest of their group. Quintus Ligarius and Marcus Spurius, though, had almost murderous looks in their eyes.

'How much longer can we bear it?' Cassius said, leaning back and sipping his wine.

'As long as we must, I suppose,' Ruga grunted.

'And how long is that? How long can any citizen of the republic worth his salt sit back and watch monarchy return to Rome in the guise of its saviour?'

'Fine words,' Ligarius snorted, 'but words are cheap, are they not?'

Cassius growled as he sat up once more. 'Even I, who turned on Pompey when the time came, and cleaved to Caesar's side as the man who could heal the republic. Even I, who saved his life, who helped him win a war and win a queen, even *I* am spurned.'

'You're just bitter, Cassius,' Calavius Sabinus said. 'Because you were passed over for urban praetor.'

'You're fucking right I'm bitter,' Cassius snapped. 'But not because I was overlooked. Oh no. I am bitter because the praetorship was denied me and given to *Marcus Junius Brutus*, and we all know why, don't we?'

'Careful,' Calavius said. 'Hush now.'

'No, I will not be quiet. Especially not in my own home. All of Rome knows Marcus Junius Brutus to be Caesar's bastard by that whore Servilia. Caesar builds his power base constantly. But I will not be cowed, and neither should any of you. All of Rome either owes Caesar or is frightened of him. All but us. Our liberty is eroded by the day as the general becomes the dictator and then the dictator becomes the king, and no one will do anything about it, because they're all indebted to him or they're terrified. Are there no tyrannicides anymore? No Harmodius or Aristogeiton?'

'I might point out that Harmodius and Aristogeiton may have killed a tyrant, but they both died for it.'

'So? They changed their world, and they are still revered for their sacrifice even now. Well we have our own tyrant. And with no Harmodius or Aristogeiton in Rome, we must step into their shoes, my friends.'

'No.'

Cassius looked up. He'd known there would be nerves, but all these men had been sounded properly. He'd not anticipated flat refusal.

Calavius Sabinus rose from his seat. 'No. I, like all of you, am dismayed by the trend. But Caesar is one man and he is old. Soon he will pass away, and no one else has his strength. No one will follow him. When he dies an old man, the republic will recover, and it will be our place to shepherd that change when it happens.'

'You underestimate him,' Cassius snarled. 'He will have a dynasty, and they will be his successors on a throne. If not his Aegyptian runt, then Octavian, or even Brutus. The time to stop this is *now*, before he goes east.'

'I will not be a part of this,' Calavius said, flatly. 'I will not stand in your way, but I have a family to consider. I will be no Aristogeiton, tortured to death for my crime.'

With that he turned his back on them and strode from the room. Cassius' gaze darted back and forth between the others. He met a number of nervous gazes. All it would take was one slip in the wrong company, one mistake, and Caesar's men would be coming for them all. Cassius was made of sterner stuff than most, though. He simply watched Calavius depart.

The man stepped through the doorway, and he died there.

As the occupants of the room turned in shock, Calavius twisted, eyes wide, gasping, hands feeling for the three knives buried in his chest. He gave a strange squeak, and then toppled forwards into the room. Half a dozen of Cassius' guards followed him in and turned him over, removing their knives and cleaning them. They then lifted the body and carried it away, slaves hurrying forward with a bucket and cloths.

Cassius looked around at the others. 'Any chain is only as strong as its weakest link,' he said, by way of explanation.

He doubted there would be any further dissent.

JANUARY

"Some men are better served by their bitter-tongued enemies than by their sweet-smiling friends; because the former often tell the truth, the latter, never."

– Cicero: On Friendship.

CHAPTER EIGHT

'This is not a good idea,' Fronto muttered.

Caesar gave him a weary look. 'After that unfortunate little show at the new temple, I need to boost spirits once more. People need to see that the gods are with us.'

'Are they?'

'Of course they are, Fronto. What happened the other day was simple bad luck.'

Fronto forbore to answer, though the timing of Caesar's attack had been a little too neat to be luck in his opinion. Had he suffered his sickness at any other time, it would have been easy to cover up. Had he needed to be removed from public sight during the meetings with his clients, that could have been effected with the minimum of fuss, and once the senate and the consuls had left, the same could be said. That Caesar had been struck by his seizure in that very moment that the city's greatest luminaries had approached, unable to rise from his seat, forced to be terse and dismissive in order to get away, really was the very worst timing. All men, even dictators, should stand when the consuls and the senate addressed them with official business. It was the done thing. A measure of respect for the highest offices of the republic. To remain seated suggested that he was above them. He *was* above them, of course, but the strictures of republican propriety had to be at least nominally retained.

The knock to Caesar's reputation had been notable, and instant. By the end of that day, Fronto had heard more than once the story that Caesar considered himself sole ruler of Rome and that the consuls should give him deference. The senate seethed with disaffection over the slight they had perceived.

And no one could explain what had happened. The 'sacred disease' as the Greeks called it was still a stigma to bear. Caesar's affliction had been kept a closely-guarded secret all his life, even from the army for fear of ruining his reputation. Only close friends and physicians were aware of it. If Caesar's popularity had suffered as a result of that little slight at the temple, that was nothing to what would have happened if his affliction became public knowledge and people began to avoid him, protecting themselves from potentially contracting it. No, there had been no option.

Caesar, of course, always had a plan set aside to curb any slide in popularity. He was not a man to leave such things to chance. Thus today's spectacle.

Fronto's eyes slid to the haruspex in his pristine white toga, his four young attendants moving alongside him at a stately pace, faces serene as the sacrificial bull was led forward by its handler. A bull for Mars, nothing less. Fronto didn't trust haruspicy as a political tool, though. If all went well, then yes, it would look good to the people. But there was always the chance that it would go badly, and that would only make matters worse.

'Are you sure about this?'

Caesar eyed him and a small smile crept onto his face. 'Spurinna can be relied upon to make sure this goes well. Trust me.'

That was the third time Caesar had said something like that to him this morning, and it worried him. If this Spurinna was a true haruspex, then a positive outcome could not be guaranteed. He would not deny the gods. And so whatever Caesar said, the man could *not* be relied upon to make sure it went well. The alternative was that Spurinna was not a true haruspex and would reveal only what Caesar wanted him to reveal. That, of course, would create the perfect political outcome, but that made Fronto even more nervous, for lying in the face of the gods' displeasure was likely to have even more disastrous outcomes. No, he didn't like this at all.

And who was this Spurinna, anyway? The man was being treated like some sort of celebrity, as though he were a famous haruspex, yet Fronto had never heard of the man before. He had suddenly appeared when Caesar needed him, summoned from

102

somewhere, perhaps across the sea? Africa did breed prophets, seers and magicians more than any other land, after all.

The man seemed confident as he strode towards the prepared area.

Fronto blinked as they emerged from the cella of the Temple of Mars and the cold winter sunshine angled in. As his vision cleared once more, he realised just how big an event this was to be. If he'd thought there was a big crowd for that debacle at the new Temple of Venus, then this was something entirely different. Those senators who remained on good terms with Caesar, or at least who were not too offended by his recent action to attend, stood around the colonnade's edge, lictors on the steps to prevent anyone approaching unexpectedly. Below the temple podium, the streets were thronged with the people of Rome in numbers such as Fronto had not seen since that great triumph a year ago. He felt those nerves creeping in again. This had better go right, because if something went wrong this time, the effects would wash across the city in moments.

Caesar, arrayed once more in his toga, a man of the people, a son of the republic, followed on behind the haruspex and his attendants. The crowd fell into a hushed silence as Spurinna appeared atop the steps. The bull was brought forward, a pure white creature, subdued by an earlier ingestion of certain infusions that dulled its senses. It was bedecked in garlands of crimson blooms, its horns gilded, a crimson rope wound around them and the neck, used to lead it. The four attendants went about their business immediately, before Caesar appeared. One attendant brought forth the bowl of pure water, another blew upon the great brazier and added fresh fuel, sending sparks up anew. The third positioned the bull carefully, while the fourth cut a lock of hair from the beast's head and then carried it reverently across to the brazier in which he dropped it with a hiss.

Their initial jobs complete, the brazier attendant and the hair cutter collected a great heavy hammer and a fresh, gleaming knife, ready. Spurinna walked forward and took prime position, raising his hands to the air. Behind him, Caesar now walked into view, eliciting a stifled cheer from the crowd, who loved a spectacle, but were wary of interrupting such a sacred event.

As was only appropriate for this particular sacrifice, the honours would go entirely to Spurinna. Caesar was here as the principle witness, not the priest. Consequently, as Caesar stood with him near the front of the temple podium, the various senators and wealthy citizens gathered behind them, it was Spurinna who turned his hands palms up in the air and spoke.

'As Rome and her dictator prepare to contend with the ancient enemy in the East, we seek the favour of the gods for this great endeavour. In the deserts of Parthia our armies will meet those of a king of kings, yet while sword meets sword and warrior meets warrior, so the gods of Rome will do battle with the gods of the Parthians. Mars, great god of war and father of warriors, patron of the legions, we sacrifice to you this pure bull and within it we seek your will. Let it be so.'

And with that, he pulled his arms back down and paced across to the bowl of water, dipping in his hands and washing them thoroughly. Drying them on a pure white towel held forth by the attendant, he stepped back across to the bull. After a stately pause, he nodded to the other attendants. One slowly, carefully, handed him the blade, while the other approached the bull, lifting the hammer. Fronto mused for a moment that sometimes it took as brave a man to be a sacrificial attendant as to fight a war. He wasn't sure that, even with it drugged, he'd have managed to maintain such a serene expression while approaching the gleaming horns of a bull.

Before the main ritual started, Spurinna began to chant the traditional prayers. Fronto didn't bother listening to them. He'd heard them plenty of times in his life, and could repeat them by rote. Instead, as was his habit, he found somewhere near the back, out of the public eye, to lean and save his bad knee, while he let his mind wander from the current tedium.

He found himself going over, once again, the numbers of troops and how he was going to divide them. In fairness, despite his arguments, Caesar had been correct. Dividing the army and sending a force against the Getae was not really a problem. It just required another set of orders to be dispatched. He had assigned five legions as well as archers, slingers, and just shy of two thousand Gallic cavalry. He wondered whether he could use the same ships to convey them across the Hellespont after that initial campaign as were assigned to transport the main army to Antioch, or whether he would need to find another fleet to assign. Calculating the times it would take for the various voyages and marches and how likely it was that ships would be available in time gave him one of those 'maths headaches', and he felt a wash of irritation as someone close by cleared their throat loudly and interrupted his thought process, losing an array of figures he'd been committing to memory. He looked around to see who had interrupted him.

The man wore a toga with a thin red border, marking him as a figure of eminence, yet Fronto did not recognise him, which was odd. He was familiar now with almost all the important men of Rome, by sight at least.

'This campaign is a mistake,' the man said, quietly, not drawing attention, not looking at Fronto, his eyes on the main action.

'Sorry?'

'Parthia. It is a mistake. It should be called off. Caesar should call it off. Or his people in the right places should *persuade* him to call it off.'

'Keep your opinion to yourself,' Fronto grunted, trying to ignore that part of his consciousness that agreed with the man.

'I remember you as a man of the republic, a true son of Rome, standing up for principles. I remember the hero Fronto, not the royal lackey who supports such usurpation of power from the state.'

That annoyed Fronto, and he turned, narrow eyed. 'Why don't you go find somewhere else to stand?'

'Taking part in this campaign could be very unhealthy. Even a quiet part, from home. *Very* unhealthy.'

'Just piss off,' Fronto said, turning back.

'It would be a shame to see such a famed republican nail his standard to the mast of a doomed ship. Step away from the Parthian command, Marcus Falerius Fronto. Step away and persuade Caesar to change his plan.'

'Will you fuck off?'

'Remember my words,' the man said, his voice quiet, oddly menacing, despite the lightness to his tone. Fronto turned back to

105

berate the man again, but could see him moving away, disappearing into the crowd. He looked around, frowning, as Spurinna finished his prayers and prepared for the main event. Fronto's eyes fell upon a familiar back-of-the-head, and he tapped Marcus Antonius, newly installed consul of Rome alongside Caesar, on the shoulder. Antonius turned, brow creasing.

'Fronto?'

He pointed at the disappearing man, the impressive bald spot in the back of his curly golden hair gleaming. 'Who is that?'

Antonius turned and followed Fronto's gesture. 'Baldy?'

'Yes.'

'That's Plautius. Publius Plautius Hypsaeus.'

Fronto blinked. He turned to get another look at the man, but he was gone from sight now, lost in the gathering of senators. *Hypsaeus.* The man with the big estate on the hill that the Pompeian veterans had visited just before they threw a good man out of a fourth floor window. Hypsaeus, who had a history of running gangs in Rome, a man of few principles, as dangerous as Milo and Clodius, but brighter than them, clever enough to stay out of major politics. A man who had been rarely seen in recent years.

A killer?

He quickly thought back over what the man had said, and the more he thought on those words, the more threatening they sounded. Damn it, but if he'd known it was Hypsaeus at the time he might have had a little more to say in reply.

Antonius had given him an odd look and then turned to pay attention to the rites once more, and Fronto followed suit. Short of pushing his way between the senators in a rather undignified manner, there was little he could do about Hypsaeus right now anyway, and he could not afford to be the man who ruined this event.

Despite his position towards the rear of the gathering, he could just see the action between the shoulders and heads of those in front, and he watched, tense, as the attendant brought the hammer down hard on the bull's pate with a crack that echoed around the streets in the reverent silence. The bull gave a weird groan as its legs gave way and it collapsed to the temple podium, its skull smashed, blood beginning to flow in rivulets from its pristine white forehead. As that attendant stepped back, Spurinna moved into his place. Knife gripped in his right hand, he used his left to lift the head. It took some effort, for Spurinna was not a big man, and the bull's lolling head would be heavy, but gritting his teeth, he managed to pull the head up so that the eyes were staring at the roof of the temple's portico. The bull had to be looking up, to Mars in his Olympian heaven. It was appropriate. With the dazed, dying creature looking upwards, he slammed the knife into one side of the bull's neck. This was a dangerous moment in any sacrifice, for the bull, wits dulled and skull smashed as they were, would still react automatically to the attack. It screamed and tried to thrash, but Spurinna proved equal to the task, shaking his head at the attendants who moved forward to help him. He held the horns tight, keeping the bull in place as he pulled the knife across the throat, a task made difficult by the bull's thick skin.

Blood sluiced down across the animal's forequarters and liberally splashed Spurinna's feet and shins as it flowed into a sizeable puddle. The creature continued to jerk, though its movements became less and less as the life ebbed from it. Blood began to cascade down the steps at the temple's front. At the bottom, kept at a distance by the lictors, a number of citizens waited with cups and bowls, hoping to collect some of the sacred blood, with which many a household would seek divine favour that night.

The bull finally stilled, and Spurinna waited a short while to let the last hint of life disappear, and then bent to his work. For this, Fronto was quite pleased that the crowd before him moved a little and obscured the action. He didn't mind watching the sacrifice, but the gutting of creatures for haruspicy always put him off his next meal. Even listening to the sawing sounds and the wet slaps and rubbery noises as things were cut away and removed made him feel a little queasy. It had always irked him that such activity had this effect. He would watch men die on the battlefield in the most gruesome fashion, but when it was animals like this, eviscerated with practiced precision, somehow it was entirely different.

Finally, Spurinna seemed to have finished. There was a satisfied murmur among the senators. Fronto, however, heard something different. Not being able to see, he had lowered his gaze, and consequently his hearing had picked up a lot more than it otherwise might. He heard the small gasp from the haruspex. It was almost inaudible, and was lost in the murmur, but Fronto had heard it, and he knew it meant something bad.

He moved a little, finding a better view, but whatever he'd been expecting, when he caught sight of Spurinna, the man was rising, the knife discarded, handed to an attendant with no sign of alarm. He had in his left hand a bronze plaque in the shape of a liver, covered in the mystical inscriptions of the magicians, his guide to what the entrails might show. In his right, he held the bull's liver, which was surprisingly large and weighty. Fronto had eaten liver often enough to recognise that the one held up by Spurinna was in good condition, unmarred and clean, a perfect colour in its glistening glory. Indeed, the haruspex was smiling benignly as he held both aloft for the audience to see.

'Let the people of Rome, and those beyond, even our enemies to the very encircling sea of the world, know that the omens are good. The gods favour Rome, the army and war with Parthia. Mars will be with the legions in the East, his arms encircling them, his blade cutting into their enemies, his rage filling their hearts. Let the Parthians quail. And the great god tells us that we need not fear the prophecies, for the Sibyl's warning shall be laid to rest as Parthia falls to Roman blades. All is good. Revel in the god's favour. Tonight Rome feasts, for tomorrow she will conquer!'

It was masterfully done. In one swift announcement, Spurinna had turned everything around, given Caesar a boost, legitimising his campaign, promising victory and even putting aside the prophecy of the Sibylline books. The people roared with pleasure and relief, and Caesar stepped to the front of the temple steps. He said nothing, but held up his arms in thanks to the god, and the people's roaring and cheering merely escalated to an ear-splitting din. Even the senators sounded relieved and cheerful. Everything was perfect.

Except it wasn't.

Fronto had heard that small gasp.

And he had noted something else, too.

In all his great speech, Spurinna had not once mentioned Caesar. He had invoked the god, the people, the army, the

108

Parthians, and even the barbarian peoples as far as the end of the world, and yet Caesar had been absent from the list. No one else seemed to have noticed, from the relieved and happy din.

They remained like this for perhaps a quarter of an hour as Spurinna burned the entrails, sending the smoke up to sustain the god, as the lictors reorganised to allow the public to collect up the blood of the beast at the bottom of the steps, and as Caesar spoke quietly and with a wide smile to the various senators. Fronto stood at the back and fretted. He kept his eyes on the two principle players in this drama, and everything he had noticed was borne out by what he saw. Spurinna was a master of spectacle, and kept his confident smile riveted to his face throughout as he answered questions from senators, made extra libations, and spoke to people about what he had seen. But every time he turned and his face was not on display, Fronto caught a hint of something dark in it, some kind of uncertainty at the very least, if not worry, plain and simple. He was clever enough, though, to keep moving and never let that expression stay visible. Similarly Caesar was all smiles and confidence, talking about the planned campaign and answering questions, but every moment he was left to himself for a heartbeat or two, he turned and threw a frustrated look at the haruspex. He, too, had noted his own absence from that list.

Then Fronto was dragged into it. Caesar had been talking about the campaign plans, and Fronto found himself being brought to the front to answer questions. Senators of all ages and statuses plied him for details, interest written on their faces. Fronto tried to sound patient and present, though in truth he was answering by rote without really paying any attention, for he was still looking at Caesar and Spurinna, and once, annoyingly, he caught sight of Hypsaeus through the crowd, the man giving him a black look.

Finally, things seemed to wind down. With a last blessing to the crowd, Spurinna turned and made his way through the gathering towards the temple, leaving bloody footprints in his wake. At the door, one of his attendants hurried over and removed his sandals, washed his legs and feet and dried them, and produced fresh sandals that he slipped on with ease. Suitably clean once more, the haruspex entered the temple. The crowds in the street remained, for there was the tradition of the bull's meat being distributed for banquets and all hoped to supplement their diet with an offcut of the sacrificial animal. The attendants went to work there, carving up the bull, clearing away the paraphernalia, cleaning up the temple, their own guards remaining in position to keep the crowd back, while the lictors moved to the temple entrance to keep the senators away, for Caesar was now following Spurinna inside.

The majority of those senators dispersed now, the interesting part done with, having shown their faces and spoken to the dictator to confirm that they were in support. A few remained, waiting to be allowed access to the temple. Fronto spotted Hirtius, both of the Brutii, Antonius, as well as Cornelius Balbus and Gaius Oppius, and a few other more important luminaries. Of Publius Plautius Hypsaeus he could see no sign, though he was in two minds as to whether that was a good thing or not. Taking a deep breath, he strode to the temple doorway. Two lictors moved to intercept, and he gave them a pointed look with an arched brow.

'Unless you want to be one fasces rod less and walking funny, back off, fellas,' Fronto growled. Still, the two heavy-set men looked prepared to intercept until Caesar called from just inside the doorway.

'Let him in.'

Fronto gave the two men an unpleasant smile as he strode between them and into the shade of the temple's cella. Caesar was standing in the middle of the room, arms folded, as Spurinna made his last libations and offerings at the altar in front of the god's statue.

'What the shit was *that* about?' Fronto snapped.

Caesar did not turn, continued to look at the haruspex.

Spurinna finished what he was doing and spent a short while still facing away, leaning with his palms flat on the altar. Finally, he drew himself up and turned. His face was carefully expressionless as he walked a few paces to face the other two men in the room.

'You brought me here because I am the best.'

'Naturally,' Caesar replied, 'but also because I consulted you in Africa and you had good things lined up in my future, all of which have come to pass. Because you can be trusted, and I needed someone the people would believe.'

'And you knew that if the omens were bad, and the god disapproved, I would tell you.'

'And yet you saw only victory for us.'

Spurinna shook his head. 'I see victory for *Rome*. Not for Caesar.'

Fronto frowned. 'Hang on a moment. I noticed that you never mentioned Caesar, but you also never mentioned *this* campaign specifically, did you?'

Spurinna continued shaking his head. 'In the coming years Rome will stand in the palaces and the holy places of Parthia. That I see. And Mars will be there and drive the legions to great victories. But not now. And not under Caesar.'

'Then what...?' Caesar began, but Spurinna silenced him with a raised hand.

'There was something else in there. The bull was not quite right. I found its heart, and there were two marks on it, like old sword wounds. Each corresponds to a marking I know well from the old Etruscan texts. Two months, they give, until the heart fails. A little more, for the second wound was larger, and resembled an X and a V.'

'I have not studied divination,' Caesar sighed. 'This is unintelligible to me.'

'But not to me. The meaning is clear, Caesar. You will not find victory in Parthia, because it is not your fate to lead the campaign there. You will be dead by then.'

Caesar faltered for a moment then, but quickly a smile of easy disbelief replaced the uncertainty. 'Come now, friend Spurinna. Interpretation is much of the game, is it not? A dozen different haruspices might read the signs differently.'

'No, Caesar. This is clear. Put your affairs in order. You will seek the boatman's crossing by the Ides of Martius.'

'Come, Spurinna, but that is just three days before I depart for Parthia.'

'Quite, Caesar.'

The dictator turned to Fronto, a question in his eyes. Fronto quailed. As the haruspex had spoken, Fronto had felt his guts flip and churn, a cold chill running across his skin. There was something in Spurinna's voice. He had heard haruspices before, and knew they came in many forms from the true mouthpiece of the gods down to the street-corner charlatan. And even the best of them would often qualify what they had seen and give room for adjustment and uncertainty. Rarely did a haruspex in a private reading such as this give a flat and certain pronouncement. Spurinna was absolutely convinced of what he had seen. And if what Fronto had just heard was the truth, then Spurinna was a respected, even revered, prognosticator, so sought after that Caesar had brought him in so as to remove all doubt.

Fronto failed to answer the dictator, instead turning to Spurinna. 'What you have seen. Is it set in stone? Have the Fates laid this out as it will come to pass? Or is there some answer to seek yet? Is there any qualification, how this can be avoided? Some solution?'

The haruspex shook his head. 'It is written in the heart of the sacred bull. I have plied my craft for three decades, and trained under the greatest haruspices in Africa. I do not dissemble and I do not lie. What I see will come to pass, and there is no doubt in my mind that this will happen, no matter what might be done in attempting to avoid it. It is the future of Caesar to pass beyond by the Ides, two months from now.'

Fronto shivered. He turned to Caesar, unsure what to say, and what he saw there floored him. For just a moment, he saw Caesar's soul laid bare for the first time. He had known the man for decades and had known him in times good and bad, facing both great things and utter disasters. He had seen the general vulnerable and weak at times, distraught even, on rare occasions. He had seen him angry and perhaps frightened. What he had never seen in Caesar's face, in all the years he'd known the man, was hopelessness.

That was what he saw in the moment he turned to the dictator. Terror, hopelessness, panic. A frightened child hearing bad news. It disappeared in an instant, and Fronto doubted Spurinna had seen it, but it chilled him to the bone. Then Caesar was back to his usual self. A look of boundless confidence appeared and he gave a low chuckle as he rocked back on his heels.

'Then I say that this time you are wrong. Or perhaps that the ancient learning upon which you rely is wrong. I have appealed to Venus on more than one occasion, and she vouchsafes that I will

112

die and old man, with my line secured, sons around me. What you have seen is a mistake.'

'No, Caesar. It is not.'

'It is, and I thank you for your excellent service today, but I charge you with keeping this false sight to yourself. I am currently in the business of rebuilding public confidence in preparation for my great campaign, and I cannot have news like this moving from lip to ear around Rome.'

'You can keep this a secret if you wish, Caesar, but it will not make it any less true.'

'Then let me worry about that, and you keep your tongue barred behind teeth, my African friend.'

Spurinna bowed low 'I will take my leave, Caesar.' He gathered up his things and made for the door. Fronto, his skin still prickling with an unnatural chill, watched him go. As the haruspex reached the door, just outside two men stepped out of his way, and Fronto momentarily caught their expressions. He winced. The damage was done. Marcus Junius Brutus and Marcus Antonius had both almost certainly heard at least some of the exchange.

He turned to Caesar. 'Whatever you say, whatever he saw, you need to start taking care, and get yourself a new, bigger, bodyguard.'

CHAPTER NINE

'I still don't know what the problem is, really,' Fronto sighed, slapping the writing tablet to the table top and leaning back, folding his arms.

'It's a combination of logistics and ego,' Brutus said, rubbing tired eyes. Thanks to the size of the fleet you have assembling in Illyricum ready for the advance in Martius, there simply is not room for the whole mass in one port, even one as major as Dyrrachium. Almost half your fleet has moved south along the coast and made their harbour at Oricum. So effectively you now have two fleets. And because you had not thought to assign a commander previously, the two preeminent naval commanders each claim control of the fleet, and each currently hold half of it. Both Calventius and Laenius expect to receive orders any day placing them in overall command of the fleet. Once they move and combine, having two matched admirals each trying to direct matters will just be a disaster. And then there's Numonius on his way from Hispania, and he was instrumental in successes in the aftermath of Africa. He's never yet seen a major reward from Caesar, but now he's coming back in from the periphery, you can bet your last coin he will be expecting to put in at Dyrrachium and be given the baton of command. And if three contenders already at sea aren't enough for you, Gellius was already nudging me the other day at the sacrifice and dropping hints that he would very much appreciate command of the fleet. One fleet, two ports and four would-be admirals.'

Fronto grunted. 'I'm beginning to see why Caesar delegated this. Why did the fleet split? If they'd assembled together, Calventius and Laenius would already have hammered this out one way or another. When we landed there a few years ago, we had a sizeable fleet, but we just used the coastline south of Dyrrachium. Why can't they?'

Brutus rolled his eyes. 'Marcus, we were landing in the middle of a military action. Disembark and launch the fight, and the fleet could then go about its business. This time, you're talking about scores of ships and thousands of personnel preparing for three months or more. They can only do that with a home port, not on some wild beach.'

'Alright, here's what we do,' Fronto said, all business as he leaned forward again and moved some of the wooden markers across the map on the table. 'Aulona is just a few miles across the bay from Oricum. Between the two places they can hold a larger fleet than Dyrrachium alone. We take these thirty ships from Dyrrachium and have them move to Aulona. Then we give Laenius at Oricum command of the larger fleet. That's the one that will put out for Antioch when the time comes. Laenius will be happy because he has the larger fleet. At the same time, the smaller fleet can stay under the command of Calventius at Dyrrachium. I was wondering how I would arrange the post-Getae movement anyway, so that smaller fleet, instead of sailing for Antioch, can make for Byzantium to collect Caesar's first force. Calventius will have a smaller fleet but will be sailing to the aid of Caesar and will be under his direct command. That will make *him* feel more important. They will both think they have the best job.'

Brutus nodded. 'And what happens when the fleet combines once more at Antioch.'

Fronto grinned. 'The beauty of that is that I'll be a thousand miles away and it'll be Caesar's problem then.'

'And what of Numonius? He'll arrive expecting command to find that two men are already above him.'

Fronto shrugged, then a thought struck him. 'He'll be putting in here on the way to Illyricum. He must have a powerful ship, given his current status. We'll assign his ship as Caesar's flagship. Instead of sailing on and joining the fleet, he can stay in Rome, moored here, and when Caesar departs for campaign, he can go on Numonius' ship. If he's captain of Caesar's flagship, that should be sufficient honour to keep him happy.'

Brutus nodded. 'That's workable. Now there's just Gellius to work out.'

Fronto let out an explosive breath. 'Gellius might have to make do with some other role. I've already magicked three commands out of one. Not sure I can do a fourth.'

A voice on the far side of the table cleared his throat. 'That just leaves the matter of command of the army in Antioch while it waits for Caesar,' Lepidus said. 'I have already had three heartfelt letters of recommendation for the position. You and I both know that whoever gets it will manage to accrue quite a small fortune even before Caesar arrives, and can expect an important role on the staff afterwards.'

Fronto sagged. 'It never ends. I've had one or two hints myself.'

He winced as he remembered the morning. His salutatio had just ended when Marcus Antonius visited. The man had been rather irritable, having heard the suggestion that his consulship might be taken from him in Martius, and he'd told Fronto flatly that if he was to have what power and honour he'd been allowed in Rome stripped away, then he would expect to find himself in a top command position in Parthia. Fronto had reminded him that Caesar had turned him down for that repeatedly, and Antonius had countered with the fact that it was Fronto making the decisions now, not Caesar. He'd managed to end the conversation with a vague and nebulous promise to look into it, but he knew he couldn't do that. Antonius had been specifically denied, and given the consulship to keep him mollified despite having no real importance any more. Fronto wondered what Antonius would say when he learned that the reason for the consulship changing was because Caesar had promised it to Fronto from Martius onwards. He winced again. That was a conversation he wasn't looking forward to.

'I'll have to think on that. I'm fairly sure we can split out command into several roles, and prevent any one man from expecting full control by maintaining the position that Caesar is overall commander, even if he's not currently with the army in Antioch. That way we can make several people quite happy instead of one ecstatic and the rest angry. For now, I've got other things I need to sort out.'

The three of them rose and stretched. Brutus nodded to him and turned with Lepidus, the two of them leaving the room together, already moving on to a new discussion. Fronto stood for a long moment looking down at the map and the many lists and letters. He scrubbed his scalp for a moment and then rolled his shoulders. Leaving the room, he could see Lepidus and Brutus already climbing into their litters, their entourages gathering around them ready to depart. He turned to the two men standing on guard outside the office he now used for all naval planning, both of them men of the fleet. 'The usual orders. No one goes in without me.'

As the two men nodded their understanding, Fronto closed the door behind him and strode across the huge flagged courtyard of the Navalia, Rome's military port on the riverside. He could see the prefect whose command the place was sitting at a table with Galronus, several others gathered around. He wandered across and watched with interest. The two men were engaged in a game of latrunculi, the stone board with its grid scattered with black and white pieces. Fronto, no mean player of the game himself, took in the situation at a glance and estimated that the good prefect was doomed, and likely to lose the match in the next four or five moves. Fronto had been playing since childhood and had fostered an interest in the game among his officers throughout his career, for latrunculi was a good tool for teaching military tactics. He was beginning to regret teaching Galronus now, though, for the Remi had taken to it like a duck to water, and was already better than Fronto.

Indeed, he watched for a while as Galronus destroyed the prefect's defences and pinned his last few pieces in the corner of the board, claiming an easy victory. The prefect let out a long deep breath and leaned back. 'I've not been thrashed like that since I let my wife play me,' he said with a shake of the head.

Galronus simply shrugged. 'If it's any consolation, I thought you were over about half an hour ago. You fought back and held on a lot longer than I expected, and better than most other people I've played.'

The prefect smiled wearily, and Fronto gestured to the man. 'Some time before the Ides of Januarius, Gaius Numonius Vala will be putting in here, returning from Hispania. I suspect he'll

117

dock with just the one ship, leaving the rest of his fleet at Ostia. As soon as he puts in, I need you to have him report to Caesar, and have a message sent to my home. His ship is to be overhauled and prepared as Caesar's flagship for the coming campaign. Understood?'

The prefect nodded. 'Perfectly, senator. I'll have messages sent as soon as he arrives.'

Thanking the man, Fronto gestured to Galronus and the two of them strolled over to the corner of the square where Fronto's own entourage awaited. It was a relatively small affair, compared with some, particularly that of Brutus, who seemed to have acquired a fearsome looking force of warriors from somewhere. Fronto and Galronus had come in a litter, carried aloft by four burly slaves. Fronto had argued against that. He hated litters. Firstly they made him feel queasy with the bouncing, swaying movement, secondly all it would take was one of the four slaves to fall for some reason and the whole vehicle would come crashing down, and thirdly he did not like the ostentatious luxury. He'd have come on a horse for preference, but Lucilia had been insistent that he at least *try* to look faintly senatorial. He'd not argued for long. He'd won the battle to wear a tunic and cloak rather than a toga, and that was a victory not to be sniffed at, after all.

Other than the four litter slaves, he and Galronus were accompanied by Aurelius, Arcadios and half a dozen of his personal mercenaries who stood poised, waiting. 'Home?' Aurelius asked, standing and rolling his shoulders.

'Indeed.'

With a sigh, Fronto climbed into the litter and took a seat, waiting as Galronus clambered in behind him. Some thoughtful soul had left a jar of wine and two cups on a tray with a deep rim to one side. Grinning, Fronto poured the drinks, noting at the wine had already been watered correctly, passed a cup to Galronus and then, wedging the jar upright between two cushions, took the other himself.

'City route or riverside, sir?' called a voice from outside.

Fronto chewed that over for a moment. The riverside was a slightly faster journey back to his home on the Aventine, but it did mean travelling past the great sewer outlet of the cloaca maxima which, even if the aroma was a little dulled in winter, could still be pungent. It also meant passing through the forum boarium, the city's cattle market, which could be even worse at times. On the other hand, the city route took longer, and other parts of Rome sometimes smelled like a sewer or a cow pat too. Before he could announce a decision, Galronus called 'River route.'

Fronto frowned a question at him, and the Remi gave him a sly smile.

'The ladies will not expect us back before dark, as we put aside the whole day for that meeting. The river route takes us past the circus. I don't think we could be blamed if we accidentally fell into it on the way home. This afternoon's races are set to be particularly good.'

Fronto gave his friend a grin. With everything that had been happening, between the troubles with Hypsaeus' collegium, the difficulties of planning the coming campaign, the vying of various important characters around the city, and with his own striving for position, pushed ever upwards by Lucilia, it would be nice to take the afternoon off at the races, untroubled by the usual issues.

'Good plan.'

The litter rose and wobbled a little as the slaves settled the carrying bars on their shoulders, the wine in their cups slopping around, not quite spilling, and Fronto and Galronus relaxed as they moved off. They could hear the men around them stomping along, nailed boots on flagstones, and heard the conversation as they passed through the archway, past the marine guards and out of the Navalia complex back into the city itself.

'What are you going to do when Caesar leaves?' Galronus said suddenly, the directness of his question coming out of nowhere and throwing Fronto for a moment. He frowned.

'What do you mean?'

'As long as I've known you, you've been Caesar's man, Marcus. So have I, of course, but to him I will always be an ally who proved useful. You've been the closest thing he has to a friend, I think.'

'I suspect "useful ally" covers me pretty well too.'

'You know what I mean. Caesar relies upon you, and you've always held yourself close. But we all know no matter what he tries, you're not going east. You're done with wars, and I can see that. So when Caesar starts a whole new campaign, which will probably see him occupied for at least the next half decade, what are you going to do? As long as I've known you, you've never had a year without fighting his wars.'

Fronto nodded sagely. In truth it was a question that had struck him one night a while ago and which he'd been brushing aside ever since, trying not to think of it.

'I don't know. Raise the boys. Be a senator. Lucilia wants me to make my mark. And no matter how much I grumble about it, I know why. It's not her ambition. She wants the boys to have the best possible start, and I can't argue with that. So I'll play the game in Rome as long as I must, and when the boys are old enough that they can navigate their own way and my status makes no difference, I'll retire. I don't know where, though. Puteoli or Tarraco. Which do you think? Both have a circus, after all.'

Galronus fixed him with a level look. 'It doesn't matter. I won't be there, Marcus.'

Fronto blinked. 'What?'

'Think about it, Marcus. We've been together all these years because we were both fighting the wars together. And because of Faleria in later years, of course. But I cannot stay in your house forever, and I have no desire for a Roman townhouse of my own.'

'Then Puteoli. Or Tarraco.'

'No, Marcus. I'll be going home.'

'Home? Galronus you're more Roman than most Romans. You *are* home.'

'No, Marcus. I've talked it over with Faleria. My home is slowly recovering. It will be generations before most of what you call Gaul will be free of the scars of war, but the Remi are better off than most. Because we backed Caesar from the start, we have little destruction, our people are well off and growing. And they are moving down from the old oppida and building towns now, with all the trappings of the Roman world. In a generation's time, you won't be able to tell Remi lands from northern Italia or Hispania. And if the Remi are ever to flourish in that new world, they will need men like me. Faleria and I will return to Durocortorum and retire there. Think about it. If we're wealthy

120

here, and I am, with Caesar's gifts to put me in the senate, imagine how rich that makes us back home. And I miss it, Marcus. I miss the green, the hills, the fresh rains of Spring. Rome is glorious, but my homeland calls me.'

Fronto suddenly felt hollow. He'd never contemplated Galronus having a life of his own, elsewhere. Fronto had rarely been close to people, even Caesar. Just his almost brother-in-law Verginius, dead in that quarry in Hispania, Priscus, the stalwart primus pilus of the Tenth, felled by an arrow on the ramparts of Alesia, and then Galronus.

He couldn't think of anything to say – other than to rant and rage, and tell the Remi not to be so bloody selfish, which, of course, would be the very apex of hypocrisy. Galronus must have realised the trouble he was having, for the man gave him a reassuring smile. 'Durocortorum is maybe six hundred miles from Rome, and from Tarraco even less. With good horses that's not much more than half a month's travel. You won't be rid of me. We will come to you, for Saturnalia if nothing else. And you can come to us. No one could teach your boys to ride like the Remi.'

Fronto just nodded in silence.

It would never work like that. That was what happened when friends parted over such distances. Once or twice they would meet, and then, slowly, they would drift apart until they only even remembered one another on important dates. He was having tremendous trouble processing this piece of news, and certainly didn't trust himself to speak just yet.

He was saved the trouble when there was an odd noise outside and the whole world suddenly turned upside down.

The litter hit the pavement one corner first, and Fronto was thrown back into his seat, the dregs of his wine spattering across his fine tunic. Before he could do any more than grunt, Galronus smashed into him, thrown forwards just as Fronto had been thrown back. The whole vehicle rocked once more as the corner behind Galronus now smashed down too, and in another heartbeat the whole thing flipped over to land on its side. The jar of wine had gone over and was glopping its contents out across the expensive interior, but Fronto was moving now, not worried about appearances. His confusion had gone, as had his shock and misery over the news, all pushed back by a sudden realisation. The first lurch had come as a surprise, but even as Galronus pulled himself back away and that second corner had hit, Fronto had recognised the noises outside. The man holding up that corner of the litter had been hit with something heavy and had gone down with a squawk that had been almost lost beneath the noise of the vehicle's crash.

They were under attack.

He had no weapon. Just his eating knife, and he'd have to work hard to do much fighting with that. Galronus was in a similar position. The litter bearers were unarmed, of course. That just left Arcadios, Aurelius and the six men outside. Aurelius at least showed little sign of his head wound now, and Arcadios merely sported a pronounced limp. Ten of them altogether. If their attackers were who Fronto suspected, they were unlikely to be present in such small numbers.

Shit.

He really should start travelling surrounded by an army.

Teeth clenched, he pulled himself up, standing on the inside wall of the vehicle as he reached up and undid the catch on the far door, which now formed the roof. Readying himself, he pushed it out and swung it open until it slapped back against the wall/roof. He pulled his hand back in and waited. Nothing was happening. Outside, he could hear shouts occasionally, but they were more urgent cries than commands or warnings, and served little to let him know what was actually happening. With a quick glance at Galronus who, all business once more, nodded back, he pulled himself up and stuck his head out of the doorway.

A small rock or bullet ricocheted off the wooden side of the litter close to his head, and as a second came close enough to part his hair, he dropped back inside.

'Slings. They can't carry big blades or bows in the city without attracting trouble, but a sling is easy to hide. They're good, too. Quick and accurate. Bet it was slings that brought down the slaves.'

'Then we're trapped.'

Fronto thought back. 'Maybe not. All the shouting I can hear is from one side, and both the bullets aimed at me came from the other. The enemy are only on one side, and I reckon the others are hiding behind the litter, pinned down.'

'Then I can think of a way out, but we'd best move quickly,' Galronus noted. 'Street fights get dealt with fairly quickly, and they'll want to finish this before they draw too much attention. They'll be moving round to flank the vehicle already. Help me.'

'What?' Fronto said, but in that moment he realised what Galronus was doing. The Remi had already undone the catch on the door that now lay underneath them on the cobbles. Realising what was to come, Fronto risked injury once more as he reached up and pulled the door closed above him, clicking the latch. The doors both opened outwards, which made things awkward for Galronus, but the Remi was equal to the task, for he simply heaved and pulled at the other door until the top came free, broken. Fronto added his strength and, a moment later, they had pulled the entire wine-soaked door off and discarded it inside the vehicle. The cold, wet cobbles lay beneath, and both men stepped onto them and bent, gripping the litter. In moments they were straining, heaving, pulling it up, and finally, as they reached the point of balance, the vehicle tipped over.

Aurelius and Arcadios were there with four other guards and a litter slave, crouching, sheltering behind the vehicle, which was just as much cover upright as it had been on its side. Thuds announced a fresh volley of slingshots against the vehicle, and stones skipped and bounced across the pavement to either side. Distant shouts suggested the enemy were on the move. They would be fanning out, trying to cut off any escape and then rush them. Likely they already had sufficient coverage to stop the fugitives reaching any other cover. Damn it. What now?

He turned and glanced the way they'd come. They must have done at least half a mile while chatting before the attack, maybe nearer a mile. He could see the Tiber Island and the bridge not far away. They had to be close to the circus and the forum boarium, then. Why had he not smelled the cattle market? He realised now that they were actually *in* the market place. Of course, it was the seventh day of the nundinae. Tomorrow was the main market day across the whole city, and that meant that the forum boarium had been empty and unused for two days to allow it to be cleaned and prepared. There was still a faint aroma of dung now that he thought about it, but that smell was prevalent enough city wide that he'd not paid attention to it.

He could see figures approaching from the direction of the bridge. No escape that way, then. Running out of options, he looked the other way. He could see the far end of the square, the old city gate, the emporium and the slopes of the Aventine that meant home and safety. He could also see figures between there and his current position.

Sling bullets came again now, and just as he ducked back out of sight, he spotted a familiar figure. He just had time to see Salvius Cursor hurl a half-brick in their direction before he was out of sight once more.

'Was that who I think it was?' Galronus breathed.

'Yes.'

'Think he'll help us?'

'If he tries, they'll kill him. He has to look like one of them, after all. No help there. But at least we know damn well who we're dealing with now. I mean, I knew anyway, but now we have the proof.'

'Much good it does. We're trapped and they're closing on from all sides.'

'Not *all* sides,' Fronto corrected him, eyes going to the slope that led down to the water.

'You're joking?'

'That's why the attack only came from one side, Galronus. We were moving along the river bank.'

The Remi eyed the Tiber. It was just past midwinter, the worst possible time for rivers. The Tiber was flowing with the speed of a launched ballista bolt, terrifyingly swift. Not only that, but it was also a dark greeny-brown with the run-off from the fields of Latium, and was deep enough that it lapped the piles of the nearby bridges worryingly close to the top of the arches.

'I can swim,' Galronus said, 'but probably not in that. I think I'd rather take my chances with the slings.'

'You're missing the point,' Fronto grinned. 'We're right above the cloaca maxima.'

Galronus frowned. 'The sewer?'

'Sewers can be really useful, my Remi friend. One day I'll tell you how I used them when I was a kid to get away from some really angry Vestals. Come on.'

And with that he stepped across to the top of the riverbank. There had been plans to put good flood walls in place along this whole stretch, from the Navalia to the Emporium, but they had been bandied about for at least thirty years now with still nothing having been done. Consequently the bank was muddy and churned, by passers-by and also by the cattle that were gathered here six days in every eight. There was no solid paving, and very little survived in the way of grass. As he reached the edge, Fronto looked down, spotted what he wanted, and edged half a dozen paces to his left. Below him now, the slope fell for perhaps five feet and then there was a channel where the great sewer emptied into the river, held open in the bank with its own ancient stone walls.

He turned and waved the others over. A slingshot whipped through the cold air not far from his ear and, spurred on by the ever-increasing danger, Fronto slid those five feet and disappeared into the channel with a splash.

This close to the outlet, the water was as much river as sewer, though as he resurfaced his relief at this fact that was rather overcome by the current. He found himself flailing at the stone-lined channel while kicking his feet and pulling himself forward just to stay in place and not be swept out into the mid-river, where drowning would be almost a given. Only when his fingers found solid purchase did he manage to start pulling himself in. The further he went, the easier it became, and he heard a splash behind him followed by a stream of curses in the Gallic tongue, confirming that Galronus had joined him. Other splashes followed soon after as the others threw themselves into the dubious safety of the water.

The sewer was armpit deep in brown water, but the flow was only light, for it had been very cold in Rome for the past month, with little in the way of rain, and most of what they were standing it was actually river water that had back-flooded from the current into the sewer. With some difficulty, Fronto began pulling himself up into the darker heart of the sewers, the others following on behind him, cursing in three different languages.

'Will they not follow us?' Galronus coughed, catching up.

'Would you?'

'Good point. And what if they go and wait for us at the other end?'

'Not likely, my Remi friend. There are side-tunnels and connections to other sewers all the way along. There's hatches up to the surface all over the place, too. There are at least a dozen in the forum alone, and one in particular that very few people will know about. It's not in a very open place, and I only know about it because the engineers rebuilding the Basilica Sempronia for Caesar came across the channel. And best of all, it's the closest. Come on.'

Ignoring all the various short side passages and apertures leading up to the surface, they ploughed on, their journey gradually getting a little easier as they walked, for as the tunnel sloped up, so the depth of the water was reduced. By the time they reached the tunnel that marched off to their left, it had come down to below waist level, which was a relief, but consisted more of general effluent than of river water, which was less so.

The whole journey was done in near darkness, their way lit only periodically by drains high up that allowed a little cold white sunshine to permeate the gloom. Finally, as the water level dropped to knee height, Fronto held up a hand and paused those following in his wake. Moving to the side of the tunnel, he ascended a rough, slippery set of stone steps that led up to an aperture in the arched ceiling. He peered through the small holes in the drain cover and, angling his view, was rewarded with a difficult glimpse of the Temple of Saturn. Relief filling him, he pushed his fingers into the holes, the eyes, nose and mouth of an ornate face carved into a large stone disc. Heaving, he managed to push it up for around a hand-width, and slid it to the side. Taking a breath of fresh, cold air, he clambered up and out into the open, looking around. He was in the narrow alley behind the temples at the base of the Capitoline, below the tabularium. The only life to be found were a scabby stray dog busy curling out its latest addition to the forum, an old beggar slouched against a wall and a young couple canoodling in the shade.

Stretching, he waited for the others to appear, each taking a relieved breath of clean air.

'What now?' Galronus muttered.

'Now, we brace ourselves for a little embarrassment, cross the forum smelling of shit, and head for home, where I shall bathe thoroughly, and then begin to plot what I'm going to do to Hypsaeus and his men, and how I'm going to do it.'

CHAPTER TEN

Fronto sat shivering, ironically, in Caesar's summer dining room, looking out of the wide apse with its open windows at the frost-rimed gardens stretching across the hill, with their own springs, fountains, woodland, lawns, hedges and shrines. Those in the know were predicting that the weather would become warmer, if a little damper, soon, but for the past two days a frost had settled each morning that had only been chased off by golden sun as the afternoon took hold, the ground barely clearing before nightfall brought a fresh drop in temperature. Rome shivered under its white sheen.

He could see some of his entourage out there. It irked him having to travel like this. He'd been born into the last days of the old Rome, the noble republic before men of power like Marius and Sulla began tearing it apart and corruption set in, but he'd been raised and weaned in the Rome of despots and criminals. Still, despite that, he'd never felt truly unsafe in the city's streets. Oh, there were always thieves, killers, gangs and the like, but Fronto liked to think he knew the city, that he knew where to avoid and what signs to watch for. He'd always walked the streets of Rome alone or with friends, afeared of nothing, for these were *his* streets.

Things had changed.

Not only was he unable to travel anywhere in the city without a litter, slaves, a secretary, a nomenclator and all the trappings of a senator, but since it seemed a certain collegium had begun to target him directly he now had to travel with at least a score of brutal killers, and Lucilia was urging him to double that. Moreover, Fronto was now arguably breaking one of Rome's oldest laws. It was, by ancient rule, illegal to carry a weapon of war within the pomerium, the sacred boundary of the original city. Many had argued over the years what classed as a weapon of war, and clubs and suchlike were now generally accepted as viable, as were utility and eating blades. Fronto was pushing the boundary. He wore at his side a blade that was officially a hunting knife, though, unless he planned to hunt lions or elephants, it was unlikely he would need anything of the size and strength of the thing at his hip. After that incident by the river, he was determined not to be caught out again. Equally, he had armed most of his men with similar blades, and made sure that each and every one had either a sling or some sort of dart to throw. Many were even armoured in a leather subarmalis of the sort worn by the more sensible legionaries. No more risks.

He leaned back and sighed, still waiting for the dictator to put in an appearance. The slave had asked him to wait in the unused summer triclinium while Caesar finished his current business, but Fronto had already been waiting half an hour. At least he was *relatively* warm. His soldiers were outside in the frost.

It had been a difficult few days. After their sewage-clad journey across the city, drawing startled looks and wrinkled noses from those around them as they sloshed and trudged their way home, it had taken two hours in the baths to cleanse sufficiently to remove even a trace of the scent of the cloaca. Lucilia had then fussed about him, all worries. She had elicited from him promises that he would move his personal safety to the top of the list of his priorities, that he would take sufficient strength with him wherever he went. He had also stepped up his security at the house. If he was to take a small army with him wherever he went, that reduced the men guarding the house, and he could not rule out an attack on his family or his people. Though he could rely upon the collegium of Caesar's veterans when he called on them, the truth was that the members were people with their own lives and jobs, and could only be called when they were available. They could hardly abandon their own families to protect his full time, so they were of no use as a permanent guard. As such, he had spent a small fortune – *another* one – but this at least with Lucilia's blessing, on another two dozen mercenaries, each of them a checked and approved veteran of Caesar's legions, to protect his house.

He did, at times, wonder where this would end, the escalation of trained killers being employed in the houses and streets of Rome. Certainly no good would come of it, he was sure.

It transpired that the Pompeian veterans had finally discovered Fronto's men watching their meeting house. He knew this, because the latest one had been left outside his house in five different pieces. He very much suspected that this discovery was also behind their latest attack on him, given the timing, which would put the blame directly with the collegium rather than the shadowy villain who he believed to be controlling them. A personal revenge attack in response to his surveillance, rather than an ordered and planned assassination attempt. As such, he was rather frustrated. Assigning a new watcher was likely to be little more than a death sentence for any man he assigned. Confronting Hypsaeus would do no good. Even if the man was aware of the attack or bore any guilt, he would deny it. Short of launching a full-scale attack on the Pompeian house, Fronto could think of no useful act he could undertake. He'd considered that, more than once, but had finally settled for increased strength and security on his own part and to hope and pray that Salvius Cursor in his hidden role would turn up something helpful.

Instead, he had concentrated on other work.

Finally, as he mused once more on how to deal with Hypsaeus, he heard the house's owner approaching. Caesar was dictating some legal document to his clerk as he clacked through the house, his boots rapping on the marble with each determined step. Fronto listened to the high-speed monologue for a moment, but his attention soon drifted from the interminable legalese.

He rose as Caesar entered, but the dictator waved him back to his seat as he completed his text and the clerk clicked the tablet shut and withdrew. Half a dozen slaves and attendants were waved away, and Caesar eyed Fronto with interest. 'Is this private? Should I have the door closed?'

'Parthia,' Fronto said by way of answer. Caesar nodded and strolled over to the window, standing and looking out, hands clasped behind his back, rocking on his heels. The door remained open. Nothing concerning the coming Parthian campaign should be sensitive enough to avoid stray ears in Caesar's own house.

'Lepidus was by yesterday,' Caesar noted conversationally. 'He mentioned your ideas about the fleet command. Ingenious. That is why I placed this task in your hands, Fronto. The mind that brought us success all across Gaul and beyond, working to make Parthia a victory before we even embark. I have had a thought about your fourth candidate, though, that might perhaps settle the matter for you?'

'Oh?' Fronto leaned forward. This could be useful. He'd been quite pleased with himself over his creation of three roles for three would-be admirals, but what to offer Gellius that would make him happy was a question he'd been working on ever since.

'Can we spare half a dozen ships?'

Fronto frowned. 'Tough. I've called in almost every military ship that's available. There are small fleets on other duties still, of course, such as the grain fleet escorts. At a push, I could probably gather six ships from them without leaving them in too much danger. Drawing them from the gathering fleet in Illyricum would be troublesome, though.'

'Do it,' Caesar said. 'The grain fleets are as safe as they ever have been these days. No pirates or enemies threaten them. I have a special command we can offer Gellius. You know he was at Munda?'

Fronto nodded. The man had been a staff officer in both Africa and Hispania, though he'd not done anything to greatly distinguish himself.

'He's formed something of a dislike of our enemies there. He was one of the men who went out hunting the Pompey brothers, and they made rather a fool of him. My latest intelligence puts the last survivor of Munda's architects in Sicilia.'

'Sextus Pompey?'

Caesar nodded. 'I understand that he continues attempts to raise support against me, though his pleas fall on deaf ears these days. It is, however, inevitable that eventually he will find someone who will listen, and we cannot afford to have a whole new rebel army growing out there. He was last seen in Hispania at the end of the summer, and if he is now in Sicilia, then he has transport, and likely a ship or more at his command. I'll give Gellius his chance at revenge. I'll assign him six ships and send him to Sicilia to hunt down Sextus Pompey. That'll satisfy him as much as any wartime command.'

Fronto nodded with a smile. 'And it has the added bonus that if he succeeds, Pompey's last playing piece is removed from the board.'

'Quite. Now what did you want to talk about?' The general turned, unclasping his hands and rubbing them together.

'Your campaign bases.' He held up his hands defensively. 'I understand your point on Alexandria, and I've not mentioned it to anyone.' He glanced at the door. Perhaps this should have been more private after all, but then he'd not meant to discuss Alexandria. He decided he needed to be rather circumspect. 'You can carry out your plans without basing yourself there. Once the Getae campaign is over, it will take time to move the army into position to take the next step into Parthia, probably the rest of the campaigning year. If you take a liburnian from Byzantium after the Getae, you could travel south, complete that little plan of yours and, everything in place, sail back to Antioch to begin the proper invasion as pharaoh. After all, it is highly likely that by the time you've finished with the Getae and plans in Alexandria the campaign season will be at an end, and you can spend the winter moving into position.'

Caesar tapped his lip. 'It has merit. I foresee the whole campaign as nothing less than three years, so rushing into the second stage is perhaps unnecessary.'

'To that effect, I think, your Getae campaign gives us an opportunity I had not previously considered. With eleven legions and support gathering in Antioch by summer and your five legions coming down from the north in the wake of the Getae, we have the opportunity for a pincer movement. The Parthian king of kings will, of course, be aware of the build-up at Antioch, and will be preparing his defences appropriately. Currently, the king of Armenia holds to his Roman alliance. When the Getae are suppressed, while you move to Aegyptus and all eyes are on there and Antioch, your second army could ship across the Euxine Sea and put ashore in northern Armenia. If we are careful, that force could move through Armenia to the northern border of Parthia without the king of kings being aware of them. As the Parthians brace themselves to defend against the army marching east from Antioch, a second force could move down the Euphrates from Armenia and flank them.'

A smile spread across Caesar's face. 'Excellent. It relies upon Armenia's loyalty, of course. If the king decides suddenly that a Parthian future looks brighter, he could turn on us and ruin the surprise.'

'With five legions and as many auxilia marching through his lands, I doubt he will be in a hurry to throw down the eagle and raise a Parthian standard.'

Caesar nodded. 'True, true. That force would need a second commander. Tell me, Marcus…'

'No.'

Caesar frowned, and Fronto folded his arms.

'I've already said many times that I'm not coming east.'

Caesar let out a light laugh. 'Some might think that a little big-headed Marcus. Actually I wasn't going to ask you. I will hold up my end of our bargain. The consulship is yours by Aprilis, and I will not drag you east. No, I was going to ask what you thought of Octavian as a potential commander.'

Fronto sucked on his teeth, leaning back and folding his arms. 'He's clever, and he knows his strategy. He's brave, devious and dangerous. And he's ambitious. All those are good traits in a commander, unless they're taken too far. But he's untested, Caesar. Apart from a little mopping up in the aftermath of Munda, he's never led an army. I would easily assign him as a staff officer and give him small commands to test his ability, but until then I wouldn't place him in a position where half an invasion relied upon his success.'

Caesar nodded. 'I have already decided to send him to Apollonia. He can go under the guise of learning, for that city is known for its philosophers. But it also happens to be mere days from both our fleets and the gathering army. I will take him with me against the Getae. Perhaps there I can test him enough to decide whether to assign him the Armenian command.'

Fronto nodded. Given everything, it might be nice to have the clever little bastard away from Rome for a while. Let him kill Parthians instead of competition Romans. That still left the question of the Armenian command, though. 'You *could* still assign Marcus Antonius,' he said.

Caesar shook his head. 'No.'

'In Martius you plan to give me the consulship, and that means that Antonius will lose it. He will be directionless, powerless, in limbo. He will have neither a role in Rome, nor a place on your campaign. I know he can be a little hot-headed, and that the relationship between the two of you is currently a little strained, but you also know that he is a brilliant strategist and an excellent cavalry commander. Better still, he is horribly likeable. If you want a man with your legions in Armenia who can make the king there feel like it is an honour to host Rome's military, you could do a lot worse than Antonius.'

'No. Fronto, I need Antonius to step back for a while. The more he has involved himself in my business, the more and more he is ruled by his emotions, causing me headaches and difficulties. I *like* Antonius. He is one of my oldest friends, after all. But as long as his anger and the wine jar drive him, I cannot trust him, neither militarily nor politically. I need him to take some time to reassess his life and come back the Antonius I remember of old, the hungry commander who joined us for Alesia. Until then, he needs to step back.'

Fronto sighed. Antonius was not going to like this. In a way, Fronto agreed with Caesar, for Antonius could certainly be unpredictable. But when he was good, by the *gods* he was good. He took a deep breath. Maybe there was a way he could persuade Caesar to allow Antonius a small command. Perhaps Gellius could be sent to Armenia instead, and Antonius be given the mandate to hunt down Sextus Pompey. After all, how much damage could Antonius do in Sicilia with six ships? He winced as a hundred answers assailed him.

Before he could put the question to the dictator, though, he became aware of new voices out there in the rest of the house. He and Caesar shared a glance at the sound of hobnailed boots on marble, and the voice of a worried slave. Moments later, two men armed with short curved swords stepped into the room, their tunics betraying no identity. Fronto rose for a moment, his hand going to his own blade for a moment, ready to fight for his life, but the two

134

fighters simply looked around the room, checking for danger, then stepped to either side of the door. Half a heartbeat later Decimus Brutus strolled in, a blade at his side too. Behind him, out in the corridor, Fronto could see more killers, armed with sharp blades.

'Decimus,' Caesar greeted Brutus warmly, stepping forward. The two met and embraced for a moment. As Caesar stepped back, Fronto nodded a greeting to Brutus.

'Who in Jove's name are these?' he asked, gesturing to the armed men.

Brutus shrugged. 'Given the apparent danger to Caesar's supporters, since some of them keep getting jumped in the streets, I decided it was time to increase my own bodyguard. One of my most dependable clients is a lanista with his own thriving school of gladiators. He has assigned me a number of them on a semi-permanent basis.'

'Sensible,' Fronto noted, then turned to the dictator. 'Take note, Caesar. Both I and Brutus can now field a small army in the streets. It is becoming a requirement just for personal safety. Yet you rely on a dozen lictors. You need to be more careful. Your doorman just let in a small force of armed men. Look, even Brutus has a sword.'

'Fronto, this is *Brutus*. There is no man in Rome with whom I am safer.'

Fronto shrugged. The haruspex…'

'Spurinna.'

'Yes, Spurinna. He told you your life was in danger in the coming days. You need to improve your security.'

Caesar gave him a rather dark laugh. 'Actually, Fronto, Spurinna did not tell me I was in danger. He told me I would be *dead* by the Ides of Martius.'

'Even more so, then.'

'Fronto, if the gods want me dead, there is nothing I can do about it. I make my libations and offerings to the gods in the hope of overturning this fate, but only the gods can change such a thing. If Mars has sealed my fate, only he and his kin can stop it. Certainly a dozen men with blades will do nothing. I will appease the gods, but otherwise I will go about my business as if there was no danger. A man who hides from a certain fate is simply wasting what time he has.'

'I could call you up a bodyguard of your Hispanic veterans,' Fronto said. 'There are plenty in the city. It might not help in the end, but they can certainly do no harm trying.'

Caesar shook his head. 'No, Marcus. How would it look to the people if their saviour had to travel the streets of his own city with an army surrounding him? If I had an entourage it took a small convoy to move about? No, I shall trust in my lictors, my common sense and the gods. Besides, have you any idea how much such a good bodyguard costs?'

Fronto nodded. 'Gods, yes. I'm sweating sestertii at the moment maintaining my own men.'

'Perhaps I have interrupted something important?' Brutus said.

Caesar shook his head. 'Actually, I think Fronto has already dealt with what he came to discuss. Do you seek privacy?'

Brutus shook his head. 'No. This is not private. Not from Fronto, at least. I've come to ask you to do the unthinkable.'

'Oh?'

'Step away from the Parthian campaign, Caesar.'

Fronto turned a surprised look on the younger man. A flash of memory of Hypsaeus saying almost the same thing at the sacrifice popped into his mind, and for a moment he couldn't help but equate the two men. That was swiftly pushed aside, though. Decimus Junius Brutus Albinus was one of their oldest friends and allies and, if rumour were true, actually Caesar's unacknowledged illegitimate son. He wanted for nothing, and had never shown anything but support and loyalty.

Caesar folded his arms again. 'I am hearing this from more than one source, Brutus.'

'Caesar, you don't need the war. Before Gaul you owed money, but now your coffers are as full as those of Croesus. You do not need the booty. The people are yours, heart and soul. You are gathering honours from the senate like a farmer gathers wheat. You do not need the fame or validation. Your victories are enough for any man for a whole life. Your fame will live on long beyond your span. In short, you do not need Parthia, nor this proposed Getae campaign.'

'Brutus…'

'I'm not saying that the campaigns are not necessary. The Getae are a threat and they need to be taught a lesson and to stay where they are. The Parthians have needed to be conquered for centuries, and we need retribution for what they did to Crassus at Carrhae, and the adding of Alexander's empire to the republic would be the greatest single acquisition of all time. But it does not need to be you who commands them. You have plenty of solid men you could assign to the task.'

'You said it yourself, Brutus,' Caesar smiled. 'The greatest single acquisition of all time. How can I hand that away to another?'

'Caesar, the glory will go to you anyway, no matter who you assign. Whoever commands the armies, it will always be your campaign and your victory. But the senate fears your plans. They fear that you intend to relocate to Aegyptus with your pet queen. They fear you intend to move the focus of their power to Alexandria. If you go east you will just feed their fears. If, however, you hand over the campaign to someone else, you can stay in Rome and allay their fears. Caesar, the senate once opposed you, driven by men like Pompey and Cato and their ilk, and it took the march across the Rubicon and fighting the senate's armies across half Italia to remove them and to replace them with a new senate. Can you really afford to turn your new senate against you the way the old one was?'

'The senate are, by and large, a gathering of greedy and sycophantic old men,' Caesar said dismissively, 'current company excepted, of course. There are few voices within it with the strength of a Pompey or a Cato. Almost anyone whose backside polishes a seat in the curia now can be bought, if need be.'

'You underestimate them.'

'I think not,' Caesar replied.

'Grant one of your lieutenants the Parthian command.'

'If you are about to push Marcus Antonius on me, Brutus, think again. Fronto has already tried that.'

Brutus shrugged. 'If not Antonius, there are others. Even with men like Lepidus and myself,' he gestured across the room, 'and Fronto, of course, retained in Rome in positions of authority, you

137

still have a good stock of command experience to call upon. Gods, but you could kill two birds with one stone – assign a good man, and with it silence one of the main voices raised in warning against you. Cassius Longinus is a proven general. Jove, Caesar, but he was the only commander to walk away from Carrhae alive. He is the only commander in the entire republic with a proven military record who has fought the Parthians and lived. He might just jump at the chance to get even with them.'

Fronto broke into a grin. 'Gods, he's right, Caesar. Cassius is the man for the job. You could honour him, prove your loyalty to the republic for the senate, and send the one man who has the best chance of victory, all in one move. It's brilliant.'

In the silence that followed, Caesar turned his glance slowly between Fronto and Brutus.

'And what of the Sibylline prophecy?'

Brutus frowned, dumbfounded. 'What?'

'I am certain you have heard what the quindecemviri found in the Sibylline books?'

Brutus nodded. 'Of course. Only a king can best the king of kings, or something along those lines. But clearly you don't believe that anyway, or you wouldn't be launching your war. You don't believe that any more than you believe Spurinna's warning, surely?'

Caesar glanced at Fronto, who sagged back into the seat. The dictator turned to Brutus. 'Whether I believe it or not, the common man does, and that includes the senate. If I wish to defeat Rome's oldest enemy and add their greatness to ours I must employ every tool and my disposal.'

Brutus' eyes narrowed. 'Do not say what I think you plan to say.'

'Fear not, Decimus, for I will remain a senator of Rome, her dictator for now. I will only take the crown in Aegyptus, and even then only for the duration of the campaign, following which I shall set it aside and return to Rome *primus inter pares*.'

'If you take a crown, you will set half the senate against you, whether it be a crown in Rome or a crown in Aegyptus, and no matter your intention to put it back down. A king is a king, and you know how Rome feels about kings. Do you think that the senate

138

would accept among them the king of Armenia, simply because he is a friend of Rome and does not purport to rule them? I charge you now, Caesar, never to pick up a crown. *Never.*'

The dictator's own eyes hardened. 'You are my ally and my friend, Brutus, and I respect you. *All Rome* respects you. After all, was it not your illustrious forebear who ejected the last king of Rome and instituted the republic we so revere? But I will do what I have to do to make Rome ever greater. And if I must wear a bauble for a few paltry months to add the lands of Alexander to the republic, then I shall do so gladly and with lightness of heart.'

'I am a loyal son of the republic, Caesar, but I am also your man. I have always been your man. Do not make me choose between you.'

'There is no choice to be made, Brutus, for I also am a son of the republic.'

Brutus turned and threw an imploring look at Fronto. 'I can do no more, apparently. *You* explain it to him.' And with that, without even a farewell, Brutus turned and marched from the room, his pet gladiators following in his wake.

Fronto waited until he had been gone for a moment. Caesar had gone a funny colour and was trembling. For a moment, Fronto wondered it there might be another fit coming on, but decided it was simply anger.

'He will calm down, Caesar. But I do wonder if he is right.'

Caesar rounded on him, breathing fast and heavy in his irritation. '*You* know why I am doing this, Fronto. The crown of Aegyptus will be mine solely to allow me to conquer Parthia. Alexander crushed the Persians, but no man since his day has come close, and now the Sibyl tells us why. *I* will be the next man to conquer that empire, and once it is part of Rome, it shall ever be so. Think of it, Fronto: the spice and incense routes are controlled by Parthia and we pay huge sums to our enemy to get what we need. And when they fall out with us, we find many sources cut off. And they control the silk road to Seres, too. Imagine if we had control of that. Parthia *must* be conquered, Fronto, and if not me, then who?'

Fronto shrugged. Make someone else king of Aegyptus and send them. Make Cassius Longinus the pharaoh for a few years.

Who cares? It's the solution, after all. It's your plan for monarchic conquest and Brutus's plan to assign someone else combined.'

'No.'

'Why? Why not? Why must it be you who wears that southern crown?'

Caesar simply fell silent, glaring at him.

Fronto nodded, a snide expression on his face. 'Because then the crown cannot pass to Caesarion. It must be you, so that your descendants with that woman will rule Aegyptus. I always knew she had her hooks into you – Cassius said as much to me – but you cannot put the whole republic in jeopardy to sit a bastard on a throne, no matter who he is. And you have other heirs, who deserve your attention, who will *not* set the senate against you, remember?'

Caesar nodded slowly, his face expressionless. 'They will be taken into account in my will. They all will. All of Rome seems bent on changing my mind, Fronto, but it will not be changed. Finalise your plans for Parthia and the Getae, and then I will reward you appropriately. Beyond that I will do what I must do, as always.'

Fronto let out a slow breath and rose.

'We live in difficult times, Gaius Julius Caesar.'

'That we do, Fronto, that we do. Before you go, though, I have a favour to ask. Since taking up the consulship I have not yet had the chance to pay the required trip to Lavinium and give thanks to Vesta. The Vestalis Maxima has sent me a number of increasingly forthright reminders. I intend to ride south in two days for the sacrifice, and, since I will be in the east by the time of the Latin Festival at Alba, I shall stop there on the return journey and sacrifice a bull to Jupiter. It would be fitting to have my consilia with me on both occasions. Are you free to attend?'

Fronto shrugged. He could imagine what Lucilia would say if he turned it down. 'I think so, Caesar.'

With that, he turned, a nodded farewell, and left the room, two slaves pattering to his side to see him out of the villa. In the vestibule Masgava, Aurelius and Arcadios waited, the rest of the gaggle outside.

'Did you see that lot?' Aurelius murmured, his eyes slipping to the door through which Brutus had so recently departed.

'I did. Gladiators from a ludus, I understand.'

'Not good ones,' Masgava said with a wrinkled lip. Fronto grinned at the big Numidian who had once fought his way across the arena's sands. Masgava shrugged. 'Still training. They don't know the tricks yet, you can see it from the way they carry their weapons, even from their walk. And they're far too pretty for a veteran.'

That made Fronto laugh, given how often he'd seen Andala, Lucilia's Gaulish friend-cum-bodyguard, watching Masgava exercise from the shade of a colonnade. Andala clearly thought a veteran gladiator could be pretty enough.

'I think we might want to expand our forces again,' Fronto said. 'Rome has the feeling of a latrunculi board with the pieces moving to a conclusion. Soon, I fear the collegium of our enemy must make a major move, and I wonder if we might not be better moving against them first. At the very least I want to be able to face them if they come.'

An image of Galronus' last game popped into his head, that one piece in the corner, surrounded and beaten.

Hopefully that piece was not Caesar.

Or Fronto...

CHAPTER ELEVEN

It had been an odd trip, Fronto reflected. It was tradition for anyone taking high office to sacrifice to Vesta in her patron city, Lavinium, and the people there had been beside themselves with joy to see Caesar and his entourage of noble notables. But it struck Fronto as a little odd to give thanks for the consulship when the man already held the position of dictator, outranking any consul. But that wasn't why it had been odd. It was the change in attitude that had struck him.

In Rome, Fronto was surrounded generally by senators and the rich, politically motivated section of society. As such, much of the time those around him found cause to complain, or at least fret, about the scale of the power being heaped into Caesar's hands, though many of those doing the complaining were also those handing him the power, Fronto noted drily. But the simple fact was that while Caesar was still popular in Rome, there were increasingly loud voices speaking against him, and they were the voices that mattered in the city. In Lavinium, however, the only such men were those Caesar took with him, and so the universal mood in that city had been one of praise, joy and optimism at the great man they were honouring. It had felt a little more like the old days, when they had faced off against a corrupt senate and marched across Italia, liberating towns from Pompeian control, those cities cheering the victor as they celebrated.

Fronto had felt his nerves tighten as Caesar offered sacrifice to Vesta, half expecting some dreadful portent in the process, but the whole ceremony had gone without a hitch, and some local soothsayer had predicted great things, a boost to Caesar given recent warnings. They had left Lavinium in refreshingly good spirits.

Then had come Alba. Once more, Fronto had prepared for the worst, and once more he'd been pleasantly surprised by the result. The sacrifice and the associated festive events had gone perfectly, and the city and its population had nothing but cheers for the dictator and his people. In fact, by the end of the day in Alba, Fronto felt almost light-hearted, the troubles in Rome nearly forgotten, just lurking in the back of his mind, festering.

Then, this morning, they had said farewell to their hosts in Alba and prepared for the fifteen mile ride back to Rome along the queen of roads, the Via Appia. A score of great men, including Marcus Junius Brutus, Antonius, Cornelius and Oppius and as well as Epidius Marullus and Caesetius Flavus, the plebeian tribunes, rode in Caesar's wake. No litters in evidence here, despite the power and money of these men, each riding a horse proudly. And then the entourage of servants, slaves and guards for each of them, as well as enough lictors to crew a trireme, marching alongside with their bundles of rods and axes. It had to be a magnificent sight, almost an army on the march, but clad in rich and gleaming clothes instead of armour. Certainly at the farms and hamlets they passed, the people turned out cheering and waving as the column moved slowly northwards once more.

But Fronto was not feeling so cheery now.

From the moment they left Alba, every mile they rode brought his mood that little bit lower, for every mile brought them a little closer to Rome. Closer to ongoing war in the streets, perpetrated by the Pompeian collegium. Closer to the tedious difficulty of campaign planning. Closer to the question of Caesar's base on campaign. Closer to those men who were grumbling with resentment over perceived troubles, their blame cast at Caesar. Closer to having to be a senator.

Closer to Lucilia and the boys… there were at least bright spots.

But on the whole the return was stripping all that relief and buoyancy back out of him, preparing to plunge him once more into a dangerous and difficult world.

'You look positively angry,' Galronus muttered as he rode alongside, the outskirts of Rome growing more and more visible just ahead.

'Just looking forward to being back in Rome.'

The Remi gave him an odd smile. 'You know what this is? This is you missing campaigns and battles. The city just doesn't suit you.'

And that didn't help. A little accidental reminder there that Galronus intended to leave for the north later in the year. Fabulous. Fronto just grunted. A small part of him would have to admit to the truth of his friend's words. He'd just about settled into life in Rome, though he wasn't sure he was particularly enjoying it. But at least he had settled. Now, though, riding out in the countryside, he was reminded of what it was like to be away from the city, moving with purpose. He did miss it. Not enough to go back to it, mind. He was well aware of the limitations age was beginning to place on his martial career. But that didn't mean he didn't miss it.

His mood dropped a little more.

Galronus tried a couple of times to make light conversation, and finally gave up in the face of sullen silence, and rode on in his own shell of quiet. The column moved between the great tombs and mausolea that lined the road close to the city, some grander than most people's houses. Then, as they neared the first habitation, they passed the great temple of Mars and the porticoed carriage stables. Word had clearly gone ahead that Caesar was returning, for even before reaching that first house, they could see the crowds thronging the roadside, waiting to see the great man. Though the lictors with them would hold the crowd back as they passed, it suddenly occurred to Fronto that if a man wanted to kill Caesar, it was a simple matter. One man in that crowd who managed to sneak a bow and an arrow? Maybe on one of the rooftops?

His gaze began to play across their surroundings, picking out anywhere a would-be assassin might take position, ready to make their move.

'What are you doing?' Galronus hissed.

'What?'

'You look suspicious, like you're expecting trouble.'

'I always expect trouble. I'm usually right.'

The Remi simply frowned and pursed his lips, but moments later he too was looking this way and that. They moved into the streets now, the city proper growing up round them, and the noise increased at the same rate as the height and closeness of the buildings. A din of cheers and shouts, the actual words virtually inaudible, lost as they were in the tapestry of sounds.

Then one thread suddenly caught their ears. By some ill-timed miracle, a half-heartbeat's lull in the noise allowed a single voice to cut through it all and reach them.

'Salve Rex!'

The column of riders stopped dead, that phrase echoing in every ear. Fronto, already alert, turned his eyes in the direction of the voice. They had heard plenty of 'Salve Caesar's as they rode this last crowded part of the journey, but to hail a king?

Unless...

Fronto caught sight of the speaker, apparently just some ordinary citizen, still grinning madly, and wondered whether the man had a friend by the name of Rex, for it was not unknown. Perhaps the man had been merely greeting a friend?

No. The speaker was looking directly at Caesar, who was looking back at him, startled. Now, another figure nearby joined in.

'Salve Rex!'

And in a heartbeat the two men were shouting it again and again, a call taken up by half a dozen others, and then a small section of the crowd. Oddly, the rest of the mass lining the street had fallen silent and were looking at this small group apparently hailing a king.

Fronto's glance slid to Caesar. This was dangerous. Even if it was a joke, in particularly bad taste, any acknowledgement of them on the dictator's part would look like agreement, as though he did, indeed, covet a crown of Rome. Word would reach the senate like a burning hillside in a low wind, and even those loyal to the dictator would begin to waver.

Caesar stepped his horse towards that part of the crowd, holding up a hand for silence, and that chanting faltered, and died away. The general was frowning as though in utter confusion.

'You mistake me for someone,' he said, as though chatting to a friend, rather than Rome's most powerful man addressing a nobody. 'My name is not Rex. It is Caesar. And I am no king.' He gave a light chuckle.

Fronto shivered. It was well done, really. He had given the best answer a man could hope for. And yet where they might anticipate a mirth-filled response as the tension eased, in fact the silence became complete, no one speaking, neither in the crowd nor among the travellers.

Caesar gave another small chuckle, perhaps hoping it would catch like a spark among the watchers. It did not.

'Seize those men,' someone shouted suddenly.

Lictors, taken by surprise, turned to see Marullus, the plebeian tribune, his face like thunder, pointing into the crowd at those figures who had hailed a king. His co-tribune, Flavus, joined him, gesturing angrily.

There was an odd moment of silence and inactivity, and then suddenly half a dozen of the lictors pushed into the crowd. Three figures were suddenly in their way, whether by design or mere bad luck, it was impossible to tell, and the lictors did that for which they were employed, pushing them aside, battering them out of the way with their rod bundles. In moments they had seized the two men who had started the chant and were dragging them by the shoulders and elbows out into the street.

Fronto felt his heart racing. Moments like this could start riots. But still no one in the crowd moved.

'Take them to the carcer,' Marullus demanded.

'They shall be tried,' Flavus added, 'for incitement to create a monarchy.'

It was too much really. The two men were clearly terrified. They had perhaps thought to make a joke, but it had rather fallen flat, and Caesar was silent, staring at what was going on around him. His attempt to solve the problem with easy humour had failed, and arrests and threats were being levelled around him. Fronto glared at him, willing the man to intervene, to say something. Those two men should not be made to suffer the way he suspected they would.

'Hail Marullus,' someone shouted from the crowd. 'Hail Flavus.'

And suddenly the crowd were *all* shouting.

Fronto stared.

He'd expected the arrest of the two men to trigger some sort of fury among the crowd, but instead they were cheering the tribunes. Then, the names Marullus and Flavus were being joined by the name Brutus. Fronto turned to find Marcus Junius Brutus in the entourage, wondering what he had done, but from the white, shocked face of Brutus, the answer was nothing. He understood, then. The crowd were hailing the tribunes as new Brutuses, painting them as the great Brutus who had ejected the last king from Rome.

'Forward,' Caesar snapped, starting to lose his easy manner. The lictors moved the two prisoners into the midst of the column among the many mercenary guards of the senators, where they were more or less lost to view from the public. In moments, the column was moving on.

If Caesar had hoped the silence and the shock was localised, he was wrong. Fronto suspected the dictator had expected that as they passed further into Rome, they would leave the incident behind and the crowd would cheer once more.

He was mistaken.

Rumour, as Aeschylus had noted, has wings.

As they moved ever closer to the heart of the city, all they met was an uncomfortable, tense silence from the crowd. News of the incident had gone ahead.

'No one dares cheer now,' Fronto muttered, chills running up his spine at the atmosphere through which they rode. He'd only really been talking to himself, and had assumed if anyone heard and replied it would be Galronus. It surprised him, therefore, when it was Caesar who spoke.

'Quite. The tribunes acted rashly. The men spoke in light-hearted jest. They should have been cautioned at most.'

Fronto's lip twitched. The time for Caesar to come to such a conclusion had been when it happened, when Fronto had been willing him to intervene. Now, it was too late. The silence became all the more oppressive as they passed the end of the great Circus Maximus and rode below the heights of the Palatine. Caesar had planned to end their journey at the temples on the Capitol, where he could libate and give offerings to the triad of gods most venerated in Rome, and they had all expected a raucous journey towards the end. Instead, there was still that eerie, dangerous silence as they rounded the Palatine and began to make their way along the Via Sacra and through the forum.

'*Do something*, Caesar,' hissed Oppius from close by as they rode slowly.

Caesar did not immediately reply, but nodded to himself, deep in thought.

'To the rostra,' he said, suddenly. 'I will speak to the people.'

'Be careful, then,' Fronto urged him. 'Don't try jokes. Apparently you're not as funny as you think you are today.'

Caesar shot him a dark look, then turned back to the forum as they rode. Fronto could see the looming shape of the rostra at the far end, in front of the temple of Saturn and the slope of the Capitol. It was perhaps just the right thing to do. As long as he said the right things. He needed to appease the people, to make them appreciate him again, to ease the tension.

Or possibly just to appeal to the lowest common denominator: greed...

'Announce a festival,' Fronto said, suddenly, the idea leaping from his tongue before he'd properly thought it through. But it was a good idea, and he could see Caesar grasping it like a drowning man clawing at a raft. The city loved a good festival, with entertainment, food and drink, and all at the expense of some rich benefactor. And with his recent raising to the consulship, the impending campaign in Parthia and the completion of so many new monuments and structures in Rome, it should not be hard to find a good reason for a festival.

New constructions like the rostra, of course.

Oh, it wasn't new, really. The great public speaking platform of Rome, formed from the prows of captured Carthaginian warships, had simply been taken apart and moved a little, reconstructed on a slightly grander scale in a more convenient position. But it had gained a little decoration in the process, some marble facing with festoon motifs, the odd inscription and, most important right now, a statue of Caesar on one end, reminding all of who had paid for this great work, and a statue of Venus at the other, reminding them of that man's divine blood.

Fronto smiled a small smile. In fact, the speech was a stroke of genius really. If Caesar said the right things, and Fronto allowed himself the conceit that he had come up with a brilliant option, then with the visual reminders of greatness, speaking from such a hallowed place, the dictator could bring people around in an instant. Caesar might just be able to repair the damage done as they'd entered the city.

If Fronto had been paying more attention, he would have noticed that despite all this, his uneasiness remained, that chill still in his spine, and he might have questioned why he still felt nervous.

Because the most likely time for any disaster is when those involved are at their most complacent. Caesar, Fronto and the rest of the entourage closed on the rostra, the crowd still gathered at the periphery in disapproving, uncomfortable silence. The great brick platform with its ship beaks, marble festoons and intricate carvings stood like a fortress of oratory before them, and Fronto's gaze, like those of the riders around him, went up to the statues flanking the podium at both ends. The nearest side, Venus, in her painted marble glory, was one of the best likenesses in the city, her form that of the perfect female shape, clad only in a diaphanous garment that clung in the right places, one breast bared like an amazon, her face a picture of obsessive beauty, the whole putting forth a confusing meld of erotic desire and aloof, divine power. It was masterful.

His eyes darted to the far end, and there beheld the disaster that awaited them. He was the first to see it, but only by a fraction of a heartbeat, judging by the strangled gasps behind him.

The statue of Caesar was equally masterfully produced. It stood tall, dressed in the armour of a conquering general. His skin tone was perfect, and his posture spoke of command and strength. If Fronto had one negative comment about the statue it would be that the hair was slightly unrealistic, not half as thinning and receded as the real article. But overall it was an excellent likeness, and conveyed to the viewer everything its subject could hope for. Combined with the statue of Venus, it would add immense weight to any speech by Caesar on that platform.

Or it would have done.

Had someone not put a crown upon it.

The wreath rested upon Caesar's slightly receded pate on the statue, challenging anyone who looked at it. And there was no mistaking what this was. It was no grass crown for military

149

victory, or simple laurel wreath for sporting success. This was a diadem of golden metal, with a wreath of laurels woven around it, the metal gleaming out between the green, but it was the white that was damning. The kings of Rome centuries before had been marked out by their simple corona of white, and it was the white of the poplar leaves, cunningly placed among the laurel to form a solid circlet that proclaimed to anyone who saw it that this was the crown of a victorious king of Rome, sitting atop the head of Gaius Julius Caesar.

The whole column stopped, as each set of eyes swivelled, widening, to take in this offensive symbol.

Fronto stared. Whatever had happened at the outskirts, be it joke, accident or deliberate act, there could be no mistaking this. This *was* deliberate, provocative. Dangerous.

He turned to Caesar. The dictator had gone pale. That, more than anything he'd seen today, unnerved Fronto. Caesar looked genuinely worried, and that was such an impossible notion that it in turn worried Fronto. Nine times in ten the great man was ahead of the game, an answer ready before the question was asked, a solution in place before the problem arose. And on the odd occasions when he was surprised or ambushed and could not simply whip a solution out of his bag, Caesar was always up to the challenge, able to turn the tide in an instant, his brilliant mind untangling the problem and providing the answer in moments. And because of his ability to deal with things in such a manner, he had never been anything less than supremely confident in his own abilities and his success. Even with Spurinna having given him a finite lifespan and forewarning of a prophesied death, Caesar had not faltered in his confidence.

This was uncharted waters for Fronto. Caesar did not know what to do, how to respond. He was at a loss. Unfortunately, before Fronto could step in and do anything to help, the figures of the two tribunes of the plebs, Caesetius Flavus and Epidius Marullus, were suddenly out front, hauling on their reins, faces puce with rage, fingers pointing angrily.

'Who is responsible for this abomination?' Flavus demanded, looking around the gathered crowd.

Caesar still said nothing, staring at the 'abomination', which, in the tribune's context, could as easily have referred to Caesar's statue as to the crown atop it.

Marullus was there too, shouting. 'One hundred denarii for the man who gives us the culprit's name.'

There was still an uncomfortable silence, though there was now an odd aura of greed flittering about the crowd. Fronto moved his horse close to Caesar's. '*Do* something,' he hissed. '*Say* something.'

But still the general was as quiet as the crowd, and perhaps as shocked.

'*Two* hundred denarii,' upped Flavus, and finally the silence ended, murmurs rippling around the gathered people of Rome. Not a surprise, Fronto thought bitterly. Two hundred denarii might be a pittance to a senator, but to the ordinary man in the street it was a fortune, the annual wage of a legionary.

As Flavus sat waiting, gaze strafing the crowd, Marullus rode over to the rostra and leapt from his horse to the steps, bounding up them and storming across to the statue. Snarling, he ripped the crown from the brow and crushed it between his hands, the metal bending, the leaves scattering away like an autumn tree.

As he did so, Fronto noted that the supposed gold diadem in the centre was actually cheap brass, bending until it cracked and broke. Not the work of a rich man, then, but also something that would take time to create. It was not a sudden joke, sprung on a notion, and therefore not a result of what had happened in the outskirts. That, of course, begged the question of whether the two events *were* connected, but the other way round. Had whoever had placed the crown then instituted the dangerous calls in the outskirts?

He shuddered at the underlying implications of that.

There was a sudden roar, and a man was dragged from the crowd, protesting and fighting back. The man hauling him forward was addressing the tribune, denouncing his captive as the man responsible for the crown.

Fronto looked at the man in question and formed the immediate opinion that the poor bastard was completely innocent and had been the first victim his captor could find in the desperate desire to claim the money. If there had been any hope for the man, it was dashed a moment later, when others stepped from the crowd, adding their accusations, also naming the poor, panicked man, claiming to have various spurious fragments of circumstantial evidence, each hoping for some share in the bounty.

Marullus glared at the prisoner, his lip twitching, then gestured to the lictors nearby. 'Another one for trial. Another for the carcer.'

The man was hauled away, bellowing his innocence, and now all three captives were escorted by lictors up the slope past the rostra towards that squat, unobtrusive doorway that led to a hell, of which Fronto had plenty of vivid memories.

Fronto watched the disasters unfolding with a sense of helplessness. Caesar was silent, still.

Then, the great man's lip began to twitch. He began to tremble, and his eyes flashed dangerously. As though suddenly waking from a dream, or his wits returning from afar, he turned in his saddle and looked across the gaggle of accompanying notables. He singled out Helvius Cinna, the most eminent of the senators among them, and he gestured to the man.

Cinna rode forward and reined in close to him. 'Caesar?'

'Go to the senate. Call an extraordinary meeting immediately. Caesetius Flavus and Epidius Marullus are hereby stripped of their tribuneship, and dismissed from the ranks of the senate.'

Cinna blinked. Fronto stared.

The two tribunes, one still busy tearing at a leafy crown, the other watching the prisoners being led away, both turned to Caesar in astonishment.

'You cannot,' Flavus snapped.

'I think you will find,' Caesar growled, 'that I can.'

And he could. As dictator, Caesar's commands could not be overturned by any political power in the city. The tribunes realised that now, and blanched.

'You would punish those of us who do you honour by saving you from the taint of monarchy? You know that even to promulgate the idea of kingship is abhorrent. That it is against our very principles, our oldest laws. Those men deserve nothing short of the Tarpeian Rock.

'And it is *my* place to refuse even the idea of a diadem,' barked Caesar furiously. '*Mine*. Not yours. You overstep the mark, both of you, and have done so more than once. No more. You are stripped of your titles. Get out of my sight before I change my mind, for there are worse fates than demotion.'

Fronto sat in the saddle and looked this way and that, his heart pounding. The two tribunes were sloping off together, arguing, their retinue close on their heel now. The three prisoners were still being led towards the carcer to await their chosen fate, whatever it was. Caesar was still trembling with rage, though now his gaze was locked on the statue atop the rostra, once more bare-headed.

The crowd had gone silent again, but this was different. The silence when they had arrived had been pensive, worried, uncertain. Now it was disapproving, bordering on angry.

Fronto closed his eyes. How many disasters could one day bring.

He knew what was in Caesar's mind, or at least he thought he did. He thought to downplay the whole situation. Even back at the start, when the man had called him Rex, he had thought to downplay it. He had attempted to brush the whole incident aside without further trouble, by making a light-hearted joke of it. When that had gone wrong, and the tribunes had arrested the men, he had been so taken aback by the failure that he'd done nothing about it. Then this business with the crown had struck, and before he could turn things around, the tribunes had leapt into action and arrested a man who was probably entirely innocent. And, just as Caesar had said, it had been *his* place to refuse a crown. Knowing the man, almost certainly he had hoped to make a big show of refusing the crown, throw out a few quips to amuse the crowd, remove the diadem and destroy it himself, and show how little he cared for monarchy. They had denied him that opportunity, and in venting their anger on the ordinary man in the crowd, they had removed any hope of turning this event around to a positive. Caesar had, maybe, been correct in dismissing them, but if he had to do so, he should have done it later, quietly, elsewhere, when he was less angry.

Because whatever had been in his mind, how it now looked to the people of Rome was that Caesar had been admiring his head with a crown atop it, and when they had removed it, the removal had angered him. By nightfall a hundred stories would be circulating in the city about how Caesar had so desired a crown that he had dismissed the tribunes for denying him.

He glanced at the statue of Caesar again, and then back to the real man. Caesar's expression was no longer one of anger. It held a bleakness of unpleasant realisation, now. Fronto pinched the bridge of his nose as he understood why.

Caesar's hope for both the succession of his only son, and of successful conquest in Parthia, hinged upon him taking on, for however short a time, the crown of Aegyptus. Until now, while that might have pissed off a large number of senators, there would be plenty of people who would still support him, and the mob, as always, would have been his.

Now, perhaps he could no longer guarantee the support of the ordinary folk of Rome, that one constant that had maintained him throughout a tumultuous political career.

Fronto shivered. All was not well in Rome.

CHAPTER TWELVE

S alvius Cursor edged along the corridor, keeping his breathing shallow, tiny, almost silent wisps of air. His left hand gripped extra tight the wooden tablet case that was his excuse should he be caught. It was an inane document. A bill of sale for two modii of grain. He'd cooked up a story about being short changed by a merchant in the forum and was prepared to ask if there was any help, legal or financial, he could get from the collegium to sort the problem. Whether it would be seen through as a flimsy excuse, he didn't know, but he'd not planned on getting caught anyway.

He was getting used to the routine in the place now. Claiming terrible living conditions and no work, he spent most of his time at the meeting house, but he was far from alone. Others were genuinely in that same state, so there was nothing suspicious about it. He'd been taken on two 'jobs' so far, the first to put pressure on a local merchant who supplied foodstuffs for Caesar's villa. The man had steadfastly refused to allow the collegium to add their own people to his staff, and bribery and cajoling had failed. The visit on which Salvius went was more of a direct threat of violence, and to give the merchant his due, he had braved his way through it, steadfast in his refusal. Salvius rather hoped he didn't have to join them on the next visit, when they planned to crucify one of the man's slaves in his warehouse, stepping up the threat.

The other job had turned up the surprise that Fronto was their target. He'd watched with considerable relief as the former legate had disappeared into the sewer with his friends. In the end they'd only taken out a handful of mercenaries and slaves, which didn't bother Salvius' rather atrophied conscience a great deal.

He was beginning to feel accepted. Many of the ordinary members of the collegium now spoke to him in a comradely

155

fashion on a semi-regular basis. He wasn't taken on every job, of course, only ones as yet that were either unimportant, or on which he could prove his loyalty. And that suited him fine, for it meant that when jobs were on and he *wasn't* required, he was left in the house with a much diminished population. That was the very best time for investigation, and this was one of those times.

He'd watched as two groups left this morning, one large and the other small and consisting only of the best men available. One of this morning's jobs was a bit special. The majority of the collegium had been called in, along with large numbers of members of two allied groups, all in order to put pressure on a fourth collegium to join what appeared to be a growing coalition. The collegium of dock workers had come onside easily. Caesar's announcement of plans to expand the harbour of Ostia and make it the only viable port for Rome would impact jobs in the city's emporium, and so they had bent to the will of this collegium readily. Similarly, a collegium from the Transtiberim region had been easy to acquire the loyalty of. Consisting of former workers in a number of structures on the hillside there, all of which had been demolished and replaced by Caesar's grand villa, they were not a powerful collegium, but were viciously anti-Caesarian.

Of the other job, and the small group assigned to it, Salvius had heard nothing at all.

The coalition was growing in numbers and power. But today, most of them were out. Consequently, Salvius had waited until they had all been gone for some time, and the house occupied only by those either too important or too unimportant to take part in what was likely to be an immense punch up. He had then gathered his excuse and made his move.

There were three offices of importance in the house, each belonging to one of the top three men in the collegium. When not occupied they were locked up tight, but between the locks and being in a house of trustworthy compatriots, no guard was ever placed on them. As he'd turned the corner and moved along the corridor towards the offices, Salvius had felt initial irritation. He'd hoped, in the circumstances, to find the places all empty and locked up. He had, in his belt pouch, a collection of keys, and there was at least a reasonable chance that one of them would be sufficiently close to the door locks here to open one of them. The chance to rifle through the room's contents while the mass were away was too good an opportunity to miss.

Unfortunately, it seemed that would not be possible, for as he'd turned the corner, he'd heard voices from the third of the rooms. He'd dithered for a moment. Getting any closer was extremely dangerous, even with his flimsy excuse in hand. If he was found sneaking around, he suspected, he would end his days a pale, bloated shape, bobbing and eddying in the Tiber. He'd almost turned and gone back, and then he'd heard Fronto's name in mid-flow of the muted conversation, and that had decided the matter.

He'd crept forward, grateful for soft, calfskin boots that made almost no sound as he paced across the stone flags. He passed the first office and paused, listening. It seemed to be little more than a debrief in the aftermath of the attack on Fronto's litter the other day. He took in what he could hear, but it was still quite muffled by the door, and the information that did leak through was of neither great interest, nor importance. He did recognise one of the voices now, though. The owner of the office, the second in command of the collegium, the leader being out with that small group. Steadying, he'd slipped onwards, reaching the firmly locked door of the second office. Once more he paused, and once his breathing slowed again, listened carefully. The exchange was clearer now and as he listened it became evident that the second man was not part of the collegium.

'…need to talk to Fuscus,' the second voice said. Salvius pursed his lips. Fuscus was the top man here, the one who made the final decisions, and who had led the smaller party out this morning.

'Fuscus will not be back until noon. You are welcome to wait in the triclinium until then.'

'I don't have that sort of time. I'm a busy man.'

'Oh, I know. It is your choice. Take my word for things now, wait in the triclinium, or go home and come back another time.'

'I shall speak to my superiors. They will not be happy.'

'I don't give two shits about the happiness of your superiors. Or your master for that matter. Men who change their allegiance like they change their tunic are not overly worthy of consideration.'

'Sir, I am offended.'

'And I am bored. The triclinium offer is withdrawn. Come back another day.'

In a slightly panicky moment, Salvius Cursor realised that the visitor was about to leave. If he walked out and straight into a man lurking outside, there would be trouble. He looked around. Too far back to the corner now, and no hope of unlocking a door. Ahead, another door led to the cellars, as he'd found some time ago. The door was always locked when not in use, but there was a corner there filled with shadow, and trusting to the noise inside the room masking his own, Salvius padded quickly past the occupied office and into the shadows, where he pressed his back against the wall.

Not a moment too soon, either, for in that moment, the door opened and an angry looking man in a miscellaneous tunic and boots and civilian belt emerged, pulling his cloak about him.

'You are not all-powerful,' he said to the doorway behind him. 'There are other collegia, you know?'

'Not for what you want. Good day.'

Huffing, the man paced away. Salvius waited until he turned the corner, and wondered what to do. The office door was still open, so he could hardly sneak back past it, but then he couldn't spend the day pressed back in this narrow, dark corner. His heart leapt as the office's owner stepped out into the corridor. Fortunately, he did not look this way, but leaned towards the far corner and cupped a hand to his mouth.

'Falco? I need you.'

With that, he stepped back into the office. Still, Salvius fretted over what to do, and his options certainly didn't expand as Falco, one of the officers of the house, appeared around the corner at a fast walk and approached, reaching the office door and stopping there, gripping the frame and leaning in.

'Yes?'

'Longinus' man is no longer welcome here. If he turns up at the door again without my sending for him, have a knee broken and throw him out again.'

Falco simply nodded. 'I was coming to see you anyway. I looked in on our new friend, and he's not in his room. Doorman says he hasn't left, and I checked the latrines and the triclinium. He's somewhere in the building, though, lurking.'

Salvius again felt his pulse begin to thunder. That did not sound good.

'I didn't like the look of him from the start. Shifty.'

Falco shrugged lightly. 'He was definitely one of Pompey's men. The tattoo was genuine. There could be any number of reasons he lied about his address.'

Salvius cursed silently. Why hadn't he been more careful? If he'd planned it more in the first place, he could actually have rented an apartment and have a more convincing back story. For a moment he tried to decide what excuse he would cook up, but swiftly abandoned that with the next words from the office.

'I don't care. When he's found, have the truth beaten out of him. Lock all the doors and set guards. Things are too important and delicate right now to allow an unknown potential enemy to mess around here.'

'I'll have him found, broken and disposed of.'

'No. I want him alive. If he's not just some poor piece of shit after all, then that raises the questions of who he is, where he's from, who sent him, and what he's after. I want to hear his life story before you chop him up and dump him in the river.'

Falco nodded and grinned. 'I'll have the butcher on standby. He's preparing for Hypsaeus anyway.'

Salvius, whose mind had been racing through the floorplans of the meeting house, trying to work out his next move, suddenly blinked in surprise. The last message he'd had from Fronto had named Hypsaeus as the probably employer of the collegium. Fronto seemed to have been pretty convinced. If the butcher, an ex-soldier with a love of blood and meat and a collection of large blades, was preparing for a session with Hypsaeus, then one thing was clear: it was *not* Hypsaeus who was calling the shots.

'Hopefully he won't have to.'

'Oh?' Falco straightened a little.

'That's where Fuscus has gone. To put pressure on him. If the fool can be persuaded to stay out of the way, it would be better. Hypsaeus is too high-profile for comfort. Killing him would draw undue attention from new sources. Besides, there may come a time when he's of use. He still has a number of connections.'

159

Falco snorted. 'Given our current selection of targets, Hypsaeus looks like small fry to me.'

'No. There'll be no more attempts on Caesar's men. No killings, anyway. Orders from the new boss.'

'Good job he's paying well. The lads don't like all this pissing about. They like a good, direct fight.'

'The lads will do what they're told, and they'll get rich doing it. Now go find that sneaky shit.'

Falco nodded and withdrew his arms, turning and pacing off down the corridor towards the corner. Salvius swore silently again. The man might have gone, but he'd still left the office door open, and the chances of sneaking past unnoticed were minimal. He was still trapped in this small, dark corner, and now Falco was locking the place down and starting a search for him. Things were beginning to look a little bleak.

What to do?

Well, if he couldn't go back along the corridor, and he couldn't stay here, that left one option. He turned to the cellar door. He wasn't sure what he planned to do, even if he could open the door. The cellar consisted of two large chambers, connected through a wide arch, shelving round the edge to contain what stores the house needed. There was a single aperture in the place, but that was at best a troublesome option. It was little more than a foot across, too narrow for Salvius' shoulders, covered with an iron grille, and even if he could get through it, it just dropped into a three foot tall sewer channel that ran under the house's latrines. Neither feasible nor desirable.

But it was maybe the only possibility.

Just in case, he held his breath and padded back to the doorway. As he approached, the sound of scribbling stopped, and a voice called softly 'Falco?'

Another silent curse. He'd been right about the office. The bastard was at his desk, facing the door. If he'd heard Salvius sneaking close, he'd most certainly see him cross the doorway. He waited until the scribbling started again, and then moved as quietly as possible back to the cellar door. There, he tucked the wooden writing tablet into his belt and very, very slowly opened his pouch and reached among the strips of linen that prevented things from clinking together. He found one of the keys and removed it quietly. He paused, then, looking at the lock. The size ruled out at least half his keys.

Fortuna seemed to be watching him, for a moment later, the office's occupant rose, with a scrape of chair legs and began opening and closing cupboard doors. Salvius grinned and tried the key, timing his movements to coincide with noises from the office.

The key did not fit, but from the distance it entered, he could estimate roughly the size of key he was looking for. Crouching, he peered into the hole with what little light there was. From the pouch he produced a long pin and began to manoeuvre it and turn it. Two teeth to the key, he reckoned, one thin, one fat. A little quiet rummaging, and he found the one he was looking for. The scraping of the chair in the office once more announced the man had stopped with cupboard doors and returned to his seat. Salvius waited, tense. The scribbling began again. He was just wondering whether he would end up standing like this for an hour or so before he was caught, when a new noise began. The man was humming. The scribbling had stopped, but a rhythmic ticking along to the song suggested he was tapping the stilus on the desk, deep in thought.

Taking a chance, Salvius slid the key into the lock and turned it, slowly. It was not quite right, but almost. Fretting, praying, Salvius moved the key a little and finally it turned with a gentle click.

He stopped, tense. The humming and tapping had also stopped.

He paused. The chair scraped again, and Salvius braced, waiting for the man to appear in the corridor and look his way. He tensed his muscles ready to act. As soon as the man appeared, he would run and hit him hard, taking him down, hopefully before he could shout.

No one appeared.

Then there came the rattling and clinking of wine and water jugs and cups.

Salvius took a deep breath and pushed the door, holding down the latch. It opened surprisingly quietly. The steps led down into the darkness, and a waft of musty storeroom air hit him in the face. He winced and started to make his way down the stairs. He had only gone three steps down before the idea struck him, and he broke out into a wide grin. Carefully, he padded back up and slipped into his dark corner. He retrieved the wooden tablet case from his belt and waited.

A moment or two later, the wine had been retrieved and the chair scraped again. Silence returned.

Salvius pulled back his hand and threw the case hard. He was rewarded with an echoing series of clacks and thuds as it bounced down the stone steps into the musty darkness.

'What now?' grunted the voice from the office, accompanied by the scrape of the chair. In a heartbeat the man was in the corridor looking this way and that. Salvius was sufficiently concealed by the darkness, and the man spotted the open cellar door next to him, turning and moving towards it.

'Falco?'

Salvius tensed, breath held, as the second most important man in the collegium stepped through the door, frowning. He paused at the top step, and then, grunting curses, began to descend into the cellar. Salvius waited until he could no longer hear the footsteps, and then burst into action. Reaching out, he pulled the door shut and turned the key, removing it once it clicked into place. As the trapped man in the dark cellar suddenly bellowed with rage and shock, little more than a muffled grunt through the thick door, Salvius dipped back along the corridor. He would have loved to have searched the office, but he knew time was now short, and speed paramount. Still, he allowed himself long enough to dip inside, sweep into a bag whatever the man had been working on, pull the drawstring shut, and prepare to leave. As he turned, he spotted, out of the corner of his eye, a gleaming blade. A legionary gladius hung on the wall next to a centurion's vine stick, evidence of the office owner's former rank. With a grin, he slung the bag over his shoulder and took the weapons one in each hand.

Up. That was the only choice. There were two exits from this place at ground level, and by now both would be sealed. He assumed there were two guards on each, since that's what he would do, and was fairly convinced he could put them down quickly. But they would have locked the doors and removed the keys, and by the time me managed to open them, half the house would be on him. The doors were out. The windows were all too high to reach without standing on furniture or a ladder, for the meeting house was private and passers-by were not to be allowed to see in. No reasonable exit by door or window, and the cellar and sewers he had already ruled out.

That left only up.

Again, he cursed his tendency to jump into things with insufficient planning. If he could go back and relive his days in this place, he'd devote at least a couple of them to forming an escape plan. The idea had not occurred to him until he needed it, though.

He tried to think about the house and its surroundings as he moved through the building, reaching corners and peeking around then before moving on. There was a staircase not far from here. The meeting house had two floors. Up the street, the next building was at least a storey higher, if not two. That would mean a climb, at least. To the other side was a warehouse, but he couldn't remember the roof line at all. Behind was the temple of Mercury, which opened onto the next street. Ah well, he'd have to solve that problem when he got to it.

He looked around the next corner and ducked back. A short, wiry man with a club was pacing his way, a look of determined anger on his face. Salvius sheathed his blade in his belt for a moment and pressed his back against the wall, lifting the centurion's vitis, a hand gripping each end. Better not to kill too many people if he could avoid it, given that he'd just heard they were to stop killing Caesar's men under their new master's orders.

He waited, and a moment later the Pompeian turned the corner, unaware of the danger awaiting him. Salvius let the man walk in front of him, then threw his arms aroundthe man's head, the vine stick suddenly at the man's neck, under his chin. He jerked in, cutting off the man's air, preventing him from crying out and alerting his friends. He kept the pressure on, holding tight as the man gasped, waiting for him to pass out.

Then the man started to fight back. A bony elbow caught Salvius in the ribs, driving the air from him. It was only through sheer will Salvius kept tight hold, but the man was struggling now, fighting to be free. Salvius sighed. He couldn't keep up the fight for long. He'd still not even half recovered from the atrophying of his muscles over months of inactivity. Ah well. He'd tried.

Honestly, he'd tried. No man could say he hadn't tried. With gritted teeth, he pulled hard, suddenly. He heard the snapping of cartilage and bone as the man's throat was crushed. He let go, experience telling him the man was done for, and the Pompeian collapsed to the floor, eyes bulging, clawing at his throat, his club slipping away.

Salvius' eyes rose to the door opposite. It was just a closet, he believed. He stepped across and opened it. A small, dark room that smelled of mould. Perfect. He propped his stick against the wall, reached down and grabbed the dying man. Neatly and quickly he smacked the man's head back against the stone floor with an audible crack, and as the man went limp, he dragged him across to the doorway and threw the twitching body into the closet. He had just tossed the club in too and was preparing to close the door and move on, when a shocked voice gasped 'wait,' in a near whisper.

He looked up sharply at the man who'd rounded the corner to find him disposing of a body. The gods never let him have anything easy, did they? He leapt. The man managed to get a single strange vowel sound out before the sword, whipped from Salvius' belt as he jumped, slammed into his chest, sliding between ribs and pinning his heart. As the man gasped, Salvius slapped a hand over his mouth and grabbed him, letting go of the hilt and keeping the sword jammed where it was. He walked the dead-man-standing to the closet and threw him in, where he fell, gurgling, on top of the man with the crushed throat.

With a sigh, Salvius closed the door. He looked down. There was a splash of blood on the front of his tunic now, and spatters up his arm. It was going to be hard to explain them away easily. And what had been a kill with no evidence until the second man turned up now looked a little like a butcher's floor.

He was careful to step around the blood as he swept up the vitis and moved on. Leaving a trail of bloody footprints would be stupid, after all.

He managed two more turns and reached the stairs without bumping into anyone else. Starting to feel the effort of all this activity on his unpractised muscles, he panted and puffed his way up the steps, turning at the first landing. He could hear voices above, at the stair top. He paused for a moment, and the

164

conversation ended. Predictably, one set of footsteps faded into the distance as the other increased in volume, coming closer.

He ducked back around the rough brick corner and waited as he listened to the descending footsteps. He estimated how close the man was coming, and when he believed him to be closing on the corner, he lifted the vitis, grip reversed so that the heavy, iron-hard knobbly end pointed down, just beneath his grip, the stick standing up above, and leapt. He turned the corner and the vitis came down hard. Luckily the man wasn't too tall, given that he was up a step, and the heavy vine wood hit the top of the man's skull with a nasty thud. The man made a strangely child-like sound and folded up instantly, all wits driven from him, eyes rolling white.

Nowhere convenient to hide the body this time, and the stairs were too easy a place to find him. If they found him here, they would assume Salvius had gone up. grumbling about his luck, Salvius hauled the body onto his shoulder, again the weight evidence that he was still not quite back to normal. Puffing and cursing quietly, he hauled the body up the stairs. He could no longer hear anyone there, but still, as he neared the top, he paused and listened. Nothing.

Turning, he moved along the corridor. At the end was a wide triple window, the three apertures separated by slender columns. It seemed the gods were not in favour of a blood-free escape. Twice already he'd tried to leave men alive and failed, and now that he had an unconscious victim, it seemed the man was doomed anyway. Salvius couldn't leave evidence of his movements, after all. With a sigh, he tossed the body out of the window and listened until he heard the wet crunch from the cobbles below and the screams of passing ladies almost flattened by the falling corpse.

Time to go.

From the view across the street through the window, he confirmed that he was at the front of the building now, and there would be no exit from here, and probably not to left or right either. Swiftly, aware that every passing moment brought discovery that little bit closer, and that with the body count he was racking up they were unlikely to go easy on him, he jogged along the corridor and turned. Two men at the far end were deep in conversation and behind them he could see another window and, through it, that most blessed thing: a dome. The temple of Mercury.

He ran.

It was not a well thought-through attack, even for Salvius Cursor, and anything but elegant, but it had the twin advantages of being fast and unexpected. He was already half way along the corridor before the two men turned, faces painted with surprise, and spotted the blood-spattered madman pelting towards them with a centurion's stick in hand.

One recovered faster than the other, a big brute of a man. He was unarmed, but with biceps like beef carcasses and a chest like a bull, he would be a fearsome proposition, especially for a man weakened by months of bed rest.

And that was why Salvius had no intention of fighting the man. The brute turned, grinning, great hairy arms out to the side, blocking the window that would be his escape, and Salvius hit him at full pelt. The man had clearly been expecting him to stop and use the vitis, and let out a squawk of shock as, at the last moment, Salvius turned side on and hit him with a shoulder as fast and as hard as he could. The two men, carried by momentum, sailed through the open window. As they passed the second, flabbergasted, man, and hurtled out into thin air, Salvius had three distinct advantages over the great ape. Firstly this was planned, insofar as anyone could realistically call it a plan, and he at least was prepared for what would happen, while the brute was shocked and horrified. Secondly, the other man was huge and very heavy, while Salvius was surprisingly small and light after his coma and recuperation. Thirdly, his momentum was still good, despite having hit the big man and taken him with him.

Consequently, as the great hairy brute plummeted to the rooftop of the single storey temple twelve feet below, hitting with a symphony of cracks and crunches that suggested his landing site was destined to be his grave, Salvius hurtled on through the air, hands flailing.

He hit the edge of the temple's domed roof, and almost bounced off to follow the same fate as his victim. His left hand grasped and scrabbled at a jutting piece of stone and he almost fell several times before he managed to get the vine stick wedged in a crack with his other hand. Safe for now, muscles screaming at him, he carefully lowered himself down until he was hanging from the stone by his fingertips and then dropped the other five feet to the rooftop, close to the pile of bleeding human that was his last opponent.

He looked up. The other man back in that corridor was still at the window, and was bellowing warnings, hands round his mouth. Salvius felt a certain satisfaction. No matter what they did now, they wouldn't catch him. He'd escaped. And he'd escaped with what he was fairly sure was vital information for Fronto and Caesar. Moreover, he still had a bag on his back, held there with a drawstring, that contained whatever documents the collegium officer had been working on.

All in all a very satisfactory day's work.

And with only four corpses to show for it.

He grinned. Four? He was clearly losing his touch.

With a cheery wave at the frantic man in the window, he rounded the temple roof to the other side of the dome and there looked down to the street. A colonnaded front, again maybe twelve feet high. Grunting with the effort, he crouched and then hung out over the edge, gripping the stone. He dropped the four or five feet to the cobbles and turned to see that the population of the street had stopped in their tracks to stare at the blood-spattered man who'd just dropped from the temple roof.

With a shrug, he turned, and ran.

CHAPTER THIRTEEN

Fronto paused to allow the kitchen slaves to distribute their trays and platters of snacks around the table between the four of them. Another mixed wine and water in Fronto's favourite krater, the large vessel displaying Priapus chasing a number of nubile young ladies around the surface, a piece of tableware that Lucilia kept hiding in a cupboard, but which kept mysteriously reappearing. Finally, the slaves left and closed the door, and Fronto picked up a chicken leg, took a bite, chewed, and then leaned back.

'So we six, yes? Only six of us know Caesar's plan?'

There was a chorus of nods and affirmative noises, and Fronto's gaze jumped from one to another around the table. Galronus, of course, knew what Fronto knew. Decimus Junius Brutus had been told of Caesar's temporary monarchical aspirations in Fronto's presence, but it had come to light through subtle conversations that the same was now true of these other people. Octavian was something of a surprise inclusion, though given that Caesar was considering allowing him a command on the campaign and the young man was preparing to go east ahead of him, perhaps that shouldn't have been a surprise. Lepidus was naturally in the know, being Caesar's Magister Equitum, his second in command, to be left in control of Rome during the campaign, and much the same could be said for Marcus Antonius, as his co-consul.

Six people who knew Caesar would take up the crown of Aegyptus. The unspoken question on every lip was whether he would be willing to put it down afterwards, as he had said he would.

'*You* should know his mind better than any of us,' he noted, gesturing at Octavian, 'as his heir and one of the prime staff officers on his campaign.'

168

He found it hard to ignore the bitter look Antonius threw at Octavian over that, but he tried anyway.

The young man shrugged. 'I'm not his heir yet, Fronto. Or not more than one among many, at least. And he's been careful to make it clear that my military assignment is to be a small command against the Getae, testing me. It is possible the command will go no further than that. But to answer the general question that no one dare raise, I believe him. A new will is imminent. He's told me plain that the new will should be written, witnessed and filed before he leaves for Illyricum, and I doubt he will wait until after I've gone next month.'

Octavian took a cup of wine and sipped it thoughtfully. 'The will, he tells me, will nod in the direction of my cousins for the sake of formality, but the lion's share and direct succession as pater familias will fall to me. No mention of my half-brother, in particular, yet I know what the young Aegyptian means to Caesar. He has a delicate balancing act to carry out: allowing his son to inherit and go on, while not putting him in the centre of politics in the city. Clearly he intends for me to take on his estates in Rome, and leave Caesarion in Alexandria as a client king, just as he says. And if that is the case, then he cannot hold on to the Aegyptian crown himself beyond the campaign, for if he died wearing it, there would be a great deal of debate as to what happened thereafter. No, if he wants Caesarion on that throne, he will have to do it as soon as he returns to Rome.'

Fronto nodded. 'The question now, then, is what we do in preparation. For years, he's enjoyed overwhelming popularity. Even when we were fighting other Romans, putting out the fires of Pompey's rebellion to east, south and west, the people of Rome were his, both high-born and low. He's been beloved of the people for so long, he doesn't remember what it was like before Gaul, when he was relatively poor and facing political disaster. But now, he keeps letting things slip, and that popularity is waning.'

'Though we cannot rule out a campaign of defamation,' Brutus put in.

'What?'

'It is remarkably convenient that someone should refer to him as a king as he enters Rome, and then there be a crown on his statue by the time he reach the forum. Some things are too neat to be coincidence. That suggests, to me, that someone was trying to make him look bad.'

'Or look good,' Antonius put in.

'Sorry?'

'You've known Caesar long enough to put that together. I would not put it past him to organise two such events himself just to give him the opportunity to refuse them and distance himself from the kingship in the eyes of the public. That it failed spectacularly does not preclude such a possibility.'

Fronto frowned, recalling Caesar's reactions. He'd been genuinely surprised, Fronto, thought, unable to react fast enough. Or had he? He'd quickly made a light quip, but his humour had missed its mark. Then he had become angry with the tribunes in the forum and snapped that the decision to remove the crown should have been his. It did sound like something the man would do.

'Anyway,' he said, shaking his head, 'whatever the intention and the result, the fact is that the people are wavering in their support at the moment, especially the senate. We might know that he has the good of Rome at heart, as well as a healthy dose of self-aggrandisement, but rumour still burns around the city like an army's cook-fires. If Caesar goes east in the current climate and accepts the crown of Aegyptus, those fires of discontent will become an inferno. It matters not what he promises, for the senate and even the people will just see his current activity and see him becoming a king. We all know how that will end. The only way he's going to come out of this looking good after that stupid day with the statue is if he manages to humble himself and bring the whole of Rome onside again before he leaves. And he's too busy with his great plans at the moment to think in such detail. It'll come down to us.'

Octavian shrugged. 'I've little time to make any difference. In half a month I'll be in Apollonia, preparing for the campaign, and before then I have much to arrange. We may have to trust to his luck and charisma for now. Don't forget that he'll have a victory against the Getae to boost Rome's mood before he ever gets to Alexandria.'

Fronto nodded. There was some truth to that last, at least.

'You keep dropping in how we all know that Caesar does plan to put down the crown,' Antonius said quietly, taking the jar of unwatered wine and filling his cup from that. You say that we all believe him. I am as yet not fully convinced. He seems to be doing his best to keep those of us who supported him through his rise safely back here, while he goes east. Current company excepted,' he added, with a sharp look at Octavian. 'If he was planning something unexpected, if he had something to hide, he would want to keep some of us out of reach, where we couldn't stop him.'

Fronto shivered, frowning at Antonius. 'You really think he's deceiving us all?'

Antonius sniffed. 'I'm not saying that he *is*. I'm just saying that it's a long way from proven that he's *not*.'

Lepidus straightened. 'If he did try to reinstitute the monarchy, or move Rome's power east, even I, as his magister equitum, would defy him. All true Romans would,' he added, with a momentary glance in the direction of Octavian. The young man either had not noticed how people kept making dubious points and looking his way, or he was bright enough not to draw attention to it. The latter, Fronto decided, knowing Octavian.

Before anyone else could speak, they were interrupted by a knock at the door.

'Yes?'

The door crept open, and the face of Fronto's major domo appeared. 'Apologies for the interruption, Domine, but you have a visitor.'

'Worth interrupting this for?'

'I believe so, sir.'

The man was pulled back out of the way with an 'awk,' sound, and a red-faced, blood-spattered Salvius Cursor appeared in his place, panting.

'Salvius?'

'I have *news*, Fronto,' the man huffed, stressing the word as he looked around the gathered faces.

'News that can't be shared among these men?'

Salvius Cursor thought on this, looking around them again. His eyes lingered on Octavian for a moment, and slid to the bowl of

171

mushrooms on the table in front of him. His lip twitched, and Fronto realised then that whatever the man might have said, he remembered damn well what Octavian had done to him. 'I suppose not,' Salvius admitted finally, stepping into the room, a last, unreadable look lingering on Octavian.

'I take it from the state of you, you ran into difficulty?'

'You could say that. The assignment is now over.'

'Assignment?' Brutus asked.

Fronto nodded as he poured a cup of wine and passed it to Salvius to help him recover. 'Our friend here, being a good former Pompeian officer, took it upon himself to infiltrate the collegium that's been causing trouble.'

Antonius blinked. 'The one that attacked my people?'

Fronto nodded. 'And mine. And Caesar's.'

'Well I don't think you need to worry about that any more,' Salvius said between swigs.

'Oh?'

'The collegium has new orders not to kill Caesar's men. I'm not sure whether it was not to attack us, but certainly not to kill us. And that's where it gets interesting.'

Fronto shuffled in his seat. 'Go on.'

'I overheard their second in command. The leader is away with his best men at Hypsaeus's house.'

'New orders?' Antonius asked, intent.

Salvius shook his head. 'That's the thing. It seems that Hypsaeus is not their employer. They went to put the frighteners on him to keep him out of the way. Someone else is now paying the collegium.'

Fronto took a deep breath and exhaled slowly. 'Well if it's someone who doesn't want us killed, that has to be an improvement, right?' He sucked on his lip. 'I wonder how long it's been since Hypsaeus lost control of them.'

Salvius took another sip. 'The way they talked about him, it sounded like he was unconnected with them, and they were keeping him around only because he might be of use. Oh, and they're expanding, bringing other collegia in on their side.'

Fronto sighed. 'This problem gets ever more complex.'

'Quite.'

They fell silent and it was only as he heard the laughter of the boys across the house that Fronto realised Salvius had not closed the door as he came in. In the silence of the room he could hear the boys, the murmur of life across the household, and now, something new.

'Can you hear that?' he asked.

The others stilled, listening. 'Sounds like a riot somewhere nearby,' Lepidus said.

Fronto's eyes narrowed. 'How did you get covered in blood?'

'They found out about me in the collegium and sealed the place,' Salvius said. 'I was forced to cause a few casualties during my escape.'

'And you made sure you weren't followed back,' Fronto replied meaningfully.

Salvius Cursor frowned. 'I got away across a temple roof and into a crowded street. The only man who followed me onto the roof died there.'

'Is that a yes?'

'I didn't check. I was sore, exhausted and in danger. I had to get here and tell you all this. And I brought some records I swiped from their office,' he added, unslinging the bag around his shoulders and dropping it to the tiled floor, where it landed with the crash of a dozen wooden tablet cases.

Fronto put a hand to his ear, somewhat theatrically. 'Hark, but I suspect I can hear the gentle sound of pursuit.'

The din, reminiscent of mob violence in the streets, definitely sounded closer.

'How secure is your house,' Brutus asked.

'Pretty secure. I've a good sized force based here these days, especially when I'm home. And with the guards you all brought, we should be well-defended.'

There would be litters and their bearers outside belonging to the men in this room, but their escorts were inside now, including Brutus' gladiators. They would be handy. Here, on the slopes of the Aventine, they were outside the pomerium, and the carrying of weapons was permissible, though the visitors had all come through that sacred boundary, and so their men would all be armed with knives and clubs at best. Fronto's mercenaries, of course, were fully armed.

'Come on,' he said, rising and crossing the room. In the atrium, he gestured at a passing servant and said 'sword.'

With the others in tow, he moved towards the vestibule to the front door. His men were already there, a score of armed killers filling the wide corridor. As Fronto and the guests approached, they moved aside to leave passage for him, and moments later the servant reappeared with Fronto's sword, proffering it. Fronto grabbed it, unsheathed it and handed the scabbard back to the man before approaching the front door. As he came closer, he realised he was hearing a different sound outside now. What they had heard in the triclinium, filtering through from the open peristyle garden, had sounded like an angry mob surging through the streets. What he could hear now, muffled by the door, sounded more like actual warfare.

The others' groups of guards were now joining them, hurrying through from the large rooms off the gardens where they'd been entertained during the visit.

'The litter bearers fighting back?' Fronto mused as he gestured to the doorman in his cubby to open up.

'Doubtful,' Brutus replied.

The doorman pulled the door open nervously, and Fronto peered out. The large group of former Pompeian veterans filled the street some thirty paces away, but they were already fighting off someone else. Other figures had gathered on the roof tops and were throwing tiles and bricks down on them, causing a surprisingly large amount of damage. Collegium members were collapsing with a cry every other heartbeat, clutching broken arms or bleeding heads.

'I don't think we'll be called upon to defend ourselves today,' Brutus grinned.

'Who are they?' Fronto muttered.

'The collegium of builders on the Aventine,' Galronus replied. 'You don't employ them, but I might have mentioned in passing to a number of local collegia that angry veterans burning down streets in the region would be bad for business.'

Fronto laughed as the Pompeians hurried this way and that, grabbing what they could from the street corners and alleys to lift above their heads and protect them from falling debris. There weren't as many as there had been in the last few attacks, just as many as they could gather quickly to follow Salvius and see where he went. Four managed to get out of the way of the falling missiles and close on Fronto's door. One of them, a leader of some sort gestured to Fronto.

'We want the spy. Hand him over.'

Fronto gave the man an unpleasant smile and stepped out into the street. This allowed his armed men to pour out of the doorway behind him and line up across the front of the house. The other visitors also joined him, standing side by side. The speaker took in the large array of armed men and the luminaries facing him: Fronto, Galronus, Lepidus, Octavian, Brutus and Antonius. His confidence, already shaken by the unexpected attack from above, crumbled completely.

'His name,' the man insisted, eyes nervous now.

Fronto simply shook his head.

'Look, we don't want trouble.'

'Coming as a mob, armed with clubs, to my house suggests otherwise,' Fronto replied.

'We have our rights. The collegium has been trespassed upon under false pretences by a criminal, who has stolen collegium property and murdered our members, and the villain is in your house, senator. It is our right to see him in court for his actions. I would know his name.'

'And I would tell you again, piss off.'

In light of the conversation, the attack from above had tailed off, and now Pompeians were helping up their wounded companions while keeping a wary eye out at the surrounding rooves. The leader turned, taking in the extensive damage done to his people, then turned back noting how outnumbered and out-armed he was, as well as the importance of the men standing before him. He sagged. With a weary breath, he wagged a finger at Fronto. 'He will pay for this. And so will anyone who harbours him. We have good lawyers.'

'Not good enough,' Antonius said with a sneer.

175

The man actually flinched, as though the words had been a whip cracked at him. He gave Fronto one last powerless glare, then turned with his men and marched back to his wounded. Gathering the fallen, including two corpses, they disappeared along the street. Fronto waited until they were no longer in sight and waved up to the gathered men on the rooftops.

'Thank you for your timely assistance. I will see to it that a number of jars of my best wine are sent to your meeting house by sunset.'

This brought a number of cheers from the men up there as they began to disperse, leaving their cast debris all over the street, amid puddles of blood. Fronto waited until they had gone, and then gestured for the others to follow him back inside. They returned to the triclinium and to Salvius, who was now washing off the last of the blood with a bowl and cloth a slave had brought. As he towelled himself dry, they took their seats once more.

'You make friends easily,' Fronto snorted. 'Just how many men did you kill getting out?'

'Four that I remember.'

'Add another couple in the street out there. A few more incidents like this and there won't be enough of them left to be a threat anyway.' Reaching down, he gathered up the bag from the floor, pulling open the drawstring and tipping the contents onto the table between the bowls of nibbles. He swept up one of the tablets and opened it.

'A list of the sick and wounded of the collegium. How ironic. And how out of date,' he added, dropping it and collecting another. 'This one's more interesting. It confirms an appointment in three days' time. Lucius Caninius Gallus is invited to attend the collegium's meeting house, but is reminded that his entourage and guards must remain outside. The letter's not finished. I guess this is what he was busy writing when you made your escape.'

'What was that name again?' Octavian said, frowning.

'Lucius Caninius Gallus. Why?'

'I know that name,' the young man said, drumming his fingers on his knee. 'Correspondence with Caesar, I think. I'm sure I've seen his name around the house. Who is he?'

Fronto shrugged. 'Don't know him overly well. I used to know him a score of years ago, in my Hispania days.'

Antonius waved a hand. 'He's a bit of an opportunist, Caninius Gallus. I remember him too. He was good friends with Caesar back when they were both small fish. They came up together, one from a consular family, one a patrician, but both a little short of coin. But he nailed his vexillum to Pompey's mast, back while we were all in Gaul. Then, when Caesar crossed the Rubicon and it looked clear that the rebels were going to run, he stepped back and cut his ties, trying to be neutral and see who came out on top. Since we came back to Rome, he's made his support for Caesar known again, but at the same time he's a good friend of Cicero, and that wily old bastard is no friend of Caesar himself. Personally I wouldn't trust Caninius Gallus as far as I could spit a ballista ball.'

Fronto nodded. 'And it would appear he's up to his old tricks again, if he's lobbying Caesar and at the same time in communication with the Pompeian collegium.'

'I should tell my uncle,' Octavian said.

'Yes, might not be a bad idea. Caesar is becoming a little too lax with his own security for my liking, especially the way he's making enemies at the moment.'

The rest of the tablets proved to be of peripheral importance or interest at best, and Fronto snapped the last one shut and looked across at Salvius. 'You'd best get yourself cleaned up and change. I was going to suggest that now you're well, you might want to move back to your own house, but in light of the fact that the Pompeians will probably be looking for you now, you might be safer staying here. The physician who looked after you is still here in my pay. Do you need him?'

Salvius shook his head. 'It's all other people's blood. I have a few aches and bruises. That's all.'

With that, the man turned and left, and Fronto sighed. 'Something is going to have to be done about the situation with the collegia. If they are retaining other groups too, maybe on behalf of whoever's currently paying them, that's a sizeable army building in the city's streets. I know I've got my own men, and Brutus has his gladiators – we've *all* got a guard, in fact – but that's not a long-term solution.'

'Oh?' Lepidus asked.

'Sooner or later, every collegium or mercenary group in Rome is going to be signed up, probably on one side or another, pro-Caesarian or anti-Caesarian. And that's most of the able fighting population of the city. I presume I don't need to suggest how dangerous it could be to have two armies prowling the streets of Rome, facing off against one another?'

Octavian nodded. 'Another civil war, but this one *inside* the city.'

'Exactly. I don't know what the solution is, but I certainly don't think it lies in escalation.'

The six of them leaned back, each pondering the situation, and for the next hour or so discussed the problems of policing a city the size of Rome with no security force other than the lictors of those men in positions of power, at least half of whom were probably involved with the various gangs and collegia anyway, even if only through clients or patrons. In the end, no solution had been hit upon by the time Antonius announced that he had to leave for a meeting with his own clients. The sentiment was echoed by others, and so each thanked Fronto for his hospitality, dropped in to pay their respects to Lucilia, and then left the house with their guards and entourage, heading back their own way. Each followed close on the heels of the other until they were down the Aventine slopes and past the cippi stones that marked the pomerium. Once across that and passing the circus, they were comparatively safe, especially with their private armies to hand.

Fronto waited for a while once they were gone, and then visited Lucilia.

'Do you mind if I nip out for an hour or so?'

She shook her head. 'Be careful. Very careful. And if you happen to be near the Vicus Tuscus on your travels, visit that bakery we like and get something for the evening.'

Fronto smiled, kissed his wife, then became all business, gathering up his cloak and his favourite 'hunting knife'. He called for his men, and in moments he was exiting the house with Galronus, Masgava, Aurelius, Arcadios and twenty trained ex-soldiers.

178

'Where are we going?' Galronus said, still throwing on his cloak, so hurried had been their departure.

'To visit Publius Plautius Hypsaeus. I think, in light of new information, it might be time to have a little chat.'

'If he was never the patron of the collegium, why did they visit him before they went to kill that clerk?' Galronus mused.

'Maybe to threaten him. Sounds like that's what they're doing again now. I'd just like to hear his side of the story, I think.'

With the others nodding their agreement, they passed the boundary of the pomerium at the bottom of the hill and crossed into the city proper. The streets were busy, but that presented no obstacle for a man with an entourage and two dozen trained killers, and the crowd melted out of their way as they marched. On they moved, past the Palatine and Caelian hills, past the high, incendiary timber insulae that crowded the street, crossing the stream that ran through the valley bottom below the Velia and passing the houses of a number of rich men on the ridge there, and began to climb the Viminal. Despite his desire to achieve as normal a journey as possible these days, Fronto had to admit that he was growing used to a litter. Certainly his knee was beginning to ache more than it had in some time by the time they crested the Viminal and made it to the Vicus Porta Collina. It did not take long to reach the house, and Fronto brushed aside his friends who all tried to step in front, protecting him, and rap on the door knocker.

After the briefest of pauses, the door crept open a little and a suspicious eye filled the gap, the face behind it oversized and ugly.

'Yeah?'

'Tell your master that Marcus Falerius Fronto is here to see him.'

The thing at the door grunted and shut it once more. There followed a silence long enough for Fronto to begin wondering whether the man had, in fact, not bothered and simply gone back to his room, leaving them waiting outside. Then, when he was considering knocking again, and more forcefully this time, he heard footsteps approaching, muffled by the door.

When it opened again, it did so wider, revealing the full huge ugliness of the creature Hypsaeus employed as his doorman. As the thing told him to follow, but only him and without weapons,

Fronto winced and leaned back in the blast of halitosis, wondering if the man had been hired specifically to keep everyone out by breathing on them. As he made to move, the others were urging him to let them join him, but he shook his head, unsheathed his knife and passed it to Galronus. 'I'll be back soon.'

With that, he entered, and the brute shut the door behind him.

He followed it through the house, trying not to breathe too hard, and not just because of the doorman's smell. The whole place had an odd musty odour, reminiscent of a building that had stood empty for some time. He remembered then that Hypsaeus had disappeared from the centre of public life when Caesar had risen to power. He was willing to bet that Hypsaeus had conveniently exiled himself from the city for a while, and had only been back in this house for a short time.

But that also did not explain the echo. The place felt empty and hollow, and apart from the doorman, he'd neither seen nor heard another person. That seemed odd. At home you had to tune out the murmur of life in the house to concentrate on anything. Big houses usually had anywhere between forty and sixty slaves.

The triclinium into which he was shown was tasteful and opulent, if a little faded. Hypsaeus reclined at a table, plucking at grapes, and gestured for Fronto to join him.

'Have you thought on what I said?' he began, as Fronto lowered himself to the couch opposite.

'What?'

'At the sacrifice. I warned you to back away. Warned Caesar too.'

'Oh, your threat.'

'Threat?' Hypsaeus paused, grape in hand, and looked up at him, brow wrinkling. He looked genuinely confused, which threw Fronto.

'Your not-so-subtle veiled threat at the temple,' he clarified.

'No threat, you fool. I gave you a friendly warning.' He snorted a derisive laugh. 'As if I had the power to threaten.'

Fronto was properly baffled now. He thought back over what was said at the sacrifice, rolling the words in his mind. *Parthia is a mistake that should be called off. You were a true son of Rome, standing up for principles. I remember Fronto, not this lackey.*

Fronto had a horrible feeling. Now that he thought back over it, though he'd assumed the words to be a threat, they could also be seen as a genuine warning. *Taking part in this campaign could be very unhealthy. Even a quiet part, from home.*

Damn the man. He should have made himself more clear.

'I assumed, what with you paying the collegium, that...'

Now, Hypsaeus broke into a wild laugh. 'Collegium?'

'Yes,' replied Fronto, though a little shakily, less sure of himself.

'Fronto, I haven't run a collegium since Milo died. Gods, but since Caesar rebuilt the senate and saw off the old crowd, most of my income has dried up to nil. I've hardly two sesterces to rub together. I've sold all but my worst slaves, and I might soon have to sell this place and move away. Have you any idea how much money it takes to run a gang?'

As it happened, Fronto *did* know that. A lot, as Lucilia was keen on reminding him.

'So you weren't in touch with the collegium of Pompey's veterans when they started on us?'

Again, Hypsaeus snorted, though this time with a bitterness and no humour. 'That lot? Jove man, but I'd pay money, if I had it, to see that lot sewn in a sack and drowned in the Tiber. No, I've no love for them. And no love for Caesar really. Or you. But if I ever hope to pull myself out of this hole, it will be with Caesar's goodwill, and that way alone, for he is master of Rome. That's why I was trying to warn you all. There are plenty of people who are waiting for Caesar to fall, and a good few who are working to make it happen. I thought if I could be instrumental in saving him, Caesar's gratitude might be shown in the form of coin. And you? You're his man through and through.'

Fronto sighed. He'd apparently got this all wrong from the beginning. The collegium was not Hypsaeus' and never had been. They had a master *now*, but it still was not him. He frowned, thinking back over what the man had said.

'You mentioned people who were trying to bring Caesar down.'

The house's owner gave him a sly laugh. 'I might be able to produce a few names, were my loyalty to be brought to the attention of Caesar and gain a suitable reward.'

Fronto nodded eagerly. 'Tell me.'

'When I have something in my hand to make it worthwhile. These are not people to fuck with lightly.'

'Then I will return soon,' Fronto said, rising. 'I have much to organise.'

CHAPTER FOURTEEN

G aius Julius Caesar pursed his lips. His great nephew sat opposite, eyes darting this way and that as he scanned the lists of troops rosters Fronto had delivered that morning, the final numbers of all the forces gathered and still gathering in Illyricum ready for the campaign. Between them, a rough shape of the east was drawn out on wooden board, with the principle sites of importance marked.

'You have a preference?' he said.

'For more than one legion, yes,' Octavian replied.

Caesar allowed his eyebrow to rise quizzically. He'd expected that, of course. 'Why?' Not a real question, more a test, or challenge.

'When part of a larger force, a legate commands at unit level, uncle. He is responsible for the formation and disposition of his legion, but little more than that. Oh, if that legion is on its own, or he is given a more expansive command, then it becomes something far greater, but as a single legate among several in a force, he is somewhat robbed of responsibility.'

'Tell that to Fronto,' Caesar said with flat humour, remembering the many times in Gaul a certain legate had turned the tide or changed a war. Still, he had to concede the point. He didn't particularly like it himself when his legates decided to extemporise.

'And the in-action command all falls to the centurionate,' Octavian went on. 'So you see, command of one legion for me is worthless, unless you intend to separate that one legion and assign it a task all its own.' He looked up from the lists. 'But then you knew that, and you knew that *I* knew that, so I find myself wondering why you ask.'

'To see your reaction.'

183

'Do I pass your test?'

'You do. Had you been too pushy, I would have worried that you were not ready for command, that you would be hasty in the field, which is the problem I tend to have with Antonius, and why I must leave him behind this time. On the other hand, had you been too accepting, I would have suspected you too weak to do what you must. You are, however, straightforward and stoic, as I had hoped, and this bodes well.'

'So?'

'So I give you the First, the Fourteenth and the Twenty Second, along with appropriate auxiliary units. Prove yourself against the Getae and we'll see what Parthia holds.' He looked at the rough map, largely beyond Roman territory, cartography cobbled together from Greek accounts and those of the more adventurous Roman traders. More of it was blank than he'd have liked.

'The lands beyond our control are somewhat mysterious and unknown, but the Getae are based around the lower Danubius region. From the muster, I shall take half the army across northern Greece to Amphipolis on the Aegean coast, and from there march them northeast, moving through Thracian lands, while your legions will travel northeast directly from Dyrrachium, through Dardania.'

'A pincer movement,' Octavian noted. 'You from the east and I from the west. It would have to be well timed and executed, of course.'

'Most definitely. Fronto has already worked out the distances and the times for us, so we simply have to stay close to his planned timeline, and all should work out more or less. This is one reason I put him in charge of planning. His experience of marching legions on tight schedules makes him an expert at logistical estimations.'

He pointed at the map. 'You will strike west through Dardania, march along the Danubius to the Thracian town of Pristi on the edge of Getae territory, and from there send half your force around the south of their lands. Their territory seems to be more or less bounded by the Loma River, and your men can follow it and garrison as they go. I shall strike at the Getae from the east and do the same, heading to Odessos on the Euxine Coast and sending my men along the line of the Haemus Mountains. This way we can encircle them, then tighten the noose and drive them to the banks of the Danubius. There are too many of them to consider conquest and settlement at this time, for our focus must remain Parthia, but they have been coming close enough to threaten Rome's control of the region, and we must push them hard enough back towards the north that it is years before they think of expansion once more.'

He sat back and folded his arms, watching Octavian, watching for his reaction.

'I hope Fronto's timing is accurate. It will take your forces longer to spread out along a range of mountains than for mine to march along a river bank.'

Caesar smiled. Good. He was thinking ahead. 'My forces are given two days for every one of yours.'

Now, Octavian also sat back, nodding, and silence fell, broken a moment later.

'Pardon me, Domine,' a voice cut in politely from the doorway, 'but you have a visitor.'

Caesar looked up at his slave. Always interruptions, especially when it was something that required a great deal of concentration. 'Who is it?'

'Lucius Caninius Gallus, Domine. And his entourage.'

Caninius Gallus? Caesar frowned, thinking back. He couldn't even remember the last time he'd seen the man. Certainly he could think of nothing Gallus might say that was important enough to interrupt work for. He shook his head, 'Tell him I am busy and to come back another time.'

His gaze fell upon Octavian, whose expression had become odd, unreadable but hard-looking.

'Speak.'

The younger man shrugged. 'There is nothing here that cannot wait, uncle. By all means see your visitor. I have things to attend to for now.'

There was something in his voice that Caesar wasn't sure about, but he couldn't quite put his finger on it. He had always thought himself fairly inscrutable, but it was disconcerting to realise that his nephew was even more so. He looked up past Octavian at the doorway, frowned for a moment over the decision, then shrugged.

'Show him in. His entourage and guards can wait outside, of course.'

The slave bowed low and retreated.

'I shall return in due course,' Octavian said, rising, still holding one of the lists and the stilus he'd been tapping idly on it.

'You can stay.'

'I won't be long,' the younger man said with a strange smile, turning and pacing from the room.

Caesar watched him go. What was he up to? Octavian was certainly clever, and Caesar liked clever men. He was also calm and detached, which, again, Caesar admired. But he was also devious and inscrutable, and while that was something else of which Caesar might approve, when all those characteristics were combined, they could create a very dangerous man. He'd known Octavian to be his only realistic heir since the man was but a boy, and he had grown into a very strong character. Would he be the one to finish the work?

Caesar mused for a rare moment, alone in his office. There were some things that could not be said, only thought, and even then only in solitude. Dangerous things. Important things.

Despite everything he said, even to his closest friends, despite every promise he made, he knew the republic was done. A sad fact, but a rather obvious one if you examined the facts. The republic was a fish on dry land, flopping and gasping its last. Strictures put in place centuries ago to prevent any one man from gaining sole power had failed time and again, and each time there had been war, assassinations, bloodbaths that had torn the republic apart. The Gracchi, and then Sulla, then Pompey and Crassus, with Caesar the junior in all that, admittedly. Once, he had seen himself as leading the change, dragging the dying republic out of the chaos of war and into a new era. But that would not happen. The time was not yet right, and he was getting too old now for such things. But if Rome was to endure and to grow once more, it had to change, and whether or not he was at the helm of the new ship, he had to do what he could to smooth that course. He had now brought to heel those who would tear Rome apart, removing the last real obstacle in the form of Pompey and his cronies, for men like Cicero might moan and complain, but they would never stand in the fact of change. And the senate had proved to have even less spine, continually granting further powers to the man they claimed was saving the republic, while knowing damn well that he was now controlling it alone. Who needed a crown, for the might of a king lay in power, not trappings?

He'd not long left, though. He still hoped Spurinna was wrong, of course, but even if he was, Caesar knew he was starting to slip. The attacks were coming more and more often now, and the last one, just two days ago, he'd had in his private bath, alone. He'd taken a chunk out of his finger in the attempt to stop himself biting through his own tongue. He'd almost drowned, and his personal slaves had just saved him in time. But he'd lost at least an hour after the attack, unconscious on the bath house floor, and when he'd finally awoken it took another hour before he could even say his own name. Not only were the attacks coming more often, but their severity was becoming far worse.

Was Octavian the one to take his place?

Almost certainly. But then, at least he would have a spare. His will was already written, just not lodged officially, and not witnessed. Pedius and Pinarius would have a little sinecure thrown their way, but Octavian would be the next Julius Caesar. Yet if he was not up to the task, there would be another heir in Alexandria, with all the wealth and power of the kingdom of Aegyptus at his fingertips. If Octavian proved not to be what Caesar hoped for, then perhaps Caesarion would.

His musings were brushed aside swiftly as the slave reappeared in the doorway, eyes appropriately locked on the floor as he came to a halt. He stepped aside then, announcing the guest, and Caninius Gallus strode in, stopping halfway between the door and the room's occupant. He was dressed togate, impressive and distinguished. But then he'd always been able to put that impression across, even while he betrayed people. You had to watch his eyes to catch any hint of his true intentions.

'Caninius.'

'Caesar.'

'You have something to say to me?'

'Caesar, I have ever been your friend and ally...'

The man stopped, sentence unfinished, as Caesar let out a short bark of a laugh.

Caninius straightened. 'Perhaps it is fairer to say I have never been your enemy. I might have had dealings with those who opposed you, but I have never done so myself. At times I have been at your side, and at others I have stood back and refused to take a side.'

'Yes. Your sense of self-preservation is legendary.'

A tic appeared below the man's eye. Good. Caesar tried not to smile. He did like it when smug and untrustworthy people were caught wrong-footed.

Caninius recovered quickly. 'I have been petitioned by a number of mutual acquaintances to put to you a plea. The senate seems unable to stop voting you new honours and powers.'

Caesar frowned. Perhaps there was a spine there after all. It was a surprise to find it in Caninius Gallus, though. He let the man go on, listening with interest.

'You have always been the people's champion, and that is, I believe, at the root of their desire to heap rewards upon you. But those people are beginning to turn on you with every bauble and title that settles on your brow. There are those in the senate who fear you, or dislike you. There are those who love you and support you. I am here to represent the rest, those who remember the Caesar who brought us Gaul, the scion of the Julii, those who worry about the direction Rome is taking under your control, but would love nothing more than to support you, if only *you* seemed to support *them*.'

Caninius Gallus straightened a little. 'Caesar, lay down your dictatorship. Retain your consulship for the year, but relinquish your total control of the state. Granting you a decade of dictatorship was ridiculous, as you well know, and utterly pointless now that the civil war is over. Laying down the dictatorship is the *sensible* thing to do, and it is the *safe* thing to do. If you do not, then soon dissident voices in the senate will demand it anyway.'

'That sounded awfully like a threat, Caninius,' Caesar said quietly.

'In that it is a certainty, it is as much threat as warning, I suppose,' the man said, but the tic was jumping in his cheek still, and his voice had become hard, bitter. 'I do not wish to make demands. My plan was but to beseech you to come to the correct conclusion yourself. I...'

Caninius paused in his diatribe, frowning. He turned his head.

Caesar could hear it too. Shouts, angry, frightened. The guest took a few steps towards the doorway as Caesar rose from his seat, and at that moment Octavian reappeared in the doorway with his writing tablet and bronze stilus.

'What is happening?' Caninius demanded.

Octavian gave him a strange smile and stepped forward. His hand moved so fast it was little more than a blur, and then he stepped back into the doorway once more.

Caesar stared as Caninius turned back to him, face white with shock, eyes wide, the sharp bronze stilus jutting from his neck. The point had been rammed in so deep the pen was buried in flesh to almost halfway. Blood began to pump, jetting around the makeshift weapon with every movement Caninius made. He let out a strange, hoarse whimper and his hand came up to touch the stilus. Even the gentlest of touches opened up the wound in his artery, and a jet of blood arced through the air, splashing onto the mosaic below.

Caesar was rarely shocked or surprised, but right now he was stunned silent. All he could do was watch as Caninius made horrified, agonised noises, and every sound moved that pen and sent more gouts of blood out into the air. The mortally wounded man turned several times, facing now Octavian, now Caesar, and so on. Again he touched the stilus, and again the blood sprayed free. He gasped, his hands coming out and up in supplication, and that move only brought a fresh wash of crimson.

'It's almost as tedious watching you die as listening to you talk,' Octavian said in a bored voice, then stepped forward and reached up.

Caninius Gallus flinched for a moment, but it did not stop the young man. Octavian grasped the stilus and yanked it free, stepping back swiftly to avoid being soaked as the arterial spray began in earnest. The dying man reached up and clamped his hand over his neck, though the blood was running free between his fingers, and already his skin tone was beginning to change.

Caesar took a couple of steps forward, though not close enough to become involved in the gruesome display. He felt his shock receding, being replaced with a cold anger. He edged to one side, and Octavian did the same in response, the two of them meeting just out of Caninius' reach as the man continued to stagger around, clutching his neck, adding to the growing lake of blood on the floor.

'Explain,' Caesar said in a clipped tone, keeping control of his anger, but only just.

'He was neither ally, nor friend,' Octavian replied calmly.

'So you murdered him?'

Octavian produced a cloth from his belt and wiped the blood from the stilus. Old bloodstains on the rag only raised more worrying questions. 'Caesar, we are at war already. Not on a battlefield and with the Getae, but in the senate and on the streets of Rome, and with an insidious opponent whose face we cannot see. Caninius Gallus was a soldier of that opponent. He was an enemy and he fell in battle. This was not murder, but justifiable execution.'

Caesar frowned. 'You have proof of wrongdoing, beyond his frankly feeble threats?'

'He consorts with a collegium who is opposed to you. The one that has launched attacks on your people. Moreover, I hear now that he has been visiting Cicero recently, and you are, presumably, aware that Cicero is your enemy?'

Caesar felt that cold anger settling into him.

'Cicero has been an opponent for most of my career, but we have an agreement now. Today is perhaps the first time in our history when I *cannot* call him my enemy, for he works to put my laws and edicts in place. And as for the activity of some shady gang…'

'He was your *enemy*, uncle, and he was far from alone, and far from harmless.'

'I will have to answer for this, or *you* will.'

Octavian sniffed. 'I think not. Just another victim of crime. I will have him disposed of. He will wash up, bloated and bloodless, on the banks of the Tiber south of the city in the coming days. And you must have heard the rumours in the city about plots against you? With him gone, the plots against you are one man lighter.'

Caesar rounded on him, the anger now tinging his voice. 'People are seeing plots *everywhere* now, since Spurinna's announcement. I tell you that nothing is amiss. And the next time you decide to kill someone in my house, you had better be prepared to defend yourself.'

At that moment, Caninius, almost entirely pale grey now, staggered between them, slipping and sliding, careened into a wall and slumped to the floor, where he lay in a heap, shaking for a few moments before falling still. Caesar took no notice, he and Octavian still locked eye-to-eye across the blood-streaked floor.

'*You* might not care about your own safety, uncle, but we do. You know damn well that you're in danger even if you won't admit it. If you are so intent on death, if you are so happy to invite danger into your life and flaunt yourself at the assassin's blade, then by all means do so, but remember those of us who will follow.'

Caesar's eyes narrowed again.

'This is about the will?'

'It *wasn't*,' Octavian snapped. 'It has *become* that, but this was about protecting you from your enemies. Since you are clearly in a suicidal and argumentative mood, I shall come back later.'

With that, the younger man turned and strode from the room, careful to step around the blood. Caesar could feel his skin prickling with anger. 'Oh no, you don't. Come back here.'

Skirting the lake of blood, he followed Octavian. His nephew crossed the atrium at an impressive pace and marched along the entrance hall towards the open doors. Caesar followed, displeased, if not surprised, by what had clearly happened outside.

Like all men of position in Rome, Caninius Gallus had come to Caesar's villa in a litter carried by flour burly slaves, with an entourage of half a dozen other attendants and a dozen mercenary guards, largely of military veterans or freed gladiators. Every last one had been slaughtered on the gravel outside Caesar's door, the whole area a lake of blood filled with hacked and torn corpses, even the man's personal slave, little more than a child. Caesar's own guards, the men whose task was the security of his villa, were standing among them, spattered and stained. Gallus' men had fought a valiant defence, but they'd had only ash rods, having come through the heart of the city, while Caesar's men carried gladius and pugio, safely outside the pomerium. The result had been one-sided and predictable. Only one of Caesar's men lay among the fallen.

He had to nod to himself silently and unseen. Octavian had to learn that he couldn't simply kill, and certainly not in Caesar's house and without permission, but at least if he was going to kill, he'd had the foresight to do away with Gallus' men first, so there would be neither reprisal not witnesses. Still unacceptable, but at least efficiently so.

'Clear these away,' he told the guards. 'I want them off my property, and have this and my office cleaned thoroughly, too. Octavian will oversee the clean-up,' he added, turning his flinty eyes on his great nephew. 'Following which you will escort him back to his mother's house in the city, where he will stay and not return here until summoned.'

Octavian's answering look was no less hard and unyielding, and the two remained locked in angry silence for a moment before the latter spoke.

'You had better learn to start watching your back, uncle, if you are determined not to have me around to do it for you.'

With that, Octavian stomped away towards the leader of Caesar's guard unit. The dictator watched him for a moment, then skirted the carnage and strode back inside, his pace given speed and strength by cold anger. When he reached the atrium, slaves were already cleaning the blood in the doorway of his public office, but he strode straight past them and towards the smaller private office towards the back of the house, which remained locked at all times, windowless and with the only key on a ring on Caesar's finger. He reached the office, slid the key into the lock, turned and entered the room, closing the door behind him. In moments he'd struck the flint and ignited the three oil lamps that lit the room.

He stomped across to the desk and opened the cupboard behind it, reaching in and pulling out a sheet of high quality expensive vellum. Stepping back into middle of the room, he unrolled it and let his gaze play across the first few lines of text.

'To my great nephew Gaius Octavianus, henceforth to be known as Gaius Julius Caesar Octavianus, I leave my estate, including all property, goods and currency.'

It went on to set a number of conditions and stipulations, and then to secure provision for his wife (not mentioned by name, should he not have managed to divorce Calpurnia and marry Cleopatra by the time it was needed), his other great nephews, and his natural son. There was even a small sum put aside for Brutus.

He read it, top to bottom. Then again.

Then he closed his eyes and pictured Caninius Gallus turning slowly like some child's toy, a bronze stilus jutting from his neck as blood sprayed. He pictured the swathe of bodies outside his front door. And he pictured Octavian looking back at him, showing not a hint of humility, remorse or apology. Just cold certainty.

With a growl, Caesar crossed the room with the will.

He might have to rethink this, he decided, as he held the corner of the document over the guttering lamp, not quite in the flame. To burn it, or not? It was not yet official lodged, and his instinct was to cut Octavian out, though he recognised that his anger might be driving him to unnecessary extremes.

Damn the lad.

ROME. LATE JANUARIUS.

'You are being complacent,' Cassius growled. 'The time to move is now.'

Trebonius shook his head. 'All things come in time, as the gods will, and what the gods will is Caesar's death. We know that now.'

Casca nodded at that. 'Spurinna confirmed it. The gods turn on the despot, clearly, for even the man he brought from Africa to prove his worthiness can prophesy only death. It will happen now. Perhaps we need not even bare a blade.'

'I'd not taken either of you for fools. How blind of me' Cassius said.

'There is no need for insults,' Trebonius snapped. 'Caesar will die. We are free of obligation.'

'No, we are not, you fools. Spurinna speaks for the gods, yes, and he tells us that Caesar will die by the Ides of Martius, but that does not mean we can sit back and cross our arms and wait. It means we must step up plans. There are only two sessions of the senate before he leaves for Parthia, and that will be too late. The second session is out, because it is *on* the Ides of Martius. Clearly that will be too late. But the session before that is in a matter of mere days, and though I cannot see how we can put everything in place in time, do that we must.'

'Why? *Why* must we?' insisted Casca.

'Because it must be us, man. The blow must be struck by us. We play the tyrannicides, and we must do it openly, publicly, with pride and with clarity of action. It must be a blow struck *for* the people, *in front* of the people. That is why we decided upon a senate session, where everyone can witness the tyrant's fall. If we simply wait and trust that the gods will act for us, yes Caesar will die by the Ides of Martius, but it may be from one of his fits that he pretends do not happen. Or it may be some gutter thief's blade. Or an accident. A drowning in the Tiber, or a fall, perhaps. And any of those deaths are the deaths of a normal man. Such a death would take Caesar, but not his legacy. The ideals that he promotes, of one man rule, of an oriental monarchy like the Macedonians, of ultimate power, would not die with him. We could wait for him to die and suddenly find ourselves with a king in the form of Octavian, or Antonius, or even, gods help us, that half Aegyptian bastard. That is why it must be us. He must die by the common will of the republic and its senate, and be seen to do so.'

'We are too few for such an enterprise. Caesar is no fool. He surrounds himself with men even while claiming to have dismissed his guard. Even without his lictors, there are noble men who cleave to him and who have veritable armies to prevent us coming close. Gods, but Decimus Brutus even has a stable of gladiators.'

'Then we must thin his ranks and swell ours,' Cassius said, leaning back.

'I will not kill others,' Casca said, with a shocked expression. 'I agreed to be part of this, because Caesar must be removed. But I am a tyrannicide, not a common murderer. I will not kill noble men like Brutus just because they stand by Caesar.'

Cassius' lip curled. 'I am not suggesting we start murdering senators. With sufficient planning, we can neutralise most of these forces of which you speak. But the prime matter is bringing in more men to our work.'

'More is dangerous,' Trebonius said quietly. 'That is why we kept it small from the start. The bigger a conspiracy becomes, the more danger there is of discovery and failure.'

'We need more,' insisted Cassius, 'for two reasons. Firstly to counterbalance those who would protect him. But more importantly, we need men who are above reproach. We need men who even the most reticent senator respects. Men whose very presence among us grants us legitimacy.'

'Such as?'

'Such as Brutus,' he said, eyeing Trebonius. 'It was you who advocated approaching him.'

'You are mad,' Casca breathed. 'He is Caesar's man. Gods, but is he not actually Caesar's *son*?'

'And yet he is a staunch republican, scion of a line of tyrannicides. And he and Caesar are not currently on the best of terms, from what I understand. And though you lobbied Marcus Antonius back in Narbo in the autumn, I suggest we approach him again. His relationship with Caesar has only become progressively worse since then, and the pair are at odds constantly. Moreover, he knew of the plot and yet he has not revealed it to Caesar. There are plenty of men who might not see Caesar as a would-be monarch, but who can see him as corrupt and dangerous regardless. Such men need to be with us.'

'You are mad if you think you can bring to our side Caesar's closest.'

'Oh I think you will be surprised. Leave it to me.'

The three men took a sip and clacked their cups together. Three expressions of determination now, even if two were tinged with worry.

Tyrannicide.

FEBRUARY

"Not only did he accept excessive honours, such as an uninterrupted consulship, the dictatorship for life, and the censorship of public morals, as well as the forename Imperator, the title Father of his Country, a statue among those of the kings, and a raised couch in the orchestra, but he also allowed honours to be bestowed on him which were too great for mortal man

– Suetonius: Life of Caesar 76.

CHAPTER FIFTEEN

Fronto looked left and right carefully, crossing the street towards the imposing gate in the boundary wall of Caesar's estate. He had twenty armed men with him, let alone the usual senatorial entourage, and his hand rested permanently on the hilt of his favoured hunting knife beneath the folds of his cloak, which protected him from the gentle Februarius drizzle but also hid the military leather tunic he was wearing beneath it.

There had not been an attack on anyone, at least as far as he knew, since the day Salvius Cursor had arrived, exhausted at his house. It seemed that the collegium's claim that there would be no more killings was holding up, though for how long he did not know, and just because they had been told not to kill did not preclude many other forms of trouble. Killing could sometimes be the less disruptive option for a miscreant. The fact that Fronto had not left the house without feeling eyes on him from the shadows made it clear that Caesarians were still under observation, and it would not take much for that to expand again into violence, he was sure.

Indeed, even as his man hammered on the gate, he could feel the malevolent watchers somewhere nearby. Some days he missed the battlefield, if for no other reason that there you could generally see your enemy, identify him and protect yourself. This kind of war was something else, even if it had paused. This was insidious. Difficult. Frustrating.

The gate opened and they moved inside, out of view of the collegium spies.

Caesar's men bowed low and led the way, and as he followed, Fronto wondered briefly what Galronus was up to. Probably at the races, he thought wistfully. Faleria seemed to dote on the man sufficiently to make no complaints that she shared his love

198

apparently on equal terms with the circus. Lucilia, he suspected, would be less accommodating should he keep disappearing to drink wine and watch chariots. Would that he were there now. Fronto had made a habit of spending as much time as possible with Galronus recently, knowing now what the future seemed to hold. But Caesar had sent the request with a specification that it was for Fronto's attendance alone. Curious.

Following the slaves, he climbed that seemingly endless staircase for speed. The winding roadway was much easier, but took at least twice as long, and Fronto suspected he was already late. Arguments with Salvius Cursor had eaten into his journey time, the former tribune, and more importantly Caesar's guard commander, insistent that he should come, and having to be restrained by Masgava and Aurelius so Fronto could leave alone. He turned his face upwards and regretted it. The drizzle was only light, but it was that sort of miscellaneous rain that you barely noticed until you realised you were soaked. By the time he emerged at the top of the stair, on the hill that overlooked the city, an impressive viewpoint, his knee was shaky and aching, his lungs burned, and his breath was coming in gasps. And his cloak was sodden.

He waved his men to stop then, placing his hands on his hips and trying to recover his breath, turning slowly. The city seemed so peaceful and ordered from up here, like some beautiful model. From here you couldn't see the limbless veterans begging, the corpses of stray dogs amid the manure, the thieves and arsonists and murderers and, worse still, politicians.

Turning back, he blinked and paused again.

He wasn't alone after all, despite the invitation.

He recognised Antonius' horse, stamping impatiently, and Hirtius' litter, its bearers looking miserable and soggy, and some of the various slaves and guards gathered there waiting, gradually becoming drenched. Fronto, Antonius and Hirtius? Curiouser still.

Gesturing for his men to join the others, he followed Caesar's slaves in through the door and into the great marble vestibule with its shrine to the household gods, dominated by a beautifully painted statue of Venus Genetrix. Slaves were bustling in the atrium, going about their work, and he spotted Marcus Antonius and Aulus Hirtius standing in the peristyle garden under the shelter of the portico, the light, misty rain drifting down through the air before them. The pair were involved in low conversation, which stopped abruptly at the sound of approaching footsteps, both pairs of eyes darting around, expressions relaxing once more as they recognised Fronto as the owner of the feet. When had even Caesar's house become a place of guarded exchanges?

'Gentlemen.'

'You're late,' Antonius grumbled. 'We've been waiting quarter of an hour.' He didn't look happy, but then he and Caesar had rarely been at ease together recently.

'Nice to see you too,' Fronto smiled. 'I had to unclasp Salvius Cursor from my leg. He was rather insistent.'

Antonius laughed. 'That man must be twitching without a war to fight. Never seen anyone so at home covered in blood. Apart from you, of course.'

Fronto snorted and turned to the other waiting man. Hirtius gave him a nod of greeting.

'What's this about?' he asked.

The two earlier arrivals shrugged, and at that moment a slave hurried over to them, eyes on the gravel, rain saturating his wispy hair. 'If you would follow me, Domini?'

With that, the old man hurried away around the portico, skirting the gardens and allowing them to cross the wide square without stepping out into the rain. They followed together, to the door of Caesar's office, lit by oil lamps from within, the warm glow of a brazier adding to the golden hue. As they stepped inside, slaves offered to take their cloaks, and the three men relinquished the damp garments readily, shaking themselves and adjusting to both the warmth and the gloom of the windowless office.

'Expecting trouble, Fronto?' Hirtius smiled wryly, eying the leather tunic.

'Always,' he replied.

'Probably sensible, given this winter's events,' Antonius added. 'But I always find it chafes under the armpits.'

'Then it's sized wrong,' Fronto replied, recipient of a thousands grazes and bruises from ill-fitting armour in his time.

Smalltalk over, they turned to look at the room's occupant. Caesar was seated behind the desk, leaning back. At the man's slightly wavering gesture, the slaves departed, closing the door behind them, shutting out the cold draft, but lowering the light once more. Three lamps was just about enough to read by, but was hardly bright.

Fronto looked the dictator up and down, and narrowed his eyes.

'When did you last sleep?' he asked.

'I caught a few hours last night,' Caesar said in a soothing tone.

'So what happened? Another attack?'

'I invited you here to pool your opinions.'

'You had another attack,' Fronto insisted. 'A bad one. Not long ago.'

Caesar sighed. 'Yes, I did. Move on, Fronto. We have much to discuss.'

'They're happening a lot,' Fronto persisted. 'Back in Gaul, months at a time would pass, but you're having them every other day now. What does the physician say?'

'He says shut up and pay attention,' Caesar snapped.

Fronto pursed his lips and frowned, but did so, nonetheless. On the table were three vellum documents, each folded neatly, none yet sealed. 'Your will?'

Caesar nodded.

'Three copies?' Antonius said.

'Three *wills*,' Caesar replied, steepling his fingers. 'Until recent events, I was comfortable and confident with what I would do, but now I find myself torn. I have my old will still lodged and witnessed, of course, though it is now hopelessly out of date, referencing men who are no longer with us. I am pressed constantly to produce a *new* will, and I have done so, *more* than once, and each time I am driven to discard it and draw up a new one, only to find that something happens to make its contents less than desirable. Once, I was decisive, sharp. Now I find I need encouragement. Support. Help,' he said finally, looking oddly weak.

The three visitors shared a look.

'Who pressed you, Caesar?' Hirtius asked.

The dictator gave an odd sigh. 'Mothers. Wives. Nephews. It is a subject that seems to arise over every meal now.'

'I was under the impression that you had settled upon Octavian,' Fronto said. 'You've told me more than once that he would be the natural choice.'

Caesar nodded slowly. 'I was under that impression too. Tell me what you think of him. Frankly. Hold nothing back.'

Fronto shrugged. 'He's more dangerous than an army of howling Germans. More dangerous than a plague in a packed camp. He shows no sign of guilt or remorse, or even *regret*, at the most appalling of acts. I suspect Hades himself trembles at the mention of Octavian's name. But he has absolute focus, one of the most intelligent and intuitive minds I have ever come across, and if you are in his camp, then you are safe as can be. He makes me nervous, and I am his *ally*. I would hate to be his enemy.'

He stopped talking and was suddenly aware that Hirtius and Antonius were staring at him in shock. He shrugged. 'He said hold nothing back. I like Octavius, I do, but he's as slippery as an eel and as perilous as a scorpion.'

Caesar gave a low chuckle. 'Gods, Fronto, but were you here somewhere, hidden, watching him the other day?'

Fronto frowned for a moment in incomprehension, then sighed. 'I've been watching him for *years*, Caesar. Ever since he became old enough to wield a knife, or... poison mushrooms. Even last year alone I could not count on one hand the number of important people who died at his command.'

'How does he view *Rome*, do you think?'

'Like a game board, I'd say. I think he views *everything* in life as a game, and he's determined to win it.'

'And if he won Rome?'

That was a worrying concept, as far as Fronto was concerned. He took a deep breath. It would be a lie to say he hadn't thought about it, though. 'I think he would see it as his personal property. I suspect he already does.'

Caesar nodded, and turned to the next man. 'Antonius?'

Marcus Antonius gave Fronto a sidelong look, as though Fronto had taken the best seat at the theatre, and now he was sitting behind someone tall while the world's best comedy went on unseen. 'Frankly, I'm surprised you bother asking me, since you seem to think my opinion counts for naught.' The angers passed quickly, though, and he sighed. 'I would say that Octavian and I have not often seen eye to eye, Caesar. Perhaps I am not the best man to give judgement.'

Fronto winced. That was something of an understatement. Fronto had watched the pair in his own house only a few days ago, and Antonius had looked ready to gut his friend's nephew over their perceived changes in status.

'On the contrary,' Caesar said, 'I would *value* such an opinion. My arguments with you, Antonius are always over your precipitous nature, not your mind or skills.'

'Then I think he is dangerous. More dangerous even than Fronto seems to think. I think he is self-obsessed, focused only on what benefits him, and woe betide anyone who gets in his way. I cannot pretend to be able to predict what that would mean for Rome, should he ever find himself in your position.'

Caesar nodded, moving on, as though all this was not condemning his own flesh and blood. 'Aulus?'

Hirtius looked uncomfortable with the discussion. 'If I were to be frank, Caesar, I would say that I see in him that which I see in you, though perhaps with the additional hunger of youth.'

'Diplomatically put,' Fronto snorted.

Caesar nodded. 'Very well. Octavian *is* clever. And by all the gods he is dangerous, I concur. But I have to base my decision on more than likeability and whether he will be a good successor to me. When I am no more, I will leave a Rome with no strong guidance at the rudder, and I need to be sure who will step into my place.'

Fronto was content with his minor place in the grand scheme of things, but he knew damn well that at least someone in the room saw himself as just such a politician. His eyes skipped past Hirtius and fell on Antonius, just in time to see the fury burn in the man's eyes at being so nonchalantly excluded before Antonius pushed down the anger and adopted a strangely accepting smile.

'And my son?' Caesar said.

'Caesarion?'

'Ptolemy Caesar Philopator,' Caesar corrected. 'I am not sure I like this diminution of his name, which is becoming so common I find myself thinking it now.'

Fronto coughed. 'He's not three years old yet. Certainly not enough to form an opinion of him.'

'But not an opinion of his place in things.'

Fronto glanced at the others. No way was he going first here. Antonius', his lip wrinkling, folded his arms. 'He's a handsome enough boy, and given his parentage he should be sharp enough to cut himself. He may even, in time, be bright enough to give Octavian a run. Any legitimacy you give him, though, will kill any remaining relationship you have with the senate. His mother fosters in him a staunch belief that he is a king by divine right, heir to the great Macedonian, through hundreds of years of rule on the Nile. The senate stand as ever against royalty. The notion of acknowledging a king who is a Roman citizen will be abhorrent among them. I have already warned you as much in relation to other... plans.' He glanced sidelong at Hirtius, for the room's other three occupants were well aware of Caesar's intention to adopt the pharaoh's crown long enough, at least, to defeat Parthia, but with Hirtius unaware, such a thing could not be mentioned.

Hirtius nodded. 'You simply cannot acknowledge him. He is a *foreigner*, the son of a *queen*. He cannot be allowed Roman citizenship, and should you acknowledge him your heir, even in small part, you will drive an unmovable wedge between the senate and yourself.'

Fronto waited until Caesar laid his gaze upon him. 'They said it all,' he shrugged. 'On that, I think we are unanimous. Caesarion is an impossible choice. I might add that his mother is at least as much a danger in herself. She's clever and powerful, and as long as she's in Rome, she becomes an unpredictable piece in any game. You would be best served sending them back to Alexandria now. Perhaps if they are gone from Rome for half a year their presence will have been forgotten enough to allow you to take... the next step.'

There was an odd silence for a moment and all eyes fell upon the table between them.

'The *third* document?' Hirtius noted, frowning. 'Pinarius? Pedius?'

Caesar shook his head. 'Both of them are solid, certainly. Good men, and they will be provided for, just like Calpurnia, but they lack the *imagination*, I fear, to truly push Rome forward, and Rome must move forward lest it stagnate and begin to moulder.'

'So?'

'There is, of course, another who could be adopted into the line, and with good reason.'

There was a thoughtful pause, and Antonius frowned. His eyes narrowed and when he spoke, it was with a suspicious tone. 'If you mean Decimus Brutus, then think again. We all know the rumour, but...'

Caesar spoke then, over the top of him, drowning him out. 'Decimus is alone now. His father died years ago. His mother has been gone for a time. Even his adoptive father, Postumius Albinus, is gone now. It would do him no dishonour to accept adoption into the Julii, and would be far from damaging for us, given the illustrious line of his ancestors. He is a proven general, bright and shrewd, politically sound, loyal to the core. Could any senator argue with Brutus as my heir?'

'And it would put to rest forever the question of his paternity,' Antonius said flatly, a challenge in his tone.

Caesar shot him a dark look, recovering slowly before replying. 'The whole question nags me. Octavian, needless to say, sees himself as the only choice, and his mother Atia badgers me repeatedly, for written confirmation of his succession in the house. I was almost ready to lodge such a will, but Octavian's recent activity gives me pause. He displayed the very brutality of which you all are wary. Cleopatra, of course, lobbies daily for Ptolemy to be given everything I can give him, regardless of the fact that to do so would be divisive at the least. And Calpurnia, on the days she will still talk to me, can see only Brutus as a possibility, despite that he is no relation.' Another meaningful look at Antonius. 'She has never got on well with Atia, and that turns her against Octavian, and there can be little doubt, of course, as to why she will not favour young Ptolemy. Everywhere I turn I find a new opinion. Yet I must lodge a will before I go east, for a man who goes to war without setting a will is a short-sighted man indeed, and the will currently lodged is pointless.'

'There can be little doubt,' Antonius said. 'Despite my fears, you should adopt Brutus. Octavian is too dangerous and Caesarion too divisive.'

'On the contrary,' Hirtius corrected him, 'I feel that Octavian is the *only* choice. He is of your family's blood, legitimate, and acceptable to the senate.'

Caesar looked to Fronto. Damn it. He *liked* Decimus Brutus. The younger man was one of the very best officers, even the best *men*, Fronto had ever served with. But Hirtius was right. Whatever the man might be, Caesar's great nephew was the clear choice.

'Octavian,' he sighed. 'It has to be Octavian. Make provisions for them all, but whoever inherits the lion's share will be a man to guide Rome in due course.' He gave a mirthless laugh. 'Besides, think of the body count that would build up if Octavian were not first in line anyway.'

This time it was Fronto who earned a cold glare from Caesar, but the look soon crumbled. Fronto was right, and Caesar knew it.

'Perhaps a few years of war in the east will tame him,' Antonius grunted.

'I will continue to ponder the matter. As my anger subsides, I find myself favouring Octavian once more, and that appears to be the consensus, but I must think on all the ramifications of my decision. I trust that when the decision is made I can count upon the three of you to take your place among the witnesses of the will?'

'Of course, sir,' Hirtius said swiftly, apparently speaking for all of them.

Caesar gave a curt nod and gathered up the wills from the table into a stack. Fronto could not help but notice the shakiness still afflicting the man's hands as he did so. This latest attack of his sickness must have been appalling.

'I suppose I should apologise for dragging the three of you half way across the city for what turned out to be a quarter of an hour's conversation. You must, of course, stay for a drink and a bite to eat. I put aside two hours of my day for this, and I have just purchased the most exquisite Syrian dancing girl and a Lusitanian dwarf with a divine lyre.'

'Before we go any further,' Antonius said, 'I've been wanting to discuss that business with the crown on your statue.'

Before Caesar could reply, Aulus Hirtius, ever Caesar's ablest administrator, turned to them and spoke. 'That matter is very easily settled. The miscreants who called Caesar's name as king have been exonerated. Their intention was never serious, and any punishment for their deeds would be hugely out of proportion. Similarly, the man we had in custody for the crown who, it turns out, is a baker who was in his shop until just before our arrival and who could not have done the deed and so is clearly innocent. All of them are free. The two tribunes,' a disapproving look cast at Caesar here, 'have been removed from all offices. Other than that they are untouched.'

Fronto snorted. For an ambitious Roman politician, to be removed from the plebeian tribunate and the senate together might as well be being handed a sword and told to throw yourself on it. Their families had probably already disowned them.

'So you see, all is fine,' Hirtius concluded with spread palms.

'No it isn't,' Antonius answered, wagging a finger at Hirtius. 'Fine, if that man *didn't* do it, but were the hecklers interrogated? Do we know who *did* put the crown on the statue if the baker didn't?'

'I believe,' Hirtius said, starting to falter a little and with a momentary glance at Caesar, 'that the true miscreant has been identified as a vagrant. A nobody.'

Fronto had been feeling increasingly irritable as he listened to Hirtius' blatant lies, wondering what the man was covering up for Caesar. This last, though, was too much. 'Bollocks,' he snorted. 'Some impoverished beggar on the streets of Rome managed to fashion a brass circlet with unusual foliage, and snuck it onto a statue, and just for fun? Come on, Aulus, *no one* would believe that.' He turned to Caesar. 'It *was* you, wasn't it?'

The dictator managed to hold an innocent expression, and anyone who hadn't known him for decades would have missed the tells that made a lie of it as he replied easily. 'It would be unthinkable for a man in my position to promote his own image in a regal manner, even just as a ploy to be able to refute it, wouldn't you agree?'

Fronto gave a hollow laugh. 'So it's true. I thought so, you old goat. Antonius here suggested it first, but I didn't really give it credence until I thought back over the years and all the times I've seen you do the unthinkable and get away with it. This one was a bold move. If it had worked, it would have changed everything. It would have countered that business with the seat at the Venus temple that really fucked with your reputation. Even you could see how far that had dragged you down, and you came up with this convoluted damn way to make yourself look good by having people hail you as king, just so you could turn it down and look like a good old republican senator. But it went wrong, didn't it? What should have rebuilt your reputation dragged it further into the mire, and now you're really in the shit. A month or two ago, you wouldn't have given a moment's thought to how choosing an heir would affect your reputation. You'd just have done it, because enough of the senators were yours that the whole bunch would fold in a moment, and the rest of the people loved you, anyway. Now there are enough voices raised against you that you have to consider every move you make.'

He realised something, and stepped back, head tilting. 'I bet that's what's behind your recent increase in attacks too. All the stress and trouble are getting to you. Is it possible that's what's behind you handing over the campaign planning to me in the first place?'

Caesar's expression said it all, and Fronto let out a victorious snort. He couldn't quite decide whether he was pleased that he'd confirmed his suspicions or simply angry at Caesar's blasé cock ups. 'See,' he snapped, 'you can get so twisted at times that you even screw *yourself.*'

'Thank you for that precis,' Caesar said, lip curling, eyes flinty. 'I find that I am suddenly weary after my attack. Perhaps we will save our socialising for another time.'

'That's right. Brush it under the mat again. Can't see it, so it's not a problem. You used to be brighter than that, Caesar.'

'And you used to be considerably more polite.'

Fronto could feel the anger building, and he let it come, relishing it. It had been a while since he'd been properly angry, and sometimes he needed that release, in place of the exhilaration of battle. 'It's true. Spurinna gives you a very finite lifespan and you blithely ignore it and go on as though nothing's changed...'

'Fronto...'

'And your serious miscalculation with the crown on the statue? Well between that and you staying seated to meet the consuls, you've done possibly irreparable damage to your own reputation...'

'Fronto...'

'And now you're planning to leave the city in a month or so and by the end of the year you'll be sitting in Alexandria and wearing a crown. And what have you done to pave the way for that so that the people don't disown you? Nothing.'

'Fronto...'

'And all those around you who you could be bringing to your side, you're pushing away. Cassius could be bought over with a command in Parthia. So could Antonius here. Shit knows what he thinks about your plans for the consulship.'

'FRONTO!'

Caesar's fury finally tore through the room and silenced him. Fronto was breathing heavily now, trembling slightly, and feeling much better for it. He did know, through the fog of anger, that what he'd just said was stupid. That shouldn't have slipped out, but still...

'*What* plans for the consulship?' Antonius said quietly into the silence that followed.

Caesar threw the most furious glare at Fronto, then turned to Antonius. 'I may have to make changes later in the year. Needless to say, if you are inconvenienced, you will be compensated in every way possible.'

'Except a military command,' Antonius replied in leaden tones. 'Or appointment as your magister equitum. Or anything of real value.'

Caesar looked frustrated, then turned to Fronto. 'Get out.'

'Gladly,' Fronto snapped, and turned, marching from the room.

Hirtius glanced in a worried manner at the other men in the room, as Antonius and Caesar glared at one another for a moment before the former turned on his heel and marched from the room behind the departing senator.

'Fronto,' Antonius called as he caught up at the front door. The rain had stopped and the clouds were clearing, leaving a clear, cold, blue sky.

'Fuck him.'

'What did you mean by the consulship thing?'

Fronto paused for a moment, then started to march on again. What difference did it make? Antonius was going to find out sooner or later. 'Caesar promised me your consulship after Martius when he leaves.'

Antonius stared. 'That was already planned? You knew?'

'I had hoped that I could persuade him that that would free you up to take command in Parthia,' Fronto replied, still angry, and plucking untruths from the air with wild abandon. In truth he'd not really thought on it at all. '*You* should be leading the army, not Caesar. *I* know that. *You* know that. Even *he* knows that. He's losing his touch, Antonius. A decade ago, he'd have had answers to all these problems before they arose. Now he's scrabbling around for solutions and pretending the problems don't exist. I didn't really believe Spurinna's prediction, but the longer we go on, the more I come to feel the truth of it. I think he's heading for a monumental fall.'

'He's lucky to still have friends like us,' the man said, climbing into the saddle and kicking his mount on as the whole double entourage began to descend the hill.

Fronto snorted. 'I'm not sure he ever had friends. Just more and less useful tools.'

'We are his friends,' Antonius insisted. 'Even if the man pisses me off at every turn, I'm his friend. And I will make him pay me back for this insult, but in order to do so, he has to be alive. Fronto, what are we going to do to save him?'

'Fuck him,' Fronto said again, though despite his anger, he wasn't quite so sure where it needed to be aimed. He sighed as Antonius rode beside him. 'Is there a solution? Pray really hard. Or find every man who stands against him and put a blade in each of them.'

'Would that we could,' Antonius agreed.

They hardly spoke for the rest of the descent, nor as they moved out of the estate and into the street, though Fronto found himself seething, listing Caesar's enemies and wondering how they could be neutralised. He could feel that anger tumultuous inside him, swirling and directionless, tinged with additional frustration at his inability to do anything useful. Rome was becoming chaos and violence, and Fronto simply drifted through it these days. As they moved through the streets, the populace stayed back in the archways and pressed themselves against the walls as the large, lightly-armed party passed, but here and there Fronto could see someone watching them with less than adorating looks. Each alone and unobtrusive, unless you knew they would be there. Collegium men.

As they crossed the Aemilian Bridge, his roving eyes picked out a figure sitting on the parapet. The man was watching him just like the others had been, though there was something about this man that singularly pissed Fronto off, particularly right now, when his anger was a formless, directionless thing looking for a target. As soon as their eyes met, the watcher's gaze dropped to the ground, but moments later he looked again to see if Fronto was still watching. He was.

'Stay here,' Fronto said to the others, and stepped out of the group, raising a warning look from Antonius that he promptly ignored. He stomped over to the bridge parapet, where the man sitting watching suddenly looked rather startled, his head whipping this way and that nervously.

'Why are you watching us?'

'Sorry?'

Fronto reached up and grabbed the man's tunic below the throat, bunching it in his fist. If he'd needed any confirmation that the man was one of the Pompeian veterans, he received it as the tunic sleeve pulled upwards and the tattoo was revealed.

'You and your lot. You're not attacking anyone at the moment, but you're still watching us all. I told your leader in your own house that if I had cause to come after you, you'd all regret it. So

211

tell me now. Tell me why you're watching us, and tell me who's paying you to do it.'

The man's expression moved one step towards panic as he shook his head. 'I don't know what you're talking about.'

'Oh?' Fronto suddenly pushed his hand out and the man found himself leaning back over a twenty foot drop into the fast, murky winter waters below. 'Know how many bodies wash up on the Tiber's banks every day?' he grinned, noting the man's panic. 'No, neither do I. But it's a lot, and we both know that. *Tell* me.'

'Just orders. To watch and report back,' the man gasped. 'Don't know anything else.'

'I don't believe you,' Fronto snarled, and let go for just a moment before grabbing the man again and stopping his fall. Whimpering with fear, the man suddenly looked up past Fronto's shoulder, and a strong hand came from one side, gripped him and pulled him back to safety. Fronto turned, angry, to see Antonius beside him.

'You're going too far, Fronto. Senators don't go around murdering people, no matter what the reason.'

Fronto glared at Antonius for a moment, and then let go of the man's tunic. For a moment he almost fell, before Antonius grabbed him with a second hand and pulled him to safety. Fronto was already walking away.

'Fronto?'

'No. This has got to stop. Once and for all.'

And he was moving with purpose, the strength of Mars in his veins. His anger had found a target.

CHAPTER SIXTEEN

Antonius had to move at a fast trot to catch up, such was Fronto's purposeful stride. The guards marching alongside their master allowed the horseman to come close, given who it was, and Fronto looked up only briefly at him and then set his sights ahead and marched on.

'What are you going to do, Fronto?'

'I'm going to sort this out.'

'What? And how?'

Fronto turned again to look at the man on the horse. 'There is so little I can make a difference with now. I'm a senator, just one voice among hundreds, and even those are powerless in the face of the dictatorship. And I can't stop Spurinna's prediction, can I? And I can't do anything to persuade Caesar to stop what he's doing. I can't change him. Or Octavian. Or Cleopatra. But there is just one thing I *can* do.'

'Oh?'

'I'm a soldier, Antonius, always have been, and whatever I wear, I always will be. If there's something I know anything about, it's war. And Rome is at war. People keep saying as much. There's war in the streets, but I can end it.'

Antonius shook his head. 'There's *peace*, Fronto. Remember that. The collegium has said there will be no more killings.'

'For now. But it doesn't mean there's be no more fighting or trouble. Just no deliberate assassinations. And even then, the peace is only temporary. The Pompeians want their old enemies to pay for their victory, and only the order of their new paymaster is stopping the killings. Well I want to know who that is, and I want the Pompeian Collegium powerless. And if I have to ram a sword through every last bastard there to do it, that's exactly what I'm going to do.'

'Fronto, you decry war in the streets, and here you are *planning* it. You're going too far. You'll start something terrible.'

'No. I'll *end* it. That's what I do. I win wars.'

He continued to march, that same determination in his step.

'You can't do this, Fronto.'

'Watch me.'

'It'll be like Sulla's bloodbath all over again.'

'You were always a warhorse, Antonius. I'm surprised you're not *joining* me.'

'This isn't a battlefield, Fronto. This is Rome. I'll have no part in killing Romans in the street.'

'Then get out of my way.'

'And what happens when you find out who's running them? Will you march into one of the big houses of Rome and gut a senator?'

'It's all connected, Antonius. The whole city's heard the rumours that there's a plot brewing to kill Caesar. I think we've all expected it for a while. The collegium focused on Caesar's officers and his guards. Do you not think there's a good chance that whoever is paying them is involved in that plot? If these bastards want to live, they give up their master to me, and then I'll leave them alone. If not, I'll leave them in pieces.'

Antonius winced. 'Turn back.'

'No.'

'Then I'll have no part of this. I shall return to Caesar and explain what's happening. You can be *his* problem.'

'Fine.'

Antonius threw him a last disapproving look and veered off, turning back to meet with his own entourage. Peace or no peace, it was still too dangerous in the streets to move about unprotected. Fronto turned to the head of his guards. 'Take two men back to the house. Gather everyone you can, armed for the pomerium, but leave a dozen to protect the house. On the way, get a message to the Caesarian collegium and have them muster in the square by the stream north of the Velia. We'll meet you there.'

The man nodded and gestured to a couple of the others, turning and jogging off at speed.

Fronto marched on. His mind was whirling. What was he doing? Was it stupid? Dangerous? The simple fact was that *something* had to change. He'd offered the collegium a very good deal, offered to see them receive restitution through the senate, but they'd shunned it. They had killed innocent veterans and attacked Rome's brightest and best in the streets, and innocents, too, like Catháin. Whoever was paying them right now had apparently instituted a rule that no more Caesarians were to be killed, but they were still to be watched and their movements noted, and that suggested an escalation was possible at any time. It also meant that the killings were likely far from over. This was a lull. Whoever was paying them was surely someone intent on bringing down Caesar. And Spurinna had set the great man's death date by the ides of next month. That was just a little more than thirty days away, and it seemed hard to believe that Caesar's demise would not be linked to those who plotted against him, and therefore to the collegium. It was, as he'd pointed out to Antonius, all connected. It had to be. He would make one last demand of the collegium, and if it was refused, he would *force* the name from them.

His strategic brain reminded him that even if he mustered everyone he could, the odds were still tipped numerically in the enemy's favour. But then the enemy were spread out across the city watching Caesar's close friends and allies, so there would be a limited number of them in their meeting house.

By the time he reached the square beyond the Velia, his blood had cooled a little, but his resolve was as strong as ever. With less anger had come more focus. At the square, he set the small number of men he had with him in position, watching all the approaches, and waited.

It didn't take long for the first arrivals. Galronus, Masgava, Arcadios and Aurelius had all ridden for speed and dismounted in the square, handing the reins to one of the worried-looking slaves that had been wandering along in Fronto's wake, unsure what to do.

'You seriously intend to go up against the collegium?' Galronus said, face full of concern.

'I want their paymaster. I want to know who it is. If they give him up, we'll walk away, but I'm prepared to beat it out of them if

I have to. I'm not walking away today unless I have their paymaster's name, or their member list is empty.'

'I know it's not my place to say,' Aurelius added, 'but you do realise this could cause huge trouble, whether we succeed or not?'

Fronto nodded. He did. But sometimes you had to take the risk if there was to be any hope.

'Then what's the plan?'

Fronto scratched his chin. 'We go there, we knock on the door. When they open it, we rush in and beat the living shit out of every Pompeian veteran we find until someone gives us a name. I don't like complicated plans.'

'Well it's not complicated, certainly,' Masgava said. 'Almost *stupidly* simple, you might say.'

'What about numbers?' Galronus asked.

'Don't know. I reckon they'll be down to about one hundred and eighty men, if they can pull in the whole membership. But Salvius said they had links with other collegia now, so that could put huge numbers against us.'

'Fabulous. And *our* numbers?'

'About a hundred and fifty, between all the men that can be spared from home, and the Caesarian collegium.'

Aurelius pulled a face, suggesting he was not at all fond of the odds. They stood in silence, each contemplating what was to come, until the sound of an approaching gang cut through the general murmur of life in the square. The ordinary people, who had been going about their business with the occasional interested glance at Fronto and his men, now melted away into doors and side alleys as the rest of Fronto's household guards arrived, each carrying a knife that was just short enough to get away with inside the pomerium, or a stout cudgel. At their head strode Salvius Cursor.

'Are you well enough for this?' Fronto asked, a formality, since he knew what the answer would be.

'I'll be wearing one of the bastards for a coat by nightfall,' Salvius answered with a belligerent sneer.

'Alright. But we're not all here yet, so settled down. We wait, still, for the others.'

And they did. Time passed, and after perhaps half an hour, Fronto was starting to wonder whether the others would be coming at all. In fact, his ire was continuing to cool, and he was beginning to wonder whether this was a good idea after all, when scores of Caesar's veterans stomped out of a side street, armed and ready, and joined the growing ranks in the square. Carbo was there, leading them, his pink shiny pate almost glowing in the winter sunshine. His expression was troubled as he approached Fronto.

'I don't like this,' he said.

Fronto fought the growing urge to back down. 'Something needs to be done.'

'We could lose our legal status for fighting in the streets.'

'Then why did you come?' Fronto snapped, his irritation starting to build again.

'Because we put it to a house vote and the lads were not far off unanimous. I don't think they care what legal ramifications this has. Enough of our lads had been taken out in the streets now that the rest want revenge. They've been ready to level the enemy meeting house for a month. You've just given them the excuse. But I don't like it, Fronto. It's dangerous.'

'Then stay here.'

Carbo glared at him. 'I don't mean the fighting is dangerous. I mean it's dangerous to even consider this.'

'I know. It still needs to be done, though.'

Before anyone could argue further, Fronto waved his arm at the gathered force. 'Come on.'

The army, roughly one hundred and fifty strong, surged forward with Fronto at the head. As he moved into the narrower streets of the Subura, the tall insulae crowding in around him, his officers moved to his side, forming the front of the force. The street gangs of Rome may be largely disorderly mobs, but this one moved with an almost military precision, nearly in formation, for few among them had not served in the legions, and most of them with Fronto, in fact.

Carbo, former primus pilus and a man with whom Fronto had stormed many a fortification. Galronus, who had been with him on every battlefield for over a decade now. Aurelius, Arcadios and Masgava, who had protected Fronto and his household for that same decade, who had marched into enemy territory with him, hunting renegade Gallic kings. Salvius, the blood-crazed lunatic who he'd spent so long hating that he hadn't realised how much he actually liked. The streets ahead of them cleared as the denizens of this dangerous region melted out of the way, and in no time at all they were at the Clivus Suburanus, beginning to climb the road that led up the slope of the Esquiline Hill.

Side streets passed with monotony as they marched, all purpose, but the surprise came when the street curved with the slope of the hill, turning eastwards towards the old, crumbling city gate.

The way ahead was thronged.

Fronto held up a hand and his men halted. His mind whirled. This was unexpected. He'd planned on marching to their meeting house, bursting in and battering everyone he met until someone told him who was paying them. To find them blocking the street in huge numbers some way from their house was something of a shock. It shouldn't have been, of course, and he kicked himself as he realised why. They'd been watching the Caesarians for days. Fronto had spent a while near the Velia gathering his force, and any one of the bastards watching him or his people would have known what was happening in plenty of time to get a message to the Pompeians and for them to start their own muster in response.

'Shit,' Aurelius said quietly.

'We could still walk away,' Carbo reminded them.

Fronto nodded. He was starting to think that might be a rather good idea. There were clearly more than twice as many of them as of Fronto's own men. Of course, his men would be better, but would it be enough? The decision, however, clearly wasn't his to make, for even as he considered whether to give the order to fall back, he heard three blasts of a centurion's whistle up the street ahead and, with a roar, the Pompeian collegium and their allies surged down the street like a tidal wave, racing towards Fronto's force with daggers and clubs raised ready.

'You can still go,' Fronto said to Carbo, but one glance at the former centurion told him that the man was in no mood to back away now. In the face of enemy belligerence, his training had taken hold. He was already throwing out pointed fingers, telling his men what to do, then he turned to Fronto. 'When this reaches the courts, *they* started it. We were only defending ourselves. There will be hundreds of witnesses.'

Fronto nodded at the logic, although he knew the people of the Roman streets. He doubted they'd find any single voice who would stand up in public and admit what they'd seen. Keeping quiet was the way to avoid making enemies in the poor streets.

It almost made him smile to see how his men were reacting. Carbo had dropped straight back into his centurionate mindset, assuming that every man in the gathering was his to command. And they were obeying, as though they were in chain shirts and gripping shields and pila, watching a horde of Belgae racing towards them. Such was the life of the soldier that even years into retirement, it only took that bellow of command from an authoritative voice, and they were forming into lines, men armed in one fashion interspersing with men armed other ways, so that blades and clubs were more or less evenly placed across the street.

'Back, Fronto,' Carbo said, and again, such was the tone of voice that Fronto almost obeyed automatically without thinking. But he resisted, and shook his head.

'I'm not your legate now. My place isn't at the back.'

'It never was, if I remember right,' Aurelius grinned.

'But now you're a senator,' Salvius added. 'Your place isn't here at all.' But that was little more than a jibe. Salvius shouldn't be here either, and there would be no dragging *him* away from the fray.

Fronto had no intention of moving, now. He'd been wavering, before. It had been an odd day. He'd started calm, and even upbeat, but then that visit to Caesar had got him angry, and the ire had risen and risen ever since, until the army was gathered and moving. Then he'd begun to worry, and waver.

But now, all doubt and confusion had gone. He was precisely where he was supposed to be, where his very soul cried out to be. Since the day he'd left Hispania and returned to Rome, he'd been craving it, no matter what he said. One last fight. One really big fight. No arguments or devious senators, no mysterious assassins or political chicanery. Just him with a pointy blade and a screaming, angry enemy, running at him, full-pelt.

It felt almost glorious. He experienced the adrenaline surge, eyed the figures pounding towards him. There were half a dozen men there who were clearly leaders of some sort, either from the

Pompeian collegium or one of their allied mobs. But there was one man, almost opposite him, that he recognised. He'd stood before the man in their house and delivered an ultimatum when all this had begun. 'I will end you all,' he'd said. 'That is a promise.'

Time to deliver on his promise.

'See the tall bastard with the blond hair and the green tunic?' he said, looking left and right.

The others nodded or murmured their acknowledgement.

'He's mine.'

Again, that murmur. Fronto sized the man up, clearer with every step and now only twenty paces away. He was a good foot taller than Fronto, and wider in the shoulder, too. But he also carried more weight around his midriff, while Fronto, thanks largely to Masgava's ongoing exercise regime, carried little extra fat at all. He would be slower, Fronto decided, for all his extra size. Each pounding step showed a favouring of the left leg, though was his right hand that held a knife not a lot different from Fronto's. A leftie, Fronto suspected. He showed every evidence of being right handed, because the legions had trained him that way, but his leading favoured leg gave the game away. Fronto adjusted his thinking to counteract that difference. The man was clean-shaven, but in need of a haircut. His belt still had the leather strops of a cingulum, but missing the metal décor and looking old and of poor quality.

Fronto set himself ready. Carbo was right, even if there would be no witnesses willing to tell a court what they had seen. Letting them charge gave Fronto and his men the legal and moral high ground, even if the enemy held it physically. There should be less comeback on them.

Ten paces.

Five paces.

The man brought his right hand up to shoulder height, grip tight on the knife hilt. Fronto watched the left, just as carefully, which seemed innocuously held down at belt level. The man hit him hard and struck instantly. Fronto reacted, partly through instinct, but partly with his careful preparation for the enemy he faced. The man's right hand came out, turning sideways, the blade levelled and aimed for Fronto's throat, where it could cut and then slice, opening his windpipe in a single blow. But Fronto was ready, and his left arm came up at the same time, inside the blow, knocking the knife aside. His own hand may be empty, and the other man's his weapon hand, but it was also his weaker hand, for all his years of retraining, and Fronto had the edge, pushing that blade out of reach with relative ease. At the same time, the man struck with his left, a move that may have caught out most opponents, had they not recognised the danger in advance. As the hand lunged into a stomach punch, Fronto's blade scythed down and slashed across the back of his wrist.

The man cried out as he hit Fronto, his dagger out to one side, harmless, his left hand now injured and welling up with blood. Fronto's knife was the nastiest he'd thought he could get away with inside the pomerium, slightly curved and with one serrated edge. As his assailant floundered, his wrist in agony, Fronto struck again. Rather than trying to resist the charging man's momentum, he turned with the barge, allowing the man to fall past him. As the man tried to recover his balance, bellowing fury, Fronto spun and lanced out with his knife, this time using the inner, serrated side. He managed to get it inside the elbow of the man's extended knife arm, slapped it against the flesh and pulled down, hard.

As the enemy fell into the men behind Fronto, the blade tore through the tendons inside his elbow, making his arm utterly useless. The dagger fell from suddenly lifeless fingers.

But Fronto wasn't done, even though the man probably was. The ex-soldier behind the man was just lifting a club to smash it down on the injured leader's head, and Fronto knocked it aside, shaking his head. He reached to the howling, stricken enemy and hauled him back up with some difficulty, until they were eye-to-eye, the Pompeian shaking wildly, eyes wide.

'Who is paying you?'

'Piss off,' the man said, then spat at him. Fronto was jostled for a moment as the fighting knocked him from behind, but then other men swarmed around him, the fight intensifying, keeping the other enemies off his back. Fronto gave the nastiest grin he could muster, let go of the man now and pushed his thumb into his deeply-slashed wrist. He screamed again.

'Who's paying you?'

221

'No one.'

'That's not true,' Fronto smiled, and punched him in the ruined elbow. The man almost collapsed, then, but a helpful soldier behind grabbed him and held him up. Fronto brought his other hand up, displaying the horrible knife, dripping crimson. 'Maybe you'd like to reconsider your answer.'

The man had been brave, Fronto had to admit. Many men, even ex-soldiers, would already be ready to sell out their own mother with damage like this, yet the man had done well. He'd taken all he could now, though. Every man has a breaking point, and the stone cold realisation that Fronto was entirely capable of using that knife again and again had snapped his final resistance.

'He's called the horseman.'

'What?'

'That's all I know.'

'Bollocks,' Fronto snarled.

'It's true. Everything's done through middle-men, and we don't know their names either. Never the same one twice.'

'So how do you get in touch with him?' Fronto snorted.

'We don't. He gets in touch with us.'

Fronto looked deep into the man's eyes. Just for good measure, he pressed on that cut again, to be sure, but even as the man yelped he could see no reticence or defiance in the man's eyes. He was telling the truth. He didn't know who the paymaster was.

He stepped away, not sure what to do with the man, now. He'd assumed at least there was a name to learn. To realise now that this was as far as he was going to get was incredibly frustrating. And he was comfortable that if this man didn't know, then neither did anyone here. As the struggle surged on around him, Fronto let himself be slowly moved towards the rear, where there was no fighting.

They didn't know who their paymaster was, and with a different middle-man each time, never with a name, there would be no trail to follow, unless he happened to be there the next time such a message was brought. The horseman. That suggested a member of the equestrian class, which made sense. He would probably be a senator, then, and would certainly be able to afford to run such a gang, given that equestrians had to own property alone worth fifty thousand denarii.

He was on the verge of a new plan when the fighting stopped. He'd reasoned that the Pompeians must receive regular payments from their benefactor, and that trail should be easier to follow. He just had to have someone watch the meeting house for any deliveries and follow the visitor. Large amounts of coin would probably have to come by cart, and carts were illegal in the streets during daylight hours, so the deliveries would be at night. A plan was forming.

Then everything stopped. The sound of a military horn was blaring out over the brawl in the streets, and both sides were reacting to the call, decades of military experience making it automatic. The two sides were pulling apart now, leaving scores of bodies in the street, some moving, some not, along with a veritable lake of blood.

Fronto pushed his way to the fore to see that two men with horns were standing at the side of the street. Behind them were a number of lictors in white with their bundles of sticks in arms, and between them stood Marcus Antonius, a look of absolute fury on his face. Once the fighting had ended and the only sounds to be heard atop the hum of city life were the groans and cries of the wounded, Antonius took a couple of steps forward.

'By order of Gaius Julius Caesar, Consul with Dictatorial powers, and myself, Marcus Antonius, Consul of Rome, you are hereby ordered to cease this fracas immediately, under threat of prosecution. Further action is to be taken against you all in light of this appalling behaviour, but until such time as that has been ratified in the senate, you will gather your dead and wounded and return to your houses.'

Fronto stood there, breathing heavily in the aftermath of the fight, watching Antonius. He'd seen the man angry plenty of times, for Antonius was never one to hide his emotions, but he'd rarely seen him as furious as this. And, clearly, he had warned Caesar.

Carbo appeared, nursing an arm with a red line along it, his expression worried. Perhaps the centurion had been right from the start? With just one apologetic look at Fronto, he called for the men of the Caesarian Collegium, and they began to gather the

223

fallen. The enemy were doing the same, and a number of small scuffles and shoving matches occurred as the two sides met again among the bodies, though each time a barked demand from Antonius put a stop to it. Before long, the street was clear, if soaked with blood, and the two sides were departing, heading back to their meeting houses with faces lowered, silent and worried.

Fronto was hardly surprised when Salvius Cursor appeared by his side, so covered in blood he might as well have been swimming in it.

'I found out nothing,' the man spat irritably.

'I fared a little better, though not enough.'

'Walk with me,' Antonius called, pointing at Fronto.

He edged round the worst of the mess, his diminished force falling in and grouping together, consisting now solely of men from his own house. Antonius' expression was cold as the two men met, and Antonius started striding down the slope without waiting for Fronto to follow.

'I made progress,' Fronto said, defensively, falling into step and trying to throw out a positive to start with.

'Oh?'

'They don't know their own benefactor, but I think he's one of the equites.'

Antonius snorted. 'Do you have any idea how many equestrians there are in Rome.'

Fronto nodded. 'But it's a step forward.'

'With an unacceptable level of violence. I warned you, Fronto, that this was not the way. War in the street is not to be permitted. There will be repercussions.'

'Like what?'

'Caesar is disbanding the collegia.'

Fronto blinked, stopping in his tracks. Antonius did likewise and turned to him.

'He's doing what?'

'Disbanding them. If they are being used as mob armies by criminals, then they are no longer to be tolerated. Oh, some will remain. The oldest ones. The priesthoods and the like. But regional, military and civic collegia will be illegal. He's already writing up the new edicts for presentation to the senate, and that's a formality. He is the dictator, after all.'

Fronto bit into his lip. At first listen, that sounded like a great thing. With the collegia disbanded and illegal, the bastards that had been facing them would be gone. Even if they remained a tight-knit group, they would lose all their legal status, and any wrongdoing could be prosecuted on an individual level. But there were two problems. Firstly, that meant Carbo's veterans were out of their club, too, which would not go down well, and would likely come back to bite Fronto. And secondly, he was as close as ever to learning who was behind the gathering force, which was probably set against Caesar, but with the disbanding of the collegia, that whole avenue of investigation was gone, and he would never find out.

Damn it. It seemed he had interfered with his own plan by accident.

'I think I need a drink,' he grunted.

'I thought you'd never ask,' Antonius said with a relieved smile.

CHAPTER SEVENTEEN

Galronus moved the last stone into place. The game was won. He'd surrounded the last piece on young Marcus's team, but he had to admit that it was, at least, a challenging game. He'd found that, although Latrunculi was a game of Roman invention, precious few Romans could play it worth a damn, and he had to have been drinking all day for Fronto even to stand a chance. That the man's eight year old son might be a genius and far outstripped his father made Galronus smile.

'You almost had me.'

'That's rather patronising, Uncle,' Marcus replied. 'Not once did I have you cornered.'

'No. But you gave me a challenge. And twice you could have turned it all to your advantage. You're better than your father.'

Marcus gave him a look that suggested this was not a difficult thing.

'Next time, archery.'

'But I don't use a bow,' Galronus frowned.

'Exactly.' With that, Marcus Falerius rose, rounded the table, hugged his 'uncle', and then left the room. Galronus watched him go with a smile. He knew that the Romans added names based on habits and physical characteristics, and given the lad's abilities at games, he wondered whether Marcus Falerius Ludus was a good name.

He leaned back and sighed. He would miss this, and the boys. And he would miss Fronto. But things had changed. Everything that had happened in the whirlwind decade since Caesar had marched into Belgae lands had sort of dragged him along with it until now. He'd taken an oath and his horse and sword and ridden out with the Remi to aid Caesar, never thinking for a moment that would be more or less the last he would see of his home for so

226

many years. And even though Fronto had repeatedly talked of retirement these past few seasons, Galronus hadn't really given it thought, concentrating instead on what they were doing as the civil wars took them this way and that across the republic and beyond.

But all that was over. Caesar didn't really need Galronus any more. He didn't need a Remi rider in his army, and he didn't need him in the senate now to direct matters, either. And now that Galronus was of no real use to Caesar, the man had seemingly all but forgotten about him, which had left the Remi directionless and forced him to think of his future for the first time in years.

The more he'd thought about it, the more he realised that he missed home. Of course, there was more to life than just him to consider. There was Faleria the younger, Fronto's sister and his own beloved, for a start. So he'd sat down with her one night not long after the return to Rome, and talked it through. He'd expected her to fly at him, to rant about the advantages of Rome and life in the republic's heart, of her family and so on. She had surprised him by nodding earnestly and laying it out bare.

'Marcus has his own family now,' she'd said. 'And when he finally cuts that tie with Caesar, he will not stay in Rome. He will go to Puteoli, or to Tarragona. And unless you feel like retiring to the seaside, we will be left here, you and I. Rome is not what it once was. It is changing. It has become dangerous to walk the streets, and simply trying to make a difference makes a man a target. Perhaps what is happening with Caesar's increasing autocracy will improve things, or perhaps it will make things worse. Either way, I am as done with Rome as Marcus is. And you and I are bound now. Where you go, I go. You speak of your home like a lost love, with reverence and beauty. I have never seen such a place. Have never felt that call. Perhaps it is time I did.'

'Durocortorum is not Rome, though,' he'd replied. 'There are no theatres, fountains, arches and basilicae.'

'Is there bread and wine? Are there roofs and walls? Is there water and earth? Galronus, you may think Romans soft, but remember we are bred from farming stock, and no matter how far we have come since those days, the earth is still in our blood. We still value that. If we can eat, we can live. And the gods will still watch us there as they do here. Besides,' she added with a sly look at him, 'it won't be long before Durocortorum has a circus, I'm sure, when a Remi son moves back there with a senator's wage.'

That had made him laugh. They had talked about it the rest of the night, and by the end his mind had been made up. He would go home, and she would go with him, and where he had left a Remi town he would return to make it a haven befitting her. But he was determined that they would make a trip to see Fronto and family at least every year. At *least*.

He gathered the coloured stones from the game board and slipped them back into the bag, pulling the string tight and returning it to the table. Turning he looked out of the door once again into the colonnaded peristyle garden. It was a beautiful place, designed by Lucilia, who had an eye for such things. It was tasteful and understated, given what most Roman houses were like in Galronus' opinion. He would perhaps be the man to bring the peristyle to Durocortorum. Tastefully.

He couldn't decide whether there was the slightest mist of rain out there. The world was a pale grey and the temperature chilly enough to frost the breath. If it did precipitate, it might just as easily be sleet or snow as rain. He smiled to himself as he heard, across the gentle murmur of the house, the distinctive sound of Fronto mollifying Lucilia. His friend's voice apologetic, and low, hers as frosty as the weather. What had he done this time, Galronus wondered with a grin.

Then there was another sound. A knock at the door, the hammering of the knocker forceful and repetitive. The gentle argument across the house ended abruptly and there came the muffled sounds of the doorman interrogating a visitor. The new voice sounded familiar, though Galronus couldn't quite place it out of context. Rising, he crossed the room and then the peristyle, making for the atrium and the front door. The rain was little more than a gentle mist.

As he reached the vestibule, Fronto was already ahead and waiting while the doorman and a slave ushered the visitor inside. Of course, Galronus realised, now placing the voice. The bald, stocky figure of Carbo, former centurion and friend and ally. Carbo looked worried.

Fronto gestured for their old friend to follow and strode towards his office. As he turned and spotted Galronus, he nodded, and so the Remi followed on, entering the room with the pair, and then closing the door behind them.

'I think I can guess,' said Fronto.

Carbo, nodding seriously, fell into that traditional centurion's pose, legs slightly apart, shoulders back, hands behind him, where they would normally be gripping his vine stick.

'The law has been passed, Fronto. Collegia have been made illegal without senatorial approval, and ours, like most, has been disbanded. Our meeting house has been claimed as public property, we've lost our legal representatives, and certain tax benefits. Most of all, we've lost the security of having each other's back. We were warned by the senate's representative that any attempt to gather in a like manner would be taken as a recreation of the collegium, in defiance with the law, so we cannot even form any other kind of brotherhood.'

'And your lads sent you, because you're their leader, but also because you know me.'

Carbo shook his head. 'The lads didn't send me at all. They can't, remember? They can't gather together, so there's no way for them to make such a decision. But the ones I've spoken to were not asking for anything. They got themselves into this. They came with you because they wanted revenge, not because you asked them, or paid them. No one holds you accountable.'

Fronto's face was troubled, and Galronus knew his friend felt a little relief there, but also a healthy dose of guilt. Whatever Carbo might say, they all knew that Fronto had been the driving force, as usual.

'Then why are you here?' Galronus asked.

Carbo turned to look at him, then back to Fronto. 'Just because the lads won't ask for something doesn't mean they don't need it. I'm fine. I have the pension of a centurion and camp prefect. In fact, I own a town house and two country estates. I don't need anything. And others among us have an adequate pension or are making sufficient money in our own businesses. But a lot of the lads are men whose legion was stood down after the wars and they were decommissioned early. They don't have the small fortune I have, and many are either manual labourers for little pay or just reliant on the grain dole. And now this new law has stripped them of financial and legal security, and that's already causing trouble. It's been a single day since the law was passed, and already former Pompeians are dragging our lads into court cases over the street fight and the deaths and injuries. Somehow they still seem to have sufficient money to hire high quality lawyers, while my lads are scrabbling around. We're a target still, and we're suffering.'

Fronto huffed. 'What to do? They can't band together, and I can't just go around hiring lawyers for people individually.'

Galronus frowned. 'Why not? It strikes me that that's exactly what the man paying the other collegium is doing.'

Fronto turned to him. 'True.'

'Though I think you have an opportunity here.'

'Oh?' Now Fronto and Carbo both turned to him.

'No matter the law, the Pompeians must still be in touch with each other, and the man paying them must still be in contact with them. If they can flaunt the rules so blatantly, then we can. And a bit more subtly.'

'Go on.'

'You were paying them a stipend to come to our aid when we needed them. And you pay your own guards to be there all the time. Why not just hire the collegium members into your household?'

Fronto leaned back. 'Because that would cost a fortune.'

'You've *got* a fortune.'

'Not for long, if I hire a hundred and fifty extra men. Lucilia would go mad.'

'Lucilia is the daughter of a legate. She understands soldiers better than you think,' Galronus said. 'Yes, it will cost more to hire them directly and to pay their court costs and so on. But you'll have them with you here all the time, which is far better.'

Carbo nodded. 'And it's not a hundred and fifty, Fronto. Not all the lads are in such a state, remember? Many have jobs or pensions. It's maybe fifty or so who are in dire straits now.'

'That's a bit more feasible.'

Galronus shrugged. 'I'll share the cost.'

Fronto looked across at him. 'I think you need to ask Faleria first. I know I'll need to ask Lucilia.'

'Faleria would agree with me. And so will Lucilia.'

Still the house's owner chewed on his lip, deep in thought. Finally, he straightened again. 'Alright. Make the offer to every one of them. Twenty denarii a month. That's slightly over the pay of a legionary. Anyone with family can do a ten hour shift for me. Anyone without can take free rooms here. This is a short-term, ad hoc thing, though. A monthly contract. This whole thing has been caused by our Pompeian friends, and when they're no longer a threat, I think the senate and Caesar can be persuaded to retract this new law and allow the collegia again.'

He sighed and turned to Galronus. 'She wants me to be a senator, a senator has plenty of clients. That's what these lot are, now: new clients. She can't argue with that.'

Galronus chuckled, then settled into quiet thought. Something occurred to him, and he drummed his fingers on the table. 'If the Pompeians are still receiving orders and payment, then they have to still be meeting as a group.'

'Makes sense,' Fronto agreed.

'And if they're meeting as a group, then they're breaking this law just like Carbo would be if he called the lads back together.'

'True.'

'So if we could find evidence of it, we could maybe use that?'

Fronto grinned. 'Take the whole lot of them to court? That appeals. But how to find them? They have to be meeting in secret now, their meeting house gone at the senate's order. We don't know any of them or their addresses.'

'Won't they be in that big records place?'

Fronto mused for a moment. 'The tabularium? They will have been. But if they're now disbanded, those records won't be kept. They may still exist somewhere, or they may have been burned. And even if they still exist, it's only been a day, so they'll not be accessible while the law is being enacted and enforced. It'll take days to get them.'

Galronus smiled. 'I might have another way.'

'Oh?'

'Let me go and find them.'

'Take a dozen men with you.'

'Better not,' Galronus replied.

'It's dangerous out there.'

'They're not targeting us specifically now, and it's very hard to be subtle with a dozen armed men following you round. I want to be subtle.'

'Never expected to hear that from the Belgae.'

Galronus flashed his friends a grin. 'I'll be back by nightfall.'

Nodding a goodbye to them, he left the room and paced back to his own quarters in a different part of the sprawling house. There, he found his most ordinary, nondescript tunic, a simple leather belt and a pair of scuffed boots. He looked into the slightly distorted bronze mirror, approved of the chin, for he hadn't shaved yet today, and it showed, and then spent a few moments restyling his hair to look more like the cheap, short cuts the ordinary people of Rome had. He removed his torc and armlet, and took stock. Perfect. He was so ordinary even he would walk past himself in the street. He reached up for his cloak, but changed his mind. The rain was little more than a mist anyway, and his cloak was clearly a military cut. Better without.

On the way back through the house, he dropped into the kitchens and borrowed a knife and sheath, which he attached to his belt. He might well be outside the pomerium for most of this, but if he had to cross the sacred boundary, he didn't want to have to throw away a good sword. Hence: the knife.

Looking like an ordinary Roman citizen in almost every way, he wandered back through the house towards the vestibule. He had to wave away slaves and guards who tried to accompany him, but once the doorman opened up and he stepped into the street, he felt oddly exhilarated. He hadn't quite realised how tedious life had become recently until that fight in the street had woken him up. It felt good to be out in the open alone again, without an entourage, ignored by the populace. Indeed, as he turned into the street, he looked about for a sign of the ever-present watchers they had experienced for so long, and could find no evidence of a single pair of eyes intent upon him. Whatever ills had been caused by the banning of collegia, it seemed to have removed their watchers at least.

Even the very faint misty drizzle seemed to be fading out. Feeling unusually active and light, he strolled down the street, without the people of Rome moving out of his way. In fact, he actually had to fight his way through here and there. He had a plan, and he had a backup plan. Before long, he had descended from the Aventine, passed the carceres of the circus, the Palatine and the Velia, crossed into the subura, and then took the walk up the same street they'd tried yesterday when the fight had broken out. Before long, he was at the site of the scrap, and even with the mizzle and the constant barrage of refuse in the streets, there were still signs of the blood here and there. Another short walk and he found the meeting house of the Pompeians. A wooden board hung over the knocker on the door, proclaiming the building to be the property of the senate of Rome and warning people to keep out.

Nodding to himself, he looked around and spotted the nearest shop. Across the road, and down a little, a man was stacking baskets on his counter, prices scribbled on the rough plaster of the wall beneath. Galronus waved to him as he neared.

'I don't suppose you know where the people from over there who died yesterday are buried?'

The man frowned at the strange question, then his forehead creased in thought. 'A few were taken away by family members yesterday. The rest were loaded on a wagon after dark and taken away.'

'Where?'

'Dunno. Probably the burial pits up the hill. Ask Secundus. He'll know. It was his cart.' He pointed down the street a little way to a livery with a large archway. Galronus thanked the man and dropped him a couple of coins, then turned and strode down the street. Reaching that arch, he passed inside and found a slave, asking him to see Secundus. He was directed to a small office and told to wait, and a quarter of an hour later a portly man with a rosy complexion arrived.

'You asked for me?'

'You took the bodies away after the fight last night. I need to know where.'

Secundus' eyes narrowed. 'You family?'

'Of sorts.' Just to be sure, he placed two silver coins on the table, and any hint of suspicion in the man's expression and tone vanished instantly.

'There's a place up the top of the Esquiline, near the burial pits. It's a big hall, run by a man called Paccius. You can leave bodies there for up to eight days. That gives relatives time to track down missing family and reclaim them for a fee. If no one claims them in eight days, they get tossed in the pit and whatever goods they had are claimed by Paccius.'

'Excellent. Thank you. Can you direct me to it?'

Secundus did just that, and in no time the Remi was striding up the slope towards the very edge of the city. It was not difficult to tell when he was approaching the puticuli, the wide pits dug outside the city's boundary for the disposal of the poor and unwanted. Any time the wind suddenly switched, he was treated to a smell that defied description, at the same time stomach-churningly revolting, and yet oddly sweet. But the real giveaway was the carrion birds above the pits, that were so thick they almost filled the sky, like an undulating black cloud.

He pulled his scarf up to his nose as he closed on the place, and tried to breathe shallow. Paccius' warehouse was not hard to find. It was a huge place, constructed of rough, cheap brick, with a large, plain door upon which were crude pictures of skulls and bones. The doors were open, and if Galronus had thought the stench of the pits dreadful, he'd not been prepared for the warehouse. He stopped at the door and removed his scarf long enough to throw up outside, three times, and then covered up again and walked in. He didn't have to ask for anyone this time, as a smiling thing shambled over to him. It looked little more than an ageing cadaver itself, but it must have been alive, since it moved. It stopped in Front of Galronus.

'Can I 'elps you.'

'Secundus of Lampmakers Street brought a cart of bodies in last night. I need to see them.'

The man nodded. 'Oh yes. One bronze fer a viewin'. Two silver to take one.'

Galronus slipped a small bronze coin to the man, who guided him into the miasma formed from scores of decomposing bodies

234

crammed into one room. Gagging, he followed, and when he was shown an array of corpses, glanced at them quickly. They appeared to be the ones he was looking for. He thanked the man, turned, and hurried back to the door. The man followed. 'Want one?'

'No. Thank you,' Galronus replied, sucking in the slightly less revolting air outside. 'Not the one I was looking for. Mind if I stay here a while?'

'One copper to watch,' the man replied with a sly grin.

Galronus gave the man another coin and leaned against the wall. The walking cadaver bowed, turned and disappeared to accost a tearful old woman who had just arrived.

The Remi settled in to wait, making sure he was in a position to spot the bodies. He was there almost an hour before the first visitor came. He was alert for a while as the bereaved examined the bodies and then burst into wailing cries, clutching at one of the dead. In a short while she was leaving the place, her friend with a hand-cart bracing himself as the body was loaded atop it, and the pair wheeled away the fallen.

He contemplated following, but decided against it. She was a widow, and that body would just be going home and then for burial or cremation. What he wanted, he was sure would come, if he waited patiently.

The next two hours took their toll, though, and he began to wonder if his plan had been poorly-thought out after all. At least the drizzle had started again, thicker than before. Though it didn't take long to soak him to the bone, it did, however, suppress much of the area's stench, so he still blessed Jupiter Pluvius and Taranis for the rain.

He even dozed off, briefly, and almost missed his chance. Only one of the new visitors coughing loudly startled him from his snooze, and his eyes snapped open to see four burly men with the build of ex-soldiers engaged in a muttered conversation with the strange old man. He pulled himself together and paid attention, watching carefully while still maintaining the appearance of being asleep.

The four men entered the building and went straight to the bodies. They examined the fallen, and then engaged the man in conversation again. This seemed to quickly devolve into an argument, and there was the distinct sound of threat being made. Other helpers hurried over to support the cadaverous man, but the four soldiers still had the edge. In the end, it seemed the old man caved in to their demands, and a bag was brought forward. The four men rummaged in it, checking the contents, occasionally holding them up to what little light there was. Rings, mainly. A few coins. The personal effects of the dead.

Content that they had what they came for, the four ex-soldiers shoved the old man roughly away and left the building once more. Galronus, stifling a smile of self-congratulation, took careful note of their faces as they left, waited until they were thirty paces down the road, and then began to follow. He was careful, and stopped here and there at appropriate shops, ducking into side roads. Halfway down the street, he stopped in a clothiers and bought a cheap cloak, which he then drew about himself and pulled over his head in a makeshift hood. Newly-disguised, he hurried and caught up with the four men and their bag of prizes, and then followed them carefully again.

It was a long trail, for they clearly were not heading back to their impounded meeting house. They descended to the Velia and then crossed and climbed the streets of the Caelian Hill, their Remi shadow never far behind. Galronus narrowed his eyes as they slowed and pulled across to the side of the street atop the hill. Their destination had a sign next to the door, and the four men knocked and then entered. Galronus crossed once the door had shut again, and read the sign, which revealed the building to be one of the many bathhouses across the city that were privately owned but open to the public for coin. He waited a suitable time and once he was content the four men would be engaged in their new pursuits, he knocked.

'Four sestertii,' the man said as he opened the door. Galronus nodded, dropped the coins into the man's hand and, once he stepped aside, made his way into the baths. A slave hurried over, offering him a towel and a tag with a number on it. The slave accompanied him into the spacious, circular changing room, and once he had slipped from his sodden clothes and wrapped the towel around him, the slave gave him the tag and took away his clothes for safe keeping. The slave gave him a quick precis of the baths' layout, and then stepped back to wait for the next customer.

Galronus made his way inside. Attired in a towel, he blended in well among the other customers, and began to stroll around the place as though he was enjoying himself. He paused here and there, having a slave apply oil and then scrape him down. He visited the hot bath and had a dip, similarly the cold bath, all the time keeping a careful eye out for the four faces he would recognise. He spent a while in the steam room, as it was rather more difficult to make out faces clearly there, and finally went for a swim in the pool. Having used all the bathing facilities, he had found not a sign of the four men.

He somehow doubted they would be in the library, but he checked it in passing, just in case, and then had a brief pause in the caupona where visitors could buy wine and snacks. It was as he was about to go outside and peruse the gardens that he heard it. Perhaps it would be meaningless to the bulk of the Roman population, but Galronus had spent enough of his life now in Roman army camps to recognise the sound instantly.

Training. Not just exercise, but military training.

He mooched quietly around the gardens until he found a nice observation position by a fountain and behind a neatly-trimmed hedge. He looked through the foliage to the racing track on the other side. A dozen or so men were busy lifting weights off to one side, but the majority of the visitors here were standing in the middle of the track. They were in perfect lines and columns, like a legion on the battlefield, and with a series of shouted phrases were working through uniform combat moves with five foot lengths of wood. As he watched, they bellowed, jabbed, bellowed, spun, bellowed, back-stepped, turned, bellowed and smashed down. His eyes slid to the side, and he could see a man leading the training at the far end. He was in a simple grey tunic and holding a stick, but he might as well have had 'Centurion' tattooed written on his chest, for that was so clearly what he was.

There was little doubt, then, that Galronus had found where they were now meeting. It was a touch worrying that they appeared to be training for war, but he couldn't just waste time standing and watching them. He had things to do now. He paced back through the baths to the changing room, and handed his tag to a slave, who brought him his clothes. He was impressed. He'd been here little more than an hour, and his clothes had been dried, pressed, and folded. He put them on with relish, and passed his towel to the slave. Before the little fellow could leave, he tapped him on the shoulder.

'I'd been hoping to use the running track, but it was occupied.'

The slave bowed lower, an impressive feat since his eyes had never left the floor in the entire exchange anyway. 'A thousand apologies, Dominus. Any other day would be fine, but those athletes use the track every week on the second day after market day. I'm afraid, we cannot ask paying customers not to use the facilities…'

Galronus nodded dismissively. 'That's fine. I shall come another day.'

In no time he was outside once more, and wrapping up against the rain. It was only a short walk from here back to Fronto's house on the Aventine, and as he strode through the damp, he thought over what he'd learned. The Pompeians were meeting at the baths on the Caelian, at least every eight days, on the same day each cycle. They would not be hard to find, then, when he needed to. On the other hand, they were not clearly meeting as a collegium any more, or not overtly, anyway. They were meeting in a public place, in the exercise yards of a bath house, which was innocuous. Fronto might want to take this information to the courts, but there was little point. The men were simply exercising in public. Any lawyer worth even a pittance could see the lot of them walk away from that. Any legal challenge seemed out of reach now. But at least he knew where to find them and, though they were apparently training for something, at least he now knew that.

The question now, then, was what for?

CHAPTER EIGHTEEN

Fronto lurked in the doorway of the small room in which he'd been hiding, gaze playing across the many luminaries drifting about his atrium with glasses of wine, all red-striped togas and rich tunics, gold sandals and expensive coiffure. In the months he had been playing this senator game, he had never felt more out of place than this evening. Briefly, amid the cackling and squawking mob, he caught sight of Lucilia, drifting about like a mortal Venus, delicate and beautiful, wearing a warm smile that she turned on every notable she passed. Inside, he knew, she would be seething, wondering where he was. He would have to get out and socialise soon. If she found him hiding, he would never hear the end of it.

Across the other side of the atrium, Galronus smiled politely as a dry-looking senator cornered him and began to ask him dull questions. Serves him right. He should have stayed hidden with Fronto. There was less danger of being in trouble with the wives if they lurked together, but Fronto had kept his friend busy speculating on the plans of the Pompeians as long as he could, and the Remi had left him there, commenting that he, at least, would be out there where Faleria could see him.

Nothing else for it. He had to brave the tedium.

Taking a deep breath, he stepped out into the atrium, emerging from the shadows of the storeroom, and bolted a smile to his face. He managed three steps before Acilius Labeo turned and smiled, indicating his desire to bore Fronto to tears by a sweep of the hand. Fronto turned sharply and stepped away, ducking past a trio of cackling women and making for the triclinium, where at least there would be wine to dull the dullness.

'Marcus, there you are.'

He kept that smile rigidly in place as he turned to his wife. 'Of course, my love.'

'Where have you been hiding.'

'I was in conversation with Acilius Labeo,' he lied glibly.

'Rubbish. Firstly, Labeo has asked me where you were three times in the past hour, and secondly I know that you would walk through a wall to avoid talking to the man.'

She placed balled fists on her hips, always a bad sign. Fronto winced.

'You can do penance for sneaking away and hiding in slave quarters by finding Acilius Labeo and making him feel welcome. And then you need to circulate. Without Caesar, the whole purpose of this gathering is shaky.'

Fronto frowned. 'He's not here?'

That was strange. This whole horrid party had been Lucilia's great senatorial gesture to celebrate the latest round of ridiculous honours bestowed upon the man, including the one that had people talking. Caesar had been here when Fronto scuttled off to hide, the moment the meal was over and people would want to occupy his time. Where had he gone?

'Good grief, Marcus, how long have you been hiding?'

'Err…'

'He left after the meal,' she said with strained patience. 'He said he had acquired rather a bad headache. Made sure everyone knew neither the food nor the company were to blame, but he left early. And without him, the next person people want to talk to is you, being the host.'

'Being the hostess's husband is not the same thing as being the host,' he muttered. A suspicion fell over him, and his eyes narrowed. 'I bet he left Calpurnia here, though?'

'He did, and rightly so. She was enjoying her evening. No need to stop just because he left.'

Fronto snorted. 'I suspect his headache will be gone before he gets home.'

She frowned. 'You don't mean…'

'Well it cannot have escaped your notice that Cleopatra is not here.'

'Of course not. He couldn't bring her to this. He has his reputation to maintain.'

'I suspect he's exercising his reputation a little about now,' Fronto replied with a meaningful waggle of his eyebrows.

'Marcus!'

'Trying for another heir, eh?'

'Marcus, you are shocking.'

He grinned, but it slipped a little as he caught the sound of argument cutting through the murmur of the party. 'Uh oh. Sounds like trouble.'

'Go. Sort it. Then speak to Labeo.'

Fronto nodded at his wife, and then hurried through the gathering, nudging and shoving his way past some of the richest and most important men and women in Rome. There was some consternation, though no one complained, it being the house's owner making his way like a ship at sea, leaving a wake of spilled drinks and sharp comments. He reached the far side of the large atrium to find a gathering of senators pressed into the doorway of the library, whence the raised voices were coming. His spirits sank as he recognised the voices of Decimus Brutus and young Octavian, along with two or three others. With no preamble, knowing that this sort of thing could ruin the night swiftly, and that he couldn't let that happen after all Lucilia's hard work, he pulled the senators aside and stepped into the room.

'Stop,' he snapped, and his tone was sufficient to halt the argument instantly.

Half a dozen people were red-faced and glaring, but it was Brutus and Octavian that were but three feet apart, paused in the act of wagging fingers at one another. As they turned to Fronto he realised that far from stopping them arguing, all he was going to do was give them another player and get himself dragged into it. Well, if that was the case, he was going to take them out of the public's earshot.

'Come with me,' he barked, a tone he used on the battlefield that had men falling into line before they'd even thought about it. Not giving them the chance to argue, he turned on his heel and pushed back through the spectators. Lucilia was drifting towards them with a look of concern. He headed her off and leaned in close.

'I'm going to knock two heads together, then I'll be back. Tell Galronus to start circulating the story of the Pompeians using a bath house for illegal collegium meetings. That'll give everyone something exciting to talk about and get their minds off this.'

She nodded, and moved off to find the Remi. That was perhaps a gamble. He'd been wondering what to do with that information. Revealing it would probably result in the Pompeians changing their routine, and he'd lose track of them again, but at least in the meantime they would find their meetings impossible and they would have all the inconvenience of changing their plans.

He glanced over his shoulder as he walked out into the gardens, and noted that Octavian and Brutus were following, at least, the others left behind.

It was chilly in the garden, but bright enough, for torches burned to hold back the night, and at least it was dry. There were fewer people out here, mostly those seeking a little solitude, and he stormed past them all without having to acknowledge anyone. Moments later he reached his personal office, which was far from the main house, near the baths and the slave quarters, flanked by storerooms that were kept locked, the perfect place for a little solitude. Two of the men he now hired from the Caesarian Veterans' Collegium stood guard, keeping any stray guests away, though with a cup of wine in hand, too. It *was* a party, after all. He nodded at them. 'Keep people away,' he said, then stepped between them, fumbling with a key and unlocking the door.

The office was a little chilly, but not too bad. He'd not had the braziers on in here today, but the furnace for the baths was just behind the rear wall, which meant the room never dropped too low in temperature. He lit two oil lamps, waited for the other men to halt in the middle of the room, then shut the door behind them.

'Alright, what is all this about?'

'This new ridiculous honour,' Decimus Brutus said, lip curling.

'And you waited until Caesar wasn't here to start on it?'

Octavian snorted. 'Of course he did. Didn't want to spoil his chances of being given rich sinecures, did he?'

'I was trying to be polite,' Brutus snapped. 'We *are* at a social occasion, if you hadn't noticed. I didn't want to ruin Fronto and Lucilia's evening, but then you went and opened your mouth.'

Octavian's own lip twitched a little at that. 'This party is to celebrate Caesar's honours. If we're not supposed to talk about them, it's all a little pointless.'

'But there's no need to bang on about it, Octavian. There are plenty of people here who agree with me.'

'About what?' Fronto asked, and then regretted it as Brutus turned to him.

'The whole point of the dictatorship is to grant it to one capable man in a time of crisis, to *resolve* that crisis. It is not a position in the governance of Rome. It is not an honour to be bestowed upon a man like a victor's wreath. It is a job, with a specific task and purpose.'

'Yes,' Fronto agreed.

'And what was Caesar granted the dictatorship for again? Perhaps you could remind me, Marcus?'

'To resolve the crisis of civil war, caused by the Pompeian factions in the senate.'

Fronto coughed uncomfortably. It was convenient these days to lay every ounce of the blame at Pompey's feet and not mention that fact that it had been Caesar who had crossed the Rubicon with his legion and marched on Rome, no matter that he had been forced into it.

Brutus was nodding, but angrily. 'He was granted the dictatorship to solve that problem. To end the war and bring peace to Rome. And I remember it. Only the consuls can appoint a dictator, but there were no consuls, because they'd fled with Pompey, so it was faithful Lepidus who proposed him, illegally. But legal or not, there was no argument, because it needed doing. The war had to end, and peace had to be restored.'

'Exactly,' Octavian said, still breathing heavily.

'But the war is *over*,' Brutus said. 'Peace is restored.'

'The war is *not* over,' Octavian said.

'Yes it *is*. The crisis has passed. A dictatorship of limited duration to see the problem solved.'

'And the problem is *not* solved,' Octavian said again.

243

'Yes it *is*.'

'No it *isn't*. There's still a Pompey out there. Sextus, believed to be in Sicilia seeking support for a new revolt.'

'One man, with one ship and hardly any funds,' Brutus snorted. He has nowhere to go, and no one in Rome will stand with him now. That's hardly a crisis. I stand by Caesar, I always have. He's as close as family to me. But I am also a loyal son of the republic, Octavian, as you should be. Caesar should be laying down his dictatorship. There is nothing happening in the whole republic now that two consuls and the senate cannot handle.'

'A rebel seeking support so close to Rome?' Octavian sneered. 'The Getae pressing west in Thrace? The Parthians feeling dangerously powerful after humiliating Rome at Carrhae? And this is not a crisis?'

'They gave it to him *in Perpetuo*, Octavian,' Brutus said with an expression of distaste. 'Dictator for life! We don't need to worry about him seeking to be king now, because the senate have already made him one in all but name.'

Fronto had been trying to get a word in edgeways, but now he found that he didn't really want to. The problem was that he rather agreed with Brutus. Dictator in perpetuity was not a long way from royalty. The man was only really missing a crown. A thought struck him, and he took his chance in that moment of silence.

'But a king has a succession. The dictatorship will not pass on. It ends with him.'

Octavian's face as he turned to Fronto was a complex mix of emotions. Fronto had just given him an angle of support, but at the same time he had confirmed that no matter what Octavian inherited, he wouldn't have half the power of his uncle.

'I almost didn't come,' Brutus said, turning to Fronto. 'I actually considered it in quite poor taste to celebrate Caesar being given almost ultimate power. I find it horribly ironic that so many senators who just made themselves redundant should be here celebrating their self-defeating move.'

'It's not ultimate power,' spat Octavian. 'A dictator is not above the law.'

'A dictator *makes* the law,' Brutus growled, turning back to him.

'No. He must devote himself to his duties, and he is liable for prosecution for any crimes he might commit.'

'Now you're just talking for the sake of talking,' said Brutus. 'Anyone with imperium is liable for such prosecution, but only once their term of power is over. I'm sure the senate will have great fun prosecuting Caesar the day after he dies. Dictator for *life*, remember?'

'And there are those who can still vote against him. The tribunes of the plebs, for instance, and there are *ten* of them.'

'Eight,' Brutus corrected him. 'Remember that Caesar had two of them removed from office. Where was the opposition then? Who among the other tribunes stood up to Caesar and saved their colleagues? No one. Because there is only one voice in the whole bunch who ever speaks against Caesar, and that's Cassius Longinus. The rest are all Caesar's people. Gods, but even Antonius' brother Lucius is one of them. No one is going to deny Caesar, and yes, he can be made to pay for anything he does, but only when he's dead. How convenient, eh?'

'That won't be long, then,' Fronto said.

Both the others stopped and turned to him, expressions suddenly confused. Fronto shrugged. 'By the Ides of Martius, if the haruspex is to be believed.'

There was an uncomfortable moment of silence, and then it was broken as the argument picked up once more. 'The senate can hardly complain,' Octavian snorted, 'when it was them who gave him the position. He never sought it. Never asked for this.'

'Nor did he argue or refuse it.'

'What man refuses honours and advances?'

'Anyone who values the republic,' Brutus replied, straightening.

The uncomfortable silence returned, and Fronto stood there, fretting, wondering what he could say to end this. These men were two of Caesar's best supporters and closest friends. To see them at odds like this was more than a little unsettling. His job was done for him, then, as the silence was broken by the muted sounds of more trouble. Fronto shook his head in disbelief, huffing.

'What now? What is going on around here? Has someone done something with the wine?' He jabbed a finger towards the pair. 'Knock this off. My house. My party. My rules. And the first rule is that you two stay out of sight of each other for the rest of the night.'

With that, he turned and ripped open the door, marching out into the cold. His spirits sank a little further to see that a crowd had moved out of the house into the gardens, and were gathered around like spectators at some event. The sounds of a scuffle were coming from the heart of it. Leaving Octavian and Brutus and hoping they did as they were told, he marched at pace over to that gathering, bellowing for people to make way. They did so, senators and rich merchants stepping aside to let him through, and Fronto found himself at the centre of the peristyle next to the fountain and the statue of Fortuna.

Gaius Oppius, amicus of Caesar, lay on the gravel, his clothes in disarray, blood smeared across his split lip and cut eye, but also his knuckles. He was snarling like a hungry wolf, while his regular companion, Cornelius Balbus, reached down, trying to help him up. A few feet away, the outspoken senator Lucius Pontius Aquila was also snapping and growling like a feral animal, blood pouring from his nose, fists balled and bloodied. He was far from done and kept lunging, lurching to get at his fallen opponent, though Sulpicius Galba and Tillius Cimber were holding him back, one on each shoulder.

'This isn't over, Oppius,' snarled Aquila. 'Your time will come.'

'Any time you like, you fucking animal,' grunted Oppius as he rose slowly, with the help of Cornelius. 'I'll be waiting, though, next time. You won't get another chance to blindside me.'

'Your precious dictator can't protect *everyone*,' Aquila said.

'I don't need Caesar's protection. I can put you down myself.'

As Oppius reached up to his lip and winced, Aquila, aware that Fronto's guards were now close too, pulled himself out of his friends' grip and jabbed a finger at his opponent. 'Next time,' he said and turned, marching off and shouting for someone to warn his litter bearers that they were leaving. In the usual nature of parties, the moment he was out of sight and the entertainment was over, the crowd started to break up, the various senators began to murmur their discussions about what they had just witnessed, and the gentle hum of social life resumed.

In the midst of the normality, Oppius limped over to a bench and sank to it, with Cornelius at his side. Fronto crossed to them and behind him his men made sure the crowd did not come too close.

'What was that about?'

Cornelius Balbus shrugged. 'If you put together a list of people who spoke openly against Caesar, Aquila would be at the top. Why he was invited I will never know.'

Fronto frowned. Good question. Lucilia should know who was an appropriate guest and who wasn't, and Cimber was another name that should probably not have made it to the guest list. Sulpicius Galba, too, for that matter.

'Who slung the first insult?'

Oppius looked up. 'I'm afraid it may have been I. They were being surprisingly silent, given their usual activity. They'd not denounced Caesar or anything. Then I saw them in a corner, speaking to Marcus Junius Brutus. There was something just sort of conspiratorial about it. I can't say what it was, it just looked very suspicious. I told them to stop their plotting and leave good men alone. They told me to stay out of it, so I may have used a couple of slightly more insulting phrases. Then it sort of spiralled out of control. I can only apologise. I'd had no intention of spoiling your delightful evening.'

Fronto nodded. He'd not been too sure about Oppius before, suspecting that the man had only cleaved so to Caesar for personal gain. That he had intervened in such a manner and taken his lumps from Aquila spoke of more character than Fronto had suspected. He found himself amending his opinion.

Leaving the two men to recover, he made his way back through the party, once more spotted Acilius Labeo looking around hopefully, ducked out of sight, and finally, in the summer dining room, he found Lucilia.

'What made you invite that lot?'

She frowned. 'Who?'

'Cimber, Aquila and Galba at least.'

Her furrowed brow only deepened. 'I didn't. I assumed you did.'

'No.'

'*I* did,' said a voice from behind them. Fronto turned to see Octavian leaning against a door frame.

'What?'

'I know. An awful liberty. You will have to forgive me for my impromptu additions and for the audacity to invite people to someone else's house.'

'Why? You know they hate Caesar. Why bring them to celebrate him?'

Octavian shrugged. 'I invited others too. Cassius Longinus. Trebonius. Cicero. Pretty much everyone who I know speaks openly against him.'

'Why?' Fronto persisted.

'Two reasons, really. Firstly, I wanted them to see the number of people here who *support* Caesar. A show of strength. If they realise the minority they're in it might minimise the risk of them doing something precipitous. And secondly, in company and with enough wine, they might let out something they shouldn't.'

'Not that you'd hear, since you were busy arguing with Decimus Brutus and trying to ruin the evening.'

'Fronto, you are a marvel. Do you really think I am so careless to get into such an argument with Brutus in public? I provoked him deliberately, and within earshot of Aquila, to try and trigger a reaction. Looks like I succeeded, too. While I used one Brutus to start it all, they were busy with the other Brutus, probably trying to draw him into their plans.'

'Gods, but the way your mind works is horrifying, Octavian.'

The younger man grinned and raised his cup of wine in salute.

'Any other little surprises you have planned you'd like to tell us about?'

'Only that I dropped a little powdered camellia sinensis into Caesar's wine to give him a headache and send him home.'

Fronto's eyes widened. 'You did what?'

'I know that leaf gives him headaches. I wanted to observe his enemies so I needed him gone, since they were hardly going to speak their mind with him around. The camellia was extremely expensive. Came all the way from India via Parthia. Maybe when we conquer them it will be cheaper, eh?'

248

His blasé manner was astonishing. Fronto shook his head and turned, marching away. He didn't want to hear any more of the young nobleman's machinations, else he might be tempted to plant a punch in his face. He came to regret that decision swiftly, as he rounded a corner and found Acilius Labeo waiting for him. With a sigh, knowing he was not going to get away with it all night, he ratcheted a smile up onto his face and approached the world's most tedious senator.

The party lasted two more hours, and without further incident, for which Fronto thanked Fortuna, though he was aware that all incidents he had encountered had been Octavian's doing, not that of luck or fate. He spent an hour of that time listening to Acilius Labeo waxing lyrical about Caesar's plans and what part he might have in them, given that Fronto was so involved and blah, blah, blah, blah.

When the last guests had been ushered out, giving their warmest thanks and congratulations to their host and hostess for a very enjoyable evening, with some unexpected entertainment, Lucilia began her post-party tasks, directing the slaves in their work. Fronto, however, found himself staying out of the way in one of the house's lesser rooms, sharing a jar of wine with Galronus and Salvius Cursor.

'I hear more and more rumours of plots, you know?' Galronus said between sips. 'It's common talk across the city, now. That and Spurinna's prediction.'

Salvius leaned back, cradling his cup. 'I've been thinking on that. It's odd that any plot could be so openly suspected and yet not be uncovered. I wonder whether Caesar's enemies might not have been a little devious and sown seeds of plots all over the place. With so much suspicion it is harder to pin down the truth, after all.'

Fronto nodded. 'Good point. Well, we have plots against Caesar that may be fictitious, but I think we have to assume there's a core of truth in there. We have people we know stand against him. Cimber, Aquila and Sulpicius Galba at the least. I would be tempted to add Cassius Longinus to that list, too. And we cannot rule out Cicero, for all that he seems to have gone quiet. And we have a collegium that I simply cannot fathom. Someone wealthy, and probably of the equestrian class, is paying them. But although they're watching us all when they can, they're not killing Caesar's men any more. Yet they do seem to be training and preparing. What for? Who controls them? It's frustrating.'

'When does Caesar sail, again?' Galronus asked.

'Three days after the Ides of Martius,' Salvius replied. 'And he's assigned me to command his bodyguard once more, but only on campaign. He still refuses to have an armed guard in the city, which is far too short sighted.'

'Then it's down to us. To his friends,' Fronto said. 'We have to hold off all danger and keep him alive. In a few days it will be the Ides of Februarius. In a month or so's time, Spurinna's prediction will have been proven or disproven. If Caesar is still alive then, his allotted date has passed. And then three days and he will be heading east with the army, where I doubt he will be in danger, other than from the Getae and the Parthians. One month and three days. That's all. Can we keep him safe that long?'

'We will,' Salvius yawned. 'We have to. Anyway, I'm for bed. See you in the morning.' With that, he rose and left the room. Fronto sat in silence for a long moment, Galronus opposite, the two men staring down into their cups. After a while, with only silence laid like a blanket upon this side of the house, Fronto looked up.

'I'm having doubts, my old friend.'

The Remi frowned. 'What about?'

'I am Caesar's man. I'm loyal. I'll no more plot against him than I will you, but sometimes, somewhere deep down, I find myself agreeing with these men. With Aquila. With Decimus Brutus. With Cicero. Every time Caesar talks to me about his plans, I come away comforted and reassured. But we both know that's how Caesar works. If he wanted me to believe the sky was green, he could persuade me with little effort. And then I come home, and I hear things, and I sit alone, and I start to wonder whether I'm wrong. Whether I'm being fooled. Caesar is certainly capable of it.' He leaned forward. 'Galronus, what if they're right? What if Caesar really *does* seek a crown? What if all these explanations we've been spun are just obfuscation to stop us seeing what he's really doing? Because every day he becomes more powerful, and every day there is less opposition to him. Gods, but most kings I know of actually have *less* power than Caesar does right now. There's only really the question of succession, and then he might as well be wearing a crown.'

Galronus shrugged. 'We have a saying in the north. 'You can call it anything you like, but if you get wet, it's still rain.'

Fronto rolled his eyes. 'Utter bollocks. What's that supposed to mean?'

'It means that whatever you're led to think, the reality will show itself in the end.'

'So you advocate waiting to see if he gets crowned?'

'What other choice is there? You either take a stand against him like these others have, or you stand by him and hope. That's all there is.'

'It must be very simple living in that Remi mind of yours.'

Galronus shrugged. 'Complication is overrated.'

'Do you remember Verginius? My old friend?'

The Remi snorted. 'Hard to forget. Him and his friends gave us a bit of trouble at the end.'

Fronto nodded. 'Verginius was always a good man. Not at the end, of course. But in his soul, he'd always been the better of us. He was so republican it might as well have been tattooed on his forehead. He hated the very idea of monarchy. To him, Sulla and Marius were curses. And upon a time, I was no different.'

'Yes you were.'

'No I wasn't. But I changed. He didn't. Back at the end, when we were facing off and only one of us would make it, he said things. He'd vowed to bring down Caesar and prevent a repeat of the civil wars of Marius and Sulla. He failed, of course, and guess what? We had a civil war. But Verginius was obsessed with Caesar having used us both and left us to die. He begged me to join him and turn on Caesar.'

Galronus just nodded, watching Fronto intently, silent.

'I said no, of course. I told him how the senate had turned on both Caesar and me. I told him how I'd seen the alternatives. That Pompey was a monster behind a smiling face.'

'I remember, Fronto. I was there for that conversation.'

'Not all of it. He ranted for a while, yes, about what Caesar had done, what he was capable of, what he *would* do. And I'm not

251

wholly sure he was wrong. And I've spent years avoiding thinking about that quarry in Tarraco. About that conversation, but the more these events are building, the harder it is to avoid it.'

'What did he say to you, Fronto. In that quarry, at the end. What did he say?'

Fronto sighed. 'He demanded that I take on his vow. Begged me. Told me he could never rest until it was fulfilled. And I can imagine that he's still out there, a lemure in the night, a restless spirit, unable to go because his vow is unfulfilled. Maybe he's somehow still influencing all this.'

'Fronto that's just fantasy.'

'Maybe. But he was like a brother to me once. We were family. I owed him so much.'

Galronus put his cup down. 'You said yes, didn't you?'

Fronto sagged back into his chair. 'What else could I do? At the time it was a comfort for a dying man I still loved like a brother for all we'd been through. I said yes. I said his vow was my vow.'

'Shit, Marcus, that's bad.'

'I know. Years now, that's been hanging over me. I vowed to kill Caesar. But I can't. And I know that breaking that oath might damn me to a nightmare world in the end, too, just like him. But how can I not?'

Galronus closed his eyes. 'I'd always wondered what you said to him at the end. I'd never have believed you'd say yes, though.'

'Where does it leave me?'

Galronus chewed his lip for a moment, and finally sat back. 'Neck deep in the shit. And upside down.'

CHAPTER NINETEEN

The senate's latest meeting had not improved Fronto's mood at all, as far as Galronus could see. He was starting to worry about his old friend. One thing he'd always admired about Fronto was his purpose and his certainty. Rarely did he dither on anything of remote importance. Sometimes his actions were planned, and sometimes they were spur-of-the-moment reactions, but they were rarely worried over. This problem was gnawing at him, though, and he couldn't tell anyone about it, other than Galronus, of course. He'd not even mentioned it to Lucilia, for she would only adopt the worry herself, then.

And Fronto had fretted over it all morning, after raising it last night. He'd worried about it all the way to Pompey's Theatre and the temporary senate curia there, and he'd worried about it during the tedious opening stages of the session. He'd been uncharacteristically quiet.

In fact, the only thing he had said during the entire sitting, leaning close to Galronus and muttering quietly, was 'if we have many more of these meetings, even Jupiter's going to be looking up to him. Venus will be building a temple to Caesar instead.'

Though, in fairness, he had a point. Every time the senate sat these days, the main order of business seemed to be finding new honours and roles to heap on Caesar. Galronus had foolishly assumed that unless they made him king, there was nowhere higher he could really go than dictator for life. Then today had happened.

Cornelius Balbus had stood, cleared his throat, and proposed new business. 'As you may be aware, Marcus Urbinius Victor passed away a few days ago, may the gods grant him peace. This, of course, leaves only one censor for the whole republic, and his new colleague needs to be selected. I would propose that the office be granted to Caesar, for as consul and dictator, the duties of the censor would naturally complement his current roles and give him a wider access to the tools of state.'

'I can think of a number of problems with that,' called another voice, and they'd all turned to see Aquila standing, a black eye and a reddened nose evidence of his recent fight.

'Oh?'

'You know it is not the senate's job to elect the censors. That is the task of a centuriate assembly.'

'But we can advise, replied Cornelius Balbus with a conciliatory smile. I doubt that any recommendation made with the backing of the senate would be refused in the assembly. It would be little more than a formality.'

'And the law,' Aquila snapped, 'states that no man can serve as a censor twice. Caesar was elected censor some sixteen years ago.'

'Seventeen,' Balbus smiled with ease. 'But as dictator, it is within his power to amend that law and allow the appointment.'

Galronus had shifted his attention to Caesar, who was seated on a curule chair at the far side of the room, facing the seated senators, as though this was his meeting and they had been asked to attend. The dictator's expression was entirely unreadable.

'Then why not go all the way,' snarled Aquila, 'and let him change the law so that the censor can be elected directly by the senate?'

'I don't think we need go that far,' Balbus laughed. 'We are in the business of saving and preserving the republic, not corrupting it.'

Aquila was too incensed to respond, blustering for a moment, and by the time he had recovered, the senate were in general nodding. 'How you can say that with a straight face and not be struck by Jove's own thunderbolt, I cannot imagine,' he said, and with that sat, glowering.

'Censor for life,' a senator called from across the room.

'For life,' others shouted.

'To preserve the sanctity of political appointments,' Cornelius Balbus said, eying Aquila, 'the title should perhaps be changed. Perhaps something like "Prefect of Public Morals", he smiled.' Aquila snorted, but remained in his seat.

'And Pater Patriae,' another senator called.

Father of the country, Galronus sighed, rolling his eyes. He knew Caesar had been something of a womaniser in his time, and there were several rumours of illegitimate children, but father of a *country* was pushing it.

'Shall we take the vote?' Balbus called.

'Is there any point?' Aquila threw a barbed reply. 'I can count on one hand the people who would vote against anything in this room.'

'A vote, then.'

Galronus had watched as these two honours were heaped on the great man's shoulders, a small gaggle of unhappy senators gathered together watching with distaste. But that was not the end of it. Cornelius Balbus having already done far too much, now Gaius Oppius stood in the silence that followed, brow and lip still miscoloured.

'I propose that the month of Quintilis be renamed in honour of its most illustrious son. Gaius Julius Caesar being born then, it is my proposal that henceforth that month be known as Julius.'

'Oh be reasonable,' snorted Sulpicius Galba from where he stood shoulder to shoulder with Aquila.

'I am perfectly serious,' Oppius replied. 'And if you or your friend there feel like arguing the point, I would happily batter the idea into his face once more.'

'A vote,' someone called.

Galronus had watched with disappointment, though with little surprise, as the rest of the session unfolded. Other, lesser, honours were granted Caesar as the session went on, and the portion of business that did not centre around the dictator came at the end, as though it were tagged on as an afterthought, a small amount of work on the actual business of state. The lictors of several of the more important and sensible attendees made sure that as the session ended and the senators left the building, Oppius and Aquila were kept well apart, for fear of the pair returning to their fist fight in public and cheapening the name of the senate in the people's eyes.

Galronus had walked with Fronto, whose face looked bitter, as though he'd been sucking on pepper. He was not at all happy with what they had just witnessed.

'Cornelius and Oppius should not have done that,' Galronus said quietly.

'Caesar should not have let them,' Fronto rumbled. 'He sat there like the master of all he surveyed and said not a single word in the entire session. Just sat there and watched the senate falling over itself to ingratiate its members with Caesar. What a piss-poor show it was. I almost voted against it on principle, not that it would have made much difference.'

Galronus nodded quietly. He was right. One could only blame the senators so much for kissing the feet of the man who all but ruled Rome alone. Eventually, the blame had to rest with Caesar for accepting all this madness. He was going too far, and everyone seemed to see that but him.

The Remi's eyes swivelled to take in Caesar's exit from the building. His lictors had come first, and then the man himself, toga wrapped around him, eyes glinting, chin high. He looked regal. Galronus had known plenty of chiefs, kings even, back in his own land, and they had looked far less regal than Caesar.

'Stop that man,' someone called, and Galronus' gaze snapped this way and that, looking for anyone putting the dictator in danger. Foolish, really, since no one would get near him past his lictors, and the gathered senators, and because he had immediately assumed it was Caesar who was in danger, he had been looking the wrong way. He saw men flock to Caesar's side, and even an archer would have had trouble landing a shot between them all. Caesar was so permanently surrounded by people, he had no need, really, of an extra guard.

Galronus turned and saw what was really happening.

From the steps of a temple, four men had burst at a run. Galronus was moving immediately, Fronto too, as well as many others, though most had also assumed it to be a threat to Caesar and had been late to spot the real danger. The four men seemed to be making directly for Gaius Oppius, who had now turned and realised what was happening.

Galronus was running now, along with the rest, but Oppius had been out ahead of everyone, on his own, and an easy target. Galronus and Fronto pounded across the open road, their togas unwinding and falling away like some discarded rag as they ran on in belted tunics alone. As the four men descended on the senator, Galronus realised with some surprise that they were not as a group intent on violence, for three of them were trying to grasp at the fourth and pull him back, though they were failing, as he kept running and pulled from their grips.

He was out ahead and now had a length of timber held tight, yanked from the folds of his tunic.

Fronto was shouting, little more than incoherent curses really, and other lictors and private guards were moving to intercept the man, but they wouldn't be quite fast enough. Nor would Fronto and Galronus. The other three assailants had realised they couldn't stop their companion, and also that tough men were on the way, and had pulled back, moving off towards that temple's steps.

Galronus felt torn. Everyone was moving to intercept the attack, and no one seemed interested in the three who were now retreating. But something caught Galronus' eye. He knew one of those men. One of the three now heading back to the temple was a man he'd recently seen in that grisly warehouse up near the burial pits. That was too much of a coincidence to ignore, and too much of an opportunity to overlook, given that the enemy were now having to meet elsewhere, and that he and Fronto had lost track of them.

He watched the assailant reach Oppius, saw him thump the senator on the bicep with his club. There was the crack of an arm breaking, and Oppius howled like a lunatic, clutching his injury, but that was the worst he was going to suffer, for his attacker was doomed. Even the lictors would not get to him in time, for the private guards who had been lax in their duty were finally involved, dragging the man to the ground and thumping, battering, kicking, beating the man to death while his victim lurched around, clutching his broken arm and screaming for a medicus.

Galronus was decided. The man was doomed. The guards would kill him, so incensed were they, and there was nothing the Remi could do to either help or prevent it. His gaze shifted to the other three. They were not stupid. Knowing that they had been seen and were involved in some way, and knowing that with their friend already down, armed men would then come for them, they split up, each of the three running for another alley or doorway.

Galronus could do nothing else. He set his sights on the one man he recognised, and raced after him. Off to the side, Fronto seemed to have come to a similar conclusion, and was following suit. For a while, he was running alongside Galronus, then he seemed to change his mind and peeled off, chasing another of the three. The two of them seemed to be alone in their work, though. Everyone else had been purely concerned with the injured Oppius and his assailant, and only Fronto and Galronus were running after the others. Perhaps they thought that, since the three had been trying to stop the attacker, they were just concerned citizens doing their public duty. Galronus knew otherwise, since he'd recognised one of them, and Fronto simply trusted his friend enough to follow.

The man from the warehouse disappeared between two of the temples that dominated this huge square, and Galronus ran after him, breathing hard as he tried to pick up the pace and catch up. As he dipped in between the grand, yet austere buildings, he lost sight of Fronto, who had raced off after another, and so he focused solely on his own prey. The man was relatively athletic. More than the average man in the street, anyway, for he was an ex-legionary and had recently been training with his friends. But he had also spent years retired in the city, and that had taken the edge off his military fitness, enough that his new exercise regime had not quite brought him back to peak yet. Galronus, on the other hand, was Belgae. Back home, the only men who were fat and unfit were those who were either too ill or too old to ride and fight. Even in these weeks of slow politics back in Rome, Galronus had been running, exercising and riding. He was as fit as he'd ever been.

And that meant that he was gaining.

The man he was chasing realised this at about the same time as Galronus, and turned into a narrow street, slowing to grab a trestle table outside a shop and overturn it behind him. Copper pots and pans clanged and bounced across the stones of the street as the man ran on. Galronus bore down on the obstacle, judging it. It was a risk. Puffing and panting like an Olympian, he extended his stride the last three steps before he reached the overturned table and its clonking, rolling contents, and leapt.

He cleared the table impressively, though as he landed, his left foot caught one of the fallen pots and he almost fell. Stumbling, arms cartwheeling, legs wobbly, he managed somehow to stay on his feet and regained his pace in a moment, just as the shopkeeper emerged from his door, shouting his fury, assuming Galronus to be the culprit. There was little he could do, though. The Remi was already past and racing after his quarry.

The man turned a sharp left ahead, and vanished from sight. Galronus' lungs were burning, but time was more of the essence than ever now, and so he pushed on, past the discomfort and pain, and forced himself to run even faster.

Reaching that corner, he dipped around it. His heart sank. There was no one in sight, and just a few paces ahead there were three alleyways leading off from a crossroads. The man had disappeared. Worse still, there were two doors here, one to each side before the junction. Five possible places the man could have gone.

Knowing what *he* would have done, had it been him running, Galronus slowed at the doors and tried each at the same time, the alley narrow enough to grasp a handle with each hand. Neither moved. He took a single breath and then tried again. It was possible they weren't locked and barred, but that the man was on the other side, holding it closed. Still, neither shifted, which suggested they were locked after all. He discounted them and reached the junction. No sign to either side. He knew the man could not have gone ahead, for he'd have been able to see him. He tried to picture the layout of the streets and alleys, a mental map of the area. That led swiftly to a decision. The man had not used the doors, and not gone ahead. Had he gone left, he would be heading back towards those temples and the scene of the attack, and would run the risk of meeting up with his friend and with Fronto, who was on the man's heel. Or probably, at least. Galronus had to acknowledge with a tinge of regret that Fronto was not as fast these days as once he was. Hopefully he was up to the task.

That left only right. There was, of course, always the possibility that he'd misjudged it, but he was faced with empty alleys and had to do something. Had to commit. He turned right and ran. The alley was some hundred paces long and terminated in another junction, and he reached it and looked left and right.

His relief that his instincts had not played him false was almost tangible. Right was another empty alley as far as he could see, to the end, but left, the alley opened out into a street, and his prey was visible. He had seemingly run from the alley and hit someone walking past. The two were now locked in a tussle as the runner tried to get away but the angry man he had run into held tight as he gave the man a piece of his mind.

Galronus ran even as his quarry broke free. Moments later he was bursting out into the street, not twenty paces behind the man. Panic seemed to be influencing the runner now, and he was stumbling into people and knocking them out of the way, misjudging his path and having to jump over or duck beneath obstacles. Galronus smiled a tight, vicious smile. That would be the man's end, for Galronus was determined and focused, and instead dipped this way and that, avoiding people and obstacles. He was catching up rapidly.

The columns of Caesar's new temple of Venus came into view as the street curved, and he realised they were almost at the forum. He had to catch the man now, for if they hit the forum square at this time of day, the huge number of people there might just allow him to get away.

But that did not seem to be a problem. As the man reached the end of the street, now just seven or eight paces ahead, he suddenly lurched left. Galronus reached the corner, followed suit and pulled himself up sharp.

He'd assumed the three men had split up and run for safety separately. It had not occurred to him that they had not been so much running *away* from something as running *to* it. His quarry had staggered to a halt, coughing and panting, leaning on the wall of a bakery, and now suddenly two friends were there with him, and Galronus was facing three men. Another was also looking tired, and had to be one of those who had run, but the third looked fine, and had seemingly been waiting here for them.

Galronus reached to his waist. Damn it. He'd no blade or cudgel, for he'd been at a senate meeting. His hand closed on his eating knife, just a small bronze thing with a blade as long as his finger. Better than nothing, he decided, as the one rested man among the three pulled a length of oak from his belt.

'This doesn't have to end in blood,' Galronus said, holding up his hands, small knife in one. He could hear something, on the edge of his hearing, but it made him smile.

'Quite right,' the new man said. 'Fuck off and we'll let you live.'

'I would, but unfortunately, I need some answers. Give me them and I'll go in peace.'

'I don't think you're in a position to make demands,' the man sneered.

'Then you don't know me at all,' Galronus grinned.

At that moment the remaining runner burst from an alleyway nearby, but before he could join the other three, Fronto hit him from behind like a bull, slamming him to the ground, where the two men rolled around, punching and kicking.

'Two against four?' the speaker sneered.

'Two against *three*,' Fronto shouted as he stamped down on his victim and rose to his feet, standing on the body.

This seemed to unsettle the only rested man there, who rallied quickly.

'Go, and I'll forget what you've done.'

'I'll try and leave enough of you to identify,' Fronto said, with an unpleasant smile, as he stamped once more on his victim's chest for good measure and then started to pace towards the other three.

'Where are your guards when we need them?' Galronus said to his friend.

'The session finished early,' Fronto shrugged. 'I'd told them to find a caupona and have a drink while they waited.'

'For a general you have horrible lapses in tactical judgement sometimes,' Galronus snorted as he too began to advance on the man with the oak club. The other two men were pulling themselves up, ready to join in, but they were at least half spent.

The man watched them and gestured to his two tired friends. While oak-club sized up against Fronto, the other two staggered and lurched towards Galronus. Passers-by paused and looked on with interest. No one came to help. Galronus felt a smile creep onto his face. He was looking forward to going home, to be in a place where when there was trouble, the standard response was not to stand at a safe distance and watch it with interest, but rather to step in on one side or the other.

He watched the less tired of the two men approaching carefully. The man's eyes never left his. He was wearing a grey tunic of the usual above-the-knee military cut, with an old military belt. He was armed with a short, foot long club. The one Galronus had been chasing was recovering slowly, but seemed to be unarmed and was a little reticent, letting his friend edge slightly forward. Good.

Galronus came to a halt and waited, gripping his small knife tight, blade angled up. The bigger man edged towards him and pulled back his club, feeling a little comforted by the small size of Galronus' blade. The man took another step, and made his move. His left arm came out to stop any blow from the Remi, while the club came round at neck height.

Even as the man lunged, Galronus launched his own planned attack. He dropped to a crouch, under the club's sweep, and stabbed up with his small knife. The blade disappeared behind the grey folds of wool and the military belt, and buried itself deep in the man's groin. Galronus felt the warm flow of a large amount of blood across his hand as he yanked the blade back out and leapt away. Blood veritably cascaded from the man's nethers, swiftly soaking the grey wool of his tunic. The man was screaming with a high-pitched wail. His club fell from desperate fingers as he lurched away, hands going to his groin as though there was anything he could do to stop the fatal flow of life from his privates.

The other man, the one Galronus had been chasing, hit him with an ursine roar, and Galronus and his enemy hit the flagged street with all its dung and refuse, both men instantly breathless. The Remi and the Pompeian rolled this way and that, back and forth, gripping one another, Galronus' bloodied blade out to one side as he tried in the struggle to change his grip so that he could slam it down into the man's back. The man had one hand at Galronus' throat and was trying to push his chin up, head back, even as he throttled him.

The Remi's grip shifted and he stabbed.

He didn't want the man dead. He wanted answers. And therefore he was immensely grateful, as the man cried out with a dozen swear words at once, to realise he'd buried his knife not in the man's back, but in his left buttock.

Just to be sure that this was the critical moment, Galronus let go of the hilt and heaved, rolling the man onto his back so that the knife hit the ground and slammed ever deeper into the man's arse.

The hand had gone from his throat now, the man's attention entirely on the blade in his buttock. Galronus took the opportunity this created, pushing his opponent back. He reached out and grabbed the man's right hand. He remembered seeing him favouring it, both that day at the warehouse, and when trying to hold back his friend near the senate. He had to be right handed, and that was how a legionary was trained, anyway. Finding the man's flailing hand, he grabbed it and jerked the fingers sharply upward, breaking three.

The man screamed, and Galronus climbed off him.

He looked across to see that Fronto had finished with his own opponent, the man lying shaking uncontrollably on the stony ground, a huge pool of blood growing beneath him from where Fronto had smacked his head repeatedly against the street cobbles.

The four men were down, all either dead or done for. Galronus reached down and grabbed the man he'd chased, pulling him up. The man wailed as the knife caught on the flagged ground and pulled at the muscles in his arse. Blood welled up there, and the man kept his broken hand well away from Galronus, as though expecting a repeat performance.

The man struggled in his grip, but Fronto was there a moment later, and between the two of them they managed to control the Pompeian, who went limp, knowing he was caught. They walked him back to the bakery wall, and Fronto glanced at Galronus. 'Follow my lead,' the Roman said.

Galronus nodded, and helped Fronto drag the man inside.

'Tell us everything,' Fronto said as they heaved the man across towards one of the grindstones for wheat.

The man shook his head. 'There's nothing to say. Nothing you need to hear.'

'I'll be the judge of that,' Fronto growled, and as Galronus took the man's weight, the Roman shooed the slave workers away and grabbed the wooden pole that was used to turn the stone, lifting it.

The two grindstones separated, and Fronto nodded at Galronus. The Remi understood and pushed the man's good hand up until it was against the bottom stone. Fronto gently lowered the top one back into place. The man gasped in pain and panic.

'Talk,' Fronto said.

Galronus let go now. The man was trapped anyway, his hand pinned between the two stones.

'I don't know anything.'

'Wrong,' Fronto said.

Galronus nodded. 'We want to know who's paying you, what your orders are, why you're training, where you meet, and what you were doing at the senate meeting.'

The man shook his head, and Fronto gave the wooden beam the slightest shove. The man's trapped hand was ground for just a moment between the two stones, and he screamed. Fronto had moved the thing less than a finger width, but the moment the man recovered from the scream, words tumbled from his lips like a waterfall.

'Don't know. Don't know who the boss is. None of us do. We got a purse of silver and we were told to train and be ready. Whoever it is wants us to be ready for anything when he calls. That's all I know. We don't all meet anywhere now, but twelve of us at a time meet at the carceres of the circus on busy days, never the same twelve. That's where messages are left now, with a beggar there.'

'And today, at the senate?'

'Please,' gasped the man. Galronus gave Fronto a pointed look, and the Roman nodded and lifted the stone, freeing their captive. He pulled back his bloodied fingers, the broken ones on his other hand making that one useless. He pushed the newly-wounded hand into his mouth, sucking the fingers. It was only a bit of a graze, really, and some bruising. Nothing permanent. But it had clearly hurt. When he finally removed it, he sagged.

'Not everyone is happy. We're told not to attack Caesar's men, but some of our lads still want to. Lucidus just snapped. We tried to stop him. We're not all your enemy. Or not at the moment, anyway.'

Fronto nodded, and Galronus reached down and helped the stricken man up.

'Take this message back,' Fronto said. 'To your friends: stay out of it. Stay away. Don't come after us, and don't even watch us. We're done being civil. Next man I catch, I'll put his face under there and I'll turn the stone until he looks like chopped meat. Tell them all. Stay away. But give your beggar friend a message too, to pass to your employer. Tell him that I want to meet him. Tell him to find me. I have a feeling that whoever it is, he'll know my house.'

Galronus stepped back and let the man lurch away, nodding desperately. Three bodies filled the street nearby. Once, that could have been a problem, but such was the lawlessness of the city these days that neither of them worried too much, stepping over the corpses and making their way slowly back to where Fronto's guards would be scratching their head and wondering where he'd got to.

'Would you really have turned that millstone?' Galronus asked.

Fronto shrugged. 'Probably not. I'm not a monster, my friend. Just a little nudge as persuasion. If he'd not talked, I'm not sure what else I could have done.'

Galronus shrugged. 'You'd step away, and *I* would have turned it. My people are a little less squeamish.'

Fronto snorted. 'Gods, but it's a good job the Remi don't rule the world.'

'Why do you want their leader to come see you? Isn't that inviting trouble?'

'I don't know,' Fronto admitted. 'But the fact that they've been told to lay off Caesar's men suggests that maybe their new paymaster isn't our enemy. Or at least not fully, or not yet. And if he's not, then perhaps he can be made to be an ally? We have plenty of other enemies. Maybe it would be a good idea to try and bring these bastards on-side?'

'Romans are too complicated,' Galronus said, with a sniff, and walked away.

Behind him, Fronto grinned widely and followed.

CHAPTER TWENTY

T he streets of Rome were about as busy as Fronto had ever seen them this morning. Tomorrow was the Ides of Februarius, and that meant the festival of Lupercalia, an event only a little less immense than Saturnalia. The festival itself, by tradition, would be limited to the Palatine and the forum, but the festivities that surrounded and followed it for the rest of the night would spread out city-wide. As Fronto passed along the Via Sacra, he could see shopkeepers putting up wolf-based decorations, crimson garlands, and small statues of Juno. Girls and even older women were out buying new clothes, cosmetics and jewellery, in order to look their best when they attended the run.

It was so lively and chaotic, it was almost easy to forget the undercurrent of fear and danger that now pervaded the city.

Almost.

But here and there were signs, and not hard to see. As Fronto moved into the forum, Carbo, Masgava and the others striding protectively around him, such signs were in greater evidence.

The statue of the great Brutus, the man who had been instrumental in ejecting the last king of Rome and founding the republic, bore a new painted slogan across its base. Every day a new slogan, always the same theme, cleaned off by authorities and replaced nightly.

"Would that you were still alive."

A common sentiment these days, amid the ongoing tales of Caesar's desire for a crown, which were almost as regular a theme of conversation as the upcoming prediction of Spurinna. Someone would wash off that latest call to the great hero of the republic to save Rome once again from tyranny. And it would be back in a different form tomorrow morning. Statue bases were, of course, prime targets for the night-time artists, though not exclusively so.

Someone had daubed across the wall of Caesar's new basilica the line "Caesetius and Marullus for Consuls," a reference to the two tribunes of the plebs that Caesar had removed from office. The statue of Marcus Junius Brutus that stood close by proclaimed in red paint "You are not his descendant," another reference to the great liberator, condemning the noble Brutus for not already standing against Caesar. The statue of Caesar on the rostrum was, of course, the prime target, and already slaves were washing the paint from it, both the slogan on the base, and the painted diadem that crowned the thing. The words were unreadable, but Fronto could remember yesterday's pithy line.

"Caesar led the Gauls in triumph, led them to the senate house,

then the Gauls took off their trousers, and put on the striped toga."

Such sentiments suggested, of course, that it was not only the ordinary street life of Rome that was producing such works, but also men of wit and education. Fronto had never seen the republic so openly critical of Caesar. Not since the days of Sulla had such things happened.

He was distinctly uncomfortable as he moved through the city. It was a strange juxtaposition: all the air of festivity going on around the painted slogans of dissatisfaction. Once more, Fronto resolved that Caesar had to do something to bring the people back onto his side. There was little he could do about the senators that opposed him, but the ordinary people had always been Caesar's, and he had proved more than once that with the army and the mob on his side, the upper classes were of less import.

At least this morning's discovery made things seem a little more positive. The new paymaster of the Pompeian collegium had not taken up Fronto's offer of a meeting, but the message he had sent had suggested that their entire purpose was changing, which could only be for the better. Or at least that was one way of reading it.

They moved on, Fronto on horseback, most of his men on foot, past the end of the forum and the Capitol, down to the river and across it, making once more for that grand villa on the slope beyond. All the rest of the way, he brooded over the many problems they were facing, and tried again and again not to think

267

of his part in it all. At least on this side of the river, preparations for the festival were sparse, as were statues to deface.

Admitted to the grounds, they climbed the winding road up the slope to the villa proper and there Fronto dismounted and left everyone outside while he entered Caesar's house, slaves guiding him through to the office, where the dictator was studying documents with a frustrated expression. Caesar looked up as the slave showed Fronto in, bowed, and retreated.

'Marcus. Did we have business this morning? I have nothing noted. In fact, I have a meeting with Marcus Antonius presently.'

'No,' Fronto said. 'But this could be important, and I'll be quick.'

Caesar looked back down at his document, made a pained expression, and then set it aside, leaning back and steepling his fingers. 'Go on.'

'Will issues again?' Fronto muttered, gesturing at the paper.

Caesar shook his head. 'The will is settled. Octavian will be my heir. This is something else. What was it you wanted?'

'You remember the collegium? The one of Pompeian veterans, who had been attacking your supporters.'

Caesar nodded. 'And now their collegium is no more.'

'Getting rid of their meeting house doesn't get rid of them. They are still a force together, and still active. Do you remember me telling you that someone was paying them? That someone was controlling the activity of the collegium?'

Another nod. Fronto huffed and dropped into a seat. 'I think this new person who's taken over the running of the collegium is someone known to us. I've heard him referred to as 'The Horseman', which suggests an equestrian, and it has to be someone wealthy enough to afford to pay hundreds of men on a regular basis, and pay them well. Since they are Pompeians, it seems likely they would only accept as a master someone also known as your opponent.'

A third nod from Caesar as he took all this in and agreed to it.

'I sent a message asking this shadowy man to meet me.'

'Brave. And possibly foolish. Did he?'

'No,' Fronto sighed. 'In fact, he didn't. But he did reply, after a fashion.'

'Oh?'

'I had a message delivered by a beggar, which seems to be the preferred mode of delivery for this man. It arrived first thing this morning and it's somewhat enigmatic. Just three words. That's all.'

Caesar remained silent, his eyebrow arched quizzically.

'One more month,' Fronto went on. 'That's all it said. I consulted a scribe, and he said there's nothing useful to glean from the writing particularly, but he did confirm that it had to be someone well-educated. The parchment upon which it was written is extremely high quality, and there are less than half a dozen places in the city you can buy it. The scribe tells me that these places, and this parchment, are almost solely purchased and used by poets, writers, and politicians. And the message itself is horribly ambiguous. Is it a threat? A warning? Is it against us, or for us? That it's the Pompeian veterans suggests against, but that the collegium was given explicit orders to stop attacking your people suggests otherwise.'

He leaned forward and put his hands on the desk. 'If I were to say that the man we are looking for is an educated and wealthy equestrian, possibly a writer of some sort, who has a history that is opposed to you enough to entice Pompeians, yet who perhaps is not currently standing against you, is there a name that leaps out?'

Caesar's lip twitched up at the corner into an odd smile. 'You might as well be describing Cicero, might you not?'

'I'd come to the same conclusion.'

'Cicero is my ally, these days, not my enemy. He sits quietly in his house in the city and studies. When he does emerge for the business of statecraft, he enacts my edicts and wishes as though we were never opponents. What need could he have of a small private army?'

'I've been thinking on that,' Fronto said. 'The veteran we interrogated suggested that the man running the Pompeians had them training to be ready for when they're needed. Coupled with that "one more month" thing, I suspect that the man is preparing for what happens on the Ides of next month. I no longer think the collegium is directed *against* you, but nor is it *for* you. I think that whoever it is believes Spurinna's prediction and is putting everything in place for the Ides on the assumption you will die by then. Because, Caesar, whatever last will you may have lodged, you know that if you die, by whatever means, there will be absolute chaos. This person is preparing for the worst, and I think I can understand that.'

'What do you intend to do about them, then?'

Fronto shrugged. 'Nothing, I think. After months of fending them off, investigating them, and building up a counter-force, I've come to the conclusion that they're no longer a threat, or at least not for another month or so. They are a safe-guard now. I think we need to keep an eye on them, but I don't think they pose any threat for the foreseeable future.'

Caesar let out a long, slow breath. 'That is one problem hopefully resolved, then. Though I maintain that Spurinna is mistaken. I have had private readings several times since then, and no other haruspex has found such a doom in my future. And Venus watches over the house of the Julii. The Ides of Martius will come and go, Marcus, as they always do, and I shall prevail and sail east.'

'I hope you're right.'

'And no supposed plots are to be believed.'

Fronto noted with interest how Caesar's gaze dropped back to the letter he'd been reading at that comment. 'What is it?'

Caesar seemed to snap out of a reverie, focusing on him again. 'What? Oh, nothing. Alarmist notes is all.'

Fronto reached across for the letter. Caesar's hand twitched as though he had planned to swipe it away, but he did not, and Fronto lifted the note and read it, his eyes widening as they wandered down it. 'Alarmist?' he breathed in disbelief. The note was little more than a few lines to Caesar from the former consul Publius Servilius Vatia Isauricus. The man claimed to have been approached directly with a view to being drawn into a plot against Caesar. He would not name names in the letter, but made heavy-handed hints that those names would be prominent ones. He warned Caesar that the conspirators would be returning for an answer, and Vatia would attempt to divine further names from them during that meeting. Then, armed with a list of conspirators, he would visit Caesar.

'Why would they approach Vatia? I didn't see him as your enemy.'

Caesar shrugged. 'The man may not have stood with Pompey against me, but I think that was mostly a matter of his advanced age. He served with Pompey against the pirates. And while my family were tied to Marius in the wars, he was a disciple of Sulla. I can see why enemies would look to him, but I cannot see this as anything but fiction, or a mistake. A misunderstanding.'

'You know that, if this is true, the moment he sets foot outside his house, they'll kill him,' Fronto muttered.

'Vatia is hardly the most reliable source,' Caesar said dismissively. 'The man jumps at shadows and often forgets names. He is eighty five summers old or more, half deaf and barely mobile. I would not be at all surprised if this were little more than imaginings.'

Fronto shook his head. 'You can't afford to ignore things like this, especially now. In fact, looking at the anti-monarchic slogans painted all over the forum, I think you need to do something to improve your standing, and promptly.'

Caesar nodded as they both heard the sound of another visitor being admitted to the house. 'I have that in hand, Fronto. Fear not.'

At that moment, the sound of heavy boots clapping across the marble announced the arrival of Caesar's other appointment.

'Consul designate Fronto, this is a surprise,' Antonius said as he came to a halt in the doorway.

Caesar straightened, sharply, and threw a questioning look at Fronto.

'He's known for some time. Not just that you might change his status, but that I and your campaign are the reasons.'

Caesar looked past him at Antonius, his brow furrowing. 'You have known of my plan, yet you have managed not to storm into my office screaming imprecations? How uncharacteristically stoic of you, Antonius.'

The new visitor gave a slight snort. 'I am past the petty now, Caesar. You and I disagree on some matters, but we share blood, and I am too old to start a feud. We shall see whether Spurinna's prediction is true, or whether you are powerful enough to defy fate.

Either way, the world will change next month, and I will find an appropriate place in it then.'

Caesar managed a smile at that. 'This is the Antonius I remember of old, though oddly a little more sober, I might say.'

'Probably the influence of others,' Antonius said, giving Fronto a weird look.

Caesar chuckled. 'I have no doubt that your place in Rome will be secured, and I might be persuaded to be instrumental in your new rise, should you agree to do something for me.'

'Oh?'

Caesar gave Fronto a smile now, then turned back to Antonius. 'I have made attempts to bring the people on side before, only to have them go wrong with the unexpected interference of others. I have a new plan, and I need this to go right. There is now a new collegium of Luperci, a third brotherhood, named in my honour. I would like you, Antonius, to lead it as head priest. And then I have a job for you, and if everything goes right, perhaps we can come to some new arrangement.'

Fronto rolled his eyes. 'Whatever you're planning, it doesn't involve me. I'll leave you to it.'

'Where are you bound?' Antonius asked.

'A few social visits. Cicero, I think, and perhaps Publius Servilius Vatia Isauricus.'

'Vatia?' Antonius snorted. 'That old lech? And waffling old Cicero? Strange bedfellows you're keeping, Fronto.'

'Just to check on a few things.'

He nodded his farewell to the two men and left them to their machinations, exiting the room and striding back out towards his entourage. Despite this news about Vatia, he felt oddly encouraged. Caesar had a plan, which could only be a good thing. He might not be taking the danger to him seriously, but at least now he was focusing on rebuilding his popularity. And he and Antonius seemed to be working out their problems, and were on good speaking terms again. Antonius appeared to have found a new inner peace, which was a welcome surprise. And the Pompeian collegium seemed to have been neutralised by their new master, removing one major danger. If it weren't for Spurinna's prediction that remained hanging over them like the sword of Damocles, Fronto might think that everything was on the up.

Even the weather seemed to be improving. This morning had been the first of the year in which the temperature had been welcoming, and he'd not felt the need for a cloak. In fact, there was almost a spring in his step as he emerged into the open once more and climbed onto his horse. With the rest of his people gathering close behind, he rode slowly down the winding road once more and out into the streets of Transtiberim. The house of Marcus Tullius Cicero, statesman, writer and lawyer, stood proud on the western edge of the Palatine, looking out over the city below. It was no small property and even though Clodius had managed to acquire a tenth of it for his new portico during the years of Cicero's exile, it was still an imposing place.

Fronto's party crossed the river and rounded the Capitol, passing the heart of the city once more, where preparations for the festival were still underway. As they climbed the ancient, busy streets to the Palatine, Fronto pondered the best way to approach Cicero. He'd not a great deal of experience with the man, and despite them both enjoying a certain level of prominence in the city, their paths had only crossed rarely. Quite simply, Cicero had ever moved in different circles to Fronto. His oft-time opposition to Caesar had put distance between them, of course, but as much as anything, they hardly met for Fronto's world had always centred on the army and kept him away from the city, while Cicero was a true politician of Rome, and was always at its heart.

Thus, as they approached the imposing frontage of the great house, he wondered not only how he was going to approach his subject, but even what the man was really like. After all, he'd assumed Pompey to be a great man until he actually spent time with him and learned the truth.

His gaze played across the building as he dismounted outside. Oddly, though it was an immense property, its condition was not particularly good, and that surprised him. Equally, when he was admitted inside, he was surprised at the house's staff. A normal Roman town house of the wealthy would need some fifty or so slaves just to function, and this house was far bigger than that, yet clearly staff were scarce, and he neither saw nor heard a soul as he made his way inside, other than the doorman who'd admitted him and the house slave who escorted him to the owner.

Moreover, either Cicero was an extreme ascetic, or he'd got rid of much of the interior décor. It was the standard to have statues, busts, ornate furniture, exquisitely painted wooden screens and so on. Even Lucilia, whose tastes ran to the more austere for a Roman matron, had more lavish décor than Cicero. A suspicion began to form in Fronto as he was escorted out to the garden, where the great man sat on a simple marble bench in the Februarius sunlight, scribbling away on a wooden tablet. Cicero looked up at the crunch of boots on gravel, frowned, and lowered his pen and tablet to the bench beside him, reaching up and pushing a stray waft of grey hair away from his eye. Fronto was impressed by the man's eyebrows, which seemed to lead a life of their own, moving independently of the rest of his face. Other than that peculiarity, the man could easily be said to be the most Roman man Fronto had ever seen. He'd probably never smiled.

'Marcus Falerius Fronto, Domine,' supplied the slave helpfully, bowing low and retreating.

Fronto came to a halt opposite and adopted the easy military stance, legs slightly apart.

'Marcus Tullius Cicero,' he said.

'Fronto. Not the last person I ever expected to cross my threshold, but certainly loitering at the back of the queue. To what do I owe this dubious honour?'

Direct. Not over-friendly, but honest and straight. Fronto decided in an instant that he actually liked this man already. He also decided that, because of that, the direct approach was the only one to take.

'I am rather hoping you do not find this an insult, but I am investigating some of the recent troubles in Rome, and your name had cause to crop up. It may be nothing, but it would be remiss of me not to turn over every stone.'

Cicero nodded. 'In the search for truth, every avenue must be explored. I am intrigued. Go on.'

'You are aware of the recent troubles involving the collegia and the fighting in the streets?'

'I am. One would have to be both blind and deaf to not be.'

'Much of the trouble has been caused by a former collegium of veterans from Pompey's legions. They were actively hunting Caesar's supporters and causing trouble for the dictator. Recently, they seem to have come under the paid control of a single man, who has curtailed their former activity.'

'And you suspect me to be that man.'

'I *did*,' Fronto admitted, though he was starting to doubt his convictions already.

Cicero gave a strange smile. His eyebrows moved again, seemingly in an attempt to march away across his forehead. 'I expect I can guess why. I am known to have no love for the man. I am a figure of some eminence in the city who is not fawning to him, and there are few enough of them to make me a rarity. But I am afraid, I am not your man.'

'It must be an equestrian,' Fronto said, 'since he is known to his collegium as the "horseman", a former opponent of Caesar's, but possibly now either his supporter or someone neutral, and someone with the finances to support them.' This last was where he was now feeling less confident.

Cicero chuckled and folded his arms.

'I meet your mould in some ways, master Fronto. I do, certainly, belong to the equestrian class. I have been a very outspoken opponent of Caesars, too. These days I find that I am more inclined to peace for a number of reasons, self-preservation being an important one, but also the desire to see Rome at peace no matter the cost. Mostly, though, when my daughter died last year and took the lion's share of my heart with her, such was the chaos and distrust in Rome that hardly anyone seemed to notice or care. Men who I had trusted and known all my life left me to my grief. Of all the great men of Rome, three of them came to me and gave me their support, their hope and their friendship. Caesar was the first, and the other two were also both his men. The heart can guide the mind sometimes, Fronto, and I owe Caesar from that heart.'

He smiled oddly. The eyebrows did a dance. 'Most of all, though, I am a poor man, Fronto. If I could afford to pay a collegium to do my will, I would not be living like this. I have ever been poor, and only my marriage brought with it some healthy funds.'

'But you are a great man,' Fronto said, frowning, though his observations since his arrival did back that up. 'You must have a good income.'

Cicero laughed. 'You have spent too much time on the battlefield, Fronto, and too little time in the city. The more you live here, the more you will learn the rule that is the bane of Rome's elite.' He leaned closer, as though whispering something conspiratorial. 'The more money you have, the more you have to pay out. Being moderately wealthy is wonderful. Being rich costs far too much.'

That made Fronto laugh, for it hit horribly close to home, given the conversations he'd had with Lucilia. The deeper he'd delved into the world of senatorial life, the more money he seemed to be haemorrhaging every day, and the only way he could see to make more money to cover the costs his lifestyle was incurring was to take on more clients and seek more opportunities, both of which, it appeared, cost more money. It was, he'd concluded, like spending his days throwing bags of coin into a deep hole.

'You're not plotting against Caesar,' he said. A statement, not a question.

'Not immediately. But I'm a Roman equestrian, Fronto, and you have perhaps spent too little time yet among your peers to realise that on some level *every one of us* is plotting against everyone else. It is the only way civilisation advances.'

Somehow, Fronto found that a profoundly depressing point of view.

'When Caesar dies,' Cicero said in a worryingly flat tone, 'I shall mourn him, and I shall miss him, and I shall bemoan his loss, but I shall also be relieved. Let us put it that way.'

Fronto knew that he had nothing to say to that, or at least nothing that he was willing to admit to. It was a sentiment worryingly close to one he found lurking somewhere in his own soul.

'You believe Spurinna's prediction?'

Cicero shrugged. 'The gods are never just, Fronto. They are powerful and eternal, but they are also petty and vindictive. That is why we send so many sacrifices to them, to buy their favour. If gods were benevolent, we would not need to mollify them so much. Caesar, I think, has come too close to joining them for his own good. Gods don't like that. Look at what happened to Achilles.'

Fronto nodded, with a private shiver. Yes, he liked Cicero, but he didn't like the way the man's mind worked. What could the future hold for Rome with brains like those of Cicero and Octavian running it?

'I am pleased to have found a dead end in my work here,' Fronto said. 'I do wonder whether, if the world had been different, we might have been good friends. For now, I will take my leave and wish you good fortune in the coming days. May whatever happens fill your coffers once more.'

Cicero laughed. 'What will happen will happen. It is an old truism. You and I, I think, are too old and too set in our ways to face a new world. Better that we fade with the old one.'

Another unsettling proclamation. Fronto found himself worrying about that one as he nodded his head in respect and left the garden, crossing the massive, largely-empty house and emerging out into the open where his entourage waited for him.

There was too much going on in Rome under the surface. Too much conspiracy and distrust. He found himself ruminating, and not over-happily, over Cicero's many observations in such a short time as he crossed the city and made for the spacious villa of Publius Servilius Vatia Isauricus. Cicero had been a font of worrying ideas, and the one thing Fronto had come away with was the conviction that the great man, while he may be no great lover of Caesar, was neither part of any plot against him, nor the man controlling the collegium. He was, in fact, entirely disconnected from the whole thing, and Fronto would eat his own loincloth if he was proved wrong.

All the way across the Caelian, his mind whirled, until one of the guards announced that they were outside Vatia's house. The place was old-fashioned, plain, the walls filled with shops rented from the landowner, the house itself identifiable by just the door. As Fronto dismounted, one of his men knocked loud, and there was a long pause before the door opened.

Fronto blinked in surprise. Doorkeeper slaves in Rome, in fact across the whole republic, were almost uniformly heavy-set and humourless drones of slaves with a club. Their entire purpose was to open and close doors and smack on the head people who were not invited in. When Vatia's door was opened by a buxom blonde some six feet tall and wearing a diaphanous garment of loose netting that left absolutely nothing to the imagination, he was rather taken aback. The woman spoke to him in Latin heavily infused with what he reckoned was a Germanic dialect, and he was ushered inside. As he walked through the house behind her, he kept his eyes everywhere but on her, and repeated the mantra 'you're a married man, you're a married man, you're a married man,' over and over.

The blush-raising problem was not eased when he realised that the entire villa's staff were buxom, tall, leggy girls from all over the republic and beyond, and not one of them wearing more than a netting tunic or a see-through loincloth. By the time he was shown to Vatia's rooms, he was quite flustered.

'In there?' he asked the latest vixen, pointing to the door ahead.

She nodded and replied in a Syrian accent. 'After his noon exercise, the dominus likes an extended nap. You might have to shout to wake him.'

Fronto rapped on the door, opened it and stepped inside. He found himself musing on the fact that if he had the same exercise regime as the suspected Vatia had, then *he* would probably need an extended nap in the afternoon too. The man was in his eighties!

A lamp guttered to one side of the room, and a half-shuttered window added extra light. Vatia lay on his bed, though there was something odd about the shape. His personal slave, a pretty thing of perhaps sixteen, lay on a reed mat beside the bed, and the girl shot bolt upright at the arrival of a visitor.

A suspicion fell over Fronto and he crossed to the bed. He'd not even reached it before he settled on the opinion that the house's owner was *thoroughly* deceased. His face was a rictus of pain, his hands drawn into skeletal claws as though reaching for the gods to ask for more time. Fronto remembered his father's body. In the end it had been a heart attack that had carried the old bastard off, and he'd had a disconcertingly similar expression.

'Your master is dead.'

The slave girl blinked, stared, went very pale, then turned and examined the old man.

'You are not to blame,' Fronto reassured her. 'In fact, I suspect his noon exercise was behind it,' though a thought struck him even as he said it. It appeared so clearly to be natural causes, so clearly his heart, and in his mid eighties and with a house full of nubile sex slaves, it really was NO surprise that his heart couldn't take it.

And yet it was somewhat convenient that this man was the first to know the name of a conspirator, and had died before he could pass it on. Fronto turned to the slave.

'Who was the last person to visit your master?'

The slave frowned. 'Dee master not see people. Not maynee visitor. Two days, see Marcus Antonius.'

Fronto straightened. For just a moment, he panicked, but then realised that there were many reasons the two could meet. This man was – had *been* – the princeps senatus, the top man of the senate, and Antonius was consul. Their work would bring them into semi-regular meetings, although in truth Vatia rarely attended senate meetings these days. And it had been two days ago he had visited, while Vatia had been dead just hours.

No. Antonius was loyal. Always.

But even the thought was enough to make him shiver.

CHAPTER TWENTY ONE

Octavian rolled his shoulders, concentrating, running everything through his mind again and again. This had to be done right. It was his first time at the Lupercalia festival as a member of one of the collegia, and all eyes would be on him, or at least on him and Antonius. But as heir to Caesar – though the will had not yet been lodged, Caesar had confirmed to him that the will naming him as primary heir was written and would be lodged as soon as it was witnessed – his attendance had to be exemplary. He was still a little young for the honour, still eighteen, but tradition aside, there was no actual rule to prevent joining the priesthood before the age of twenty. And if he'd waited, it would be too late. Tomorrow, he departed for Illyricum and the army, and a first command against the Getae.

He glanced around. The three collegia were each gathered in their groups, ready. Octavian was in Antonius' new third collegium, the *Juliani*, of course. The priest of Jove was finishing up his work, his sacrificial animals now little more than bloody heaps on the floor of the grotto. The flickering lights of the braziers and lamps gave the cave an eerie glow, and the metallic smell of all the blood was heady, intoxicating. It was easy to find the mind wandering into wild imaginings in this place.

All around, the cave was decorated with mosaic designs, the whole creation sufficient in the dancing golden light to trick the eye and change even the general shape of the place. Once, long ago, this had been the cave where the infants Romulus and Remus were suckled, and here was one of the most sacred places in all of Rome. Of course, these days it resembled a temple more than a cave, formed into a smooth domed room, plastered and decorated on every surface.

His mind was wandering again. He concentrated. The young men of the Quinctiliani were moving now, stepping forward solemnly, one after another, to make their offerings. He watched, shivering slightly. The cave was relatively warm, what with the lamps and the braziers that gave it light, but the breeze that sporadically gusted in through the entrance still carried the chill of late winter rolling into early spring. And, of course, he was naked. That didn't help.

He was not shy. Not afraid of this, of displaying his physique. People went about their business at the baths naked, after all, and so public nudity was nothing new. But he could see one or two of the others looking rather self conscious. He forced himself not to smile at that. This part of the festival was austere, important. Not something for humour, not yet. Another chill and he shivered again as the last of the Quinctiliani finished and stepped back into their group. The Fabiani came next, one after the other, and he watched and waited patiently. Finally it was the turn of the Juliani.

Octavian gripped the salted meal cake carefully, dusty powder drifting down from the hand into which the Vestal virgin had placed it half an hour ago and, following the others, at the rear of the line being both the newest and youngest priest, he approached the altar and made his offering, murmuring the ritual words at a low hum as the others had done and adding his cake to the teetering pile. Stepping back, he took the blade up from the table beside the altar and, just as all the others had done, bent to the sacrificial carcass and cut a thong of hide free from it. The task was not an easy one, for both animals had been almost flayed clean by the others before him, but with a little work and care, he managed to hack free a foot-long strip of hide, the blood still warm as he worked, coating his hands.

Gripping his precious prize, he returned to position and, with the others, waited. He knew it would be him. He might be too young and new really, but such was his eminence in Rome that there was little chance of the honour passing him by. Sure enough, as the priest made his selection, his pointing finger fell upon a young man of the Aemilian gens and then upon Octavian.

The two men, trying not to let their pride show, faces as austere and expressionless as possible, stepped forward, approaching the altar. They stood side by side, eyes locked on the priest before them, as the man began the intonation of his prayer to Jupiter and to all the gods of Rome. Rite complete, he reached down for the knife he had used in the sacrifice, still bloody upon the altar, and lifted it. Solemnly, he wiped blood from the blade with his thumb and then reached up and smeared that blood across Octavian's forehead, repeating the gesture with the other young man.

In the silence that followed, the older man lowered the blade once more, and then intoned the ancient words, thanking the she wolf for her service to the founders of the city and devoting the attentions of the luperci to her, in particular the two representatives before him, tonight the embodiment of Romulus and Remus. He lifted a wad of milk-soaked wool and wiped the smears on their heads, which did not so much clean their foreheads as turn the blood into a watery pink paste. The priest smiled, cracking his veneer of austerity at last, and, freed of their constraint, the two chosen men laughed aloud as they turned and embraced.

'Go,' the Jovian priest called, his voice echoing around the domed cave. 'Bring joy and bounty to Rome.'

Released, the entire cave of Luperci erupted into howls and cries, the place sounding like the echoing den of a wolf pack, and then, their individual collegia forgotten, they piled into the cave mouth and emerged into the wide corridor already at a jog. The smooth flags beneath Octavian's feet were comfortable, and he made the most of it, knowing that he would feel every pebble and crack outside. But naked was naked, and that also meant no shoes.

They burst out into the late afternoon, the light fading, the sun already lost behind the buildings to the west. Torches and lamps were being lit around the city, but fires had already been set and lit along their route, illuminating the path. Beside the mouth of the cave stood two of the lictors who had been assigned to the Jovian priest for the occasion, preventing anyone unauthorised from entering the Lupercal, which would be cleared, cleaned and locked once the evening's events were done with.

Now, Octavian was running with the rest. He didn't look back, didn't need to. He would see the cave again soon enough. A circuit of the Palatine, and then back to the cave, following which they would be allowed to don tunics and boots once more for the festive meal.

He ran. They all ran. Howling like wolves, shrieking and laughing, naked as the day they were born, they ran. Beneath their bare feet, the streets were cold, but at least clean, for every flag had been meticulously swept of debris and gravel earlier, and washed thoroughly, all the way around the hill, the route they would take. But it was cold, and here and there a crack or a raised bump between flags would cause minor injury. Even stumbling, though, perhaps even bleeding, not one of them would stop. Broken toes would hamper no one this night, for this was a thing of the gods.

But also a thing of men.

And of women.

For as they ran, the crowds that had amassed to observe the run pressed close, as close as they *dared*, to the runners, each of whom was a noble son of Rome from a great house, but also an anointed priest, sacred to the gods. The only figures who dared to get in the way were the women, the young hopefuls and the recently married matrons, all of whom hoped for the intervention of the Luperci in their quest for childbirth. For to be struck by one of the runners was almost a guarantee of fertility.

A scrawny young woman in a green stola, wearing her very best jewellery, stepped into Octavian's path, and he howled, face raised to the darkening sky, baying at the heavens, and ducked around her, making sure to whip her across the midriff with the shaggy, bloody thong held tight in his grip. The woman shrieked with delight at the spattered red mark the thong left on the belly of her dress, and stepped back into the crowd to the cheers and delight of her family.

Ahead, someone had the worst night of their life, for one of the runners had dropped his thong, lost his grip from numb fingers, and had stopped, face white with horror. He bent to pick the thong back up, and looked around, guiltily, wondering if he could get away with pretending it had never happened, but people were pointing and shouting. His failure had been seen. The thong was no longer pure, no longer a thing of magic and sacredness. It could no longer help the barren. He would be doing penance for this all year, stripped of his priesthood, his family ashamed. Poor bastard. Octavian's grip on his own wolf tail tightened, just to be sure.

Another woman stepped out, and he struck her too, leaving marks, before he reached the corner of the Palatine and turned north, racing along between it and the Caelian hill. His throat was getting dry and sore now from all the howling, and his breath was coming sharply. Like many others, he started regulating his breathing for a while between howls, and slowed his pace slightly. The run had begun in a din and at a breakneck pace, the excitement hard to deny, but there was a long way to go, yet, and they had to conserve their breath and energy. His colleague for the year, the Aemilian fellow who'd been marked with him, stumbled suddenly, a stray flagged corner tearing a hole in the sole of his foot. He cried out with the sharp pain, flailing and almost falling, but determination won through. The lad was never going to let mere pain ruin this for him. Foot spattered with his own blood, he ran on, teeth clenched. Octavian approved, liked to think he would have done exactly the same.

More women stepped out now, and he managed to get two, though the third he missed, and she yelped in disappointment and tried to get struck by another, failing again and retreating into the crowd in tears. Puffing now, and aware that his thong had become a dry and ragged thing that would leave no more bloody marks, Octavian ran on, approaching the north eastern Palatine corner now. The bonfires lit the way ahead, where they would follow the Via Sacra along the lower northern slope of the hill, and the crowds were becoming larger and noisier here, where they approached the forum in the wider open spaces.

Octavian was running well, staying the course, while many of the others were lagging a little, dropping back, and he was now with the front dozen or so runners. He was rather impressed to see the heavy-set, gleaming naked figure of Marcus Antonius, head of the Juliani, close to the front. The man was neither thin, nor young, yet he was clearly as fit as any runner in this crowd. If ever Caesar had a war horse in his stable, Antonius was that horse.

It was as he watched Antonius that he saw something odd. As they passed the junction where the Via Nova arced off up the hill, Antonius suddenly slowed and dipped out to the left, the opposite

284

side to the gathered crowds that pressed for his attention. Octavian, curious, followed suit, allowing others to run past. They jogged along below the colonnaded steps of the temple of Jupiter Stator and Antonius slowed further. A half-hidden movement caught Octavian's eye and he saw the other man, where most would not. A shadowy figure, lurking behind the columns of the temple took two steps out into the open and threw something before disappearing from view once more.

Antonius caught what had been thrown to him and sped up once more.

Octavian picked up his pace in an effort to catch up, and in moments was running along not far from Antonius' heel. He squinted in the poor light, and his eyes widened at what he saw. Antonius was now carrying a diadem of gleaming gold, wrapped with a laurel wreath threaded with white poplar leaves, very similar to the one that had been placed on Caesar's statue a month ago. Antonius had a strange look on his face as he turned and realised that Octavian was with him. The younger man frowned, unsure whether what he was seeing was determination, worry, distaste, or quite possibly a mix of all three. Whatever he was doing, he clearly wasn't sure he wanted to do it.

Octavian, a thought occurring to him, looked up ahead. The further into the forum region they were getting, the bigger and more excited the crowd. But he was suddenly in no doubt as to what was about to happen. They jogged beneath the great arch of Fabianus and emerged into the main forum area, the basilicas, temples and columns all around them, but his eyes were on one sight alone, as were Antonius'.

Gaius Julius Caesar sat on a golden curule chair on the great rostra, watching the festivities. His lictors were at the rostra steps, preventing unwanted persons from approaching, though a score of the city's most eminent men, notably ones who supported Caesar, were up there with him, standing in a knot nearby. The path of the runners followed directly in front of the rostra, and the nearest bonfire was opposite Caesar's position, illuminating he and his companions clearly for all Rome to see, despite the rapidly encroaching evening gloom.

The lead runners, the most athletic among the Luperci, ran past, howling, waving their wolf-thongs in the air, grinning at Caesar and the great and good of Rome as they passed.

But not Antonius.

Fully anticipating his actions, as Antonius slowed, Octavian also came to a halt just behind him. Their unexpected stop caused a ripple through the entire group, and the runners behind them also slowed and stopped now, the ones ahead drifting to a halt and turning to see what had happened.

'Don't do this,' Octavian hissed, just loud enough for Antonius nearby to hear but too quiet to draw attention from the crowd.

Antonius simply shot him a look, which Octavian read as 'as if I have a choice.' Then, putting on a beaming smile that never once reached his eyes, Antonius stepped away from the runners and approached the rostra. Octavian looked up at Caesar, and was impressed. The man was a master, for he managed to look a little confused and even a little surprised, while Octavian was sure that in reality this whole thing had Caesar's fingerprints all over it. Indeed, from the looks on the faces of Caesar's companions, especially Marcus Brutus and Aulus Hirtius, they had clearly formed the same opinion, looks of distaste falling across them. In fact, only Fronto looked as though he approved, which seemed odd, but then Octavian had often found Fronto to be difficult, partially because of his unpredictable nature.

Antonius passed the lictors, who did not move to stop him, and climbed the steps of the rostra, approaching Caesar. The dictator remained seated on his golden chair, and it occurred to Octavian just how carefully Caesar must have planned this. He wore a toga picta, deep purple picked out in gold thread, a garment usually reserved for a triumphant general. A precedent allowed such a thing, for Caesar had the right to wear it, given that he had triumphed, and more than once, but it was not generally done to wear it at other occasions. Beneath the toga, he also wore the tunica palmata of a triumphant general, once again purple, with palm leaves picked out in gold. It was, of course, perfectly acceptable regalia for a son of the republic, but in the right circumstances, it would escape the notice of few that purple was also the colour of kings in the east, a hue adopted by the absolute monarchs of Macedonia, of Persia, of Judea. And in case anyone was left unsure over just how powerful the purple-clad man before them was, he clutched the baton of imperium that no man could wield within the pomerium, the symbol of total military authority carried by a proconsul abroad. No governor, general, senator or even consul, could carry that baton in the sacred heart of the city.

But Caesar was none of those, and yet all, and more. He was dictator of Rome, and no man could deny him anything.

Two men moved, now, up on the raised platform. Two men, both scions of that same Brutus who had expelled the last king of Rome and founded the republic, both bearing down on Antonius to intercept him. Marcus Junius Brutus and Decimus Junius Brutus Albinus both wore horrified expressions as they went to stop this. Octavian did nothing of the sort. He could see where this was going. He might not approve, for such a display could go horribly wrong, as it had a month ago, but if it went right...

Fronto clearly knew too, for the grizzled old veteran stepped out and blocked the way for the two Brutii, bringing them to a halt, and clearing the way for the approaching naked runner.

Antonius reached the top of the steps and crossed to where Caesar sat. He still had his wolf-thong in his left hand, but in his right, he held a crown. Caesar still wore a look of worried bafflement that Octavian did not believe for a moment.

Now, the seated dictator made to rise, but Antonius was there in time to act first. With no preamble, he lowered the crown onto Caesar's head. There was a strange, tight hush across the forum as all the world watched Caesar being crowned, many with horror, a precious few with delight. The crown rested there for just a moment as Caesar maintained his confused expression, and then his face twisted into a picture of distaste and he reached up, grasped the diadem and removed it.

It was masterfully done. He'd uncrowned himself, but he had left it just long enough for the image to sink deep into the minds of every observer in the forum. Caesar, crowned, regal, seated in royal purple with a sceptre of absolute power. It was a strong image, and one that no one could possibly forget or misinterpret. Octavian knew that he would see that picture in his mind's eye for the rest of his life.

And as if subliminally planting the image of Caesar as all-powerful king into the mind of all present, the man was not yet done with his show. Now, he had removed the crown and thrust it away with distaste.

'Never,' he said, loud enough that his voice cut across the whole forum.

Octavian focused on Antonius. All the world was looking at Caesar, breathless, and would not have noticed the look of utter distaste on Antonius as he took the crown back and cleared his throat.

'The people of Rome offer you a crown,' the naked man shouted. 'Will you not accept it?'

It would be galling for Antonius, Octavian knew. He wondered what Caesar had dangled in front of the man to get him to do this. More than the consulship, clearly. Octavian's attention turned briefly to the surrounding crowd. The sound out there did not support the notion that they were offering Caesar a crown. There were a few lonely cheers among the press, a little sporadic clapping, but a lot more groans, and even more shocked and disapproving silence.

Octavian winced. It appeared to be going wrong again, just as it had that day Caesar returned from Alba, and the very reason Octavian would have counselled against the whole thing.

There was a heavy pause, a tense moment, the silence reinstating. Octavian clenched his hands, gritted his teeth, willed something positive to happen. He could see the Brutii still, and now it was clear from their faces that both of them knew this for a carefully constructed play. Marcus Junius Brutus' lip was curling up in distaste.

At some unseen and unheard cue, Antonius once more stepped forward, and once more placed the crown on Caesar's head. This time there was a distinct rumble of unhappiness all across the forum, but once again, as Antonius stepped back, Caesar reached up and removed the diadem.

'Rome is a republic,' he announced loudly. 'Take this up to the capitol and put it where it belongs, for Jupiter *alone* is king of the Romans.'

With this he thrust the crown at Antonius, who took it with head bowed. Across the forum, the crowd erupted in cheers and applause. Caesar rose as Antonius, his task complete, retreated down the rostra steps once more and out of sight of the public. As the crowd continued to show its approval for the dictator, Caesar cast his golden chair down from the rostra, a final show of his ordinariness as he stood now among his peers.

Octavian caught sight briefly of Antonius, who was now moving back around to join the runners, the crown gone already, probably to a lictor. His face was a picture of self-loathing for just a moment until he was in sight of the public once more, when that expression was suddenly gone, replaced once more by an easy smile.

Octavian let his teeth and fists unclench. The old goat had done it. This was precisely what Caesar had been aiming for that other day with a crown, a month ago. This time, though, there were no plebeian tribunes around to interfere and cause it all to go sour. This time it had all gone according to plan. It had not escaped Octavian's notice that it had *almost* messed up again, with the interference of the Brutii, but that Fronto, seemingly in on it, or at least bright enough to realise what was happening, had stepped in to prevent that.

As the crowd continued to roar and celebrate, so someone called for the festivities to resume, and moments later the runners were off again, turning and heading past Caesar's new basilica, racing along the Vicus Tuscus towards the southwest corner of the Palatine and that sacred cave once again. As he ran, just behind Antonius once more, Octavian mused over what he'd seen, occasionally pausing to smack a hopeful matron with his pelt-thong.

Caesar had been experiencing a massive decline in popularity. Many senators disliked or feared him, and even those who fawned about him and heaped honours upon him, Octavian was sure, largely did so out of fear and self-preservation, rather than loyalty or approval. And that had not particularly worried the man, despite all rumours of plots and predictions of his death, for he had been at odds with the senate before but had persevered and triumphed in the end. But he was also becoming less and less popular with the people, who feared not only a crown in the man's future, but also a move eastwards and the creation of a new Rome, who saw Caesar as under the influence of that Aegyptian witch, Cleopatra.

In one display, at an event large enough to have drawn a massive crowd, Caesar had put the latter right once more, his repeated refusal of a crown and devotion to Jupiter earning him new support, loyalty and love from the people of Rome. And those who were not here to see it would tell the rest, and over the hours and days that followed, the story would become greater and ever more noble in the retelling. The people were Caesar's once more.

Octavian could go to Apollonia safely, now, knowing that his legacy was again looking stable.

There was just one thing that nagged at him, though, as he returned to the Lupercal and found his underwear, tunic, boots and belt and began to dress for the great feast that would follow in the Basilica Iulia.

The last thing he had seen at the rostra before leaving was not the triumphant humility of Caesar, nor the bitter acceptance of Antonius. It had not been the relief on Fronto's face, nor the joy and praise among the ordinary people.

The last thing he had seen had been the two Brutii, and neither had looked either fooled or happy.

Trouble yet lay ahead.

ROME. LATE FEBRUARIUS.

The wind whipped through the window, bringing the chill with it, making the room's occupants shiver.

'We could strike at the elections in the campus martius,' mused Galba as he rose, crossed to the window, looked around to confirm yet again that no one was in earshot, and closed the shutters.

'Too crowded,' the house's owner replied.

'But we could split into two groups. Jove, Cassius, but there are nearly sixty of us now. We are more than tyrannicides now, we're practically an army.'

'Two groups,' agreed Trebonius. 'One moves up onto the voting platform with him and throws him off, while the other can be waiting below to do the deed. And the campus martius is outside the Pomerium, so we can have blades bared.'

'No. It is a meaningful spot, but still too crowded, and therefore too unpredictable. There is a high possibility of something going wrong.'

'Then how about on the sacred way?' Cimber put in. 'There is barely a day he doesn't pass along it one way or another and it's in the heart of Rome. Very visible.'

'Same problem,' Casca said. 'And not only too crowded, but not significant enough.'

'Not *significant*? The *Via Sacra*?'

'Not for our purpose. The location needs to have value in terms of both politics and Romanitas.'

'It needs to be the senate house,' Cassius said. 'That has always been our plan.'

'But the senate meets on the Ides of next month. That is too late. Spurinna's prediction…'

'Was that Caesar would die by the Ides. He did not specify whether that was the start of the Ides or the end. There is still time. The senate house represents Rome, its power, its history, its value,

291

it is the perfect place. And there is the added irony that the senate currently meets in the curia within Pompey's theatre complex, and there are still many who bemoan Pompey's loss and remember him as the last powerful general who served republican interests. Moreover, it is also outside the pomerium, and so blades can be borne there without breaking the law.'

'There may be sixty of us,' Galba said, 'but do not forget how many senators are still Caesar's creatures. We are a force to be reckoned with, but we will still be greatly outnumbered in the senate.'

'I have no intention of fighting my way through the senators to get to him,' Cassius snapped. 'The day will be carefully engineered. We will need distractions to keep his key supporters out of the way. We will need to neutralise all those private forces his allies rely upon and who they will bring to the steps that day as escorts. And we will somehow need to persuade the man himself to attend the meeting. If he has any sense, given the predictions, he will hide in his bedroom until the day is over and he has survived.'

'Yet he could die any day now and prove Spurinna right, yet he goes about his daily business as though nothing has changed.'

They fell into sudden silence at a rap on the door.

'What?' Cassius barked.

The door opened and his head slave stood on the corridor, head bowed. 'You have a visitor, sir. He would not give his name, but he is a nobleman, sir. I see a striped toga beneath his cloak.'

Casca frowned and turned, a warning look to the rest, then followed his slave out into the open, across the peristyle, through the atrium and to the house's vestibule. As his eyesight adjusted to the gloomy interior once more, he saw the cloaked figure in the hallway, examining the altar of the household gods, a man in a senator's toga. Cassius frowned. He did not like surprises.

The figure turned, a grave expression on his face.

'I'm in,' said Marcus Junius Brutus.

MARCH

"His slayers, to be sure, declared that they had shown themselves at once destroyers of Caesar and liberators of the people: but in reality they impiously plotted against him, and they threw the city into disorder when at last it possessed a stable government.

– Cassius Dio: History LXIV.1

CHAPTER TWENTY TWO

Galronus coughed uncomfortably and glanced sidelong at Salvius Cursor.

'Every passing moment makes me less sure about this.'

Salvius said nothing, just cradled his wine cup and watched the basilica.

'We should go back.'

'No,' Salvius said, this time. 'Something has to be done. I am the head of Caesar's bodyguard. Or I was, and will be, anyway.'

'One defining thing about the head of a guard,' Galronus said archly, 'is that he usually has a guard around to be head of. We're alone. They're not.'

He was definitely starting to regret going along with Salvius' plan. It had sounded like a good idea to begin with, but in practice he could now see the dangers.

The ides of Martius were now but two days away, and Caesar's departure for the east just five. The dictator was going on with his blasé approach to the world in which he seemed to disbelieve the predictions of Spurinna and worked on the assumption that all would be fine, he would attend this last meeting of the senate and then depart for Illyricum and the east. But all those around him were becoming more and more tense. Galronus, as something of an outsider, had seen it in the others, in all those who came and went from Caesar's house: Oppius, the Brutii, Hirtius, Cornelius Balbus, Antonius, and even Fronto. And as for the man's women, Cleopatra and Calpurnia, both were on edge like Galronus had never seen before. Everyone was waiting for Caesar to fall, and no one could really do anything about it. The only solution seemed to be locking Caesar in a cellar for the duration, and the man would not accept any form of hiding.

Only Octavian could not be seen to be worrying, but that was simply because he was absent from Rome now, safely over in Apollonia with the army. Fronto had thrown himself into the various last moment planning stages of the Parthian expedition, things that could really be done after the ides, and ideally even by other people, particularly Octavian. But Fronto had tried to persuade Caesar to take on more protection and be more careful so often now that the pair kept falling out. Besides, Fronto was starting to think that, plots notwithstanding, it might be natural causes that carried the man off before the ides, for he was having his fits at least every other day now. What he would be like on campaign in the east, who knew?

It had been Salvius, then, who had decided to make the move. He'd not approached Fronto, and had been busy putting together a bag of rations, tablets and stilus, coin purses and two knives when Galronus had stumbled across him in the storeroom.

'What are you doing?'

Salvius had tried to bluster his way out of the question, but Galronus had persisted and drawn from the man his plan.

They had only two days to find out what would kill Caesar and to stop it. If it were illness or an accident there was nothing they could do, but if not, then it seemed a certainty that it would be some move made by the mysterious plotters that rumour had it were conspiring in the city. With no evidence on who might be involved, Salvius had drawn up a small list of names and had decided to follow and observe them.

He'd discounted Cicero, following a short conversation with Fronto in which the man had stated that he knew for a fact Cicero was not at fault in this. But that still left a few names, and top of that list was the man who had been set against Caesar for years. Since the senate had been rebuilt following the rebels' flight from Rome, few who sat in that august body would speak out openly against Caesar, and of those, one name stood out proud.

Lucius Pontius Aquila. He'd been an open supporter of Pompey, had denounced Caesar time and again, and voted against him repeatedly in the senate, for all the good that did. There were also Sulpicius Galba and Tillius Cimber, of course, who were usually to be found in Aquila's company. But of them all, Aquila seemed to be the one to call the moves. And so, Salvius would watch Aquila. And when he uncovered the senator's plot, he would unravel it, for he was grimly content that Aquila was his man.

He had been so convincing, and the whole matter so frustrating, that Galronus had found himself nodding, agreeing, even planning to go with the man. Salvius had agreed to that. He was going incognito, with no retinue, for it would be extraordinarily difficult to follow and spy on anyone with a small armed force and a gaggle of slaves following on. However, two ordinary men in the street together might be even less conspicuous than one.

So Galronus had also gathered together a bag of things, and the two men had slipped from Fronto's house and descended the Aventine, making for the forum. This morning, three men were being tried in the Basilica Aemilia on charges of bearing false witness at state trials, and the responsibility of presiding over such a case fell on the praetor in charge of *falsum*, notably Aquila. Thus, on one rare occasion, they had foreknowledge of where and when they would find the man, outside a sitting of the senate.

They had reached the forum and checked, confirming that Aquila was, indeed, present for the trial. A little wandering around and listening to the chatter of the various groups gathered near the basilica and waiting, and it was not difficult to identify that which belonged to Aquila. The litter was plain, though of high quality, the four red-haired slaves bearing it enormous. Two other slaves stood around looking miserable, and the whole group were guarded by two lictors and ten private mercenaries.

That had been what had started Galronus fretting. Twelve armed men protecting Aquila, and he doubted that if they spotted the two observers, the ten men would baulk at putting in the boot in defence of their master. He and Salvius would have to play it very carefully.

The entourage were gathered at the south-eastern corner of the basilica, which sported three doors out into the forum, the frontage covered with small shops and cauponae. Maintaining an air of nonchalance and normality, the two men had wandered over to a small caupona next to the easternmost of the three doors, bought a jug of wine and two cups, and took a seat at the wooden trestle in front, in exactly the same manner as several other ordinary forum-goers.

Within half an hour, they had exhausted every topic of bland conversation they could come up with, hampered by the realisation that they shared almost no interests whatsoever, and so they moved on to more or less monologues, with Galronus explaining to the other man the minutiae of the current racing season, its riders, the best moments, the horses to watch and so on, while when he finished, Salvius started to blather about some new comedy that was doing the rounds in the theatre, all bare bums and fart gags. The sort of thing that would make Fronto laugh. After a while they fell silent, poured another drink and, assuming that after all this time, anyone listening in would have forgotten what they had previously said, began to trot out their limited repertoire of small talk again.

The guards, lictors and slaves of Aquila's entourage paid them absolutely no attention, but Galronus had had enough chases, attacks and other encounters in the streets these past few months to know that just because everything looked peaceful did not mean that the next moment someone would not be trying to stove your head in with a plank. He kept a careful watch, while doing his level best to look like he wasn't.

It was almost noon when the senator finally put in an appearance, stepping out of the basilica, his guards flocking to his side once more to escort him from the building. Galronus and Salvius both drained the last sip from their cups ready, but just as they were about to leave, Aquila gestured to someone in the crowd across the forum, and then beckoned, standing mere paces from where the two men sat.

Galronus forced himself to stay calm. The man had no reason to recognise Salvius at all and, though Galronus had been to plenty of sessions in the senate alongside Aquila, the Remi had never once stood and spoken, keeping his part in all activities to simply joining the 'ayes' or the 'nays' in a vote. Aquila had probably never even registered Galronus' presence there, let alone committed his face to memory. Then again, the Remi was often to be seen in Fronto's company, and Fronto, the man would remember well. Just in case, Galronus lowered his face. He was dressed in a fairly nondescript manner, and, clean-shaven and short-haired like most Romans, he would hardly stand out. He had toyed with the idea of growing it all again, and might just do that when they left for Durocortorum, but for now, he looked thoroughly average in the forum.

His heart began to pound as Aquila came closer and stood not ten paces from him, the two lictors making sure he was untouched by the populace while the figure to whom he'd gestured in the crowd emerged and crossed to join him.

Recognition of the man did little to ease Galronus' nerves, as Servilius Casca approached. Again, the Remi kept his eyes lowered. Casca, one of Caesar's old friends, keeping company with Aquila was a surprise. Casca was an occasional visitor at Caesar's house, though not often, yet he might just recognise Galronus. He found he was holding his breath.

'Not here,' was all Casca said, in a slightly offended tone. With that, he strode off.

Salvius and the Remi shared a look and refilled their cups, taking another swig, while Aquila made irritated noises and gestured for his litter, which was brought round in front of the caupona. The two men sat sipping, murmuring nothings, as the senator climbed into the litter and was heaved aloft by the red-haired slaves. Moments later he and his entourage were on the move, passing along the front of the basilica in the direction of the Argiletum, moving past the shop fronts. As soon as they were two shops away and paying more attention in front than behind, Galronus and Salvius rose, dipped back into the basilica and hurried along its length inside, hidden from their prey. At the far end, they emerged from the westernmost door, slowly and carefully, to find they were only twenty paces behind the litter as it turned left and marched off across the square below the slopes of the Capitol.

'One at a time, yes?'

Salvius nodded and dropped back a little, letting Galronus move off ahead, the two stringing out along the way, less visible if they had been noted in the bar as a pair. They followed the litter with relative ease through the crowded forum, and then onto the Vicus Jugarius, heading towards the river. Carefully, the Remi moved on along the route, occasionally pausing at shops, ducking into alleys, or changing to a different side of the street, making sure to keep more interesting looking people between him and Aquila's guards.

And so it went, slowly and carefully, through the forum holitorium, the Circus Flaminius, and along the road lined with recent construction, once little more than a grassy plain, until they found themselves below the towering curved walls of Pompey's theatre. For a moment, he thought they were making for the Baths of Fortunatus and grumbled that he seemed cursed to shadow people in bathhouses, but at the last moment, the entourage changed direction and skirted the outside of the huge complex of Pompey. The great sprawling mass of stonework was accessible only from one end, where the steps climbed from a line of ancient temples, two great archways granting access on each side of the current senate house.

The memory of his last visit to this place replayed itself as he watched the man's litter come to a halt at the base of the steps. A session of the senate, descending those very steps and then racing off past those temples in pursuit of the men of the Pompeian collegium. This time he was, again, following someone, but at a much more sedate pace.

Galronus could hear the huge murmur of a crowd in the theatre itself even from the far end of the complex, suggesting there was a play on, this afternoon. He did not like the theatre. It bored him. He liked chariots thundering across the sand. Still, there was little he could do. The Remi waited for a short while as Aquila's litter slowly and carefully climbed the steps, the bearers struggling to keep their burden level even as they ascended. He watched the litter pass the currently closed senate house and disappear into one of the arches, and then waited for Salvius to catch him up.

'What do you think?'

'I think we'd best go watch a play,' the man replied, subtly gesturing across the street. Galronus' gaze slid that way and he again spotted Casca leaning from the window of his litter as it approached.

'I hate plays.'

'You'll like this one. All tits and arse and pratfalls.'

299

Galronus rolled his eyes as the two men waited for Casca's litter to pass and climb the steps, and then followed at a distance. Through the arches, they emerged into the great portico, some two hundred paces long, which lay between the curia, with its arched entrances, and the theatre itself. The portico was surrounded by a colonnade that sheltered shops, bars and places where the public could tether animals or leave litters for a fee. The great open space was laid out as a grand garden, and already around it milled the many folk who were here as entourages of the wealthy, waiting during the performance for their masters and employers. Hurrying across the great open space, they managed to locate the litters of both Aquila and Casca, parked some distance apart as the two entourages settled in for a long wait. The lictors were not with the litter of Aquila, while many of his mercenaries were, suggesting he'd taken a minimal personal guard with him. The two hunters reached the arched entrances to the theatre itself and spoke to the man at the counter.

There were not many places left, the performance about to begin, but they secured two seats together, far up in the higher tiers, and then moved into the passageways. Galronus cursed as he realised they had lost both their quarries, but followed Salvius along endless corridors and staircases until they arrived, puffing and panting, at the top.

The theatre was almost full, and their view of the play pretty poor, the actors small, distant figures. They watched the introduction of the play and the speech of the narrator and his chorus, already full of bawdy jokes, and the sound carried well even up into this high place. But their attention was on the crowd. It took quite a while to spot their prey. Aquila was seated near the stage in one of the most expensive seats, probably one reserved for him, his name carved into the stone. The seats around him had been kept empty, his lictors close by, but it now came as no surprise to see Casca near to him. The two leaned close several times and exchanged words which were totally inaudible up here, and would likely be just as impossible to hear by the other nearby guests, given the general noise of the play and its audience. The perfect place, Galronus noted, for a clandestine conversation.

His mind raced. They had no evidence linking Aquila to a plot, of course. He was just the most obvious name that leapt to mind if you were going to suspect anyone. And Casca would never have appeared on the list. He and his brother were old friends of the Julii and had never, as far as the Remi knew, spoken out against Caesar. Yet their very manner was highly suggestive of conspiracy, and it was hard not to picture it.

If they could prove this, then they might be able to unravel it all. Casca could be the key to saving Caesar. After half an hour, knowing they would get nothing more from the pair by sitting here, the Remi gestured to Salvius that they should leave. Salvius grumbled, as he was enjoying the show, but eventually nodded, and the two slipped away into a stair corridor and descended once more to street level.

'What now?'

'Wait and watch.'

And so they did. They moved across the portico to where the litters and entourages waited, where water was available, and snacks for a price. There they bought bread and pork, and ate while they waited, drinking water from the fountain and trying to look as though they, too, were just waiting for someone. They made sure to be far from Aquila's men, yet within sight, resting on stone benches by a fountain at the centre of the portico.

It had seemed an age when there was finally a huge thunder of applause in the theatre and the play ended. Shortly thereafter, the audience began to emerge from the arched entrances and go their many ways, a number of the wealthier ones gathering in this large portico and collecting their slaves and guards.

The two men watched. Aquila appeared first, crossing to his men and giving orders. The litter was retrieved and he climbed inside, being lifted easily and borne away across the portico. Galronus' gaze swept across to the litter of Casca, as yet no sign of its owner visible. He fretted and turned again, Aquila rapidly disappearing into the crowd.

'I think we need to split up.'

Salvius Cursor nodded. 'I'll stay on Aquila. You follow Casca.'

And with that the man was off, threading his way through the crowd in pursuit of the distant litter. The Remi stood and waited. It

301

was some time before Casca finally appeared, crossing the portico, and instructed his litter bearers. They lifted him and began to carry him away from the place, towards those steps. Once again, Galronus followed on, crossing the campus martius and climbing the slopes of the Quirinal.

Finally, as he rounded a corner, carefully, eyes on his prey ahead, he saw them come to a halt outside the boundary wall of a large urban villa. The Remi cursed himself for not knowing more of the houses of the wealthy in Rome, for he had no idea whose home this could be, and it clearly wasn't Casca's from the fact that the entourage were halted at the door, rather than simply going inside. Perhaps if he got closer he might find more of a clue. Slowing, so that he could fall in line with a family who were trudging up the hill, using them as camouflage, he closed on the gathering. As he slowed once more, the door to the house opened and Casca stepped inside. Immediately, his slaves and bearers settled down to wait, but the various armed men folded their arms and turned, paying attention now to the street. Galronus flinched as he recognised fresh danger. He turned his back on the gathering, looking over a counter full of seafood outside a shop. The owner finished a transaction with a drab-looking woman, filled her small bucket and slid a live eel into it. She tottered off, heaving her bucket, bracing with the weight, and the man turned to Galronus.

The Remi was starting to feel a little queasy with the smell of all the sea life, both live and dead. He had been born and bred and had lived in Remi lands, a long way from the sea, and the most adventurous fish he'd ever eaten before the wars had been trout. He'd never liked the look of most of the things the Romans seemed to haul out of the water and push down their throats. Half of it was still moving at the time, and the rest they left to ferment so long it made the eyes water.

'What can I get you?' the shopkeeper asked.

Galronus fought the urge to say 'a bucket,' and instead looked around the counter. 'What's best.'

'I got lovely oysters.'

Galronus nodded, trying not to breathe in too deeply. 'How much are they?'

'Four denarii for ten, all good quality, brought in overnight from Portus Veneris in Liguria, fresh as it comes.'

'Freshen them with a bit of information, and I'll give you ten for ten.'

The man's brow creased for a moment, but he quickly overcame his suspicion, naked avarice taking its place. 'Go on.'

Galronus kept his gaze, intent, on the bowl full of oysters, trying not to imagine eating one. 'The house behind me, across the road. Who does it belong to? Don't look up,' he added sharply.

The man, who'd been about to look at the house, cleared his throat and looked back down at the oysters instead. 'That is the house of Cassius Longinus, my friend.'

The Remi nodded. *Cassius.* A man of whom he was well aware. He thanked the shopkeeper, produced the coins and dropped them on the counter as the man produced a net bag of rough twine and counted out ten oysters into it. 'If these are being kept for a day or two, don't let them dry out. As soon as you get home, decant them into a bowl of water, preferably water with a reasonable salt content.'

Galronus nodded, thanked the man and turned, marching on up the street as though he were about his daily business. He kept facing directly ahead, but allowed his eye to swivel enough to take in the house. The guards were still paying attention to the street about them, and he got the momentary impression that more than one of them were looking directly at him, but dare not let his gaze linger long enough to draw attention, and moments later, he was away.

A hundred paces further up the way, he turned left into a smaller side alley, and took the opportunity to give one quick sidelong glance back down the street. His heart lurched as he realised that two of Casca's men were moving up the street after him now, not running, but definitely at a fast, purposeful walk. As they saw him look back and turn, they broke into a run, and Galronus did the same.

Why in the name of all the gods had he gone along with this idiotic idea of Salvius'? Worse still, they'd told no one where they were going, and nobody therefore knew they were in danger. And then they'd split up. He'd heard more than once in the army the old joke. 'Let's split up. We'll cover more ground that way,' the intimation being 'with our blood and guts.'

Now, here he was, alone, in an area of Rome he didn't know very well, with two trained killers chasing him. And he was under no illusion that they would be unskilled thugs. Casca was important, and so any men he trusted to guard him in the city would be good. It was faintly possible that Galronus was good enough to take two of them on, but it certainly wasn't worth betting his life on. And if two of them had spotted him as potential trouble, then probably their friends were well aware of him too. And if they were, then very quickly, Casca would be. And Casca was at Cassius' house, where one of Rome's most powerful men lived, along with a strong guard drawn from the veteran survivors of the battle of Carrhae he had limped home with. In short: if he did not get away fast, he might find half the Quirinal after him.

He reached a junction and tried to turn right, further and further from the house, only to find that some sort of work was going on in the street, all the stonework torn up, the sewer beneath open to the air, workmen everywhere and piles of equipment and stone and earth making the route impassable. Cursing, he turned left instead, horribly aware that this meant he was now heading back in the direction of the house, parallel, one street back.

Still, he ran. This was news that needed to reach Fronto. There was absolutely no doubt in his mind now that they were onto the conspirators. Aquila had to be part of it – *had* to be – and if there was a second most likely man on the list, that man would be Cassius Longinus. The inclusion of Casca as a link between the two was extremely worrying, for Casca should be as loyal as anyone.

With three names, it should not be hard to uncover more. The irony did not escape him, that one of the praetors who would sit in any trial for such a crime would be Aquila himself.

The Remi shook his head. Now was not the time to untangle it all. Now was just the time to get away. He pounded on down the street towards another junction. He could see a high, bare wall opposite, and judged that, with the distance he must have already run, that would almost certainly be a side wall of Cassius' house.

Bollocks.

He had the distinct feeling he was in trouble. A glance over his shoulder and he could see his two pursuers now gaining on him. They must have realised that they had seen him at the basilica, and then, again at least once, at their destination. The odds of such a double meeting by chance were incredibly small in this city, and so even his presence twice would warrant extreme suspicion. It was, of course, possible that someone even recognised him as an oft-time companion of Fronto.

He reached the corner and skipped to a halt, trying to decide what to do. His spirits plunged as he saw two more standing in the street to his right, while other guards were approaching from the left. He was trapped.

He rolled his shoulders. 'Alright. Who's first.'

* * *

Salvius Cursor had been having a little more luck. Aquila had stopped at a small bathhouse on the edge of the campus martius and gone inside. The hunter had weighed up the possibilities. In the baths he might be able to glean a clue as to what was going on, see who his quarry met, but he would also be naked and unarmed, unable to run if he had to. But outside he would remain ignorant.

It was as he was trying to decide that his gaze played across the various attendants waiting in the small square beside the complex. A dozen men were gathered around a horse of pale grey, with expensive military harness decorations. He had the distinct feeling he knew the horse's owner, but could not quite place it, irritatingly. Could it be chance that Aquila was here, and so was another nobleman of note?

Hardly.

Sighing, Salvius Cursor approached the building and was about to step into the doorway when a familiar figure appeared, freshly bathed and primped, in his finery, leaving the baths.

'Good afternoon,' Marcus Junius Brutus said with a humourless smile.

Something hit the back of Salvius' head and everything went black.

CHAPTER TWENTY THREE

Fronto waited impatiently for the slave to admit him, and the moment the man stepped aside, the visitor marched straight past him, through the house, and into Caesar's office.

The whole villa was in chaos, though of the ordered kind. The final session of the senate was set for this afternoon, and in just three days now, Caesar was leaving for Parthia. Consequently, slaves were everywhere, gathering and packing all that would be required for the next few months, and carrying out the myriad tasks that would need to be completed before he left. Fronto marched past the carefully neutral expression of Calpurnia without acknowledging her, past the triumphant expression of Cleopatra, past the worried looking Caesarion, who was too young to remember the exotic land of his birth, to which he would now be expected to return.

Fronto didn't care.

Caesar turned in surprise at his arrival.

'Fronto? I...'

'Have you seen Galronus? Or Salvius Cursor?'

The dictator frowned, paused, shook his head. 'Not since your last visit. In fact, I don't think they were present then either. The visit before, perhaps.'

Fronto let out an explosive breath and collapsed into a chair, draping himself.

'You've lost them?' Marcus Antonius, previously unnoticed, called from another chair across the room.

'Nobody's seen them for two days. We got up yesterday morning and they'd both gone. I had people search their rooms, and we found out they'd took money, knives, writing gear and other things, but they left their armour, swords, cloaks and togas behind. Just went in tunics. There'd been no struggle, so they both left of their own accord, without telling anyone. They seem to have conveniently chosen a moment when the doorkeeper had left his post for a call of nature, though the man seems to spend half his time in the latrine, so that might have been coincidence. And they seem to have gone together. Whatever they went to do, it must be something I'd disapprove of, cos they never spoke to me before they left, and clearly deliberately so.'

'Could they be passed out in a bar somewhere?' Antonius asked.

'I don't think so. Galronus is always careful to stay sober enough to return to my sister, you've met her, so you understand, and Salvius doesn't drink a lot of wine since his illness. Doesn't agree with him so much now. I checked the cauponae where they both tend to go, anyway, and there was no sign of them. Same with the people at the circus who know Galronus, what with him being a regular. No one seems to have seen them for days.'

Caesar folded his arms. Have you checked the ports? Someone will have a list of departing passengers.'

Fronto shook his head. 'I can't speak for Salvius, but Galronus planned to stay with me until the summer, and was then heading north back into Gaul. There is no reason I can think of he'd take a ship now, especially without Faleria. I'll check next with the navalia and the emporium, but it's a long-shot at best.'

'Could they have gone to family?'

Fronto shook his head. 'Galronus doesn't *have* family in Rome, and Salvius wouldn't go to his. He only has cousins in the city, and when they thought he was dead, they cleared out his house, sold his slaves and most of his stuff. That's why he's still staying with me. I did check his house, but it was still empty and unused.'

He sighed. 'I even wondered if they'd gone to do something about the former collegium of Pompeians. I badgered some poor sod in the tabularium until he searched all the discarded records following the banning of collegia and found me the name of one of the Pompeians. I visited the man and gave a bloody nose, and the man swears blind that neither he nor any of his mates know anything about the pair. And I ended up with him held over the latrines in the baths, head first. I know when a man's panicked enough to tell the truth. I've checked the senate house, a tavern I

307

know that caters specifically for Gauls, and all our mutual friends. Nothing.'

'And I am your last port of call?' Caesar asked.

'You've been busy. And I figured if they'd come to you, I'd know it by now. I'm at the end. No idea where else to look. I even went up the Esquiline and checked the body warehouse, just in case, but they've not turned up there either. And did you know that some enterprising fellow near the temple of Portunus keeps a records of all the bodies that wash up on the riverbank, even animals? He's not seen them, either. I'm stuck.'

Caesar nodded. 'I do not fear for their life, though, Fronto. Such is the nature of those two men that had they fallen foul of enemies there would have been such bloodshed in the streets we would have heard about it.'

Fronto was less sure. He knew what the streets of Rome were like these days.

'I fear your guarantee of a reunion will be to stay close to me,' Caesar said with a wry smile.

'Oh?'

'Salvius Cursor has been champing at the bit to return to the campaigning life as my bodyguard. I have flatly refused to have such a unit in the city, as you know, but the moment we leave, our mutual friend will return to his commission, and nothing short of divine intervention will get in his way, I fear. Mark my words, by the time I set foot on that ship, Salvius Cursor will be by my side.'

Unless you're dead by then, Fronto murmured under his breath. Today was the day, if Spurinna was right. It was a testament really to the dictator's confidence. If *Fronto* had been given an end date for his life, no matter how cynical he might be in life, he would be hiding in a cupboard, clutching a sword until the moment that date had come and gone, not going about his normal business as though nothing were untoward. Better still, he would have a small army of loyal men standing in a circle fifty deep around him, not having dismissed and refused all protection but that of his lictors and close friends as Caesar had done.

'I will see what I can do to help with our missing friends,' the dictator said, 'though it must wait until the afternoon. There is less than three hours until the senate meets, and I have a number of pieces of business I wish to raise before I depart for Illyricum. In that time, I am expected at the house of Gnaeus Domitius Calvinus. He has arranged for a grand sacrifice to Jupiter in advance of the campaign in which he is to join me. I foolishly promised to attend.'

'Foolish is right,' Fronto snorted. 'On a day your own haruspex predicted your death, you plan to go swanning across Rome on social visits.'

'Foolish is right,' Antonius echoed, 'taking Calvinus. The man lost a huge army at Nicopolis a few years ago, when any half-competent general would have walked away with the victory.'

Caesar threw a warning look at Antonius. 'He was stalwart holding the centre with you at Pharsalus.' He then turned to Fronto. 'You are determined to retire?'

Fronto nodded. He'd still half expected Caesar to push for further service, but he was resolute. 'Though if I find anything has happened to my friends,' he added, 'I might start a little war of my own.'

'Even at this point,' Antonius said with more than a touch of bitterness in his voice, 'you are determined not to take me east, Caesar. You offer Calvinus and press for Fronto, while I am in the very *room*. Am to be a war-widow, burning a light in the window and waiting for you to come home? You *promised* me, Gaius, that you would find a place for me. I offered you a *crown* for such a right.'

Caesar breathed deep and turned back to his old friend. 'I will do what I can, Marcus Antonius, but I have already granted all the available commands for this season against the Getae. I can hardly ask a man to stand down so that you can sweep away his office.'

'But you are happy to sweep away your promises to me, and a lifetime of my support, in order to grant important commands to hopeless losers like Calvinus.'

'I have not got time for this, Marcus. All will be sorted. Trust me.'

'If you survive this day, Gaius Julius, then you will *owe* me. And you owe me big.'

With that, he turned. 'I will be at my house until the senate session, if you come to your senses.'

Fronto watched Antonius leave, then rubbed his eyes and sat straighter, turning to Caesar. 'Don't go.'

The dictator looked up, brow creased. 'Fronto?'

'Things are going wrong, Caesar. Something is happening. Something bad. Galronus and Salvius don't habitually disappear, and they are very competent men. I have a bad feeling about all this. And whether you believe Spurinna or not, going about *inviting* disaster is plain stupid. If you *really* disbelieve it, you should be doing everything you can to survive, and that includes not wandering around Rome going to sacrifices and sitting in the senate. Stay at home.'

Caesar stopped moving for a moment, and Fronto realised that, for the first time in a while, Caesar was actually considering it. He gave off just the faintest air of nerves, which was so unusual that Fronto had almost missed it.

'I cannot refuse Calvinus, Fronto. It is a sacrifice to Jove, and if we are to face the Parthians, we should not anger the gods. I must have them with us. I simply cannot turn my back on a sacrifice now.'

'And the senate?' Fronto said. 'In the heart of the crowded city where one man with a well-placed roof tile can end you? And for what? So that you can enact some law that can be done *for* you by any number of men who speak for you in the curia? You have no need to sit in the senate. Jove, but you're a consul. You have the right to dissolve a senate meeting at short notice. Alright, go and honour Jupiter at Calvinus' house, but there's absolutely no reason to sit in the senate. We can get to Calvinus in less than a quarter of an hour, without going near the city centre, then come home, sit in the house surrounded by your people, and prove Spurinna wrong.'

He finished with a firm silence, and Caesar, arms folded, drummed his fingers on his biceps for a moment.

'The senator is right,' added an exotic voice from just outside the doorway. Fronto turned to see Cleopatra make her way in, her walk as always a strange mix of commanding stride and alluring sashay. He tried not to look at her. It wasn't easy. He distrusted her immensely, knew her for a selfish power-monger, but she did draw the eye. He also knew she agreed, and that she needed Caesar safe, which was useful.

310

The dictator pursed his lips, then exhaled slowly. 'Very well. This morning I shall visit Calvinus and then stay home and not attend this session of the senate. Not,' he added, waving a finger, 'because I believe this nonsense, or live in fear for my life, but simply to mollify those of you who do.'

Fronto nodded. 'And I think I'll escort you to Calvinus' place. Me and the forty guards I brought with me.'

Caesar's eyebrow rose a little and Fronto shrugged. 'The streets are dangerous these days.'

He would have brought more, would have brought a *hundred*, which he could easily do these days and still leave enough at home for security there. However, for the past day, he'd had every man he felt he could spare out in the city, searching for any sign or mention of the two missing men, watching their regular haunts, and keeping an eye on the places they knew to be connected with the Pompeian veterans.

'Very well,' Caesar nodded. 'I doubt that Calvinus will be offended at you joining us. We will leave in less than half an hour.'

Fronto rose from his seat. 'I think I'll visit the facilities for a bit while I wait.' He turned, nodding a polite bow to the Aegyptian queen before stepping from the room. His mind was elsewhere, and so he only noticed the figure standing in the doorway opposite as it disappeared back into the shadows. A woman. Calpurnia, presumably, given the quality of the dress of which he'd caught a momentary glimpse.

Intrigued, he pottered across the atrium and into that corridor, turning a corner just in time to see Calpurnia rounding the next one, the corridor there bathed in bright light. He followed again, the nagging urge to urinate gone for the moment, and reached the next corner to see that Caesar's wife had emerged into a small peristyle, a private one, smaller than the main garden back near Caesar's office. He padded to the doorway quietly and leaned there, watching. Calpurnia clearly had no idea she was being followed as she crossed the garden and came to a halt at a small shrine, hemmed in by a hemicycle of well-tended trees. The shrine consisted of an altar beside a small pool, flanked by two statues of a serene goddess clutching a cornucopia, and with twin babes grasping at her legs.

Gaia. Seemingly an antique shrine that predated Caesar's villa, which had been built around it.

Caesar's wife bent at the sacred site, fumbling at her midriff, unseen as she faced away, and Fronto could just hear the low murmur of her voice as she intoned a prayer, then there was a 'plop' as something heavy disappeared beneath the surface of the water. She rose and turned sharply, and her eyes fell upon Fronto in the doorway. A distinct flash of guilt crossed her face, but it was replaced instantly with a serenity that Fronto envied.

'Senator.'

'I think we've known one another long enough for a little familiarity, Calpurnia.'

'I needed air.'

'Funny,' Fronto said as she crossed the garden towards him, 'but a good lead curse tablet makes a noise almost completely unique. Has more of a sound of finality than anything else as it passes beneath the surface, like the leaden doors of Hades closing.'

That guilty look made another momentary appearance. 'You are too clever for a senator,' Calpurnia said quietly. 'Such wit is wasted there.'

Fronto chuckled. 'I cannot see my time in the senate dragging out. I'm not a young man these days, and peaceful retirement beckons. Puteoli calls.' Calpurnia nodded her understanding, and Fronto gestured towards the shrine and the pool. 'I know what he does hurts you. And it's not just you. I remember Cornelia and Pompeia too. He was just as faithless to them. It's who he is. He is as driven by Eros as he is by his pride. He could no longer stop philandering than he could conquering. I hope you realise that sufficiently to not do anything precipitous?'

She paused now, close to him, frowning, then turned in realisation back to the pool. 'That?' She gave a dark laugh with just enough of an edge of malice to make Fronto shiver. 'No, that was for his whore. He will take her back to Aegyptus, but if the gods are kind to me, she will die there.'

Fronto nodded slowly. He was not sure whether that would be good or not, but he could certainly understand Calpurnia's actions. He gave her a reassuring smile. 'This will go no further than the garden. I saw nothing.'

'Take care of him, Marcus. I fear the worst.'

'We all do, Calpurnia. All except Caesar, I think.'

'I dreamed last night. I dreamed that the house collapsed, and the pediment fell. I dreamed that Gaius staggered into the shaking house, wounded many times, and died in my arms.' She trembled. 'He dreamed too, and badly, though he will not tell me what of.'

'If it is the gods' will, Calpurnia, then we can do nothing, but I tell you this: any *man* who wants his blood will have to get past me. I will see him to this sacrifice and safely home. This I vow.' Silently he cursed himself. He really had to stop readily making important vows that he might struggle to keep.

She smiled weakly and ducked past him, moving through the house again until she was out of sight. He breathed in the air of the garden, cleaner than almost any air to be found in Rome, here on the periphery, out across the river, and fought just the tiniest wave of sadness.

Everything was coming to an end, and that was the best of all possible outcomes. It could yet get worse. His days of soldiering were done. In fact, his days of cleaving to Caesar at all were done, he thought. Once he had taken on the mantle of consul, no matter how brief, his descendants would be among the nobiles, at the top of Rome's social order forever, and so he could retire, and even this political whirl would end. And in three days, when Caesar went east, the current tension in the city would fade and all threat would end. Then, in the summer, Galronus and Faleria would leave for the north, and without them there would be nothing really left for Fronto and his family in Rome.

Of course, that relied on Caesar being right about Spurinna's prediction, and on Galronus reappearing from somewhere, looking sheepish and nursing a hangover.

He bit down once again on the intense worry over his friend, and then forced himself not to think on that, for when he thought of what his best friend meant to him, that brought him back to memories of Verginius in that quarry in Hispania. And that meant an impossible vow he'd made to a dying man, which was a whole different and perhaps more worrying issue.

He lost track of how long he'd stood in that chilly doorway, thinking, and trying *not* to think, and by the time he wandered back through the house, Caesar was being dressed in his finest toga by his slaves in preparation for the visit to the house of Calvinus.

'Be careful,' Calpurnia was saying from another doorway.

'I am always careful,' Caesar smiled to his wife. 'And if I cannot be careful, I am always lucky.' He gave her an easy smile, which she did not easily return. 'Fronto has a small army with him,' the man said reassuringly. 'I shall be perfectly safe.'

She turned to Fronto. 'Make sure he comes back, Marcus.'

Fronto bowed his head. He had every intention of doing so.

A short while later the great man left his house, his entourage gathered, and Fronto strode from the doorway at his heel. As Caesar's horse was brought round, Fronto shook his head. 'Oh no. You go by litter today, Caesar.'

'Hark at the senator and consul designate, dictating to the dictator,' Caesar said, archly.

'Bollocks. And you can say what you like, but I'm not going to face Calpurnia over your corpse and tell her I didn't do everything I could to keep you safe.'

And not to plant a blade in you to fulfil my vow to Verginius.

Caesar frowned, but swiftly realised that Fronto was not going to be denied, so sighed and waved the horse slave away, crossing and climbing into the litter. Fronto, of course, would ride, but then it was not him that mysterious assassins across the city might be taking aim for with their poisoned arrows. To get at Caesar in the litter, they would not be able to use arrows or stones. They would have to use swords face to face, and even then they would have to get past Fronto and his men.

After a brief conflab with Masgava and Carbo, the two men currently leading his guard, he split his men four ways, Carbo would take ten as the vanguard, Masgava bringing up the rear with another ten. Fronto would ride on the right side of the litter with the third detachment, the side which held the single door, and Aurelius and Arcadios with the last on the left. They moved into formation, and began the descent. They were moving at a stately pace until Caesar urged them to a faster speed, noting that the time for their visit to Calvinus was rapidly approaching.

They emerged into the streets of Transtiberim swiftly, and Carbo led them off towards the house of the Domitii, which occupied the lower slopes of the Pincian Hill, overlooking the campus martius. As Fronto had noted, their route took them along the bank of the Tiber opposite the city, and crossed north of Pompey's great theatre, where the crowds were already building for the senate session that loomed in the afternoon and which, much to Fronto's relief, Caesar would not attend. They remained in the outskirts throughout, as they moved along the very edge of Rome's more recent building projects and closed on the garden estate of the ancient patrician family of the Domitii Calvini. Despite the fact that they had avoided the busiest regions with the narrowest streets, and that the group appeared to be Fronto and his entourage, and with no clear indication who was in the litter, Fronto was still tense throughout, his eyes darting this way and that at every perceived movement, his ears pricking at every unexpected sound. He had a bad feeling about today, and he had made a promise to Calpurnia

As they approached the house, with Fronto finally starting to relax, the gates were opened by the Domitii's private guards, and the entire entourage was escorted inside, through the most exquisite gardens and to the villa proper, an ancient residence that reeked of old money and even older blood. Calvinus may be wanting in the strategic mind department, but he certainly wasn't in noble lineage.

Instead of the usual doorkeeper and an army of slaves, as they approached the entrance to the house, they were instead met by a small woman with the most impressive dress, just staid enough to be traditional, just rich enough to be showy. The sort of dress that a woman has to spend an enormous sum on in order to look as though she hasn't done just that. She frowned as her eyes slid across the gathering, searching for the man she'd expected and not finding him, settling instead on the only nobleman present.

'Good morning,' she finally said, slightly uncertainly, but recovering well. She clearly did not know Fronto, and was looking at him carefully, perhaps trying to place him.

'Hello,' he replied with a smile, but that was the extent of his interaction, for at that moment Caesar stepped from the litter, and her face lit up like a warning beacon.

315

'Caesar, how good of you to come,' she gushed, stepping a couple of paces forward.

The dictator smiled and bowed his head in return. 'On the contrary, how good of you and your husband to invite me. It is a rare honour to be present at such a hallowed event, especially in the house of one of Rome's most illustrious families.'

His words had just the effect Fronto expected. The little woman nearly fainted with delight, blushing slightly as her smile almost reached her ears. As Caesar crossed to the door, she backed away like a slave, making way before him. Fronto fell in close by.

'I do hope I am not too presumptuous,' Caesar said, 'but I rather hoped that you and your husband would extend the invitation to our mutual friend here, Marcus Falerius Fronto, who seems to think that I need military protection, even on a social visit to a friend's house.'

'Ooh,' the lady replied, face contorting into an exaggerated expression of concern, 'you can't be too careful, Caesar. What with prophecies and conspiracies and the like. You can't be too careful.' She turned to Fronto and the smile was back. 'And I have to apologise for not recognising the famous senator here, veteran of all your wars, and companion of my own husband throughout them.'

Now, Fronto bowed his own head, and waited as the lady gushed and flattered, leading them into the house. A slave hurried out and spoke to Masgava, telling him where everyone could go to stay warm and comfortable and wait for their masters, with wine and food.

Fronto walked inside. The house was the very epitome of tradition. If it had been any more Roman it would have ripped itself from its foundations and marched off to conquer somewhere. He admired all the décor as they passed, and noted that Lucilia would approve heartily. She would also love this chatty little woman, who Fronto privately suspected would become unbearable after an hour of non-stop pleasantries. Still, he was little more than an observer here, and could step back, detached, and watch. He followed them through the house and into a large room with walls painted red and picked out with gold coloured painted festoons on three sides, the fourth a perfect trompe l'oeil showing a sea view framed with colourful plants, a series of triremes plying back and forth across the imagined waves in the distance. Looked a little like the view from Puteoli to Fronto's mind.

The room had been prepared, lamps burning in all four corners and providing plenty of light, a brazier already glowing like Vulcan's furnace. An altar had been brought in, and now stood on a low wooden platform near one of the red walls. Fronto frowned as he entered the room, neither at the décor nor at the temporary fitments for the sacrifice. The thing that had surprised him was the man standing by the altar, preparing for his work. In a way, he had hoped never to lay eyes on Spurinna again. It seemed to him that all this trouble had begun with the man's reading, what seemed a lifetime ago.

He nodded, face sullen, not trusting himself to speak, which was probably unfair. It was not the man's fault that the gods had shown him something none of them liked, after all. Fronto turned the moment he'd registered who the man was and looked back at the doorway. Caesar's reaction was interesting, and any student of the human expression would have been fascinated by it. The moment the dictator's gaze fell upon Spurinna, anyone looking into his eyes would have seen his soul laid bare.

Surprise was there, or perhaps shock, and fear, as well as a profound, if unhappy, respect, a strange understanding, and not a small amount of anger. This was all there for just a moment, the blink of an eye, replaced unexpectedly with naked panic, which was then forced away equally swiftly and replaced with a calm and welcoming smile.

Fronto had not realised until that moment just how frightened Caesar actually was, for all his bravado. The man had been maintaining a proud air of denial in order to cover his own fear. Perhaps he had even been fooling himself almost as much as he had everyone else.

'Ah, I see you've met my guest,' said Domitius Calvinus from the doorway behind them. For a heartbeat or two, Fronto wondered if Calvinus actually had some beef with Caesar and this had been done as a deliberate provocation. They turned to find their host behind them, dressed in an expensive tunic and gold-trimmed sandals, smiling warmly. No, Fronto decided, looking the man up and down. He was genuine, perhaps a little vacant. He had not invited Spurinna to goad Caesar, but rather in the foolish belief that it would impress the man.

'Good morning to you both,' Calvinus said. 'I was not expecting Senator Falerius, but he is a most welcome guest, of course. I was looking for a priest of note to perform our sacrifice to Jove, and it occurred to me that Caesar's chosen haruspex from Africa would be the perfect choice.'

Perfect. Yes. Not the word Fronto would have chosen.

Caesar, ever the politician, simply nodded with a smile and turned to Spurinna, who had looked up at him from where he was working.

'Good day, Spurinna. While I would never wish to malign your gods-given skills, it is worth noting that the Ides of March have come, and yet I am hale and hearty.'

Spurinna's eyes narrowed slightly. 'They have *come*, Caesar, but they have not yet *gone*.'

This seemed to nonplus Caesar, for he gave the man a weak smile and turned to Calvinus, striking up a fresh conversation on the subject of the coming campaign and their host's part in it. Fronto stood, uncomfortable, in the middle of it all, and tried not to speak or be involved.

Once all was ready, Spurinna began the sacrifice. A white sheep was brought in, appropriately decorated, and, when he had finished with his prayers and intonations, the man enacted the sacrifice with neatness and precision. While the man's very presence, and certainly his work, seemed to have brought with them the trigger that had changed Rome and brought on a wealth of disasters, in truth Fronto could not fault the man. He had seen plenty of priests, augurs and haruspices in his time, most of whom were either charlatans pretending to be divine magicians or unimaginative politicians rattling out prayers by rote, it was clear that Spurinna was the genuine article. He sought divine understanding and visions of what might be through his craft, knew the work of a priest beyond doubt, and carried out his devotions with the sincerity and piety of a man who truly believed in the sanctity of the gods and of his work.

Fronto stood and watched the sacrifice, rather grateful that Calvinus had not gone far enough to arrange a fresh reading. The chances of Spurinna reversing his prophecy would be miniscule, and no one wanted to hear that pronouncement again. Instead, the man carried out his duties as priest with none of the precognitive aspects of the dead animal, and he stepped back to the bowl of water, washing his hands and announcing that Jupiter would be more than pleased with the sacrifice, and with Jove's mighty approval the other gods would show favour. One thing that Fronto noticed, that it seemed everyone else missed as they hung on the man's words, waiting for word of the god's favour, was that not once did Spurinna explicitly refer to the coming campaign, referring more vaguely to Rome's warriors, and not once to Caesar, instead aiming his words at Calvinus. If the priest were to be believed, despite their host's spotty military record, the man's future was to be golden, which pleased both he and his glowing wife immensely.

The woman offered them hospitality afterwards, of course, urging Caesar to stay and partake of delicacies and their best wine, but, to Fronto's great relief the dictator demurred, claiming a lack of time, with the senate meeting looming, and soon they were once more departing from the villa. Fronto's expert gaze swept the street, looking for trouble and, finding none, he thanked the gods and prepared for the return journey, for once Caesar was home he would be safe, and only the gods or the man's own health could take him away then.

CHAPTER TWENTY FOUR

Galronus woke with a groan and sat still for a moment, running a quick check of all his body parts. He still had all his limbs, right down to the digits at the ends, and they all moved the way they should, though they also all ached like a bastard. His head ached, too like the hangover of a two day binge, and his neck was stiff as he moved it, but there appeared to be no critical damage. He was intact, just bruised and stiff. He could see nothing, and worried for a moment about his sight, but as he blinked and adjusted, he realised it was just dark. He could breathe, he did not appear to be bound, and he could both smell and hear. That last brought with it a moment of uncertainty, for what he could hear was muted shuffling somewhere in the room.

Slowly, he was adjusting. There *was* light, even though it was very low, sneaking in beneath and above an ill-fitting door, two cracks of pale grey. He could make out some detail of the room now, a plain chamber not more than ten or fifteen feet across and entirely lacking in both décor and furniture. A man sat at the far side, knees brought up under his chin, encircled by his arms, a position of defeat, of having given up.

A prison of some sort, then.

Not wanting to draw the other man's attention yet, not knowing who it was, he kept his movements tiny and his breathing quiet, thinking back. The streets near the villa where he'd been chased and cornered. He'd been trapped, and unarmed. Oh, he'd had the bag with him with the little knife in, but he'd not had time to open it and find the weapon. Instead, he'd flung the bag at the nearest man to temporarily knock him out of the fight and buy some time to either deal with the others or find a way to slip away.

He wondered where the bag was now. It certainly wouldn't be here. He *liked* that knife, too. It had a four horse chariot carved into

320

the handle, souvenir of the races a year or so back, commemorating a particularly good win for the greens, with the rider's name on it.

He'd taken down the other man waiting for him in that side street, by simple reaction and brute force rather than tactics. The man's companion floundering on the cobbles under Galronus' bag, he had been rather taken by surprise when, rather than preparing to fight like a proper soldier, Galronus had simply run at him, bellowing like a wounded bear. He'd hit the man hard, head-on, and knocked him flat. The man's skull had connected with the street and driven him into unconsciousness in an instant, but unfortunately the Remi's foot had somehow become tangled with his victim as they collided and he came down on top of the man in a graceless heap. By the time he'd made it back to his feet, the other man had removed the bag and was also up. Galronus had tried to run, but the man had leapt to block his path, and before he could get away, the rest had caught up and were closing on him from behind. Then the fighting had become intense, a struggle of fists and feet, of foreheads and teeth, and, in the case of the attackers, of clubs.

He'd fought well and done plenty of damage, and it occurred to him now that the reason he'd survived so long was because they had been attempting to capture or subdue, not to actually injure, him. That, of course, explained why it was that he'd woken up at all.

A suspicion struck him.

'Salvius?' he hissed.

'Oh, you're awake,' grunted Salvius Cursor from the far side of the room, unwrapping his arms from his legs and looking up, head wobbling slightly.

'They got you too, then?'

'A well placed blow to the back of the head,' Salvius grumbled. 'Think I can taste my brains. The cheap bastards never even gave me the chance to fight back. Good job really. I'd have gutted the lot of them.'

'Aquila's men?'

Salvius shook his head, then cursed and clutched it. Bad idea, clearly. 'Ow. No. Aquila is not alone. I followed him, and he met up with Marcus Junius Brutus. It was *his* men who got me.'

'Shit,' breathed Galronus. 'Brutus? But he's one of Caesar's closest friends; like *family*. *No one* would suspect him of any involvement. He could get right up to Caesar, even in his office, and stick the knife in. You're *sure* it was him?'

'I have his footprint on my brain. It was him.'

Galronus whistled. 'Less of a shock on my side. Casca met with Cassius Longinus, and if I were going to pluck a name out of the air to suspect, Cassius would have been that name anyway.'

'At least four, then, given Brutus, Aquila, Cassius and Casca. And probably more, besides. If Aquila is involved, then you can bet Sulpicius Galba and Tillius Cimber are in, too. They're never more than a few feet from the man, and they supported him in that fight back at Fronto's party. That's six so far. It's starting to look a lot more serious than I'd thought. Not just a mad little plot, but a major, organised conspiracy. How men of that stature could keep this hidden is beyond me.'

'Senators,' snorted Galronus. 'They spend their whole life trying to put over one appearance or another, while planning a third. It's all about lies and hidden truths. It's what they are. Probably makes them excellent plotters. Just being a senator makes you suspicious, in my opinion.'

'The question is, what we do next?'

'How long have we been here?'

'No idea,' Salvius said, 'but I've been watching the light come up since I woke, so it's at least the next morning.'

'That means we have a day, two at the most. The ides will either be today or tomorrow, depending on whether we missed a day. I'm inclined to suggest that we have, given how hungry I am.'

A muffled voice somewhere outside called to a companion. 'They're awake.'

Salvius and Galronus looked at one another. Was that good or bad?

'On the bright side,' Salvius said, 'they don't seem to want to kill us. I did wonder whether they were keeping us alive to torture us, but I can't think what we might know that they'll need. If they

322

have Marcus Junius among their number, they'll have access to everything they want from the people around Caesar. We can hardly supply anything of use.'

'I don't think they want war, or mass murder,' Galronus agreed. 'I don't know about the others, but Brutus is a good man, no matter what he's done. If he's decided Caesar has to die, it will be all about Caesar and *only* Caesar. They won't want to kill anyone else. It's politically motivated, not a crime spree.'

They fell silent at the sound of approaching footsteps, and when the door opened, the sudden change in light levels made them both blink rapidly. Two men stood in the corridor, in plain grey tunics and with clubs in hand. They had the scarred appearance of veterans, as well as the expected musculature, and Galronus immediately put aside thoughts of fighting free. They would not be the only two men here, and it would be stupid to try and run until they had better knowledge of their situation. They could bump into a veritable army in any blind corridor. Galronus had done enough running in blind alleys for one month.

'Out you come, gentlemen,' one of the guards said, his voice almost jolly.

Salvius rose, then swayed for a moment and clutched his head before righting himself and staggering towards the door. Galronus rose a little more steadily, but slowly, for almost every muscle hurt. In the corridor, one man gestured for them to follow, and walked ahead, while the other waited for them to do so, and then brought up the rear. From the architecture, Galronus leapt to the assumption that they were in the slave quarters of some large house. Not a surprise, and he would be willing to bet that whoever's house they were in, he could name the owner in four guesses.

Aquila, Brutus, Casca, Cassius.

They were led in silence through the house, past slaves and other guards, into a more decorous area, then out, across a peristyle and into the good, high-quality domus of an aristocrat. The walls were decorated with fake scenes of seaside villas, with mosaics of gods and fantastical creatures, with paintings of great events in the history of Rome and the owner's family. Very traditional.

Finally, they reached a room into which they were shown, and the two guards entered right behind them. It was a well-appointed triclinium, decorated with bright painted walls showing golden cupids, and with a three-arched window opening out onto one of the villa's peristyle gardens.

Gaius Cassius Longinus sat casually on a couch at the far side of the chamber, the room's only occupant. He had an exquisite glass filled with wine and a strange expression.

'You can go,' the man told his guards, who looked disapproving, but bowed their heads and left, closing the door behind them.

'Brave,' Salvius said. 'Stupid, but brave. Alone with your two angry prisoners.'

Cassius gave him a level look. 'I would like to think I am anything *but* stupid, Salvius Cursor. I am, after all, the only man who managed to lead a unit away from that dreadful field at Carrhae. I joined Caesar to save my men and to help the republic in the east, and I fought with him across Aegyptus, very successfully, despite his pet whore. I was also noble enough to draw the line there and not take up arms against the senate in Africa. Everything Caesar has done since then could have been settled another way, without bringing the republic to the very brink of destruction. No, I am not a stupid man, Salvius. *Never* assume that. But I *am* an honourable one. I have no issue with either of you, and though I had to have you contained for obvious reasons, I have no wish to spill your blood. Enough has been spilled on behalf of the tyrant already.'

Salvius didn't seem to know what to say to this, and Galronus too was a little taken aback by the civility of it all. In the silence that followed, Cassius Longinus gestured to couches around the room. 'Sit. Eat. Drink. Recover. Fear not.'

They glanced at one another, shrugged, and did just that, both men shovelling food from the platters into a bowl and pouring watered wine from the krater into their cups. They might have wanted to make a stand, but also both men were starving.

'It is not my intention to keep you like common criminals. Though neither of you falls within the roll of the patrician gentes or the list of the nobiles, you are both honourable men, playing your part for the good of all. As such, if I can trust you to peace and civility, you will instead be kept here in comfort as my guests.'

'Prisoners,' Salvius corrected.

'Call it what you will, but personally I would prefer a bed and wine to a dark cellar. I must simply keep you from carrying word of our little venture until it is too late to prevent it, and I would much rather do that in a civilised manner. It is a little after dawn on the ides of Martius, now,' he said, confirming Galronus' suspicion. 'By nightfall everything will be over, and you will both be free to go, as good sons of the republic. I know you both, what you are. One of you is the commander of Caesar's bodyguard, so I cannot let you go, but I also know that you were once Pompey's man, and yet you have shunned personal gain for service, which suggests to me that the republic is more important to you than the individual. And the other: Galronus, a Remi prince, no less, who has led cavalry for Caesar for a decade now, but I also know you for a man of like mind with Fronto, and the last of the Falerii, I think, is but a step from being among our ranks anyway. Indeed, there are some among our ranks who wanted to approach your friend and bring him in, myself included. But we are now so many that expanding further creates unnecessary risk. Besides, he added with a wry smile, Fronto is a little unpredictable to pin the future of the republic on.'

'Fronto would not have joined you,' Galronus said, earning a nod from Salvius, though deep down the Remi was considerably less sure of that than he'd sounded. After all, despite his personal feelings about Caesar, Fronto had made that vow to Verginius, and that was one that meant something, that tore him up at night.

'Perhaps,' Cassius sighed. 'But it is immaterial. Everything is now in place. Caesar will die today, and the whole republic will know that this was not murder, carried out by the jealous and the villainous, but tyrannicide, carried out by men who felt it was their duty to preserve the republic to which they owe all. There are so many of us now that we cannot be stopped.'

'You'd be surprised,' Salvius growled.

'No. I don't think I would. We have safeguards in place. All those who might leap in to defend the tyrant at the last moment will be kept busy, and the man himself will not be able to hide away. He will be there, ready for the executioner's blade. It will end today, and nobly so, in the full view of Rome, proudly and as a statement, not by hooded men in a dark alley.'

'You almost make murder sound noble.'

'You are clearly not listening to me. This is not *murder*, but *tyrannicide*. It is the duty of all republicans to recognise any threat to their liberty and to remove it. We are not breaking the law, Salvius Cursor. We are upholding it. *Saving* it.'

'Call it what you like, I call it murder.'

'I'm not overly concerned what you think, my friend. I have killed one man already in defence of this plot, and I found it distasteful, no matter how necessary. I do not wish to do so again, and while I will if I must, the only man who *needs* to die is the tyrant. I simply want your oath that you will not cause trouble, and you will be treated like honoured guests until nightfall, when you will be released to go your own way. Your oath, for mine.'

Salvius Cursor fixed Cassius with a look. 'I give you my oath I will cause no trouble.'

Cassius nodded. Galronus frowned at the other prisoner, caught a glint in his eye, and turned to their captor. 'You have my oath,' he added.

'Good. I have things to do, as I'm sure you appreciate. We are now on something of a tight schedule, and everything must be kept in place and unhindered. But you may have the run of the house, the baths, the gardens. There are a few private areas, of course, but my guards will be there to make sure you know where they are, and they will be posted at the exits to prevent any unauthorised disappearances. Now please stay, eat, drink, and wait. When the sun sets you will be free Romans once again.'

With that, Cassius rose. The man clearly had no fear of them, for he strode between the two, opened the door, stepped through and closed it again, leaving them alone. There was no click of a key, and his receding footsteps confirmed he had not waited outside. They waited for a moment and not even the tell-tale shuffling of guards was audible outside. They were alone.

'What now?' Galronus said.

326

'I gave my oath not to cause trouble, but it will hardly be a lot of trouble for them when we slip away unnoticed and without violence, eh?'

'I think that might be stretching definitions,' Galronus mused.

'Do you want out or not?'

'We need to get word to the others as soon as possible, but trying to get free immediately might be foolish. We need to know what we're up against first.'

Galronus nodded his agreement, and the two men sat for a time, discussing their options, eating and drinking the vittles' left out for them, confident that they would be perfectly safe. If Cassius had wanted them dead, they would be dead. The man genuinely seemed to be trying to remove Caesar without any undue bloodshed.

After almost half an hour, they finally began to move. Initially, they left the dining room and began to explore, separating and moving individually about the sprawling complex. Galronus found the baths, three gardens of varying sizes, the slave quarters and a guard house, as well as a set of offices and private rooms that were off limits. He found only one exit from the villa, which was near the slave quarters, but had its own guard post with three men on duty. It would, of course, be locked, too. There were ways up onto the roof, of course, from the colonnades of the gardens, but that was very conspicuous and dangerous, and would have to be the last resort.

In the end, he returned to the triclinium and waited a short while until Salvius cursor rejoined him.

'Plenty of places we can go,' the man replied in a defeated tone, 'but only one main exit, and a minimum of three guards and a doorman stand between us and it. And given the situation, the door's probably locked as well. And everywhere there's a chance to go out of a window or up onto a roof, there's someone watching. No sign of Cassius or his close advisors, though. I think he must have left the house.'

Galronus nodded. 'I found a couple of places we could get onto the roof, but they're both in gardens, and quite open. I doubt we'd do it without being seen.'

'Then at the moment, there's no clear path. In truth, I am not above completely breaking my oath to the man and simply butchering my way free.'

Galronus shrugged. An oath to Roman gods is less important to me than most. Toutanis would protect me. What are you thinking?'

'You said there were three men at the back door?'

'When I was there. Good men, I think.'

'That's the best chance, then. All the guards are armed with clubs, though, so we need to be armed, too. There will be an armoury, of course, for the villa's guards.'

Galronus nodded. 'I think I passed it, but its door opens onto the guards' accommodation, which is never empty. I don't think that's viable. And we could be outside the pomerium here, so they might be using swords.'

'There's the kitchens. A couple of cleavers, rolling pins, big chef knives. What do you think?'

Galronus smiled. 'Sounds feasible.'

'Let's arm up and then go and check your slave door.'

The two men took another swig of wine and a bite of salted pork and then left once more, this time following Galronus' earlier route and moving into the ancillary areas of the huge villa complex. Slaves noted them as they entered the kitchens, but their eyes immediately dropped to the ground. The had not been informed of the two men's status, and slaves did not look at or speak to a free man unless they were told to. Consequently the two prisoners moved through the kitchens freely and unquestioned, picking up blades and lengths of timber that took their fancy. They had returned to the corridor that led to the peristyle when the sounds of commotion reached them. They edged towards the doorway in time to see Cassius' guards hurrying across the gardens, gripping weapons and making for that back gate. The two prisoners exchanged a look and then waited for the last man to pass before ducking out. They shuffled along the wall and then peeked around the corner.

There appeared to be a small war going on around the back gate. The gate itself stood open, slightly damaged, broken inwards, and two slaves lay nearby on the grass, unmoving. Cassius' guards were pushing their way out through the gate, and the sounds outside were the unmistakable din of battle. A fight was going on in the street.

'Who is it?' Galronus hissed.

'Who cares? If they're killing this lot then they're on our side, right?'

'I suppose so.'

'A man with his back turned makes an easy target. And my oath was never serious.'

Galronus snorted. 'Let's cause some trouble.'

Together the two men stepped round the corner. Most of the men of Cassius Longinus were now through the gate and fighting outside in the street beyond, just a few still pushing, trying to join their mates. The two prisoners did one last quick check round, confirmed that all available men were busy at the gate and that no one else was about to come and rush them from behind, and then broke into a run, making for the gate.

The rearmost of Cassius' guards only realised the danger by the time it was too late. The fellow turned just as the two men bore down on him from behind, and managed to make an 'urk' sound before Salvius was on the man. Galronus had sheathed his big kitchen knife in his belt and was wielding a big oak meat tenderiser, but it seemed that Salvius was less concerned about killing, and had a cleaver in one hand and a serrated meat knife in the other. Galronus winced at the way the rearmost guard died, and by the time the Remi had smacked the next man on the head with the tenderiser, Salvius Cursor was already wading into the fight, shouting curses to make a sailor blush, and already covered in so much blood that he looked the stuff of nightmare. The man really was a marvel, in the most horrific way.

Galronus' victim folded up under the blow, unconscious, his wits stolen, and in moments the Remi was in the gateway alongside the blood-coated officer, laying waste to Cassius' guards in spite of their oath, one of them battering his prey and pulling their semi-conscious remains out of the way, the other carving a meaty, bloody path to freedom.

The men of Cassius Longinus never stood a chance. Concentrating on an invader from the street, they were in no position to turn and face the onslaught of two blood-crazed lunatics from behind, and it came as something of a surprise when he hit a man in the back of the neck with his makeshift hammer, heard an unpleasant crack, and found himself, as the man toppled, face to face with someone coming the other way while the body disappeared.

The two fugitives had met the invaders, Cassius' men almost entirely gone under the twin attack.

As Galronus held up his hammer, indicating that he was a friend and not one of the defenders, Salvius Cursor next to him happily ripped into two more men, screaming something about revenge through the spray of blood and the howls of the wounded. Finally, the man realised he had no more enemies to kill, was face to face with the invaders, and staggered to a halt, puffing and panting, blowing pink bubbles through the blood, eyes wide and white amid the crimson.

They were free.

One of the men facing them raised a huge length of timber with half a dozen nails driven through it, a makeshift mace of gruesome construction, already coated with blood and hair, and worse, and growled at Galronus, but the man to his left reached up and gripped his arm before it could descend, halting the blow.

'Not him, you fool,' the man hissed.

Galronus, relief flowing through him, took a deep breath. Salvius Cursor was lost to the battle gods right now and having enough trouble not tearing holes in the men before him, let alone attempt rational thought and discussion. The Remi locked his gaze on the man who'd spoken.

'We've been...' he began.

'We know,' the man cut him off. 'Come with us.' And with that, the attack broke off and the armed gang turned swiftly and began to move away. Galronus and Salvius went with them, and the Remi looked over his shoulder to see a number of the attackers picking up their dead and carrying them away, while others heaved Cassius' guards back inside the broken gate and then closed it, leaving only blood spatter on the walls and cobbles to suggest that anything had ever been amiss.

The realisation hit him then, and as they moved at speed away from the scene of the fight, he grabbed the arm of the man he'd been speaking to. 'You came for us?'

'That's our job. The boss has had us watching certain houses, and you were seen being brought to this one.'

'The boss?'

But the man said nothing after that, and, as they moved through the streets, another suspicion began to occur to Galronus. It was confirmed swiftly with just a little observation. The sleeves. The tattoos. He turned to Salvius and kept his voice in a tight whisper. 'These are the Pompeian collegium.'

'I know,' Salvius said in little more than a growl.

'What do we do?'

'How the fuck should I know,' the blood-swathed officer replied. 'Are they our enemy now? They were told not to kill us, and they broke us free, didn't they?'

'No matter what you've heard,' Galronus replied, 'the enemy of my enemy is not necessarily my friend.'

He cleared his throat and tugged at the man again. It had not escaped his notice that the forty or so men had moved as they walked through the streets, so that now the two former prisoners were right in the middle of the crowd. The man looked back at him.

'We need to get to the Aventine,' Galronus said. 'I have a message to deliver.'

'I'm afraid that won't be possible,' the man said, confirming the Remi's fears.

'What?' snapped Salvius, but Galronus sighed and threw him a look.

'I thought that might be the case. We're not free. We're just someone *else's* prisoner.'

'Only for a short time,' the man replied. 'Once we get word from the boss, you can go free, but he might need you before then. We've orders.'

'And if I decide I don't want to be a prisoner?' Salvius said quietly, indicating his carving knife and cleaver meaningfully with a tip of his blood spattered face.

331

'We only need one of you,' the man replied in a flat tone, 'and even he doesn't have to be unharmed, just intact.' He looked about at the gathered strength. 'I wouldn't fancy your chances. I fought your lot at Pharsalus and I'm doing what I'm paid to do right now, but I could very easily stove that face in for what you've done instead. And the other lads are all the same.'

Salvius made to say something else, but Galronus flashed him a warning look. Better not to provoke this lot in such numbers.

'Where are you taking us?'

'Never you mind. You're insurance. Be happy with that, and then, when the world's changed, you can go free.'

'That's a very familiar sentiment,' Galronus noted.

They moved through the city, and though the Remi was less than familiar with much of the hilly region in the north of Rome, the Viminal, the Quirinal and the Esquiline, he did note that they seemed to be moving *across* those hills, with no sign of descending toward the heart of the city. When they did begin to move downhill, it was in a westerly direction, and they passed around the northern edge of the city, reaching the river and crossing it, coming a little way down the far side.

When the gang finally came to a halt, they were on the right bank of the Tiber, with the great curve of Pompey's theatre just in sight above the bathhouses and roofs of the recently occupied campus martius opposite. They were at the gate of a large estate, and one of the men produced a set of keys, crossed to a large town house opposite, and opened it up. The place was disused, more than a modest pile, but not quite large enough to be considered the villa of an aristocrat. Empty, cold and filled with dust and cobwebs. The two men were ushered inside, and Galronus could see his friend's lip curling in distaste.

'I recognise that house over the road,' he said. 'I've been there once or twice, but I can't remember whose it is.'

'I know *damn well* whose it is,' Salvius Cursor replied darkly. 'And I know whose house *this* is, too.'

'Oh?'

'It's mine,' Salvius growled. 'And if they have the key, that means they got it from my cousins.'

Galronus shivered at the malice in his tone. Things were definitely coming to a head, and there was little chance of them getting away from this lot as they had at the house of Cassius Longinus. Looked like they were here for a while, and unless something changed unexpectedly, they were trapped.

CHAPTER TWENTY FIVE

Fronto had foregone the opportunity to be present at another sacrifice. Quite simply, there were only so many entrails, and so much animal blood a man could stand to be around before it started to seep into the pores, and the only thing he'd be able to smell for weeks would be the victim. Instead, he took to being extra vigilant.

They had returned from the house of Domitius Calvinus without incident, much to Fronto's relief, and settled in once more at Caesar's great garden villa on the right bank of the Tiber, and Caesar was safe. He'd taken a headcount, and between Caesar's own guards and the men he'd brought himself there were over two hundred soldiers here now, protecting the dictator, and they were all former Caesarian veterans, as trustworthy as a man could be. Even then, Fronto had made every man swear a fresh oath on an altar of Apollo in Caesar's private pantheon, assuring their loyalty. Moreover, he'd limited access to the man to only those among the staff who were beyond doubt, and weapons had been forbidden in the private sector of the place, where Caesar would stay until at least the end of the day. Even clubs and knives were banned. Two men were tasting Caesar's food before it went anywhere near him.

Fronto was determined. Caesar would not die on his watch.

Which left him in some difficulty with the vow he'd made to Verginius half a decade ago, but he'd decided that everything now hinged on Spurinna's warning. He would protect and save the man until the day was over and the haruspex had been proven wrong, and then that would give him the rest of Caesar's life to find a way out of his knotty problem.

And really, there was no way anyone was going to get near Caesar now. Only the gods or ill health could take him. He'd not had a fit in several days, apparently, so that was a concern. There was almost certainly one due, but they all knew how to manage the fits these days, and there was a small squad of professionals in the villa, medici, apothecaries and former capsarii, who would be on hand for the worst moments. The gods, of course, no one could do anything about, but the amount of animals that were being sacrificed should please any god, no matter how hungry.

Caesar, of course, was entirely unaware of most of these precautions. He was keeping himself busy. With having agreed not to visit the senate, much to the relief of all and sundry, he had devoted his time in the house to other work. He had been preparing the various motions he'd been planning to put forward, and the laws he intended to enact, into writing, so that in his long-term absence Antonius could do so for him as co-consul, at the next session in Aprilis. And then he'd settled into more planning for his expedition.

The senate would not meet without Caesar, of course, and Caesar was hardly going to stroll across the city and stop the session. The only other man who could call off the meeting was the other consul, and so a messenger had been sent to the house of Marcus Antonius, asking him to do just that.

There really was nothing else now but to wait, as far as Fronto could see. He leaned on the balustrade of the small square in front of the house's main door, atop the great staircase, and looked out over the city. Rome looked so peaceful and ordered from here. It was hard to believe it had become the seething den of intrigue and mayhem that it seemed to now be. He closed his eyes and breathed deeply, savouring the fresh morning air.

Perfect.

A call drew his attention, and he looked down the staircase to see a large entourage had been admitted at the gate of the villa down below. He frowned for a moment, for he'd given instructions that no one was to be admitted without his specific consent. He had taken on the mantle of the villa's security chief, and he was determined. Who the man in the litter, accompanied by a small army of slaves and armed guards, could be, to be admitted so readily against orders, he could not imagine. He straightened, and called over several of his men from nearby, as the litter began to make its way up the winding slope, the armed guards following on.

He felt a twinge of nerves, but fought them down. It had to be someone trustworthy to be admitted so. By the time the entire column was a little over halfway up the hill, he had begun to relax. He recognised the warriors now, for no other man in Rome had a guard like that. Gladiators. That meant Decimus Brutus Albinus, and there were few men in Rome Fronto trusted more. He'd fought alongside the younger officer so many times, as had Caesar, that he now understood why the guards had let him in. Brutus reached the top finally and dropped lithely from the litter, his expression light as he strode over to Fronto.

'Marcus.'

'Decimus, what's up?'

'Nothing really. I found myself with nothing to do for a few hours, and tried to visit my cousin, Marcus. He's not in, though, and everyone there was very cagey, wouldn't tell me where he was. All very strange. I thought I would come and find out what was happening here before the session. Nothing of import it seems.'

Fronto nodded. 'A sacrifice. And the session is being called off.'

'Oh?'

'Caesar is not well,' Fronto said, the excuse tripping from his tongue unexpectedly. He'd not thought about it, but the senate would expect a reason for their dismissal, after all. Illness was a simple explanation.

'Nothing serious?'

'No. He'll still be good to go east, but in the meantime, I think he needs rest. The man always runs himself ragged, but he's been worse than usual these past days.'

Decimus Brutus nodded. He knew the dictator as well as any, was rumoured to be the man's illegitimate son, and there had been hints that he had been named in Caesar's new will as the secondary heir, inheriting all should Octavian die before Caesar.

Brutus leaned on the balustrade beside him as his gladiators milled about across the square, finding places to lean or sit. He breathed in and commented on the freshness of the air out here, and the two men chatted for a time about mundanities.

'Hello, something's happening, Decimus said, straightening. Fronto looked down at the gate and saw now that someone else had been admitted, someone on a horse. As he came into full view, Fronto nodded with relieved recognition. It was the messenger they'd sent to Antonius returning. His relief evaporated, though, as the man all-but galloped up the winding road to the top and the house's frontage where the noblemen waited. Why the hurry?

The rider, one of Caesar's guards, a former optio from the Thirteenth, dropped from the saddle, face grave, and hurried over to Fronto, bowing his head, almost saluting out of habit.

'What is it?'

'Begging your pardon, sir, but I can't deliver the message to Antonius. I rode to his house, but there's an armed gang blocking the street. I told them to move aside so I could get in, even invoked Caesar's name, and they started throwing things at me. Got hit by a half brick,' he added, indicating a purpling bruise with a bloody scrape on his bicep.

Fronto frowned and turned to Brutus, who shrugged.

'This is all starting to worry me,' Fronto breathed. 'First Galronus and Salvius go missing, then Marcus Junius Brutus, and now there's a gang outside Antonius' house?' He turned back to the rider. 'How many?'

The man shrugged. 'Maybe forty, sir. No more than fifty, anyway.

Brutus chewed on his lip. 'That's more than just an ordinary street gang.'

'I'd be willing to bet I know who they are,' Fronto said, lip curling. 'The collegium's been too quiet for comfort recently. I wondered when they'd resurface. I think this is it. I need to go and deal with them.'

'Want a hand?' Decimus asked, indicating his gladiators.

Fronto shook his head. 'Me and mine know this lot. We've a history with them. I'll take my lads. We're forty too, and better than them. You keep your gladiators here and protect Caesar until I get back. Hopefully I'll settle this once and for all.'

Decimus nodded, and as Fronto called over to Carbo, who stood by the house's door, telling him to gather his men, Brutus issued commands to his own guards. In little more than moments,

Fronto's force was assembling by the veranda. Carbo gestured to Fronto. 'Armed or unarmed?' Everyone in the villa's grounds was armed for war, given that they were sufficiently far from the pomerium here.

Fronto reached down to the hilt of his own sword. 'Armed. Antonius' house is on this side of the river, so we'll not cross the pomerium.' Carbo nodded and snapped a few orders at the assembled men. Moments later Fronto and Brutus shook hands, and then they were off.

As they moved down the steps at speed, all on foot, there being no time to waste having horses readied or litters brought, Carbo and Masgava fell in beside him. Fronto winced increasingly with the descent, the pressure of the stairs on his bad knee bringing on the old familiar ache, but he fought through it, determined.

'What's the plan?'

'Plan?' Fronto replied. 'Find them. Kick them down.'

'Fronto, we need a plan,' Carbo insisted. 'Whatever you said back there, we'll be evenly matched, and their lot are ex legionaries too, trained and recently keeping in shape. This is not going to be a simple walk-over.'

Masgava clicked his tongue. 'Are we sure there is a fight to be had? I thought this lot weren't our enemies any more.'

'They threw bricks at Caesar's messenger. I think that suggests things have changed.' Fronto took a deep breath. 'But you're right. We need a plan. These men are soldiers at heart. They have ranks and leaders, and we all know that the best way to put an army in disarray is to pick off the officers. We'll confront them and demand to know their purpose. If they're hostile and refuse to back down, we'll take them on, but we'll deal with their officers first. How many men do we have with bows?'

'Four,' Carbo said, 'though one of them's only a learner.'

'He'll do.' He tried to picture the street. He'd been to the place plenty of times, visiting Antonius, but also once or twice to the deserted house of Salvius Cursor opposite.

'There's not much building this side of the river. Coming from this direction, there's a big gap on the right before Antonius' boundary wall, all the way down to the riverbank, so there's no real vantage point there, but on the left there's a shrine to Faunus.

If I remember right, it has trees to the rear, a little pond, and an apse behind the whole thing. Should be room for a few archers there. Before we're in sight of the collegium, get those four archers off into the open land on the left. They can sneak into position at the shrine, and at my signal they can bring down the leaders.'

'Will they *know* the leaders?' Masgava asked.

'*I* will. I'll indicate them. The archers can spring a surprise volley and take out their command. Then we form a wedge and plough into them, cut them into two groups and hopefully, without officers, they'll be in chaos, and we can put them down fast.'

'It's workable,' concurred Carbo.

'Right. Pass the orders back.

They emerged into the street outside Caesar's gate, and Fronto addressed the guard before they left, confirming the order that only Fronto, Caesar and Decimus Brutus should grant admittance to anyone. Other than that, everyone stayed outside, today.

This side of the river was still largely wild. Far from Rome's heart, and connected by a few bridges, along with the campus martius, this whole region had been open countryside less than a century ago, and it was only relatively recently that houses and villas had started popping up. Most of those were still down close to the river, but parts even along the banks were still open land, particularly given the flood risk they faced. Thus, Fronto and his men strode at pace along a wide road between large houses, the boundary walls of estates, and, here and there, the smaller dwellings of the less fortunate. Occasional shrines dotted the roadside, some small, others surprisingly large, for this region held some of the more sacred parts of the city, particularly those associated with wilderness deities and cults. It was easy to forget they were marching to war, and Fronto found himself repeatedly having to focus on the task at hand.

He was retired. No longer a soldier, a general, a legate, but it seemed there would be one last fight to see off his career, and ironically, it seemed to be the ghost of Pompey that led his enemy to battle even now.

He checked the fit of his sword, pulling it from the mouth of the scabbard and pushing it back, making sure it would be easy to draw when needed. He rolled his shoulders and exercised his arms.

It seemed to have been a while since he'd fought a proper fight. His knee was a worry. These days it was generally alright, but then he hadn't normally pounded down one of the longest flights of steps in the city, and it was throbbing more than usual. Still, he could rest it when he was done.

They passed one of the bridges, the sparse street life stepping out of the way of this armed gang, and Fronto noted, as they closed on the location of the house of Antonius, how the population petered out until the streets were empty. No one wanted to be in the open near the gang that had gathered ahead, and now people were running for shelter at the sight of a second gang, for a clash seemed inevitable, and the people of Rome did not want to be in the way.

At a command from Carbo, Arcadios and his three fellow archers dipped to the left, off the road, moving around the back of a sizeable house and disappearing from sight, moving into position. Accordingly, Fronto and his men halved their pace, allowing the archers to get ahead and find a place before they were needed. He counted to two hundred, decided that the four men had sufficient lead now, and sped up once more.

The Pompeian collegium came into sight before the house to which they had blocked access. The high walls of Antonius' estate stretched from the street down to the water, a gentle slope of grass and bushes before it. On the other side, Salvius' empty, unused house stood quiet and solemn, and before that, on the left, the shrine, just how Fronto remembered it: an altar and a statue by a small pool, an arc of neat cypress trees behind it, and that backed by a wall carved with festoons and bearing an inscription centuries old. He couldn't see any archers there, which was good, for they had to be in position by now, and he was pleased to note that the view of the gathered collegium from the shrine should be excellent.

The Pompeians shuffled around as Fronto and his own men slowed, coming to face them, and Fronto's heart lurched. As the front ranks parted, one of their leaders, a man he recognised from more than one encounter, stepped to the fore, but behind him came the figures of Galronus and Salvius Cursor, each with a man standing beside them, a knife to their throat.

'Marcus Falerius Fronto,' the man said, as Fronto came to a halt, waving his men to do the same.

'What is this?'

His mind was racing. The relief at the discovery that his friends were still alive was rather tempered by the knowledge that this might not be the case for long. Both men were good, but with a sharp knife at the jugular they would be foolish to try anything. One little nick and they would very likely die.

'I have a proposal for you,' the man called. 'You go home – *your* home – and you take your men with you. You stay there until dark. And if you do that, your friends here both live, and will both be set free.'

Fronto frowned. That, he had not expected. Someone wanted him out of the way. On today, of all days, that boded, and how specific was the 'until dark' bit? The collegium were either working with conspirators, or at least knew something was happening. He bit down on the uncertainty. There was too much of that at the moment, but at least he was certain of one thing: this collegium needed to be put down, and his friends needed to be saved. Any move they made, both men could die, though.

There was one chance for Galronus and Salvius, and only one that he could think of, and it depended heavily upon the skill and the quick thinking of others.

Praying they knew what they were doing, and touching the figurines of Fortuna and Nemesis around his neck, he shouted 'Now!'

In answer to his call, four arrows thrummed from the shrine off to the left.

Time slowed. The world ground to a halt, only four things moving, with seemingly infinite slowness. Immobile, frozen, Fronto watched the arrows fly. Three were seemingly on target, a fourth less so. He'd told them he'd mark the enemy leaders to target, but he'd not done so, relying on his men to have adjusted their strategy in light of the new situation.

The first arrow thudded into the throat of the man standing beside Galronus, an instant kill. The man fell away from the Remi, knife falling from his hand unused. The second arrow clattered on the cobbles near the dead man's feet. A third thudded into the man

341

who'd spoken, someone having clearly maintained the original plan, and the fourth hit the man beside Salvius Cursor…

…in the leg.

Fronto watched in horror as the razor sharp blade in the man's hand slashed into the side of Salvius' neck even as its wielder fell to the ground, screaming.

The world started to move again, in a frenzy now. Galronus had leapt away the moment his captor had been felled, and was running forward to join Fronto. Salvius had bellowed in shock and pain, and his hand had come up to his neck, where he clamped it like a bandage, even as he reached down and plucked a sword from the fallen man's hand.

Fronto bellowed an order, so fierce and reactive that he wasn't even sure what it was he had shouted. Whatever it was, though, it had the desired effect. His men charged, howling curses. Galronus was suddenly by Fronto's side, and had been given a sword by someone, which he now wielded, his face contorted with fury. The two men joined the fray, swords stabbing and hacking, swinging and chopping.

The Pompeians had miscalculated. In attempting to pressure Fronto and his men to stand down without a fight, they had, instead, given them a rage and a lust for blood that they'd have lacked in other circumstances. Each and every man of Fronto's guard was now fighting like a Titan, untouchable and unstoppable.

He was lost in the violent, all-consuming fog of war, only occasionally glimpsing Galronus fighting alongside him. His sword bit into flesh, grated on bone, thudded into leather, cut tendons. The air was filled with the warm, damp mist of blood fountaining up from a hundred wounds, and with the grunts, curses, cries and screams of men. He was being careless, and he knew it. Lucilia would berate him, but the fury was in him, anger not only at these men, but at what they had done, and at their hidden master for directing them so.

He felt the hot, agonising line of a wound across his thigh, another sharp pain in his arm, a dull ache of a blow to his shoulder from something blunt. All painful, none critical or life-threatening. Nothing enough to stop the whirl of edged death he had become.

Then, suddenly, horrifyingly, he found himself beside Salvius Cursor in the press. The man was done for. Salvius was almost grey now, crimson gushing and spraying from beneath the hand he still held to his neck, one whole side of his body soaked in his lifeblood, yet still he thrust and hacked, killing without mercy even as he died.

Fronto felt cold, furious and hollow, and he took it out on the men in front of him. If they had thought him dangerous before, then now they were learning what a true killer was. He pulled himself in among the remaining men of the collegium, their ranks now thinned drastically by the sheer fury of the Caesarians. A blur of an angry face before him. A head butt. A shock of pain and then the brief vision of a bloodied man falling away, teeth and nose shattered. His sword cut and bit, hacked and stabbed.

When he came to, from the instinctive, senseless whirl that was a true mist of war, he was shaking, ice cold, and alone atop a carpet of bodies. He blinked away a curtain of blood and turned a slow circle. Not one man remained of the collegium that had caused them so much trouble these past few months, and no small number of his own men lay among them. But more than a dozen remained, standing here and there, like him, shaking and alone, grisly scarecrows, keeping the carrion birds from the field of battle.

Galronus was nodding slowly, face dark. Carbo was staring at Fronto in shock, which said a great deal, given how many times the two had fought side by side. Salvius was not there. It took long moments for Fronto to find his friend's body among the others, and when he did, he fished at his belt for his purse and produced a rare gold coin, opening Salvius' mouth and placing it under the tongue for the ferryman.

'What about the fallen?' Carbo said in the strange silence, broken only by the groans of the dying and wounded.

Fronto looked about him again. 'Ours we'll come back for. Too many for us to carry right now.' He picked out two of his men who were nursing minor wounds, Aurelius seated with a gash under his knee, and another man holding his left arm with his right. 'You two, you going to be alright for an hour or two?'

Aurelius nodded. 'We'll not bleed out,' he said, busily tying a tourniquet.

'Then stay with the wounded. Make sure no one comes to rob and scavenge. I'll have someone sent for them as soon as I can.'

Arcadios and the archers were joining them now from where they'd remained, picking off the enemy wherever they had a clean shot, and Fronto nodded over to Masgava, who was busy dispatching the surviving enemy. 'Everyone wait here.'

Picking his way through the wounded and dead, he closed on the front gate of Antonius' house, reached it and hammered on it hard. After a few moments, a voice called from the other side.

'No visitors today.'

'Open up. I need to see Antonius.'

A small shutter next to the door opened, and beady eyes peered out from the dark, through a grill. 'Senator Falerius. I'm afraid the master is not here, Domine.'

Fronto frowned. 'Where is he?'

'I do not know, sir. Only that he left the house several hours ago.'

Fronto had no idea what to say to that and turned away, brow still creased in thought as he strode back to the others, the shutter closing behind him. Antonius was not at his house. Marcus Junius Brutus had not been home when Decimus Brutus had called. Something was happening. He could feel the motion of it, like a boat hull beneath the feet, stationary and yet moving at the same time. He could almost feel something big building, and it felt like static, crackling through his hair and across his skin.

He had a sense of anticipation.

He felt nervous.

'I don't like this,' he said out loud as he reached the others.

'Fronto?'

'I don't like this. Something's going on. Something I can't quite see. It involves Brutus in some way. And Antonius too. And me. And if it involves us, it involves Caesar, sure as blood is blood.'

'I was trying to get to you,' Galronus said. '*We* were,' he corrected. 'We followed Aquila and he met others. He's part of a plot against Caesar. They're going to kill him. Cassius is with them, but others you wouldn't expect. Casca. Marcus Junius Brutus. And Cassius said there were near sixty of them. Never mentioned Antonius, though.'

'Caesar is in danger,' Fronto said suddenly.

'Caesar is safe,' Carbo said. 'He has two hundred men around him, between his and the gladiators of Decimus. No one is getting close to him.'

Fronto felt a chill, then.

'Except Decimus Brutus,' he said quietly.

Carbo shook his head. 'That's not...'

'Yes, I know. Decimus is loyal. A close friend of Caesar's. So is Casca. So is Marcus Brutus. If *they* cannot be trusted, then of what value is the oath of Decimus. Gods, man, we came here because we thought Antonius was in danger, but this was all to keep me out of the way. And what's happening while we're here?'

Masgava blinked. 'We need to get back.'

But Fronto was already running. Behind him, the rest followed on, those who could. His old stalwarts, Carbo, Masgava, Galronus and Arcadios, as well as several survivors from his guard. Those too exhausted to run, or with leg injuries, stayed behind with the other wounded, and a dozen men pounded along the street, racing the waters of the Tiber downstream towards Caesar's villa.

Brutus? Decimus Brutus? It seemed almost impossible to believe. The man had been Caesar's right hand many times over the last decade and more, was the most loyal of friends, the most noble of officers... *the most traditional of Romans*. And that was what suddenly struck Fronto. That was what this was about, after all. It was what Verginius had warned him of back in Tarraco, what Cassius had intimated more than once, what even his long-gone father-in-law Balbus had told him in a matter-of-fact manner. Caesar was the end of the republic. Whether he did it intentionally, or was merely carried along on the crest of the wave, what was happening now with Caesar was killing off all hope of the old republic coming back. Given the last half century of despotism and disasters, Fronto was not convinced that would be a bad thing, but men like Cassius, like Aquila, like both the Brutii, were republican to the core. They had it bred in their bones, and could no longer watch the republic fall than they could fell it themselves.

As his feet and blood pounded with every pace of the journey, Fronto found himself wondering what the Brutii had been going through these past few months. If Fronto had been struggling between his need to save Caesar and his vow to kill the man, he couldn't even imagine the torture his friends had endured, watching all they loved being torn apart by a *man* they loved.

Gods, but it was going to end today.

Spurinna had been right.

He reached the gate of Caesar's villa, out of breath, wide-eyed and desperate, heart thundering, mind awhirl, the others mostly with him, some having lagged behind. A dreadful feeling falling across him, he approached the gate, and as he did so, a moment of faint hope burned anew in his soul. The place seemed calm. There was no shouting, no screaming, no clash of arms. If Decimus had killed Caesar, surely there would at least be crying. Perhaps he'd been wrong, he decided, blowing on that ember of hope, fanning the flames as he hammered on the gate. Decimus was loyal after all.

The gate opened and the doorman there frowned at him in apparent confusion.

'Let me in. Where is Caesar?'

The man's frown deepened greatly. 'Sorry, senator?'

'Caesar. Where is he. Find me a horse, I can't do those steps again.'

The man was still furrowed in confusion, though, which rang whole new alarm bells. Fronto felt that frisson of shivery, cold anticipation again. 'What?'

'Domine, Caesar left for the senate with master Brutus some half hour ago.'

The world opened up beneath Fronto's feet. He closed his eyes. Swallowed.

Brutus had been the greatest of betrayers. Of course he'd not killed Caesar in the villa. That would just be murder, and whatever he might be, Brutus was no murderer. This was to be a statement. A blow for all republicans against a tyrant. It would have to be done in public, somewhere significant. And with the old curia being demolished and Caesar's new one not yet built, the senate were currently meeting in the curia of Pompey. How fucking ironic. Caesar was to die in Pompey's building, the heart of Roman politics, in full view of all the Roman world. And worse still, Pompey's curia was in the campus martius, outside the pomerium.

Even the most traditional, law-abiding Roman could carry a sword right into the senate building.

'Shit. Find me a horse,' he shouted. *'Fast.'*

CHAPTER TWENTY SIX

Fronto had never ridden so fast. The borrowed mare's hooves clattered on the flagged road as he swung wildly from Transtiberim onto the Aemilian bridge, replaying a route he had taken so many times since returning to Rome. Past where he'd threatened to drop a man from the parapet, where his men had been attacked by the collegium, where Catháin had died, veering sharply left through the forum boarium and towards the campus martius.

As he rode, he pieced more together. The conspirators had presumably been behind the urgent business in Ostia that had taken faithful Lepidus, Caesar's deputy, from the city yesterday, safely out of the way. And where Antonius was, he couldn't say, but the man was not at his home, and there was every possibility that he, too, had been conveniently removed, being the dictator's co-consul. Then the enemy had sent the one man who Caesar would trust beyond all doubt to his house to make sure he attended. Perhaps they had somehow had wind of the message he'd sent Antonius? That was uncertain, but for sure they had sent Brutus with the specific remit to make sure Caesar attended. And Fronto? He'd been taken from Caesar's side despite his vow, for he too had trusted Decimus Brutus implicitly. How blind he had been.

Past temples and porticos he rode, beneath the shadow of the Capitol and the gate of triumphs and into the campus. He could hear it now, ahead. The meeting of the senate was always an occasion, and the people of Rome would gather in the streets to see their representatives guiding the republic through the choppy waters of life. There would be games going on in the great theatre of Pompey, as well as jugglers, acrobats, dancers, musicians.

All the world gathered to watch a tyrant fall.

Sixty men, Galronus had said. Sixty! And if they were all men of the calibre of Brutus, Cassius, Casca and Trebonius, that meant probably a quarter of the sitting senate. Gods, but how had it come to this? There had been rumour in the streets, of plots and conspiracies, but nothing concrete had ever cropped up, and with all the stuff about Spurinna's prediction, and the episodes with the crowns, the actual notion of investigating potential plotters had stupidly never cropped up until Galronus and Salvius had taken it upon themselves two days ago. Insanity.

A litter ahead, with an entourage of slaves and guards, marked a senator on his way to the session, presumably an innocent man. Anyone arriving now would be too late to prepare for a murder, after all.

He thundered along the street past the litter, which wobbled and tipped as the entourage lurched out of the wild horseman's way, along the street, making for Pompey's great theatre complex, which he could see rising over the roofs of other buildings.

The irony. Wouldn't that old bastard Pompey be laughing his arse off in Hades at the thought.

Now he was reaching the more densely crowded streets, people from all walks of life closing on the heart of the city's entertainment for the day. When Fronto had been a boy, all this area had been fields, he thought, oddly. Apart from the villa publica and a couple of shrines, nothing permanent was built there, for it was public land. The Field of Mars, as it was called, where armies gathered. Then had come the great powers of Rome, the dictators, the Mariuses and Sullas, the Sertoriuses and Crassuses, the Pompeys... and the Caesars. And now the place was becoming as urban as the heart of Rome. Perhaps that was what progress was. But he could see it through the eyes of men like Brutus and Cassius. Even such a small thing as the ever increasing urbanisation of the campus martius was a sign of the traditions and the hallowed past of Rome being eroded, and to them Caesar represented the latest incarnation of the powers that were changing the city.

It was foolish.

He growled as he rounded a corner and raced towards the temples that lay before the great Pompeian complex. Foolish. They thought that killing Caesar would change things, would halt the decay of the republic and the rise of the new masters of Rome, which only went to show that they had not paid attention to the men around Caesar. Octavian would inherit, and Fronto had a suspicion that the wily young man would be every bit of what they despised in Caesar, and a damn sight more. And even if Octavian was also removed, there would be others. Antonius was a man who could very easily slip into the same mould, and so was Lepidus to a lesser extent. Rome had not been without despots now for five decades, and if the Sullan wars had taught them anything, it should be that the removal of one tyrant merely made room for a *new* tyrant. That was the bleak truth facing the would-be liberators of the republic.

It mattered not. What happened afterwards was a thing for then gods. All that mattered was now. Spurinna had said it would happen this day, and it seemed he had been right. But had he predicted that the assassins would strike on the ides, or had the assassins struck on the ides because that was when Spurinna predicted? If it was the former, then it was in the hands of the gods and there was nothing anyone could do. If it was the latter, there might still be time to save him.

He hauled on the reins, pulling his mount to a halt, staring at the scene beyond the temples. The open space between the sacred buildings and the steps that led up to the portico and the curia of Pompey was packed to the gills with people, milling this way and that. Gritting his teeth, he drove his horse into the crowd, aiming for that great building, heart in his mouth.

He was not too late.

Senators were still arriving, ready for the session, climbing the steps and entering the doorway. The crowd were being kept back from the central stair by lictors and private guards, and Fronto could see gatherings beyond. Here and there, senators standing in pairs, talking. It was all so bloody normal, it was hard to believe what must be happening. And where was Caesar? Had he arrived yet? Had he been delayed, distracted, waylaid? Had he changed his mind? Had *Brutus* changed *his*, and warned the man, taking him into hiding?

Then he saw the men at the top of the steps to either side of the curia, in the archways that led to the portico and the theatre beyond. Gladiators. That meant Brutus' guards, and if they were here, then so was Decimus Brutus. And if Brutus was here, then so was Caesar.

It was too difficult with the horse. There are times when being mounted is actually a hinderance, especially in a crowd, and so Fronto vaulted from the saddle, cursing as the shock of landing echoed through his knee, and began to push and heave his way through the press. He'd forgotten what it was like to be ordinary, unnoticed in a crowd, without guards and slaves and lictors opening up a path, the public pulling back in awe to watch as a senator passed.

His horse he had now left behind, amid the crowds in the middle of the square.

He was alone. There had only been one horse at the gatehouse of Caesar's villa, kept there for the speedy delivery of messages, and Fronto had taken it. Others were being brought for the rest, and Galronus, Masgava, Aurelius and Arcadios would all be racing along in his wake now, but too far back to make a difference. Perhaps it was better that they were not here.

As he neared the lictors and the steps, it occurred to Fronto how foolhardy this was. Of all the senators descending on the complex, he could be the only one with the intent of saving Caesar. Any moment now, he might find himself facing sixty armed and angry senators, and what then?

He shook away that momentary doubt.

This had to be done.

As he broke free of the last of the crowd, he tore the sword from his belt. Perhaps it was another sign of how things had changed in the city that a man in a simple tunic, spattered with blood, could emerge from a crowd with sword in hand, and the episode raise only mild surprise from all present. Senators looked round at the commotion, all except one small gathering off to the right, but Fronto's attention was on the lictors, for it was the lictors and guards that were closing on him, ready to defend the various senators they served. The gladiators atop the steps made no move as yet.

Fronto held up a finger to the approaching lictors, his face grim.

'Marcus Falerius Fronto,' he barked. '*Senator* Marcus Falerius Fronto. Out of my way.'

Half the men immediately backed off, whether because they recognised him or because of his commanding tone and out of simple habit, he could not say. The others paused in their advance, looking at one another uncertainly. Then, Fronto was through them, taking advantage of their uncertainty and knocking the nearest two aside in his passage.

His eyes took in everything, now. The lictors were still unsure, variously returning to their posts to hold back the general public, or dithering, considering chasing down the blood-spattered man who'd just barged through them. The gladiators atop the steps had not moved, still, which was both surprising and a relief, but they were now looking at one another, trying to decide whether Fronto was a viable target. Most of the senators had strode in through the great bronze doors of the curia atop the steps now, the gladiators flanking the building.

His gaze fell on the remaining pair of white-robed figures that had not looked at him yet, and in that moment he recognised them. Gaius Trebonius, a stalwart of Caesar's campaigns, had been with the general in Britannia, had helped put down the revolt of Ambiorix, had besieged Massilia and taken control of Hispania, and who was now named among those who sought the death of Caesar. Fronto's anger flared. With him was Marcus Antonius, though it did not look as though they conspired. Indeed, it looked as though they were entirely at odds. Antonius was gesticulating angrily at Trebonius, and every time Antonius looked as though he were going to leave, making to step round him, Trebonius moved back in his way, even reaching up and grabbing his arm to keep him in place.

Fronto had a sinking feeling. Antonius was being kept in place, out of the way. Trebonius caught sight of Fronto approaching, sword in hand, and there was a moment of almost panicked indecision there then, faced with having to keep Antonius out of the curia, but now also with an angry Fronto. His job was made easier a moment later as Decimus Brutus emerged from the door, bellowing for his guards to surround the curia.

Fronto's heart lurched at the sight. Brutus also held a blade in his hand, and his, too, was stained red. Brutus had not immediately spotted Fronto, and his attention was on Antonius, who had finally pushed past Trebonius. The young officer held his sword out to the side, attempting a non-threatening manner, but Antonius' face took on a thunderous look.

'Marcus Antonius, hold there,' Brutus said, raising his free hand up, palm forwards.

'What have you done?'

'Saved the republic,' Brutus said. 'Brought the tyrant down.'

But a blood-curdling scream from inside the curia suggested that was not quite true. Fronto, fresh purpose squashing the horror that had been rising in him, raced up the steps. Gladiators were closing now, stepping into position to block the way, but Fronto was not to be stopped. All the gladiators in the world were not going to prevent him reaching the curia today. Brutus now realised what was happening and, leaving Antonius, who was now once again entangled with Trebonius, he hurried towards Fronto, gesturing at the gladiators. 'Leave him. Leave him, I say,' and then to the angry senator: 'Fronto, wait.'

But Fronto had no intention of waiting. Most of the gladiators had heeded their master's words and were stepping aside, holding up their weapons, but one man was still directly in Fronto's path, a small round shield on his arm and a curved, Thracian sica blade in hand. The man settled into a defensive stance, sword back at his side, ready to lance out, shield up and facing.

Fronto simply walked straight into the man. As he reached the gladiator, who was somewhat nonplussed at this curious behaviour, he stamped down and lunged with his forehead at the same time. The gladiator's foot crunched unbearably beneath the blow, while the head-butt mashed most of his face. He had lunged with the sica even at the last moment, though, years of training kicking in despite his surprise. Fronto felt the blade slide into his side, felt the agony, the hot, burning pain of the wound from the razor sharp sword, and even more as he never faltered in his advance, simply knocking the wounded gladiator out of his way, but the sword in his side cut through flesh as it came free, with an agonising pain.

The man fell to the steps, knocked aside, and Fronto was clear, marching on the curia doorway. He looked down once, saw the huge blossom of red on his tunic, and knew it for a bad wound, but somehow it didn't matter. He didn't care. He was focused.

'Fronto,' Brutus said in a conciliatory tone, hurrying to his side and reaching out, grasping his shoulder. 'Fronto, it's too late.'

Fronto ripped his shoulder free of the grip without once breaking his stride. He was nearly at the bronze doors now. The agonised howling of Caesar was still emitting from the chamber, given a tremendous echo by the sheer size of a room designed to amplify the voices of speakers. The dictator was still alive, whatever Brutus said. The throbbing in Fronto's side was becoming hard to ignore, but he managed it all the same.

Antonius was nearby now. Trebonius sat on the steps, holding his head and shaking it from where he'd been well and truly thumped. Fronto turned one last time before he entered the senate building, seeing the floored Trebonius, seeing Brutus turning, making to follow him, seeing Antonius.

There was something about that man. He looked angry. He looked furious, even. But Fronto had known hiim a lot of years, and Antonius was a man ever to wear his heart on his sleeve, not given to secrecy and obfuscation. He did well to hide it, given all that, but while everyone else might miss it, Fronto saw right through it all. Antonius had known this was coming. There was not an ounce of surprise about his whole being, for all his angry indignation. It was pretty convincing. For Antonius, it was, in fact, masterful, and Fronto noted it with a whole new anger, filing that away for later. For now, he had other matters in mind.

Gladiators were moving again, making to cut him off, but they were too late. Antonius had Brutus, Trebonius was out of it, and Fronto was in through the doors, into the curia of Pompey, leaving a trail of crimson drips.

It was rather dark, after the bright sunshine of spring outside, and it took precious moments for his eyesight to adjust, even as he kept walking. He saw the senatorial rows, seating all around three sides of the great chamber in tiers, five rows, with steps here and there granting easy access to the seating. Few of the seats were occupied, and the men who were in those seats were gripping their chairs tight, wide-eyed with shock, trembling. Others had risen from their seats, but were still in place, afraid to move.

A whole gathering of senators, however, were on the speaking floor. Fronto could see the curule chair that should be Caesar's seat for the session. As his eyesight continued to adjust to the dimness, he realised that one arm of the chair was broken, and there was blood across it, and across the floor beneath it. Men had staggered this way and that through the blood, for it was smeared and spread across the delicate marble, and a dozen tracks of prints led from there to where the senators were gathered. More blood hit the marble, this time from the newcomer, heavy drips from the wound in his side and the blood-soaked tunic, blatting to the floor. Fronto broke into a jog, for still Caesar lived. There were howls of agony echoing around the chamber, the source lost behind that collection of white-clad bodies.

Brutus had not been the only killer, for as Fronto closed on them, he could see bloodied blades in the hands of many men. Gods, but how many had it taken to fell the dictator? As he stomped across, roaring incoherent oaths, soaked in blood, both his and that of others, senators pulled back and opened a path for him. His furious gaze took in the luminaries as he passed.

Marcus Junius Brutus, one of Caesar's oldest friends. Blade red, his eyes met Fronto's with not a shred of remorse to be seen. Pontius Aquila, outspoken opponent of Caesar, nodding his satisfaction. Servilius Casca, once one of Caesar's closest, now covered in his blood. At least *he* looked guilty. Cassius Longinus, less of a shock, republican to the core and former Pompeian, though he appeared shocked at what he had done. Cimber. Basilus. Petronius. The list went on. Fronto lost count of how many bloody knives and short swords he saw as he passed through the crowd, but there must have been a score or more.

As he emerged beyond them, his own blood chilled.

Caesar had clearly taken the first few blows at his curule chair, but had lurched from the seat, bloodied and torn, and staggered away. The assassins had been merciless, attacking again and again as he weaved across the rich marble, and the great man had finally fallen, perhaps slipping in his own blood, at the foot, rather ironically, of the statue of his one-time nemesis, Gnaeus Pompey Magnus. The lamented rebel commander now looked down from his painted marble visage at the man who had vanquished him, a heap on the floor.

Yet still, Caesar was not dead. The pile of bloodied toga beneath the statue pulsated and shook, moved and thrashed, issuing horrible keening noises.

Fronto shuffled over, holding his throbbing side, and dropped to a crouch, his sword falling to the marble, clattering loud enough to echo around the chamber. Caesar's toga was little more than a blood-soaked rag, wrapped around him, and Fronto had to unwind it to assess the damage.

His shock and dismay deepened with every fold that fell away. Caesar had been stabbed many times, by many of the senators present, but Fronto's experience on the battlefield told him a horrible truth. They had not once delivered a killing blow, even with a score or more hits, and that could not be an accident. Most of these men had been soldiers at some level, and all of them would have been taught elementary swordsmanship in their youth. That a few of them could fail to produce a killing blow was no surprise. That *none* of them had managed was unfathomable. For just a moment, he wondered whether they were so vicious as to have deliberately struck to cause as much pain as possible without death, but he quickly brushed that aside. Even if men like Cassius and Aquila were capable of such cruelty, the Brutii would never have agreed to such a thing. No, that was not the reason. He realised then the horrible truth. There had been something like sixty conspirators, and each was to be allowed his blow for freedom. Had one of them killed him too quickly, the others would not have the chance to add their own blade to the event, and that was part of it. It was to be a death by universal consent, and so *all* had to have a hand in it. That meant, to Fronto's mind, that they were less than half way through! There were more than twenty wounds already, but that meant thirty some still to go.

He shuddered.

The shape was groaning, coughing, whimpering.

Leg wounds. Arm wounds. Hip. Side. Face and neck. One to the chest, but not deep enough to kill. The man was starting to go grey through loss of blood, though. If they didn't get the rest of the blades in soon, the man would die before they could. Mind you, Fronto's *own* wound was no scratch either. It probably wouldn't kill him, unless it had nicked his liver, but only if he got to a medicus soon.

'Cruel bastards,' he spat, then reached to Caesar, turning him over a little more, so that the face looked up at him. 'I will get you back to the villa. There are surgeons there for both of us. We might have time to...'

His words trailed off as the dictator blinked twice, coughed up a clot of blood and sagged even further.

'Finish... me...' the man hissed, then winced and coughed, shaking, a fresh gout of blood pouring from the wound in his neck.

Fronto felt the world change, felt the gods stop what they were doing and look down at the Curia, at the assassination, at the victim, at Fronto. He felt the shades of men long gone gathering round him at the dark edge of the room. Paetus was there, nodding. And there was Labienus, too. And other shadows, waiting.

But most of all there was Verginius.

His oldest friend simply stood, a formless shade, watching.

Fronto swallowed. The gods had gifted him a boon. It was the most horrible boon a man could be given, but it was his way out. He had promised to save Caesar, and yet he had vowed to Verginius he would kill the man. And here was a chance to do both.

Despite his words of consolation, from the moment he had crouched over the body, Fronto had known damn well that Caesar was done for. He'd lost too much blood. And even if, by some miracle, he lived, he would never be whole again. Too many organs, joints, tendons and muscles had been scythed and torn for him ever to be Caesar now. He was a corpse already, just one who could still feel and see, and smell his own death. And now, Caesar had asked him to end it.

Fronto had walked enough battlefields in his life to know that sometimes a swift blade was far more merciful than a kind word and false hope.

He leaned over Caesar, fingers fumbling for his fallen sword.

'No,' one of the senators called. '*No*. Not yet.'

But Fronto had already placed the tip of the blade over Caesar's heart, and now he pushed down with all his might. He felt the flesh give, the ribcage crack, the blade slide deep through soft tissues, and finally thud into the marble beneath. The effort caused his own wound to blossom anew, and for a moment he wondered whether he might end here, alongside the dictator. No. He had time, yet.

Caesar's eyes went wide, and he coughed again, once, twice, thrice, and then shook for a moment and fell still.

Fronto looked down. Twenty three blows, and only his had been merciful. He looked at the man he had served most of his adult life, and found that suddenly he had no words. He was beyond anger, beyond grief. *Twenty three*. Caesar's eyes looked up at him, and even now, lifeless and glassy, they were unreadable. He almost laughed at that, then reached down and gently closed the man's eyes, finding another coin to put under the great man's tongue.

He looked at the gleaming disc in his hand and it almost made him laugh out loud again. Caesar's profile was more accurate than many coins, a recent striking, in the past month or so. A denarius on which the man's head was surrounded by the legend DICT PERPETVO CAESAR. Caesar, dictator for life. The ironies seemed to be unstoppable, today. He turned the coin over to find the figure of Venus holding out Victory in her hand. Shit. He leaned over and prised the man's teeth open, sliding in the coin. What would happen now, he had no idea, but whatever it was, desecration or honour, he had made sure that Caesar could pay the ferryman.

He pulled his sword free and rose, turning slowly, empty hand going to the warm, damp tunic at his side.

A senator he didn't know was fuming angrily, jabbing a finger at him and ranting about honour and unity and other noble and currently unimportant concepts. His friends were holding him back, which was a good thing for him. Fronto turned his back on the body, letting go of his wound, took three steps, grasped the wagging hand and broke the finger without even looking at the man. The senator shrieked, which made Fronto's lip twitch. The bastard had been ready to hack a hole in a man's body, but a broken finger was apparently unacceptable.

'You *animal*,' the man snapped, and only avoided Fronto's swinging fist because his friend pulled him out of the way.

'He needs to be on display,' someone said, 'somewhere the people can see him. It is not enough to bring down a tyrant; people need to know he has fallen. On the rostra in the forum.'

Fronto stopped, turned, glared at the speaker.

'No,' someone else said, 'he is a *criminal*, and now that he has no imperium, he can be tried. We should try him in absentia, condemn him, and treat the body with the contempt it deserves. In pieces in the Tiber, I say.'

Fronto's twitching lip and stony glare turned to this man now.

'No,' called Decimus Brutus from the chamber's doorway. 'He will be borne away and mourned as he should. This was tyrannicide, not villainy.'

Fronto turned again, said nothing. He did not trust himself to say anything to Brutus. Instead, he walked between the gathered senators and across the floor of the curia, trudging through the lake of blood around the chair and leaving fresh prints all the way to the open door.

'I know you're angry,' Brutus said, standing in his way. 'One day you will understand. You may even agree.'

Still, the angry Fronto said nothing, did not slow, walked through the doorway, roughly knocking his old friend out of the way. Brutus staggered back, and Fronto emerged into the light of a bright afternoon in a new world, blinking, bleeding. The commotion all around was almost unbearable. Tidings of what had happened had apparently hit the crowd while he'd been inside, and Rome was crying, groaning, shrieking, cheering or whooping. Some were celebrating the death of a tyrant, but more were horrified, panicked, angry. Fights were already breaking out across the square.

Trebonius was on his feet and moving towards Fronto with hands up in a conciliatory manner.

Fronto came to a halt at the top of the stairs, above the crowd, and something in his expression warned Trebonius off, for the man quickly recoiled and hurried away, leaving Fronto alone, looking out over Rome. People were being wounded in the press now, probably even dying.

This, he realised, was how it would begin. The aftermath.

The fall of a man like Caesar would do more than just cause ripples. It would change *everything*.

Brutus was outside now, too, calling for calm from the crowd, but Antonius was stalking towards him, wearing an expression of righteous anger. It mattered not. Fronto hardly noticed when the two men started arguing.

They were all at it, bellowing at one another, senators inside, senators on the steps, people in the crowd, gladiators in the portico, and those who were not shouting or arguing were fighting. Fronto stood, not watching, not really seeing the crowds, the fights, not hearing the shouts or anything more than the background din. His gaze was looking out not over the city, but over the years, both back, and forward. There was going to be another war. You only had to listen to the shouting here to realise it. There would be another war, and whatever happened, whoever won, it would not change things. There would just be a new tyrant as always. Antonius, maybe, or Lepidus.

His gaze turned slowly towards the east.

Or Octavian.

But whatever happened, it was no longer Fronto's fight. He was done. He'd said it many times, but this time it was final. He was done.

The sword dropped from his open hand, clanging and clattering on the steps, and Fronto walked away.

CHAPTER TWENTY SEVEN

Fronto bounced in the vehicle along the street, listening to the sounds of a restive, troubled city outside. He travelled in the litter not through propriety, nor through fear of violence, but simply because too much walking, and particularly riding, kept opening the wound in his side a little. The medicus had assured him that he would live, unless he did anything stupid to prevent it. Lucilia had, of course, made a comment about the likelihood of her husband doing something stupid.

The city was in chaos, and Fronto could hear his men tense, ready for trouble, as they marched alongside the litter, led by Aurelius, Arcadios and Masgava. It had been three days since that dreadful moment, and he was still really no nearer to coming to terms with it, though he had resolved a few things in his mind. One, in particular, he'd thought on, long and hard, and it had taken this long to do something about it, hence his journey this morning.

Caesar's body had been taken away on a stretcher by three slaves, carried back to his villa across the river. Several of the more rabid among the assassins had tried to stop it, but Brutus and Cassius had maintained that decorum should remain, and had made sure the body could be taken away safely.

Antonius had become involved in an argument, then a fight, with Trebonius, and had finally fled for safety when the other conspirators came forward and threatened him. Fronto had not been present for anything that followed. He had lost so much blood that by the time he reached home, there had been great concern for his life, and it had taken a full day before he'd had the strength to rise from his bed. Even now, he was weak as a new-born, and it hurt when he bent. Stupid, really. He'd fought Gauls, Germans, Aegyptians, Africans, and many Roman rebels, and yet it had been a hired gladiator that had almost done for him in the end. But the

361

events that ensued were reported to him repeatedly by his friends, in particular Galronus, who had taken part in some small way, being a senator.

Following the removal of the body, the more sensible of the killers had rushed to the forum, where they had mounted the rostra and addressed the people of Rome. Notably, Marcus Brutus and Cassius Longinus took the fore, calling for Rome to remain calm, telling them that the deed was done, that the tyrant had been removed, and that Rome was free. They had called for clemency now, and for peace to allow the republic to find its way back to its course.

Some of the people heeded their words. Others were still madly enraged by the loss of a man who they saw as having saved Rome. Nothing had been truly achieved by the time the sun set that day, for the assassins were still at large, the people still troubled, Antonius in hiding, and Lepidus still away. That night, as if the gods themselves spoke their fury, there had been such a storm as few could remember, thunder and lightning and rain that hammered the roofs and turned the streets to rivers.

When dawn came and the storm had abated, it transpired that much had happened as the people cowered in their houses. A mob of pro-Caesarian partisans had attacked and sacked the houses of Marcus Brutus and Cassius Longinus, killing and looting, though both men were absent, in hiding. A poor fellow by the name of Helvius Cinna had been butchered by the mob, mistaken for the *senator* Cinna who had borne one of the assassin's blades, the innocent man's head still being carried in the morning atop a spear. Lepidus had returned, too, during the storm, bringing with him a legion of soldiers from the port. He'd stationed them at important places around the city, and taken control of the forum. When dawn arrived, he had Antonius at his side, and the two men then addressed the people, just as Brutus and Cassius had done the previous day. They, however, called for anything *but* amnesty and clemency. They called for the proscription and execution of the assassins of Caesar, and their righteous fury had fanned the flames of the mob's anger, only making matters in the city worse. That day chaos reigned, and senators and beggars alike found themselves attacked in the streets for one reason or another. The city had become a deathtrap.

The assassins then returned to public view, taking advantage of the chaos to condemn Antonius and Lepidus in turn. It had been Antonius who had called an emergency meeting of the senate the next day. Again, murders and chaos ruled the streets that second night.

The senate's meeting had been unexpectedly successful, largely down to the part played by Cicero. Despite everything, the great orator was a figure who appealed to both assassins and Caesarians, for he had been an outspoken opponent of Caesar, but he had also had no part in the conspiracy to kill him. Consequently, as men like Brutus and Cassius, Antonius and Lepidus watched each other warily across the senate house, the stains of the blood still visible on the floor, tension riding high, all were content to accept Cicero's words.

The man advocated for all sides. It was his contention that Rome had suffered enough. That any further division would only tear the city apart, and that the division between these men at the top layer of society was causing the violence and chaos in the streets. He called for the honouring of Caesar's memory, removing all taint of despotism from his reputation, but also a grand amnesty for the men who had seen their actions as for the good of the republic. It was voted upon and accepted, and as they left the senate house, on the surface it had seemed that all things could settle. Caesar was to be granted divine honours in an unprecedented fashion, greater than any man in the history of Rome, and a state funeral, while honours would also be bestowed upon every man involved in the killing, including provincial appointments that would take them from the city and make them immune to prosecution for the duration.

That afternoon, after the meeting, Caesar's body, now carefully arranged on a bier, had been carried from his house all the way to the forum, where a pyre had been raised. Though the public were kept at a distance, as the great man's body burned, the soldiers Lepidus had brought, all veterans of Caesar's legions, cast goods and trinkets into the flames in commemoration.

A shrine was raised on the rostra to the man's memory, with the bloody toga in which he'd died on full display, hardly a move to placate the public, and one that had enraged Brutus. The assassins left before the funeral games began, showing readily that no matter what the senate had voted, the division among the leading men of Rome was far from healed.

That meeting in the curia of Pompey was to be the last held there. Effort was redoubled on the new curia Caesar had begun, in the hope that it would be complete before the next session was called. The chamber where the deed had been done was to be walled up and never entered again, left as a hallowed place.

The night that followed had been little better than the previous two, more violence in the streets, more partisan activity, both Caesarians and tyrannicides hiding behind the high walls of their houses with their guards, staying far from the violence in the streets.

It had been this morning's visitor that had spurred Fronto to finally rise from his convalescence and take action, though the household was already preparing for the inevitable departure. Octavian had arrived with a large guard, looking pale, dark rings beneath his eyes. Word had reached him almost immediately following the assassination, and he had taken ship from Illyricum and then horse, riding through the night and arriving back in Rome at sunset yesterday.

'I went straight to the house of Marcus Antonius,' Octavian said as he was shown into Fronto's chamber and sank into the chair beside him. 'He's not my favourite person, nor I his, but he and Lepidus seem to have been the two men attempting to keep Caesar's legacy alive, so I did not know where else to go. I certainly wasn't going back to the villa, with Cleopatra and my cousin in residence.'

Fronto nodded. It was a knotty problem, because there was almost no one left in the city Fronto trusted, except perhaps, oddly, Cicero.

'When I got there,' Octavian continued, 'they were in the process of reading Caesar's will. Antonius had just finished and was putting it away. He claimed to have been left all of Caesar's inheritance. When I managed to get hold of the will, I looked at it.

It labels me as primary heir, inheriting three quarters of Caesar's estate, with the other quarter split between my cousins, and, somewhat ironically, Decimus Brutus named as the heir in the second degree, should I die. When I confronted Antonius, he pointed out that this will had never been officially lodged, and it was true. There were no seals attached. It had never been witnessed. But it was his will. I know his writing, and we all know this was to be his intention. I did consider having fake seals put on, post-mortem witnesses, but that would cheapen its worth. Instead, I intend to fight Antonius over the will in the courts, and I have absolutely no doubt that I will win.'

No, Fronto thought, me neither. Antonius was too hot-headed and impulsive to walk away with this one. Octavian was cleverer by half and had the advantage of being Caesar's flesh and blood. He would win.

'Besides,' Octavian added, 'everyone will be keen to see the will accepted. It gives over the gardens of the great villa to the people of Rome as a park, and vows three hundred sestertii to every man in Rome.'

Yes, Fronto agreed, that would buy an awful lot of goodwill. Antonius would struggle to oppose it.

'As such,' Octavian sat back and folded his arms, 'I am to be adopted as per the will. I shall become Gaius Julius Caesar Octavianus.'

Fronto shivered then, looking across at the young man. He remembered Caesar at a similar age, and the two men were astonishingly alike. Octavian would be a new Caesar, and, if anything, he would be more Caesar than Caesar ever was. He sighed. He'd thought that often, recently: that the death of the tyrant was only going to leave a hole to be filled by a successor. The only question now was who that successor would be. He had no doubt that Brutus and Cassius and all their allies would lose out. There might be a war, there might not, but they would never win, and the republic as it was would disappear forever. But who would be the man to rule what was left was the question, for there was no love lost between Antonius and Octavian, and a clash, he was sure, was inevitable. The only thing that kept them from open confrontation at the moment was that they shared a mutual enemy in Caesar's murderers. Fronto suspected it would be little more than days before the senate's decrees were overturned and the proscriptions and executions would begin.

Octavian had left the house this morning, and left Fronto deep in thought. The more he contemplated matters, the more he'd become convinced that this would come down to a contest between those two men, and that all those who'd been involved in the plot would be hunted and killed.

That left Fronto with two problems. Firstly, he trusted neither man. He liked them both, but trusted neither of them. Octavian might seem perfectly reasonable and an ally, but Fronto had seen another side of the man a year or so ago, casually removing anyone who he considered an obstacle to his inheritance. And Antonius *should* be trustworthy, but Fronto had seen his face on those steps yesterday and realised that the man had known what was coming, yet had done nothing to stop it. So neither were to be trusted. And the second problem, of course, was that if all the assassins were called to account, someone, at some point, would draw attention to the killing blow being delivered, and to Fronto emerging from the curia, soaked in blood, sword in hand.

When those two facts were added together, they resulted in only one conclusion. Fronto's time in Rome was done. He hadn't pieced the last bit of the puzzle together, though, until he was dressing and giving out orders to the household. Then, when Carbo had mused whether the collegia might now be reinstituted, it had begun a cascade of connections and realisations.

The horseman. The new leader of the collegium.

It was nothing to do with the equestrian order after all. It was a reference to a man who had been one of Caesar's senior cavalry commanders and his magister equitum, his 'master of the horse,' the previous year.

Within half an hour he was out in the streets, bouncing around in his litter, making for the house of the man who had prevented him from saving Caesar. He already had everything being put in place at home, but now he had to make sure that they would be safe.

A call indicated that they had arrived, and the litter came to a halt. As it was lowered, Carbo reached in and helped him, grunting and swearing, from the vehicle. It would, he grumbled, be many months before he was remotely fit again after this wound.

One of his men knocked on the door and when it was opened, Fronto was admitted to the house of Marcus Antonius without delay. He walked through the place, having been here a number of times, not needing the slave guiding him, and was shown to the room where Antonius was reclining, Lepidus and Hirtius present, similarly reclined, all drinking wine. Fronto looked at the other two visitors, then at Antonius. 'I need to speak to you.'

'Of course.'

'Alone.'

Antonius frowned, but gestured to Lepidus and Hirtius. 'Would you mind, gentlemen?'

The two nodded their consent and rose, brows furrowed in confusion, and slaves led them away, still holding their cups of wine. Fronto waited for them to go, and then turned and closed the door, shutting he and Antonius away in solitude. He listened, to be sure there was no one in earshot and, satisfied, turned to the house's master.

'When does the bloodshed start?'

Antonius, face all innocence, frowned. 'I have no idea what you...'

'Cut the shit, Antonius. You and I both know that you have no intention of letting the assassins get away with it. The republic has gone, even though its body is still here, twitching. Caesar never *needed* a crown – he was more powerful than any king. And this power vacuum will not last long, for the senate will never be able to fill it. There will be a successor, and that means that the so-called tyrannicides will all have to die.'

Antonius sat up, put his cup down and placed his hands on his knees.

'Very well, if we are to be frank, Fronto, yes. I am already pulling appropriate strings to have the list of names drawn up. You are quite right that the senate and the consuls will never again rule Rome, no matter what anyone thinks.'

'My name will be on that list.'

'I can arrange anything. I have sufficient power and authority, Fronto.'

'No you don't. Even Octavian and Lepidus cannot do that. If you condemn *one* man for this act, you must condemn them *all*. Every man has to die, and my name will not escape the list.'

'You were no murderer, Fronto,' Antonius said. 'I know what you did.'

'And I know what *you* did.'

Antonius frowned, leaning back. 'I don't follow you.'

'Yes you do, but you've become a lot better at hiding things recently. I don't know whether it's spending time with men like Caesar and Octavian, or whether it's simply plenty of practice, but you're getting much subtler in your old age.'

'Whatever you think you know, Fronto…'

Fronto interrupted, shaking his head. 'No. You listen to me, Marcus Antonius. I know you were the man paying the Pompeian collegium. I don't know how you afforded it, since you always seem to be bordering on broke. Maybe you borrowed from Caesar, but whatever the case, I know it was you. The horseman.'

'They were ordered not to hurt anyone,' Antonius said defensively.

'Yes. I had figured out that they were given new orders when you took control, though I am not entirely convinced it was not you who had the man arranging Caesar's new bodyguard killed. But you knew how strong the collegium was first-hand, for you were the first person they went for. And my men were the ones who told you that Clodius, Milo and Hypsaeus used to run the collegia as gangs. Gods, but it was when we'd been attacked by them that the idea was put in your head. By *us!*'

'I never had people killed.'

'Perhaps not by direct order, but your culpability for a lot of deaths cannot be argued. So you had your private army ready for when the deed was done, and you needed support. And I presume it was nothing to do with the assassins that I was out of the way. I think you knew I was too close to Caesar and I would save him, so it was you who drew me away. Unfortunately for you, right now you're not in the strong military position you would have been, because my men and I killed your precious private army.'

'Why would I not want you to save Caesar?' Antonius demanded, lip curling. 'He's one of my oldest friends, a relation, even. I am the man seeking retribution for his death.'

'Yes,' Fronto snorted. 'All very convenient. You knew the plot was on, and Spurinna had given you a date. The location was not really hard to guess. I suspect you already knew at least some of the conspirators and you've been watching them, so you knew where they, and we, all were. Oh, you didn't kill Caesar, Antonius, but fuck you for *letting* it happen.'

'You don't know what you're talking about.'

'Don't I? Because you've been overlooked for years now, and right now you've no more political power than any other senator. But Octavian will inherit everything and become the new Caesar. And you knew he hadn't lodged the will. If the old man died before the will was ratified, you could prevent the succession passing smoothly to Octavian. Because if that happened, then you were finished. Octavian dislikes you as much as you dislike him. And if you think *Caesar* overlooked you, imagine what it will be like when his *nephew* is dictator.'

An uncomfortable silence fell. Antonius had been caught out, and he knew it.

'There is no proof of what you say.'

'No,' Fronto agreed. 'You were pretty thorough there. But should such information reach the ears of some important folk, you would lose all your influence. Even the *suggestion* of what you did would be enough to ruin you for good. And I cannot say I haven't thought this past hour or so of letting just that happen.'

'So what do you want, Fronto?' Antonius said, coldly.

'Fronto is dead. Marcus Falerius Fronto is no more. He died of his wounds after the assassination. Of this you are in no doubt, and his family disappeared thereafter, without a trace. It ends there. No one comes after us. No one even looks for us.'

'People will ask questions,' Antonius replied. 'You were on the steps with a bloody sword.'

'Answer them. Do what you have to. I and mine are gone, dead and removed from Rome. Do not follow us, and your secret will die with Fronto. Dig him up, and that secret might see the light of day again. Do we have an agreement?'

Antonius closed his eyes, sucking his lip, then opened them and nodded.

'It's important you understand why, Fronto.'

'No it isn't.'

'Yes it is. Because I've always considered you a friend. Because I need *someone* to know. It's not greed. Yes, I need money, and I wanted a campaign in the east to pay off my debts, but it's not that. I've needed money all my life, and yet I've always managed, finding a way. And it's not hatred. Caesar had irritated me, yes, but I still loved him. He was family. And it certainly wasn't for the love of the republic which, as you noted, is a dying thing now.'

He rose, arms by his side.

'Caesar was dying, Fronto. His fits were coming all the more often, and each was worse than the last. I doubt he would have reached Getae lands before his health failed him. He was not a young man. He was ill, almost critically so, and too old for active campaigning. I very much doubt he'd have reached Alexandria or Parthia. His death then would leave a mess. And Octavian would take the reins, as you said, if his new will was accepted. You might think bad of me, but you also know the young bastard, and you know what he's capable of. The republic might be dead, but *Rome* must go on.'

Fronto simply sighed, sagged slightly, and turned, reaching for the door.

'Fronto?'

'Fronto's dead, remember?'

'Then who are *you*?'

'Best for all of us that you don't know that.'

He pulled open the doors and walked out of the room.

Half an hour later, he was back home.

'What do we do with this, Domine?' a slave asked, indicating a bust, the death mask of Fronto's father.

He shrugged. He might want it still, he supposed. 'Pack it with the rest. Leave only the furniture. Everything else goes.' He walked on through the organised chaos. Slaves and servants and guards hurried this way and that. Everything had to be readied by dusk. They had to hurry. The proscriptions might begin with little notice, and the Falerii had to no longer exist when hunters came looking.

Masgava appeared from a doorway, looking relieved. 'I've been worried about you. Everything is set. The ship is docked at the emporium ready to sail at first light. Eight wagons have been retained from a local supplier and will be here as soon as it's dark, and they're legal in the streets.'

Fronto nodded and walked on. He found Galronus and the boys in the garden, the Remi playing some sort of sword-fighting game with them as they leapt about, laughing, and Faleria looked on, a warm smile on her face.

'Dad,' Marcus shouted, dropping his wooden sword and running over, throwing his arms around Fronto, which made the wound hurt and made him wince. 'Is it true? We're leaving Rome?'

Fronto nodded. 'You remember the villa near Tarraco? We'll live there from now on. You can start your career there. It's a lovely city, and without the chaos and violence of *this* place.'

He gave another smile as the lad laughed, and turned, going back to play.

Tarraco.

The villa he had placed in the hands of his factor there, the former slave Arius Rustius. They would take up residence there once more with a new name. A new start. He would become Marcus Rustius, the boys too. Fronto and his family were dead. Time for a new world.

'I always thought I would be leaving before you,' Galronus said, crossing to him, as he leaned against a column amid the chaos and watched the boys cavort.

'Events overtook us.'

Galronus laughed. 'Just a little. And I know you think this is the end, but it isn't. We *will* come and see you. *More* than once a year, too. And you will come to us. I need you to. I cannot turn Durocortorum into a new Rome without help.' He grinned. 'And we have wineries there.'

'Ha.'

'It's *not* the end, Fronto,' he said again.

'Who's Fronto?' his friend replied, with a relieved smile.

THE END.

"ACCORDING TO HIS VIRTUE LET US USE HIM,
WITH ALL RESPECT AND RITES OF BURIAL.
WITHIN MY TENT HIS BONES TO-NIGHT SHALL
LIE,
MOST LIKE A SOLDIER, ORDER'D HONOURABLY.
SO CALL THE FIELD TO REST; AND LET'S AWAY,
TO PART THE GLORIES OF THIS HAPPY DAY.
EXEUNT"

Closing lines of "Julius Caesar" by William Shakespeare, spoken
by Octavian.

HISTORICAL NOTE

I always knew I would need to write this book, and I always knew it was going to be a difficult proposition. From the day I finished the first Marius' Mules back in 2003 and was hyped up ready to work on a book two, I conceived a series that would last 15 volumes, covering all of the Gallic and Civil Wars, and ending with the greatest event of the age: the death of Caesar. When the first book was actually finally released in 2009, and it was almost immediately, and rather surprisingly (to me), a roaring success, I realised that I was actually going to *write* all those 15 books, and I penned the part of the scene following Caesar's death back then, though it has been played about with considerably in the current plan and is not quite in its original form. And in the original draft the very final scene would have been Fronto with bloodied sword on the steps.

In the main, the sequence of events for a series seemed so neat. Gaul from 58 to 50. The Civil War, Egypt, Africa, Spain, and finally the finale in Rome in 44. It was only as I was closing in on book 15, realising that the penultimate book contained Caesar's last battle, as the title suggests, that I realised the problem I was going to have. I had written fourteen books about war. Fronto was a soldier. In every book he fought battles. Then suddenly I had the most important book of all to write, and the war was over. No battles. Just politics, a conspiracy and a murder. And it was more than just a question of whether readers of the more military titles would be interested in this one. I have come to know Fronto inside and out over the series, and I now worried how the old warhorse could be made to work in a book *not* about war. But the more I looked into the period and its events, the more I realised that just because we were not at war, did not mean I could not have warfare in the book. The streets of Rome by this time had become almost a

374

warzone of their own, with gangs at their nefarious work, powerful rich men directing crime, even the noble Brutus having acquired a force of gladiators.

Much of the background of this book is based around the planned Parthian campaign. We have plenty of record that Caesar was planning to move against the Getae and then Parthia from the Spring of 44 BC. Tubilustrium, the start of the campaigning season, was on March 23rd, and Caesar planned to sail for his army on the 18th. That means that he died just three days before he was due to sail for a new war. The importance of this event is clear, given the timings. The assassins struck at the last time they could, before he departed. Caesar was not to be allowed to launch this war. We know bits and pieces of the planned campaign through sources, but not a lot, for, of course, it never actually happened. As such, I have stamped my own mark on the campaign plan, via Fronto. In many ways, the details of that campaign are not important – how many legions, how many ships, where the campaign would move. What *is* important is that there was a solid belief in Rome that Caesar was bound for Alexandria when he left, and that once that happened, he would begin a shift of all Roman governance to the east, ruling like an eastern Divine King. That is critical to what happened in Rome. And I have long held that Caesar was, for all his faults, staunchly Roman. I cannot picture him turning Rome into an Egypto-centric republic or empire. He may have desired a crown, but it would be a Roman one. And so I could not picture what could possibly make Caesar want to go to Alexandria, despite his mistress and bastard son.

The answer came unexpectedly, for me – that little gem of the prophecy of the Sibylline books. Odd that I had read through the texts of Caesar's life time and again, and yet that particular fact had never struck me before with the importance it has. Plutarch tells us (Caesar 60.1) that from *"a report that from the Sibylline books it appeared that Parthia could be taken if the Romans went up against it with a king, but otherwise could not be assailed."* I suspect I had not looked at it in the light of Alexandria because in Suetonius we are told that *"Lucius Cotta would announce [...] that inasmuch as it was written in the books of fate that the Parthians could be conquered only by a king, Caesar should be given that title*." As such I had lumped this in with the various diadem and rex stories of Rome and not given it sufficient thought. But Caesar's mistress was a queen, his son a prince, and the throne of Egypt lay empty. Caesar planned to conquer Parthia, which could only be conquered by a king. Much of my treatment of the last three months of his life somewhat hinges on that realisation.

This was the basis around which I constructed my plot, not wanting to merely echo extant tales or to copy the bard. I had a new perspective, I think, on the plot and all the factors surrounding it.

To the wars in Rome, then. The collegia were Rome's trade unions. They existed for almost every trade, almost every part of Rome, and were of some importance. Their power had grown sufficiently that in 44 BC Caesar made them illegal, barring the most ancient and respected ones. I was led to wonder why. There are nebulous tales that the collegia had been used at times as mercenary forces for hire by the more dubious wealthy men of the city (our Milos, Clodiuses, and Hypsaeuses.) Still, I wasn't really sure how I might weave them in until I read somewhere of the existence of colleges of former soldiers. I immediately wondered whether such colleges of opposed commanders might come to blows in the city, and, of course, of all the collegia, ex-soldiers would be good at it. I had my men for war in the streets. My fixation on Hypsaeus was because I needed a fall guy Fronto could suspect, and the man had been just such a master of gangs in his time. He fit the bill. Fronto and his enemies now had a ready source of men to throw at one another. But who really was to be my bad guy?

Antonius?

Yes, I suspect you're astounded, flummoxed, disbelieving, even irritated. After all, Marcus Antonius has gone down in history as one of Caesar's greatest and closest supporters, the man who purged Rome in revenge, following Caesar's death. I invite you, however, to consider a few matters.

In Plutarch's life of Marcus Antonius (13.1) he tells us: "*This incident strengthened the party of Brutus and Cassius; and when they were taking count of the friends whom they could trust for their enterprise, they raised a question about Antony. The rest were for making him one of them, but Trebonius opposed it. For, he said, while people were going out to meet Caesar on his return from Spain, Antony had travelled with him and shared his tent, and he had sounded him quietly and cautiously; Antony had understood him, he said, but had not responded to his advances; Antony had not, however, reported the conversation to Caesar, but had faithfully kept silence about it."*

This event is not universally accepted as true, but Cicero in his Second Philippics (34) gives us a fairly unarguable *"if it be a crime to have wished that Caesar might be put to death, beware, I pray you, O Antonius, of what must be your own case, as it is notorious that you, when at Narbo, formed a plan of the same sort with Caius Trebonius"*.

So, many months before the plot comes to culmination, Antonius is made aware of it directly by one of the conspirators, and yet, though he does not join them, neither does he make Caesar aware of this plot. Moreover, he has to have kept the secret completely, for Trebonius goes on to build his conspiracy unchallenged. So the next question must be: why? Why did Antonius not tell Caesar of the plot?

The answer to this, for me at least, was rather neatly summed up recently by the fabulous Harry Sidebottom at an event we both attended. Harry gave a superb talk on why Rome grew, changed, and then stopped growing, and it was as I was listening to his explanation of the general financial system in the republic that a possible reason struck me.

To be a senator in the republic was a horribly costly business. The expenditure for anyone who needed to live in the world of the Roman elite was monstrous, and so senators haemorrhaged money on a daily basis. Where could they *get* this money, though? After all, family fortunes dwindle when used lavishly, and senators were not allowed to engage in business. So where did the money they needed come from? They could theoretically make money from land rents, but even the greatest property owners in Rome could not support such a lifestyle on that income. So where did they turn? The simple answer is conquest. A Roman nobleman would seek position in order to engage in military campaigns, securing a governorship or a special commission, with the remit to conquer offering vast opportunities. Julius Caesar belonged to a renowned family, but a far from wealthy one. He borrowed huge sums to get the leg up that his political career needed, but then he needed to solve that. The answer was Gaul. By the time that war was finished, Caesar was powerful, wealthy and in prime position in Rome.

Now think about Antonius, a relative of Caesar's, who had been profligate in his youth (and indeed throughout his life). Antonius by 58 BC had run up enormous debts. In the hope of solving this, he secured positions with Caesar several times during the Gallic wars, but not until 54, and even then only sporadically. While Caesar gained the profit from eight years of war, Antonius secured two or three at most, and as a secondary officer, not the campaign's master. Perhaps he paid off his debts entirely. Perhaps not. Even if he did, if he wanted to go on living a lavish lifestyle, and all indications are that lavish, even extravagant, was Antonius' natural state, then he would need more money. A *lot* more. Helping Caesar in several years of Civil War would not solve that. Profit could not be made out of fellow Romans like it could from foreigners. And over the ensuing years, Antonius is repeatedly shuffled into political roles in Rome by Caesar. Honourable and significant, but far from lucrative.

Then, in 44, Antonius is granted the consulship alongside Caesar. In this era, both consuls could command armies and campaign, but with Caesar now long-term dictator, with authority even over the consuls, it seems highly unlikely Antonius would be permitted to campaign anywhere while Caesar is in the east. Antonius has now been left to keep Rome settled several times, and it seems highly likely that this is simply the next of those duties. So Caesar is marching east to crush the Parthian empire, notably the richest potential enemy of Rome. If the campaign is successful, Caesar and his officers and men will accrue incredible wealth. Antonius, sitting in Rome, will not. Indeed, he will *spend* it. Moreover, though he is now consul, he is still outranked, even in Rome, for Caesar plans to leave Lepidus in the city as his Magister Equum, the dictator's second in command.

There is one event yet to consider in this particular discussion. Marcus Antonius knew there was a plot against Caesar, and knew that at the very least Trebonius was part of it. The name of Cassius would also almost certainly have leapt to his lips as a potential plotter. After the incident with Spurinna, they had a terminus ante quem for Caesar's death: March 15th. Antonius knew that Caesar was fated to die by the Ides of March. On that fateful day, when any Roman (for *all* Romans were believers) had to know that Caesar's death was imminent, Antonius accompanies Caesar to the senate meeting. Appian, in his Civil Wars II:117 tells us *"The conspirators had left Trebonius, one of their number, to engage Antony in conversation at the door."* So, on a day that Antonius knew Caesar was fated to die, he allowed himself to be waylaid at the door by the one man that he knew beyond all doubt had been part of a plot to kill Caesar? The implications of this are simply staggering. And they cast Antonius in a new, and rather unflattering, light. He may not have been involved in the conspiracy to murder Caesar, but he clearly let it happen, by withholding his knowledge of it at least, and by allowing Trebonius to waylay him at the senate steps.

I have many villains in the book. There are the violent gangs, there are the assassins planning to kill Caesar, but most of all, I have the man who Caesar trusted and who can only have let the murder happen. History paints Marcus Junius Brutus as the greatest deceiver and villain of the tale, but he was far from alone in that. Antonius is my real villain.

To the causes:

History tells us that three events turned Rome against Caesar and led to what happened. The first was the fact that when Caesar received honours from the senate at the temple of Venus, he remained seated, an insult that was noted by all. The reason for this has been explained differently by sources. Some say he was advised to stay seated, others that he was ill. I have chosen to make it part of the ongoing illness that is part of Caesar's great legacy (more on the illness to follow.) One thing I chose to avoid in this scene was relating Cassius Dio's version of the reason: *"Some who subsequently tried to defend him claimed, it is true, that owing to an attack of diarrhoea he could not control the movement of his bowels and so had remained where he was in order to avoid a flux."*

The second such cause is a sort of mish mash of two events, one being the calling of Caesar as Rex, the failed joke and the arrests, the other being the crown placed on Caesar's statue. The reasons for these events are still debated now, but given Caesar's mind, it seems impossible to believe that it was anything other than a deliberate attempt to be offered a crown and to turn it down. Especially given that the third straw that broke the camel's back was that moment at Lupercalia. Antonius tried twice to push a crown on Caesar, who refused, thrilling the public, though no one who knew him at all could have been under any illusion as to what they were seeing. This is so clearly a setup moment.

Caesar's will plays less of a part in the story than it might have done, incidentally, and is one of the most fascinating angles of the whole period. However, the actual importance of Caesar's will only becomes apparent after his death, naturally, when Octavian attempts to secure legitimacy. Thus I have largely ignored its importance, alluded to it in a number of scenes, and only really dealing with it as at the end, in passing.

A word next about superstition. All Romans believed in the gods, and all Romans were superstitious to some extent. But sources suggest that Caesar was less so than most, for even having been given a terminal date, and with disastrous dreams, knowing there were plots against him, he went on in a blasé fashion as though nothing had changed. The haruspex Spurinna, only mentioned in one source and otherwise unattested in the whole of history, had set the ides of March as Caesar's final potential day. Yet Caesar went on with senate meetings, still planning his coming campaign. At some point on that final day, he was at the house of Calvinius, where he met Spurinna again (Valerius Maximus gives us this tale.) This seems to have been the moment (though another source has it confusingly at the portico of Pompey) when Caesar famously tells the man *'The ides have come and I am still alive,'* while Spurinna replies that *'they might have come but they have not yet gone.'*

Sources have Marcus Junius Brutus being the man who persuaded Caesar to attend the senate session (and yes, one of my greatest challenges in this series has been keeping the two Brutuses separate.) History tells us that sixty men were involved in the conspiracy against Caesar, although he was stabbed only 23 times, and despite this, we only have certain names. I have left the blame chiefly with certain of them. The conspirators we know that are detailed in this book:

Marcus Junius Brutus
Gaius Cassius Longinus
Decimus Junius Brutus Albinus
Gaius Trebonius
Lucius Tillius Cimber
Publius Servilius Casca Longus
Servius Sulpicius Galba
Pontius Aquila

Others, not taking part:

Quintus Ligarius
Lucius Minucius Basilus
Gaius Cassius Parmensis
Caecilius
Bucilianus
Rubrius Ruga
Marcus Spurius
Publius Sextius Naso
Petronius
Publius Turullius
Pacuvius Labeo
Servilius Casca

Four men from this novel are conspicuously missing from the list. Cicero is even now considered a shady character in this respect, and there are people who suspect him of being the driving force behind the whole affair, despite that he later expressed regret that he was not one of the assassins. Secondly, Antonius. I think I've covered that well enough. At the least, he was an enabler of the plot. The third is one Salvius, who appears rather obliquely here in that Antonius' gang imprison Galronus and Salvius in his cousin's house with the keys. Though no Salvius appears among the lists of the killers, it is interesting that a Salvius was the very first man to be executed by Antonius' party in the proscriptions following Caesar's death. If he was not involved in the assassination as one of the unrecorded sixty, and Antonius WAS what I have intimated, then that reeks heavily of a villain covering his tracks. Interesting, no?

The last is Fronto, who I think I have now explained sufficiently. Fronto must put a blade in Caesar to fulfil his vow to Verginius, but he is a man loyal to Caesar, and so being the one who administers the coup de grace and saves Caesar his agony seems appropriate. And anyone who's been eagle eyed since book 1 will have noted something. When the cavalry officer Longinus died in book 1, Fronto visited his villa near Tarraco in Spain. In book 9, Fronto was back there again, following the episode with Verginius. He then bought the villa, and placed a freedman, Arius Rustius, in control, transferring the deeds to him. In the aftermath of the death of Caesar, Fronto tells Antonius that the Falerii are gone forever, and not to look for him again. He returns to the villa, and takes on the name of the Rustii. Anyone who has read wider in my books will have then perhaps picked up a certain Praetorian by the name of Gnaeus Marcius Rustius Rufinus, of a troubled family who live in a coastal villa near Tarraco. So yes, Fronto's family goes on, and two centuries later you can read about his descendant in the Praetorian books. But the change of name might explain why Fronto does not appear in the lists.

On the assassination itself, all four main sources are fairly succinct and generally agree, though there are differences in the details. That there were sixty conspirators and that Caesar was stabbed twenty three times, we can be content. I have tried to present the best average portrayal, given that Fronto does not actually witness the murder, so some of the detail is therefore irrelevant.

Both Plutarch and Appian tell us Caesar planned to send Antonius to dismiss the senate.

Suetonius tells us that it was approaching lunchtime when Caesar, persuaded by Decimus Brutus, attended the senate meeting. Dio instead tells us that it was dawn, and has Trebonius being the one pulling Antonius aside at the steps. Appian, similarly, names Trebonius in this role. Plutarch, in contradiction, has it being Decimus Brutus that stops Antonius outside the curia. For the record, I have selected Trebonius as the delayer, since he is cited twice and Brutus only once, and I have had the event later in the day, as per Suetonius, for the morning routine for senators would usually call for their salutatio in the morning, and so a later meeting seems likely.

Suetonius has the episode with Caesar and Spurinna, that the day had come, as they enter the senate house, though I have discarded this, since there would be no reason for a haruspex to be there. Dio also relates the exchange, but with no other details than that it was on the day of the killing. Similarly, Plutarch tells us that the exchange took place on the way to the Senate.

Suetonius has Caesar seated and Cimber striking the first blow, then Casca, Caesar fighting back and stabbing his attacker in the arm with a stilus. Plutarch echoes this depiction, though he has Caesar and Cimber locked in a struggle over the knife after the first blow is delivered. Appian, too, has Caesar seated, though he has Cimber initiating the attack, but Casca striking the first blow.

Suetonius tells us that he was stabbed twenty three times, and gives us the immortal 'Et tu Brute' line when Marcus Brutus takes his turn. He says that only the second wound to the chest was a mortal one. Dio only tells us that they gathered around Caesar and tried to allay his suspicions, then attacked him en masse. He also tells the 'Et tu Brute' tale, although he does not tell us which Brutus it was. Plutarch has Brutus delivering a blow to the groin (one of the noted killing zones). It is Plutarch who tells us that Caesar collapsed at the feet of the statue of Pompey. Appian also tells us this, having Brutus delivering the blow that sends him staggering thus.

Incidentally, there is a tale told across the sources about one Artemidoros of Cnidos, who came from the house of Brutus that morning with full details and proof of the plot, which reached Caesar, but was never read. Suetonius does not mention him by name, yet has the document put in Caesar's hand, but unread. Dio tells us he was given the message but did not read it. Plutarch gives us much detail of this episode, including the name, though the result is still the same: in hand, and unread. Appian gives us a rather garbled version, separating the unread document and the message of Artemidoros into two events. This whole thing would have added nothing to my account, and so I have not included it in the text.

The upshot is that I was never going to have Fronto as one of the assassins, and so he had to be on Caesar's side, yet he could not prevent the killing without changing history, and so I had to have him too late to do anything about it, which necessitated not actually portraying the assassination itself. I am, however, becoming adept at describing deaths in retrospective, as anyone who's read my Caligula will know.

Finally, a word on Caesar's illness. That he was struck by these attacks is historically attested, and it would certainly have been kept quiet, for Rome was superstitious, and no one would want to be thought cursed. For a long time it has been assumed that it was epilepsy that Caesar suffered, although more recently, scientists are more inclined to blame a series of mini strokes. The former is a condition that can be managed and changes little over time. The latter is indicative of failing health, and would likely gradually become worse and more debilitating. Thus I have suggested that Caesar was in decline at the end, and even had Antonius use that as an excuse.

So there you have it. Fronto's adventures with Caesar are over. And though I am regularly asked if I will continue the series, I'm afraid the answer is no. Marius' Mules has always been envisaged as an arc of fifteen books, ending on the Ides of March, 44 BC. You can follow his distant descendant in the Praetorian series. It may be that one day I yearn again for the late republic, and if I do, there are two young men ready to carry the torch into the Augustan age, but for now that is not in my plans. There are simply too many other tales waiting to be told.

But I'm hoping you have enjoyed living Fronto's adventures with him, I hope you are pleased with this final outing, and I ask you to raise a glass to his memory when next you can. I know I shall.

See you soon, with a whole new series.

Vale,

Simon Turney, February 2023

ACKNOWLEDGEMENTS

A t the end of a fifteen book run that I have been writing for twenty years, I find that there are a huge number of people that I owe in one respect or another. Firstly, it would be my wife Tracey, who has lent her support and her not inconsiderable promotional, research, editorial and administrative talents to work on the series. Then also my mother, Jenny, and my sadly-missed great aunt Lilian, both of whom took on a great deal of beta reading and proofing in the early days.

Then, there are those people who have been instrumental in the production of the covers. Dave Slaney, the amazing designer who has produced the whole series for me, and who has become a household name in the book cover business. Dave, you are a star! Garry Fitzgerald, whose face graces the covers of fourteen out of sixteen releases (the extra one being volume 6.5: Prelude to War), who was the first man I met with republican Roman kit and who has become a firm friend ever since. Paul Harston, who runs Roman Tours and Deva Victrix reenactors, and who was instrumental in that first photo shoot, and with whom I stomped around in caligae for a while, coming to understand what I was writing. (And for the record, Ian, Sumpty, Gary, Rhodri, Charlene, Cellan, Roland and all the other DV reenactors I had the privilege of marching with.) And then Graham Harris, whose stately presence provides the figure for the final cover and who you can meet at the Eboracum festival, annually.

Over the years, a number of people have lent their great talents as editors, proofers and beta readers. Perhaps foremost among these is Ben Kane, who read the very first book not long after its release and gave me comments that I value highly, given how far I have come since then. Also Barry Maxted, Sue Kitchen and Leni

McCormick, who have provided much appreciated talent at times and all of whom are truly appreciated. Thank you all.

The books would never have reached as many people as they have were it not for the help and advice of Robin Carter of Parmenion Books, and also of Julie Richards over in the States, with whom I have sadly lost touch. If you read this, Julie, please do get in contact. My wonderful agent, Sallyanne Sweeney, has made huge advances for me in getting the books into the audio market, and the incomparable Malk Williams has done sterling work in voicing them for audio releases. I know listeners love him, because more than half the fan mail I get relating to the audio books is actually for him, not me!

And then there are you guys. Readers. Without you, this whole thing would be pointless. The support of you all throughout these years has meant a great deal to me, and has been instrumental in the series flourishing, right to the end. I hope you have enjoyed it all, and I hope that this last outing, and Fronto's finale, has been satisfactory. Thank you all to the heights of Olympus.

CAESAR'S ROME

Forum of Caesar

Aemilian Bridge

Offerings in Temple to Caesar

Temple of Venus
Genetrix

Temples with site of
Pompey's Curia behind

Made in United States
North Haven, CT
16 March 2023

34142205R00243